The Collected Works of
Langston Hughes

Volume 15

The Short Stories

Projected Volumes in the Collected Works

The Poems: 1921–1940

The Poems: 1941–1950

The Poems: 1951–1967

The Novels: *Not without Laughter*
  and *Tambourines to Glory*

The Plays to 1942: *Mulatto* to *The Sun Do Move*

The Gospel Plays, Operas, and Other
  Late Dramatic Work

The Early Simple Stories

The Later Simple Stories

Essays on Art, Race, Politics, and World Affairs

Fight for Freedom and Other Writings on Civil Rights

Works for Children and Young Adults: Poetry,
  Fiction, and Other Writing

Works for Children and Young Adults: Biographies

Autobiography: *The Big Sea*

Autobiography: *I Wonder As I Wander*

The Short Stories

The Translations: Federico García Lorca, Nicolás Guillén, and
  Jacques Roumain

An Annotated Bibliography of the
  Works of Langston Hughes

Publication of

The Collected Works of Langston Hughes

has been generously assisted by

Landon and Sarah Rowland

and

Morton and Estelle Sosland

The Collected Works of

Langston Hughes

Volume 15

The Short Stories

Edited by R. Baxter Miller
Introduction by Arnold Rampersad

University of Missouri Press
Columbia and London

University of Missouri Press, Columbia, Missouri 65201
Printed and bound in the United States of America
5 4 3 2 1   06 05 04 03 02

Library of Congress Cataloging-in-Publication Data

Hughes, Langston, 1902–1967
    [Works. 2001]
    The collected works of Langston Hughes / edited by R. Baxter Miller
        p. cm.
    Includes bibliographical references and indexes.
    ISBN 0-8262-1411-8 (v. 15 : alk. paper)
    1. African Americans—Literary collections.   I. Miller, R. Baxter.   II. Title.
PS3515 .U274 2001
818'.5209—dc21   00066601

⊗™This paper meets the requirements of the
American National Standard for Permanence of Paper
for Printed Library Materials, Z39.48, 1984.

Designer: Kristie Lee
Typesetter: Bookcomp, Inc.
Printer and binder: Thomson-Shore, Inc.
Typefaces: Galliard, Optima

Contents

Acknowledgments

The University of Missouri Press is grateful for assistance from the following individuals and institutions in locating and making available copies of the original editions used in the preparation of this edition: Anne Barker and June DeWeese, Ellis Library, University of Missouri–Columbia; Teresa Gipson, Miller Nichols Library, University of Missouri–Kansas City; Ruth Carruth and Patricia C. Willis, Beinecke Rare Book and Manuscript Library, Yale University; Ann Pathega, Washington University; Marlene Allen, University of Georgia.

The *Collected Works* would not have been possible without the support and assistance of Patricia Powell, Chris Byrne, and Wendy Schmalz of Harold Ober Associates, representing the estate of Langston Hughes, and of Arnold Rampersad and Ramona Bass, co-executors of the estate of Langston Hughes.

Chronology
By Arnold Rampersad

1902   James Langston Hughes is born February 1 in Joplin, Missouri, to James Nathaniel Hughes, a stenographer for a mining company, and Carrie Mercer Langston Hughes, a former government clerk.

1903   After his father immigrates to Mexico, Langston's mother takes him to Lawrence, Kansas, the home of Mary Langston, her twice-widowed mother. Mary Langston's first husband, Lewis Sheridan Leary, died fighting alongside John Brown at Harpers Ferry. Her second, Hughes's grandfather, was Charles Langston, a former abolitionist, Republican politician, and businessman.

1907   After a failed attempt at a reconciliation in Mexico, Langston and his mother return to Lawrence.

1909   Langston starts school in Topeka, Kansas, where he lives for a while with his mother before returning to his grandmother's home in Lawrence.

1915   Following Mary Langston's death, Hughes leaves Lawrence for Lincoln, Illinois, where his mother lives with her second husband, Homer Clark, and Homer Clark's young son by another union, Gwyn "Kit" Clark.

1916   Langston, elected class poet, graduates from the eighth grade. Moves to Cleveland, Ohio, and starts at Central High School there.

1918   Publishes early poems and short stories in his school's monthly magazine.

1919   Spends the summer in Toluca, Mexico, with his father.

1920   Graduates from Central High as class poet and editor of the school annual. Returns to Mexico to live with his father.

1921   In June, Hughes publishes "The Negro Speaks of Rivers" in *Crisis* magazine. In September, sponsored by his father, he enrolls at Columbia University in New York. Meets W. E. B. Du Bois, Jessie Fauset, and Countee Cullen.

1922   Unhappy at Columbia, Hughes withdraws from school and breaks with his father.

1923   Sailing in June to western Africa on the crew of a freighter, he visits Senegal, the Gold Coast, Nigeria, the Congo, and other countries.

1924   Spends several months in Paris working in the kitchen of a nightclub.

1925   Lives in Washington for a year with his mother. His poem "The Weary Blues" wins first prize in a contest sponsored by *Opportunity* magazine, which leads to a book contract with Knopf through Carl Van Vechten. Becomes friends with several other young artists of the Harlem Renaissance, including Zora Neale Hurston, Wallace Thurman, and Arna Bontemps.

1926   In January his first book, *The Weary Blues,* appears. He enrolls at historically black Lincoln University, Pennsylvania. In June, the *Nation* weekly magazine publishes his landmark essay "The Negro Artist and the Racial Mountain."

1927   Knopf publishes his second book of verse, *Fine Clothes to the Jew,* which is condemned in the black press. Hughes meets his powerful patron Mrs. Charlotte Osgood Mason. Travels in the South with Hurston, who is also taken up by Mrs. Mason.

1929   Hughes graduates from Lincoln University.

1930   Publishes his first novel, *Not without Laughter* (Knopf). Visits Cuba and meets fellow poet Nicolás Guillén. Hughes is dismissed by Mrs. Mason in a painful break made worse by false charges of dishonesty leveled by Hurston over their play *Mule Bone.*

1931   Demoralized, he travels to Haiti. Publishes work in the communist magazine *New Masses.* Supported by the Rosenwald Foundation, he tours the South taking his poetry to the people. In Alabama, he visits some of the Scottsboro Boys in prison. His brief collection of poems *Dear Lovely Death* is privately printed in Amenia, New York. Hughes and the illustrator Prentiss Taylor publish a verse pamphlet, *The Negro Mother.*

1932   With Taylor, he publishes *Scottsboro, Limited,* a short play and four poems. From Knopf comes *The Dream Keeper,* a book of previously published poems selected for young people. Later, Macmillan brings out *Popo and Fifina,* a children's story about Haiti written with Arna Bontemps, his closest friend. In June, Hughes sails to Russia in a band of twenty-two young African

Americans to make a film about race relations in the United States. After the project collapses, he lives for a year in the Soviet Union. Publishes his most radical verse, including "Good Morning Revolution" and "Goodbye Christ."

1933   Returns home at midyear via China and Japan. Supported by a patron, Noël Sullivan of San Francisco, Hughes spends a year in Carmel writing short stories.

1934   Knopf publishes his first short story collection, *The Ways of White Folks*. After labor unrest in California threatens his safety, he leaves for Mexico following news of his father's death.

1935   Spends several months in Mexico, mainly translating short stories by local leftist writers. Lives for some time with the photographer Henri Cartier-Bresson. Returning almost destitute to the United States, he joins his mother in Oberlin, Ohio. Visits New York for the Broadway production of his play *Mulatto* and clashes with its producer over changes in the script. Unhappy, he writes the poem "Let America Be America Again."

1936   Wins a Guggenheim Foundation fellowship for work on a novel but soon turns mainly to writing plays in association with the Karamu Theater in Cleveland. Karamu stages his farce *Little Ham* and his historical drama about Haiti, *Troubled Island*.

1937   Karamu stages *Joy to My Soul*, another comedy. In July, he visits Paris for the League of American Writers. He then travels to Spain, where he spends the rest of the year reporting on the civil war for the *Baltimore Afro-American*.

1938   In New York, Hughes founds the radical Harlem Suitcase Theater, which stages his agitprop play *Don't You Want to Be Free?* The leftist International Workers Order publishes *A New Song*, a pamphlet of radical verse. Karamu stages his play *Front Porch*. His mother dies.

1939   In Hollywood he writes the script for the movie *Way Down South*, which is criticized for stereotyping black life. Hughes goes for an extended stay in Carmel, California, again as the guest of Noël Sullivan.

1940   His autobiography *The Big Sea* appears (Knopf). He is picketed by a religious group for his poem "Goodbye Christ," which he publicly renounces.

1941   With a Rosenwald Fund fellowship for playwriting, he leaves California for Chicago, where he founds the Skyloft Players. Moves on to New York in December.

1942   Knopf publishes his book of verse *Shakespeare in Harlem*. The Skyloft Players stage his play *The Sun Do Move*. In the summer he resides at the Yaddo writers' and artists' colony, New York. Hughes also works as a writer in support of the war effort. In November he starts "Here to Yonder," a weekly column in the Chicago *Defender* newspaper.

1943   "Here to Yonder" introduces Jesse B. Semple, or Simple, a comic Harlem character who quickly becomes its most popular feature. Hughes publishes *Jim Crow's Last Stand* (Negro Publication Society of America), a pamphlet of verse about the struggle for civil rights.

1944   Comes under surveillance by the FBI because of his former radicalism.

1945   With Mercer Cook, translates and later publishes *Masters of the Dew* (Reynal and Hitchcock), a novel by Jacques Roumain of Haiti.

1947   His work as librettist with Kurt Weill and Elmer Rice on the Broadway musical play *Street Scene* brings Hughes a financial windfall. He vacations in Jamaica. Knopf publishes *Fields of Wonder*, his only book composed mainly of lyric poems on nonracial topics.

1948   Hughes is denounced (erroneously) as a communist in the U.S. Senate. He buys a townhouse in Harlem and moves in with his longtime friends Toy and Emerson Harper.

1949   Doubleday publishes *Poetry of the Negro, 1746–1949,* an anthology edited with Arna Bontemps. Also published are *One-Way Ticket* (Knopf), a book of poems, and *Cuba Libre: Poems of Nicolás Guillén* (Anderson and Ritchie), translated by Hughes and Ben Frederic Carruthers. Hughes teaches for three months at the University of Chicago Lab School for children. His opera about Haiti with William Grant Still, *Troubled Island*, is presented in New York.

1950   Another opera, *The Barrier*, with music by Jan Meyerowitz, is hailed in New York but later fails on Broadway. Simon and Schuster publishes *Simple Speaks His Mind*, the first of five books based on his newspaper columns.

1951   Hughes's book of poems about life in Harlem, *Montage of a Dream Deferred*, appears (Henry Holt).

1952   His second collection of short stories, *Laughing to Keep from Crying*, is published by Henry Holt. In its "First Book" series for children, Franklin Watts publishes Hughes's *The First Book of Negroes.*

1953 In March, forced to testify before Senator Joseph McCarthy's subcommittee on subversive activities, Hughes is exonerated after repudiating his past radicalism. *Simple Takes a Wife* appears.

1954 Mainly for young readers, he publishes *Famous American Negroes* (Dodd, Mead) and *The First Book of Rhythms.*

1955 Publishes *The First Book of Jazz* and finishes *Famous Negro Music Makers* (Dodd, Mead). In November, Simon and Schuster publishes *The Sweet Flypaper of Life,* a narrative of Harlem with photographs by Roy DeCarava.

1956 Hughes's second volume of autobiography, *I Wonder As I Wander* (Rinehart), appears, as well as *A Pictorial History of the Negro* (Crown), coedited with Milton Meltzer, and *The First Book of the West Indies.*

1957 *Esther,* an opera with composer Jan Meyerowitz, has its premiere in Illinois. Rinehart publishes *Simple Stakes a Claim* as a novel. Hughes's musical play *Simply Heavenly,* based on his Simple character, runs for several weeks off and then on Broadway. Hughes translates and publishes *Selected Poems of Gabriela Mistral* (Indiana University Press).

1958 *The Langston Hughes Reader* (George Braziller) appears, as well as *The Book of Negro Folklore* (Dodd, Mead), coedited with Arna Bontemps, and another juvenile, *Famous Negro Heroes of America* (Dodd, Mead). John Day publishes a short novel, *Tambourines to Glory,* based on a Hughes gospel musical play.

1959 Hughes's *Selected Poems* published (Knopf).

1960 *The First Book of Africa* appears, along with *An African Treasury: Articles, Essays, Stories, Poems by Black Africans,* edited by Hughes (Crown).

1961 Inducted into the National Institute of Arts and Letters. Knopf publishes his book-length poem *Ask Your Mama: 12 Moods for Jazz. The Best of Simple,* drawn from the columns, appears (Hill and Wang). Hughes writes his gospel musical plays *Black Nativity* and *The Prodigal Son.* He visits Africa again.

1962 Begins a weekly column for the *New York Post.* Attends a writers' conference in Uganda. Publishes *Fight for Freedom: The Story of the NAACP,* commissioned by the organization.

1963 His third collection of short stories, *Something in Common,* appears from Hill and Wang. Indiana University Press publishes

Five Plays by Langston Hughes, edited by Webster Smalley, as well as Hughes's anthology *Poems from Black Africa, Ethiopia, and Other Countries.*

1964   His musical play *Jericho–Jim Crow,* a tribute to the civil rights movement, is staged in Greenwich Village. Indiana University Press brings out his anthology *New Negro Poets: U.S.A.,* with a foreword by Gwendolyn Brooks.

1965   With novelists Paule Marshall and William Melvin Kelley, Hughes visits Europe for the U.S. State Department. His gospel play *The Prodigal Son* and his cantata with music by David Amram, *Let Us Remember,* are staged.

1966   After twenty-three years, Hughes ends his depiction of Simple in his Chicago *Defender* column. Publishes *The Book of Negro Humor* (Dodd, Mead). In a visit sponsored by the U.S. government, he is honored in Dakar, Senegal, at the First World Festival of Negro Arts.

1967   His *The Best Short Stories by Negro Writers: An Anthology from 1899 to the Present* (Little, Brown) includes the first published story by Alice Walker. On May 22, Hughes dies at New York Polyclinic Hospital in Manhattan from complications following prostate surgery. Later that year, two books appear: *The Panther and the Lash: Poems of Our Times* (Knopf) and, with Milton Meltzer, *Black Magic: A Pictorial History of the Negro in American Entertainment* (Prentice Hall).

The Collected Works of

Langston Hughes

Volume 15

The Short Stories

Introduction
By Arnold Rampersad

Langston Hughes is celebrated as a writer in the United States and around the world mainly because of his moving poetry. Nevertheless, he also deserves to be known as an accomplished writer in areas other than verse. He is, indeed, perhaps the most representative of African American writers by virtue of his publications in virtually all areas of literary activity. Hughes was a master dramatist whose plays alone would earn him a place in African American literary history. He was the author of several books, including fiction and nonfiction, aimed at young people. He was a journalist whose work appeared on a weekly basis in important newspapers for over twenty years. He published a history of the NAACP and wrote lyrics and opera libretti. And he was also proud of his achievements in fiction, including his two novels and the three published volumes of short stories that are reprinted in this volume of his collected works.

Hughes wrote and published short fiction from virtually the beginning of his career as a writer. In fact, he credited a writer of fiction, Guy de Maupassant, with helping him decide that his life's work would be writing. As Hughes tells it in his first volume of autobiography, *The Big Sea* (1940), he was studying French in high school and trying his best to understand a text in French by Maupassant when suddenly the language and the author's style became luminously clear to him. "The soft snow was falling through one of his stories in the little book we used in school," Hughes writes, "and that I had worked over so long, before I really felt the snow falling there. Then all of a sudden one night the beauty and the meaning of the words in which he made the snow fall, came to me. I think it was de Maupassant who made me really want to be a writer and write stories about Negroes, so true that people in far-away lands would read them—even after I was dead."[1]

In his high school magazine, a monthly, Hughes published at least three short stories in addition to the verse he offered there. These were

---

1. *The Collected Works of Langston Hughes, vol. 13, Autobiography: The Big Sea*, ed. Joseph McLaren (Columbia: University of Missouri Press, 2002).

apprentice pieces, both in poetry and prose, in which Hughes gave no real glimpse of the interest he would develop in exploring topics such as African American culture and racial strife. What was clear, however, was Hughes's acute interest in the question of social justice, as well as his sympathetic feelings for the poor and downtrodden. His first published short story, "Those Who Have No Turkey," appeared in the December 1918 Central High School *Monthly,* when Hughes was sixteen. The story told about a kindhearted country girl who, on a visit to her prosperous aunt in the city, impulsively invites a poor but grateful family to Thanksgiving dinner.

In the 1920s, as his writing career developed, Hughes published relatively little fiction; instead, he concentrated on poetry and made his name with his volumes *The Weary Blues* (1926) and *Fine Clothes to the Jew* (1927). Until his novel *Not without Laughter* appeared in 1930, his output of fiction consisted mainly of a group of stories written around 1927, in which Hughes explored his memories of his weeks in 1923 as a sailor on a freighter traveling up and down the west coast of Africa. Composed at the height of the Harlem Renaissance, an exhilarating time for Hughes and other young writers, these stories explored relatively daring subjects. "Luani of the Jungles," published in the new magazine *Harlem* by the novelist Wallace Thurman, tells of the marriage of a white man to a Nigerian woman in Europe. When they return to her home in Africa, she acts independently to the point of taking an African lover, as well as hunting and fishing without her husband; he is distracted by her behavior but unable to give her up.

Although these stories, appearing in obscure magazines, made little impression on Hughes's audience, they suggest in general Hughes's technical range as a writer of short stories. No experimentalist, he relies, as Hans Ostrom points out in *Langston Hughes: A Study of the Short Fiction,* "on simple narrative forms—the tale, the sketch, the parable, and deliberately undramatic reportage." Hughes is also "interested in allowing colloquial language, the blues, gospel music, and the sound and sense of 'street speech' to inform the language of his short fiction."[2]

His first major statement as a short story writer came in 1934, when his publisher, Alfred A. Knopf, brought out Hughes's *The Ways of White Folks,* a collection of fourteen stories. Much had happened between the publication of "Luani of the Jungles" and the appearance of this book. Hughes had suffered a devastating personal blow with the collapse of his

---

2. *Langston Hughes: A Study of the Short Fiction* (New York: Macmillan, 1993).

intimate relationship with his major patron of the decade, Mrs. Rufus Osgood Mason (about which he writes in *The Big Sea*). At the same time, the Harlem Renaissance had collapsed as yet another casualty of the Great Depression in the United States. Both factors had combined to drive Hughes far to the left politically. A year in the Soviet Union between 1932 and 1933 had deepened his interest in radical socialism. By this time Hughes has ceased to write the kind of poetry, saturated in blues and jazz, that had made him well known in the 1920s. Instead, he wrote mainly revolutionary verse, such as the poems "Good Morning Revolution" and "Goodbye Christ." However, such verse could not do justice to the complex of emotions and ideas generated by the troubling events of his life in this period.

By accident, while living in Moscow in 1933 Hughes discovered an ideal outlet—the short story form, especially as practiced by the famous British writer D. H. Lawrence. Reading Lawrence's collection *The Lovely Lady*, Hughes was riveted especially by the title story and by another tale, "The Rocking Horse Winner." These stories, he recalls in his second autobiography, *I Wonder As I Wander*, "made my hair stand on end." The grasping old woman at the center of "The Lovely Lady" so resembled his former patron Mrs. Mason that "I could not put the book down, although it brought cold sweat and goose-pimples to my body."[3]

Challenged and liberated, Hughes plunged into writing stories that explored a complex of issues that touched on his own intimate experience of the white world but also went beyond it. Several stories treat matters such as white condescension to and patronizing of blacks in the name of charity, and the often painful, confusing isolation of blacks caught up in the cold machinery of white "benevolence." Hughes explored generally ignored subjects such as miscegenation, the phenomenon of white desire for the black body, and the fraudulence that racism, especially when linked to wealth and liberalism, encouraged in blacks and whites alike. His first story in this period, "Slave on the Block," is about a young white bohemian couple living in Greenwich Village, New York, who take pride in their "special" relationship to blacks. The wife, a pretentious artist, insists on painting a young black man, their employee around the house, with his shirt off; their black maid, an older woman who is sleeping with him, resents the couple's silly patronizing and helps to bring them to their moment of truth. "Cora Unashamed" tells of a black

3. *I Wonder As I Wander* (New York: Rinehart & Co., 1956), 213. Forthcoming as volume 14 of *The Collected Works of Langston Hughes*.

woman of powerful if latent emotions, isolated in a cold, white, heartless midwestern world. In "Poor Little Black Fellow," a black boy adopted by a self-righteous but sterile white family grows up to defy them and assert his independent identity, free of their condescension and their joyless Puritanism.

The longest story, "Father and Son," relates the story of a southern white planter, Colonel Norwood, and one of his mulatto children, Bert. Colonel Norwood lives openly with the young man's mother, but he refuses to acknowledge her and their mulatto children publicly. When Bert, who has been educated in the North, insists on being recognized as Norwood's son, and thus entitled to his rights of a citizen, he sets in motion a train of events that leads to his murder of his father and his own death at the hands of a lynch mob. In part, Hughes drew in this story on the life of his maternal grandfather, Charles Langston, who was one of three sons of a white Virginian planter and a black woman, Lucy Langston. But Hughes drew more immediately on his past in composing perhaps the most memorable story from *The Ways of White Folks,* "The Blues I'm Playing." This tale pits Oceola Jones, a young black woman who is a gifted pianist, against her wealthy white patron, the elderly widow Mrs. Dora Ellsworth. At first united in their interest in seeing Oceola grow and flourish as a musician, they clash over conflicting ideas about art and, just as important, about life. Oceola insists finally on both her right to play the blues as well as the classics and her right to enjoy the love of her man rather than sacrifice her emotions and sexuality to a monastic notion of the life of the artist. The story thus celebrates Hughes's own championing of the culture of poor black folks and the life-affirming values at the heart of that culture.

These stories, and others such as "Home" and "Red-Headed Baby" (the former about a black violinist respected in Europe but reviled and finally killed by whites in his southern hometown, the latter about the bastard child of a desperate liaison between a black woman and a white sailor), reflected Hughes's hardened attitudes in much of the 1930s. The sentimentality and lyricism of many of his poems of the previous decade, as well as his novel *Not without Laughter,* had more or less vanished. Instead, Hughes now showed a militant, cynical, and embittered face. This new toughness made some of the stories difficult to place when Hughes offered them individually to some of the leading American magazines. In the end, however, *The Ways of White Folks* earned sometimes grudging but on the whole respectful reviews. The *North American Review* saw it as comprising "some of the best stories that have appeared in this country in years." In the *Nation,* the prominent writer Sherwood Anderson was of two minds. He noted the bitter criticism of whites and hailed Hughes as a champion of blacks rather than of whites—"My hat is off to you in relation to your own race." Nevertheless, Anderson's respect for Hughes as a writer was clear.

The relative success of *The Ways of White Folks* did not lead immediately to new efforts in the same vein by Hughes. Perhaps if Hughes has been able to sell short stories more consistently to the leading magazines he might have continued to produce them—his need for money was urgent at this time. However, few magazines wanted fiction about the often-sordid consequences of racism. Instead, as restless as he was versatile, Hughes turned to the theater. For much of the rest of the 1930s he devoted his time to writing plays. The most prominent was undoubtedly *Mulatto,* which dramatized the story of miscegenation and patricide told in "Father and Son." *Mulatto* had its debut on Broadway in 1935 and became the longest running Broadway production by a black writer until Lorraine Hansberry's *A Raisin in the Sun* in 1959. (Later, *Mulatto* and "Father and Son" led to the opera *The Barrier,* with music by Jan Meyerowitz, which reached Broadway—and flopped there—in 1950.)

In the 1940s, Hughes wrote much short fiction—but not in the traditional vein of the short story. Starting in 1943 in his weekly column in the Chicago *Defender,* he developed in brilliant fashion the world of Jesse B. Semple, or Simple, an affable if uneducated Harlem man-about-town whose comic exploits gained Hughes renewed respect and affection in the African American world. Simple's adventures, recounted in conversations with the often stuffy narrator of the column, involved his typical dealings with the world—including his cranky landlady, his bourgeois fiancée, and his fiancée's disreputable rival for his affections, the colorful Zarita. Never shy about voicing his opinions on any subject, Simple quickly became by far the most popular aspect of Hughes's column and a major element in Hughes's reputation as a writer in the black world. Edited by Hughes, the Simple stories became the raw material for five books, the first, *Simple Speaks His Mind,* published in 1950, and the last, *Simple's Uncle Sam,* published in 1965, only two years before Hughes's death.[4]

4. The collections of Simple stories are reprinted in volumes 7 and 8 of *The Collected Works of Langston Hughes,* edited by Donna Akiba Sullivan Harper (Columbia: University of Missouri Press, 2001, 2002).

With his attention on Simple, Hughes wrote relatively few short stories during this time. In fact, eighteen years passed between the publication of *The Ways of White Folks* and that of Hughes's next collection, *Laughing to Keep from Crying*, in 1952. This new volume collected twenty-four stories, most of which had appeared earlier in various magazines. Perhaps the most noticeable difference between the two collections of stories is the extent to which the bitterness, violence, and tragedy of the former give way to a gentler form of irony and, indeed, to a more comic spirit. The emphasis, it seems, is more on laughing than on crying. For example, the first story, "Who's Passing for Who?" involves three white interlopers in a Harlem nightclub; however, two apparently turn out to be African American. The genuinely white interloper interferes in a fight between a black man and a woman who looks white; to his utter confusion, she also turns out to be black.

If this story strikes a farcical note, another story, "African Morning," is at once more ominous and yet finally optimistic. Perhaps written in the late 1920s as part of his series inspired by Africa, the story tells of a mulatto African boy whose black mother is dead and who fears for his future at the hands of his white expatriate father. He appears to be on the brink of suicide by drowning, but surfaces in a move that seems to symbolize his determination not simply to live but to prevail. "Saratoga Rain" is in yet another mode—a desultory but expert sketch of two lovers dreamily enjoying a rainy morning in Saratoga, New York—presumably near the artists' colony of Yaddo, where Hughes probably wrote the story during a stay in 1942. "Slice Him Down," set in Reno, Nevada, and written when Hughes visited the gambling city in 1934, comes close to violence, but no one is hurt in a knife fight between two blacks whose drinking gets out of hand.

The most anthologized story in the collection, and one of the most anthologized of all of Hughes's stories, is "On the Road." This story, too, was inspired by his visit to Reno in 1934. The main character, Sargeant, is a black hobo who seeks refuge from the bitter cold of a northern city in winter by pounding on the door of a white church. Disoriented, he finds himself talking to "Christ," passes out, and eventually awakens to find himself in jail. "On the Road," Hans Ostrom remarks, "is a parable that makes almost perfect use of techniques and tendencies found in Hughes's first two collections: the simple, direct style, the thirst for social criticism, the balance between satire and comedy, the basic, easily recognizable plot line, and the ability to create 'everyman' characters."[5]

5. *Langston Hughes: A Study of the Short Fiction.*

Laughing to Keep from Crying provoked only mild interest among the critics when it appeared in 1952, the same year as the acclaimed novel *Invisible Man* by Ralph Ellison. Nevertheless, Hughes's reputation and his personal prosperity grew in this decade, as he explored his versatility as a writer. Still inspired by and devoted to his Simple character, he wrote even fewer short stories than in the previous decade. Indeed, when his third and last collection, *Something in Common and Other Stories,* was published in 1963, all but ten of its stories had appeared in the previous two collections.

Nevertheless, some of these stories explore interesting themes. Perhaps the most ambitious is "The Gun." A black woman, isolated in her small town in Montana, takes to the road in search of adventure and perhaps fulfillment. In Fresno, California, she buys a gun, which leads her first to thoughts of suicide, then to a perhaps Freudian and bizarre infatuation with the weapon itself. In "Blessed Assurance," Hughes treats the intertwined themes of homosexuality and religion in a story written from the point of view of a young black man's father, who is obviously upset about his suspicion that his son might be gay. The young man's beautiful singing voice excites a male organist in the church into a state of ecstasy even as the young man's father seethes in embarrassment and disapproval. The tone of the story is satiric and perhaps even sardonic, with no clear indication about Hughes's attitude to homosexuality. However, his typical impatience with organized religion is evident, and that impatience shows again in "Rock, Church." Both "Breakfast in Virginia" and "Fine Accommodations" take place on trains. In the first, two black soldiers are barred from the dining car because of their race, but are invited by an elderly white man to eat in his private car. The second involves a black college president, a professor traveling with him, and a porter; Hughes shows here his old contempt for the lack of freedom and imagination that he had encountered in too many black colleges.

Langston Hughes's short stories together represent an impressive and indispensable part of his collected works. Here, as in other forms, he showed his determination to write about matters important to his community and to the nation, and to do so in ways accessible to the reader while at the same stylish and replete with meaning. In these stories he captures both the joys and the sorrows of life, as well as something of the complexity of race relations in America and of the lives of African Americans in general.

A Note on the Text

For this edition of the short stories of Langston Hughes, we have used the first editions of *The Ways of White Folks* (Alfred A. Knopf, 1934), *Laughing to Keep From Crying* (Henry Holt, 1952), and *Something in Common and Other Stories* (Hill and Wang, 1963). The original ordering of the stories within these volumes has been retained, allowing the reader to encounter the stores as Hughes structured and published them in book form. All spellings, capitalization, punctuation, and word compounding have been retained as they originally appeared, although obvious typographical errors have been corrected.

Hughes repeated many stories from his first two volumes in *Something in Common and Other Stories*. To eliminate the duplication of stories within this volume, these stories are given in their entirety in the volumes in which they were first published, with annotations indicating any wording that was changed when they were reprinted in the later collection. In *Something in Common*, page markers designate the placement of the repeated stories in that volume. This mode of presentation minimizes the duplication of many pages yet provides the reader with a firm sense of Hughes's volumes structured as wholes.

The texts for the uncollected stories are from *Langston Hughes: Short Stories,* edited by Akiba Sullivan Harper (Hill and Wang, 1996). Hughes's earliest known story, "Mary Winoski" was the product of an assignment for an English class at Central High School in Cleveland in 1915. The manuscript is in the James Weldon Johnson Collection of the Beinecke Rare Book and Manuscript Library at Yale University. A few years later, "Those Who Have No Turkey" was published in *Monthly* (December 1918), a school magazine at Cleveland High; it was subsequently published in *Brownie's Book,* a children's supplement to the *Crisis,* in November 1921. The manuscript for "Seventy-Five Dollars," also published in *Monthly* (January 1919), is in the archives of the Western Reserve Historical Society in Cleveland, Ohio. Published in *The Messenger* were "Bodies in the Moonlight" (April 1927), "The Young Glory of Him" (June 1927), and "The Little Virgin" (November 1927). "The Childhood of Jimmy" appeared in *Crisis* (May 1927) and "Luani of the Jungles" in *Harlem* (November 1928).

The Ways of
White Folks

(1934)

To Noël Sullivan

The ways of white folks,
I mean some *white folks.* . . .
                          Berry

Thanks are due the editors of *Esquire, The American Mercury, Scribner's, Opportunity, The Brooklyn Daily Eagle, Debate,* and *Abbott's Monthly* for permission to reprint certain of these stories first published in their pages.

Contents

Cora Unashamed

Melton was one of those miserable in-between little places, not large enough to be a town, nor small enough to be a village—that is, a village in the rural, charming sense of the word. Melton had no charm about it. It was merely a nondescript collection of houses and buildings in a region of farms—one of those sad American places with sidewalks, but no paved streets; electric lights, but no sewage; a station, but no trains that stopped, save a jerky local, morning and evening. And it was 150 miles from any city at all—even Sioux City.

Cora Jenkins was one of the least of the citizens of Melton. She was what the people referred to when they wanted to be polite, as a Negress, and when they wanted to be rude, as a nigger—sometimes adding the word "wench" for no good reason, for Cora was usually an inoffensive soul, except that she sometimes cussed.

She had been in Melton for forty years. Born there. Would die there probably. She worked for the Studevants, who treated her like a dog. She stood it. Had to stand it; or work for poorer white folks who would treat her worse; or go jobless. Cora was like a tree—once rooted, she stood, in spite of storms and strife, wind, and rocks, in the earth.

She was the Studevants' maid of all work—washing, ironing, cooking, scrubbing, taking care of kids, nursing old folks, making fires, carrying water.

Cora, bake three cakes for Mary's birthday tomorrow night. You Cora, give Rover a bath in that tar soap I bought. Cora, take Ma some jello, and don't let her have even a taste of that raisin pie. She'll keep us up all night if you do. Cora, iron my stockings. Cora, come here . . . Cora, put . . . Cora . . . Cora . . . Cora! Cora!

And Cora would answer, "Yes, m'am."

The Studevants thought they owned her, and they were perfectly right: they did. There was something about the teeth in the trap of economic circumstance that kept her in their power practically all her life—in the Studevant kitchen, cooking; in the Studevant parlor, sweeping; in the Studevant backyard, hanging clothes.

You want to know how that could be? How a trap could close so tightly? Here is the outline:

Cora was the oldest of a family of eight children—the Jenkins niggers. The only Negroes in Melton, thank God! Where they came from originally—that is, the old folks—God knows. The kids were born there. The old folks are still there now: Pa drives a junk wagon. The old woman ails around the house, ails and quarrels. Seven kids are gone. Only Cora remains. Cora simply couldn't go, with nobody else to help take care of Ma. And before that she couldn't go, with nobody to see that her brothers and sisters got through school (she the oldest, and Ma ailing). And before that—well, somebody had to help Ma look after one baby behind another that kept on coming.

As a child Cora had no playtime. She always had a little brother, or a little sister in her arms. Bad, crying, bratty babies, hungry and mean. In the eighth grade she quit school and went to work with the Studevants.

After that, she ate better. Half day's work at first, helping Ma at home the rest of the time. Then full days, bringing home her pay to feed her father's children. The old man was rather a drunkard. What little money he made from closet-cleaning, ash-hauling, and junk-dealing he spent mostly on the stuff that makes you forget you have eight kids.

He passed the evenings telling long, comical lies to the white riff-raff of the town, and drinking licker. When his horse died, Cora's money went for a new one to haul her Pa and his rickety wagon around. When the mortgage money came due, Cora's wages kept the man from taking the roof from over their heads. When Pa got in jail, Cora borrowed ten dollars from Mrs. Studevant and got him out.

Cora stinted, and Cora saved, and wore the Studevants' old clothes, and ate the Studevants' leftover food, and brought her pay home. Brothers and sisters grew up. The boys, lonesome, went away, as far as they could from Melton. One by one, the girls left too, mostly in disgrace. "Ruinin' ma name," Pa Jenkins said, "Ruinin' ma good name! They can't go out berryin' but what they come back in disgrace." There was something about the cream-and-tan Jenkins girls that attracted the white farm hands.

Even Cora, the humble, had a lover once. He came to town on a freight train (long ago now), and worked at the livery-stable. (That was before autos got to be so common.) Everybody said he was an I. W. W. Cora didn't care. He was the first man and the last she ever remembered wanting. She had never known a colored lover. There weren't any around. That was not her fault.

This white boy, Joe, he always smelt like the horses. He was some kind of foreigner. Had an accent, and yellow hair, big hands, and grey eyes.

It was summer. A few blocks beyond the Studevants' house, meadows and orchards and sweet fields stretched away to the far horizon. At night, stars in the velvet sky. Moon sometimes. Crickets and katydids and lightning bugs. The scent of grass. Cora waiting. That boy, Joe, a cigarette spark far off, whistling in the dark. Love didn't take long—Cora with the scent of the Studevants' supper about her, and a cheap perfume. Joe, big and strong and careless as the horses he took care of, smelling like the stable.

Ma would quarrel because Cora came home late, or because none of the kids had written for three or four weeks, or because Pa was drunk again. Thus the summer passed, a dream of big hands and grey eyes.

Cora didn't go anywhere to have her child. Nor tried to hide it. When the baby grew big within her, she didn't feel that it was a disgrace. The Studevants told her to go home and stay there. Joe left town. Pa cussed. Ma cried. One April morning the kid was born. She had grey eyes, and Cora called her Josephine, after Joe.

Cora was humble and shameless before the fact of the child. There were no Negroes in Melton to gossip, and she didn't care what the white people said. They were in another world. Of course, she hadn't expected to marry Joe, or keep him. He was of that other world, too. But the child was hers—a living bridge between two worlds. Let people talk.

Cora went back to work at the Studevants'—coming home at night to nurse her kid, and quarrel with Ma. About that time, Mrs. Art Studevant had a child, too, and Cora nursed it. The Studevants' little girl was named Jessie. As the two children began to walk and talk, Cora sometimes brought Josephine to play with Jessie—until the Studevants objected, saying she could get her work done better if she left her child at home.

"Yes, m'am," said Cora.

But in a little while they didn't need to tell Cora to leave her child at home, for Josephine died of whooping-cough. One rosy afternoon, Cora saw the little body go down into the ground in a white casket that cost four weeks' wages.

Since Ma was ailing, Pa, smelling of licker, stood with her at the grave. The two of them alone. Cora was not humble before the fact of death. As she turned away from the hole, tears came—but at the same time a stream of curses so violent that they made the grave-tenders look up in startled horror.

She cussed out God for taking away the life that she herself had given. She screamed, "My baby! God damn it! My baby! I bear her and you take her away!" She looked at the sky where the sun was setting and yelled in defiance. Pa was amazed and scared. He pulled her up on his rickety wagon and drove off, clattering down the road between green fields and sweet meadows that stretched away to the far horizon. All through the ugly town Cora wept and cursed, using all the bad words she had learned from Pa in his drunkenness.

The next week she went back to the Studevants. She was gentle and humble in the face of life—she loved their baby. In the afternoons on the back porch, she would pick little Jessie up and rock her to sleep, burying her dark face in the milky smell of the white child's hair.

II

The years passed. Pa and Ma Jenkins only dried up a little. Old Man Studevant died. The old lady had two strokes. Mrs. Art Studevant and her husband began to look their age, greying hair and sagging stomachs. The children were grown, or nearly so. Kenneth took over the management of the hardware store that Grandpa had left. Jack went off to college. Mary was a teacher. Only Jessie remained a child—her last year in high-school. Jessie, nineteen now, and rather slow in her studies, graduating at last. In the Fall she would go to Normal.

Cora hated to think about her going away. In her heart she had adopted Jessie. In that big and careless household it was always Cora who stood like a calm and sheltering tree for Jessie to run to in her troubles. As a child, when Mrs. Art spanked her, as soon as she could, the tears still streaming, Jessie would find her way to the kitchen and Cora. At each school term's end, when Jessie had usually failed in some of her subjects (she quite often failed, being a dull child), it was Cora who saw the report-card first with the bad marks on it. Then Cora would devise some way of breaking the news gently to the old folks.

Her mother was always a little ashamed of stupid Jessie, for Mrs. Art was the civic and social leader of Melton, president of the Woman's Club three years straight, and one of the pillars of her church. Mary, the elder, the teacher, would follow with dignity in her footsteps, but Jessie! That child! Spankings in her youth, and scoldings now, did nothing to Jessie's inner being. She remained a plump, dull, freckled girl, placid and strange. Everybody found fault with her but Cora.

In the kitchen Jessie bloomed. She laughed. She talked. She was sometimes even witty. And she learned to cook wonderfully. With Cora, everything seemed so simple—not hard and involved like algebra, or

Latin grammar, or the civic problems of Mama's club, or the sermons at church. Nowhere in Melton, nor with anyone, did Jessie feel so comfortable as with Cora in the kitchen. She knew her mother looked down on her as a stupid girl. And with her father there was no bond. He was always too busy buying and selling to bother with the kids. And often he was off in the city. Old doddering Grandma made Jessie sleepy and sick. Cousin Nora (Mother's cousin) was as stiff and prim as a minister's daughter. And Jessie's older brothers and sister went their ways, seeing Jessie hardly at all, except at the big table at mealtimes.

Like all the unpleasant things in the house, Jessie was left to Cora. And Cora was happy. To have a child to raise, a child the same age as her Josephine would have been, gave her a purpose in life, a warmth inside herself. It was Cora who nursed and mothered and petted and loved the dull little Jessie through the years. And now Jessie was a young woman, graduating (late) from high-school.

But something had happened to Jessie. Cora knew it before Mrs. Art did. Jessie was not too stupid to have a boy-friend. She told Cora about it like a mother. She was afraid to tell Mrs. Art. Afraid! Afraid! Afraid!

Cora said, "I'll tell her." So, humble and unashamed about life, one afternoon she marched into Mrs. Art's sun-porch and announced quite simply, "Jessie's going to have a baby."

Cora smiled, but Mrs. Art stiffened like a bolt. Her mouth went dry. She rose like a soldier. Sat down. Rose again. Walked straight toward the door, turned around, and whispered, "What?"

"Yes, m'am, a baby. She told me. A little child. Its father is Willie Matsoulos, whose folks runs the ice-cream stand on Main. She told me. They want to get married, but Willie ain't here now. He don't know yet about the child."

Cora would have gone on humbly and shamelessly talking about the little unborn had not Mrs. Art fallen into uncontrollable hysterics. Cousin Nora came running from the library, her glasses on a chain. Old Lady Studevant's wheel-chair rolled up, doddering and shaking with excitement. Jessie came, when called, red and sweating, but had to go out, for when her mother looked up from the couch and saw her she yelled louder than ever. There was a rush for camphor bottles and water and ice. Crying and praying followed all over the house. Scandalization! Oh, my Lord! Jessie was in trouble.

"She ain't in trouble neither," Cora insisted. "No trouble having a baby you want. I had one."

"Shut up, Cora!"

"Yes, m'am. . . . But I had one."
"Hush, I tell you."
"Yes, m'am."

III

Then it was that Cora began to be shut out. Jessie was confined to her room. That afternoon, when Miss Mary came home from school, the four white women got together behind closed doors in Mrs. Art's bedroom. For once Cora cooked supper in the kitchen without being bothered by an interfering voice. Mr. Studevant was away in Des Moines. Somehow Cora wished he was home. Big and gruff as he was, he had more sense than the women. He'd probably make a shot-gun wedding out of it. But left to Mrs. Art, Jessie would never marry the Greek boy at all. This Cora knew. No man had been found yet good enough for sister Mary to mate with. Mrs. Art had ambitions which didn't include the likes of Greek ice-cream makers' sons.

Jessie was crying when Cora brought her supper up. The black woman sat down on the bed and lifted the white girl's head in her dark hands. "Don't you mind, honey," Cora said. "Just sit tight, and when the boy comes back I'll tell him how things are. If he loves you he'll want you. And there ain't no reason why you can't marry, neither—you both white. Even if he is a foreigner, he's a right nice boy."

"He loves me," Jessie said. "I know he does. He said so."

But before the boy came back (or Mr. Studevant either) Mrs. Art and Jessie went to Kansas City. "For an Easter shopping trip," the weekly paper said.

Then Spring came in full bloom, and the fields and orchards at the edge of Melton stretched green and beautiful to the far horizon. Cora remembered her own Spring, twenty years ago, and a great sympathy and pain welled up in her heart for Jessie, who was the same age that Josephine would have been, had she lived. Sitting on the kitchen porch shelling peas, Cora thought back over her own life—years and years of working for the Studevants; years and years of going home to nobody but Ma and Pa; little Josephine dead; only Jessie to keep her heart warm. And she knew that Jessie was the dearest thing she had in the world. All the time the girl was gone now, she worried.

After ten days, Mrs. Art and her daughter came back. But Jessie was thinner and paler than she'd ever been in her life. There was no light in her eyes at all. Mrs. Art looked a little scared as they got off the train.

"She had an awful attack of indigestion in Kansas City," she told the neighbors and club women. "That's why I stayed away so long, waiting for her to be able to travel. Poor Jessie! She looks healthy, but she's never been a strong child. She's one of the worries of my life." Mrs. Art talked a lot, explained a lot, about how Jessie had eaten the wrong things in Kansas City.

At home, Jessie went to bed. She wouldn't eat. When Cora brought her food up, she whispered, "The baby's gone."

Cora's face went dark. She bit her lips to keep from cursing. She put her arms about Jessie's neck. The girl cried. Her food went untouched.

A week passed. They tried to *make* Jessie eat then. But the food wouldn't stay on her stomach. Her eyes grew yellow, her tongue white, her heart acted crazy. They called in old Doctor Brown, but within a month (as quick as that) Jessie died.

She never saw the Greek boy any more. Indeed, his father had lost his license, "due to several complaints by the mothers of children, backed by the Woman's Club," that he was selling tainted ice-cream. Mrs. Art Studevant had started a campaign to rid the town of objectionable tradespeople and questionable characters. Greeks were bound to be one or the other. For a while they even closed up Pa Jenkins' favorite boot-legger. Mrs. Studevant thought this would please Cora, but Cora only said, "Pa's been drinkin' so long he just as well keep on." She refused further to remark on her employer's campaign of purity. In the midst of this clean-up Jessie died.

On the day of the funeral, the house was stacked with flowers. (They held the funeral, not at the church, but at home, on account of old Grandma Studevant's infirmities.) All the family dressed in deep mourning. Mrs. Art was prostrate. As the hour for the services approached, she revived, however, and ate an omelette, "to help me go through the afternoon."

"And Cora," she said, "cook me a little piece of ham with it. I feel so weak."

"Yes, m'am."

The senior class from the high-school came in a body. The Woman's Club came with their badges. The Reverend Doctor McElroy had on his highest collar and longest coat. The choir sat behind the coffin, with a special soloist to sing "He Feedeth His Flocks Like a Shepherd." It was a beautiful Spring afternoon, and a beautiful funeral.

Except that Cora was there. Of course, her presence created no comment (she was the family servant), but it was what she did, and how she did it, that has remained the talk of Melton to this day—for Cora was not humble in the face of death.

When the Reverend Doctor McElroy had finished his eulogy, and the senior class had read their memorials, and the songs had been sung, and they were about to allow the relatives and friends to pass around for one last look at Jessie Studevant, Cora got up from her seat by the dining-room door. She said, "Honey, I want to say something." She spoke as if she were addressing Jessie. She approached the coffin and held out her brown hands over the white girl's body. Her face moved in agitation. People sat stone-still and there was a long pause. Suddenly she screamed. "They killed you! And for nothin'. . . . They killed your child. . . . They took you away from here in the Springtime of your life, and now you'se gone, gone, gone!"

Folks were paralyzed in their seats.

Cora went on: "They preaches you a pretty sermon and they don't say nothin'. They sings you a song, and they don't say nothin'. But Cora's here, honey, and she's gone tell 'em what they done to you. She's gonna tell 'em why they took you to Kansas City."

A loud scream rent the air. Mrs. Art fell back in her chair, stiff as a board. Cousin Nora and sister Mary sat like stones. The men of the family rushed forward to grab Cora. They stumbled over wreaths and garlands. Before they could reach her, Cora pointed her long fingers at the women in black and said, "They killed you, honey. They killed you and your child. I told 'em you loved it, but they didn't care. They killed it before it was . . ."

A strong hand went around Cora's waist. Another grabbed her arm. The Studevant males half pulled, half pushed her through the aisles of folding chairs, through the crowded dining-room, out into the empty kitchen, through the screen door into the backyard. She struggled against them all the way, accusing their women. At the door she sobbed, great tears coming for the love of Jessie.

She sat down on a wash-bench in the backyard, crying. In the parlor she could hear the choir singing weakly. In a few moments she gathered herself together, and went back into the house. Slowly, she picked up her few belongings from the kitchen and pantry, her aprons and her umbrella, and went off down the alley, home to Ma. Cora never came back to work for the Studevants.

Now she and Ma live from the little garden they raise, and from the junk Pa collects—when they can take by main force a part of his meager earnings before he buys his licker.

Anyhow, on the edge of Melton, the Jenkins niggers, Pa and Ma and Cora, somehow manage to get along.

Slave on the Block

They were people who went in for Negroes—Michael and Anne—the Carraways. But not in the social-service, philanthropic sort of way, no. They saw no use in helping a race that was already too charming and naive and lovely for words. Leave them unspoiled and just enjoy them, Michael and Anne felt. So they went in for the Art of Negroes—the dancing that had such jungle life about it, the songs that were so simple and fervent, the poetry that was so direct, so real. They never tried to influence that art, they only bought it and raved over it, and copied it. For they were artists, too.

In their collection they owned some Covarrubias originals.[1] Of course Covarrubias wasn't a Negro, but how he caught the darky spirit! They owned all the Robeson records and all the Bessie Smith. And they had a manuscript of Countee Cullen's. They saw all the plays with or about Negroes, read all the books, and adored the Hall Johnson Singers. They had met Doctor Du Bois, and longed to meet Carl Van Vechten. Of course they knew Harlem like their own backyard, that is, all the speakeasies and night clubs and dance halls, from the Cotton Club and the ritzy joints where Negroes couldn't go themselves, down to places like the Hot Dime, where white folks couldn't get in—unless they knew the man. (And tipped heavily.)

They were acquainted with lots of Negroes, too—but somehow the Negroes didn't seem to like them very much. Maybe the Carraways gushed over them too soon. Or maybe they looked a little like poor white folks, although they were really quite well off. Or maybe they tried too hard to make friends, dark friends, and the dark friends suspected something. Or perhaps their house in the Village was too far from Harlem, or too hard to find, being back in one of those queer and expensive little side streets that had once been alleys before the art invasion came. Anyway, occasionally, a furtive Negro might accept their invitation for tea, or cocktails; and sometimes a lesser Harlem celebrity or two would decorate their rather slow parties; but one seldom came back for more. As much as they loved Negroes, Negroes didn't seem to love Michael and Anne.

But they were blessed with a wonderful colored cook and maid—until she took sick and died in her room in their basement. And then the most marvellous ebony boy walked into their life, a boy as black as all the Negroes they'd ever known put together.

"He *is* the jungle," said Anne when she saw him.

"He's 'I Couldn't Hear Nobody Pray,' " said Michael.

For Anne thought in terms of pictures: she was a painter. And Michael thought in terms of music: he was a composer for the piano. And they had a most wonderful idea of painting pictures and composing music that went together, and then having a joint "concert-exhibition" as they would call it. Her pictures and his music. The Carraways, a sonata and a picture, a fugue and a picture. It would be lovely, and such a novelty, people would have to like it. And many of their things would be Negro. Anne had painted their maid six times. And Michael had composed several themes based on the spirituals, and on Louis Armstrong's jazz. Now here was this ebony boy. The essence in the flesh.

They had nearly missed the boy. He had come, when they were out, to gather up the things the cook had left, and take them to her sister in Jersey. It seems that he was the late cook's nephew. The new colored maid had let him in and given him the two suitcases of poor dear Emma's belongings, and he was on his way to the Subway. That is, he was in the hall, going out just as the Carraways, Michael and Anne, stepped in. They could hardly see the boy, it being dark in the hall, and he being dark, too.

"Hello," they said. "Is this Emma's nephew?"

"Yes'm," said the maid. "Yes'm."

"Well, come in," said Anne, "and let us see you. We loved your aunt so much. She was the best cook we ever had."

"You don't know where *I* could get a job, do you?" said the boy. This took Michael and Anne back a bit, but they rallied at once. So charming and naive to ask right away for what he wanted.

Anne burst out, "You know, I think I'd like to paint you."

Michael said, "Oh, I say now, that would be lovely! He's so utterly Negro."

The boy grinned.

Anne said, "Could you come back tomorrow?"

And the boy said, "Yes, indeed. I sure could."

The upshot of it was that they hired him. They hired him to look after the garden, which was just about as big as Michael's grand piano— only a little square behind the house. You know those Village gardens. Anne sometimes painted it. And occasionally they set the table there for four on a spring evening. Nothing grew in the garden really, practically nothing. But the boy said he could plant things. And they had to have some excuse to hire him.

The boy's name was Luther. He had come from the South to his relatives in Jersey, and had had only one job since he got there, shining shoes for a Greek in Elizabeth. But the Greek fired him because the boy wouldn't give half his tips over to the proprietor.

"I never heard of a job where I had to pay the boss, instead of the boss paying me," said Luther. "Not till I got here."

"And then what did you do?" said Anne.

"Nothing. Been looking for a job for the last four months."

"Poor boy," said Michael; "poor, dear boy."

"Yes," said Anne. "You must be hungry." And they called the cook to give him something to eat.

Luther dug around in the garden a little bit that first day, went out and bought some seeds, came back and ate some more. They made a place for him to sleep in the basement by the furnace. And the next day Anne started to paint him, after she'd bought the right colors.

"He'll be good company for Mattie," they said. "She claims she's afraid to stay alone at night when we're out, so she leaves." They suspected, though, that Mattie just liked to get up to Harlem. And they thought right. Mattie was not as settled as she looked. Once out, with the Savoy open until three in the morning, why come home? That was the way Mattie felt.

In fact, what happened was that Mattie showed Luther where the best and cheapest hot spots in Harlem were located. Luther hadn't even set foot in Harlem before, living twenty-eight miles away, as he did, in Jersey, and being a kind of quiet boy. But the second night he was there Mattie said, "Come on, let's go. Working for white folks all day, I'm tired. They needn't think I was made to answer telephones all night." So out they went.

Anne noticed that most mornings Luther would doze almost as soon as she sat him down to pose, so she eventually decided to paint Luther asleep. "The Sleeping Negro," she would call it. Dear, natural childlike people, they would sleep anywhere they wanted to. Anyway, asleep, he kept still and held the pose.

And he *was* an adorable Negro. Not tall, but with a splendid body. And a slow and lively smile that lighted up his black, black face, for his teeth were very white, and his eyes, too. Most effective in oil and canvas. Better even than Emma had been. Anne could stare at him at leisure when he was asleep. One day she decided to paint him nude, or at least half nude. A slave picture, that's what she would do. The market at New Orleans for a background. And call it "The Boy on the Block."

So one morning when Luther settled down in his sleeping pose, Anne said, "No," she had finished that picture. She wanted to paint him now representing to the full the soul and sorrow of his people. She wanted to paint him as a slave about to be sold. And since slaves in warm climates had no clothes, would he please take off his shirt.

Luther smiled a sort of embarrassed smile and took off his shirt.

"Your undershirt, too," said Anne. But it turned out that he had on a union suit, so he had to go out and change altogether. He came back and mounted the box that Anne said would serve just then for a slave block, and she began to sketch. Before luncheon Michael came in, and went into rhapsodies over Luther on the box without a shirt, about to be sold into slavery. He said he must put him into music right now. And he went to the piano and began to play something that sounded like Deep River in the jaws of a dog, but Michael said it was a modern slave plaint, 1850 in terms of 1933. Vieux Carré remembered on 135th Street. Slavery in the Cotton Club.

Anne said, "It's too marvellous!" And they painted and played till dark, with rest periods in between for Luther. Then they all knocked off for dinner. Anne and Michael went out later to one of Lew Leslie's new shows. And Luther and Mattie said, "Thank God!" and got dressed up for Harlem.

Funny, they didn't like the Carraways. They treated them nice and paid them well. "But they're too strange," said Mattie, "they makes me nervous."

"They is mighty funny," Luther agreed.

They didn't understand the vagaries of white folks, neither Luther nor Mattie, and they didn't want to be bothered trying.

"I does my work," said Mattie. "After that I don't want to be painted, or asked to sing songs, nor nothing like that."

The Carraways often asked Luther to sing, and he sang. He knew a lot of southern worksongs and reels, and spirituals and ballads.

> *"Dear Ma, I'm in hard luck:*
> *Three days since I et,*
> *And the stamp on this letter's*
> *Gwine to put me in debt."*

The Carraways allowed him to neglect the garden altogether. About all Luther did was pose and sing. And he got tired of that.

Indeed, both Luther and Mattie became a bit difficult to handle as time went on. The Carraways blamed it on Mattie. She had got hold of Luther. She was just simply spoiling a nice simple young boy. She was old enough to know better. Mattie was in love with Luther.

At least, he slept with her. The Carraways discovered this one night about one o'clock when they went to wake Luther up (the first time they'd ever done such a thing) and ask him if he wouldn't sing his own marvellous version of John Henry for a man who had just come from Saint Louis and was sailing for Paris tomorrow. But Luther wasn't in his own bed by the furnace. There was a light in Mattie's room, so Michael knocked softly. Mattie said, "Who's that?" And Michael poked his head in, and here were Luther and Mattie in bed together!

Of course, Anne condoned them. "It's so simple and natural for Negroes to make love." But Mattie, after all, was forty if she was a day. And Luther was only a kid. Besides Anne thought that Luther had been ever so much nicer when he first came than he was now. But from so many nights at the Savoy, he had become a marvellous dancer, and he was teaching Anne the Lindy Hop to Cab Calloway's records. Besides, her picture of "The Boy on the Block" wasn't anywhere near done. And he did take pretty good care of the furnace. So they kept him. At least, Anne kept him, although Michael said he was getting a little bored with the same Negro always in the way.

For Luther had grown a bit familiar lately. He smoked up all their cigarettes, drank their wine, told jokes on them to their friends, and sometimes even came upstairs singing and walking about the house when the Carraways had guests in who didn't share their enthusiasm for Negroes, natural or otherwise.

Luther and Mattie together were a pair. They quite frankly lived with one another now. Well, let that go. Anne and Michael prided themselves on being different; artists, you know, and liberal-minded people—maybe a little scatter-brained, but then (secretly, they felt) that came from genius. They were not ordinary people, bothering about the liberties of others. Certainly, the last thing they would do would be to interfere with the delightful simplicity of Negroes.

But Mattie must be giving Luther money and buying him clothes. He was really dressing awfully well. And on her Thursday afternoons off she would come back loaded down with packages. As far as the Carraways could tell, they were all for Luther.

And sometimes there were quarrels drifting up from the basement. And often, all too often, Mattie had moods. Then Luther would have moods. And it was pretty awful having two dark and glowering people around the house. Anne couldn't paint and Michael couldn't play.

One day, when she hadn't seen Luther for three days, Anne called downstairs and asked him if he wouldn't please come up and take off his shirt and get on the box. The picture was almost done. Luther came dragging his feet upstairs and humming:

> *"Before I'd be a slave*
> *I'd be buried in ma grave*
> *And go home to my Jesus*
> *And be free."*

And that afternoon he let the furnace go almost out.

That was the state of things when Michael's mother (whom Anne had never liked) arrived from Kansas City to pay them a visit. At once neither Mattie nor Luther liked her either. She was a mannish old lady, big and tall, and inclined to be bossy. Mattie, however, did spruce up her service, cooked delicious things, and treated Mrs. Carraway with a great deal more respect than she did Anne.

"I never play with servants," Mrs. Carraway had said to Michael, and Mattie must have heard her.

But Luther, he was worse than ever. Not that he did anything wrong, Anne thought, but the way he did things! For instance, he didn't need to sing now all the time, especially since Mrs. Carraway had said she didn't like singing. And certainly not songs like "You Rascal, You."

But all things end! With the Carraways and Luther it happened like this: One forenoon, quite without a shirt (for he expected to pose) Luther came sauntering through the library to change the flowers in the vase. He carried red roses. Mrs. Carraway was reading her morning scripture from the Health and Life.

"Oh, good morning," said Luther. "How long are you gonna stay in this house?"

"I never liked familiar Negroes," said Mrs. Carraway, over her nose glasses.

"Huh!" said Luther. "That's too bad! I never liked poor white folks."

Mrs. Carraway screamed, a short loud, dignified scream. Michael came running in bathrobe and pyjamas. Mrs. Carraway grew tall. There was a scene. Luther talked. Michael talked. Anne appeared.

"Never, never, never," said Mrs. Carraway, "have I suffered such impudence from servants—and a nigger servant—in my own son's house."

"Mother, Mother, Mother," said Michael. "Be calm. I'll discharge him." He turned on the nonchalant Luther. "Go!" he said, pointing toward the door. "Go, go!"

"Michael," Anne cried, "I haven't finished 'The Slave on the Block.'" Her husband looked nonplussed. For a moment he breathed deeply.

"Either he goes or I go," said Mrs. Carraway, firm as a rock.

"He goes," said Michael with strength from his mother.

"Oh!" cried Anne. She looked at Luther. His black arms were full of roses he had brought to put in the vases. He had on no shirt. "Oh!" His body was ebony.

"Don't worry 'bout me!" said Luther. "I'll go."

"Yes, we'll go," boomed Mattie from the doorway, who had come up from below, fat and belligerent. "We've stood enough foolery from you white folks! Yes, we'll go. Come on, Luther."

What could she mean, "stood enough"? What had they done to them, Anne and Michael wondered. They had tried to be kind. "Oh!"

"Sneaking around knocking on our door at night," Mattie went on. "Yes, we'll go. Pay us! Pay us! Pay us!" So she remembered the time they had come for Luther at night. That was it.

"I'll pay you," said Michael. He followed Mattie out.

Anne looked at her black boy.

"Good-bye," Luther said. "You fix the vases."

He handed her his armful of roses, glanced impudently at old Mrs. Carraway and grinned—grinned that wide, beautiful, white-toothed grin that made Anne say when she first saw him, "He looks like the jungle." Grinned, and disappeared in the dark hall, with no shirt on his back.

"Oh," Anne moaned distressfully, "my 'Boy on the Block'!"

"Huh!" snorted Mrs. Carraway.

Home

When the boy came back, there were bright stickers and tags in strange languages the home folks couldn't read all over his bags, and on his violin case. They were the marks of customs stations at far-away borders, big hotels in European cities, and steamers that crossed the ocean a long way from Hopkinsville. They made the leather-colored bags and black violin case look very gay and circus-like. They made white people on the train wonder about the brown-skinned young man to whom the baggage belonged. And when he got off at a village station in Missouri, the loafers gathered around in a crowd, staring.

Roy Williams had come home from abroad to visit his folks, his mother and sister and brothers who still remained in the old home town. Roy had been away seven or eight years, wandering the world. He came back very well dressed, but awfully thin. He wasn't well.

It was this illness that had made Roy come home, really. He had a feeling that he was going to die, and he wanted to see his mother again. This feeling about death had been coming over him gradually for two or three years now. It seemed to him that it must have started in Vienna, that gay but dying city in Central Europe where so many people were hungry, and yet some still had money to buy champagne and caviar and women in the night-clubs where Roy's orchestra played.

But the glittering curtains of Roy's jazz were lined with death. It made him sick to see people fainting in the streets of Vienna from hunger, while others stuffed themselves with wine and food. And it made him sad to refuse the young white women trailing behind him when he came home from work late at night, offering their bodies for a little money to buy something to eat.

In Vienna Roy had a room to himself because he wanted to study and keep up his music. He studied under one of the best violin teachers. But it was hard to keep beautiful and hungry women out of his place, who wanted to give themselves to a man who had a job because in turn the man might let them sleep in his room, or toss them a few bills to take home to their starving parents.

"Folks catch hell in Europe," Roy thought. "I never saw people as hungry as this, not even Negroes at home."

But it was even worse when the orchestra moved back to Berlin. Behind the apparent solidity of that great city, behind doors where tourists never passed, hunger and pain were beyond understanding. And the police were beating people who protested, or stole, or begged. Yet in the cabaret where Roy played, crowds of folks still spent good gold. They laughed and danced every night and didn't give a damn about the children sleeping in doorways outside, or the men who built houses of packing boxes, or the women who walked the streets to pick up trade.

It was in Berlin that the sadness weighed most heavily on Roy. And it was there that he began to cough. One night in Prague, he had a hemorrhage. When he got to Paris, his girl friend took care of him, and he got better. But he had all the time, from then on, that feeling that he was going to die. The cough stayed, and the sadness. So he came home to see his mother.

He landed in New York on the day that Hoover drove the veterans out of Washington.[2] He stayed a couple of days in Harlem. Most of his old friends there, musicians and actors, were hungry and out of work. When they saw Roy dressed so well, they asked him for money. And at night women whispered in the streets, "Come here, baby! I want to see you, darlin'."

"Rotten everywhere," Roy thought. "I want to go home."

That last night in Harlem, he couldn't sleep. He thought of his mother. In the morning he sent her a telegram that he was on his way.

II

"An uppty nigger," said the white loafers when they saw him standing, slim and elegant, on the station platform in the September sunlight, surrounded by his bags with the bright stickers. Roy had got off a Pullman—something unusual for a Negro in those parts.

"God damn!" said the white loafers.

Suddenly a nasal voice broke out, "Well, I'll be dogged if it ain't Roy Williams!"

Roy recognized an old playmate, Charlie Mumford, from across the alley—a tall red-necked white boy in overalls. He took off his glove and held out his hand. The white man took it, but he didn't shake it long. Roy had forgotten he wasn't in Europe, wearing gloves and shaking hands glibly with a white man! Damn!

"Where you been, boy?" the white fellow asked.

"Paris," said Roy.

"What'd yuh come back for?" a half-southern voice drawled from the edge of a baggage truck.

"I wanted to come home," said Roy, "to see my mother."

"I hope she's gladder to see yuh than we are," another white voice drawled.

Roy picked up his bags, since there were no porters, and carried them toward a rusty old Ford that seemed to be a taxi. He felt dizzy and weak. The smoke and dust of travel had made him cough a lot. The eyes of the white men about the station were not kind. He heard some one mutter, "Nigger." His skin burned. For the first time in half a dozen years he felt his color. He was home.

III

Sing a song of Dixie, cotton bursting in the sun, shade of chinaberry trees, persimmons after frost has fallen. Hounds treeing possums October nights. O, sweet potatoes, hot, with butter in their yellow hearts.

"Son, I'm glad you's done come home. What can Ma cook for you? I know you's hungry for some real food. Corn bread and greens and salt pork. Lawd! . . . You's got some mighty nice clothes, honey, but you looks right thin. . . . Chile, I hope you's gonna stay home awhile. . . . These colored girls here'll go crazy about you. They fightin' over you already. . . . Honey, when you plays that violin o' your'n it makes me right weak, it's so purty. . . . Play yo' violin, boy! God's done give you a gift! Yes, indeedy! . . . It's funny how all these Hopkinsville white folks is heard about you already. De woman where yo' sister works say she read someplace 'bout that orchestry you was playin' with in Paris. She says fo' Sister to bring you up to de house to play fo' her sometime. I told Sister, no indeedy, you don't go around playin' at nobody's house. Told her to tell that white woman de Deacon's Board's arrangin' a concert at de church fo' you where everybody can come and pay twenty-five cents to de glory of God and hear you play. Ain't that right, son? You gwine play fo' de Lawd here in Hopkinsville. You been playin' fo' de devil every night all over Europy. . . . Jesus have mercy! Lemme go and get ma washin' out! And whiles you's practicin', I'm gonna make you a pumpkin pie this afternoon. I can see yo' mouth waterin' now. . . . Honey, Ma's sho glad you's done come home. . . . Play yo' violin, son!"

IV

CAPRICE VIENNOIS
AIR FOR G STRING
SONATA IN A
AVE MARIA
THE GYPSY DANCES

What little house anywhere was ever big enough to hold Brahms and Beethoven, Bach and César Franck? Certainly not Sister Sarah Williams's house in Hopkinsville. When Roy played, ill as he was, the notes went bursting out the windows and the colored folks and white folks in the street heard them. The classic Mr. Brahms coming out of a nigger's house in the southern end of Missouri. O, my God! Play yo' violin, Roy! Tonight's your concert.

The Deacons and the Ladies' Aid sold a lot of tickets to the white folks they worked for. Roy's home-coming concert at Shiloh Church was a financial success. The front rows were fifty cents and filled with white folks. The rest of the seats were a quarter and filled with Negroes. Methodist and Baptist both came, forgetting churchly rivalry. And there were lots of colored girls with powdered bonbon faces—sweet black and brown and yellow girls with red mouths pointed at Roy. There was lots of bustle and perfume and smothered giggling and whispered talk as the drab little church filled. New shoes screeched up and down the aisles. People applauded because it was past the hour, but the concert started colored folks' time anyhow—late. The church was crowded.

V

Hello, Mr. Brahms on a violin from Vienna at a colored church in Hopkinsville, Missouri. The slender brown-skin hands of a sick young man making you sing for an audience of poor white folks and even poorer Negroes. Good-evenin', Mr. Brahms, a long ways from home, travellin' in answer to your dream, singin' across the world. I had a dream, too, Mr. Brahms, a big dream that can't come true, now. Dream of a great stage in a huge hall, like Carnegie Hall or the Salle Gaveau. And you, Mr. Brahms, singin' out into the darkness, singin' so strong and true that a thousand people look up at me like they do at Roland Hayes singing the Crucifixion.³ Jesus, I dreamed like that once before I got sick and had to come home.

And here I am giving my first concert in America for my mother and the Deacons of Shiloh Church and the quarters and fifty cent pieces they've collected from Brahms and me for the glory of God. This ain't Carnegie Hall. I've only just come home. . . . But they're looking at me. They're all looking at me. The white folks in the front rows and the Negroes in the back. Like one pair of eyes looking at me.

This, my friends . . . I should say, *Ladies and Gentlemen.* (There are white folks in the audience who are not my friends.) . . . This is the *Meditation from Thaïs* by Massenet. . . . This is the broken heart of a dream come true not true. This is music, and me, sitting on the door-step of the world needing you. . . . O, body of life and love with black hands and brown limbs and white breasts and a golden face with lips like a violin bowed for singing. . . . Steady, Roy! It's hot in this crowded church, and you're sick as hell. . . . This, the dream and the dreamer, wandering in the desert from Hopkinsville to Vienna in love with a street-walker named Music. . . . Listen, you bitch, I want you to be beautiful as the moon in the night on the edge of the Missouri hills. I'll make you beautiful. . . . The *Meditation from Thaïs.* . . . You remember, Ma (even to hear me play, you've got your seat in the amen corner tonight like on Sunday mornings when you come to talk to God), you remember that Kreisler record we had on the phonograph with the big horn when I was a kid? Nobody liked it but me, but you didn't care how many times I played it, over and over. . . . Where'd you get my violin? Half the time you didn't have the money to pay old man Miller for my lesson every week. . . . God rest his unpaid soul, as the Catholics say. . . . Why did you cry, Ma, when I went away with the minstrel show, playing coon songs through the South instead of hymns? What did you cry for, Ma, when I wrote you I had a job with a night-club jazz band on State Street in Chicago? . . . Why did you pray all night when I told you we had a contract to go to Berlin and work in a cabaret there? I tried to explain to you that the best violin teachers in the world were in Berlin and that I'd come back playing like that Kreisler record on the old victrola. . . . And didn't I send you money home? . . . Spray like sand in the eyes. . . . O, dream on the door-step of the world! Thaïs! Thaïs! . . . You sure don't look like Thaïs, you scrawny white woman in a cheap coat and red hat staring up at me from the first row. You don't look a bit like Thaïs. What is it you want the music to give you? What do you want from me? . . . This is Hopkinsville, Missouri. . . . Look at all those brown girls back there in the crowd of Negroes, leaning toward me and the music. First time most of them ever saw a man in evening clothes, black or white.

First time most of them ever heard the *Meditation from Thaïs*. First time they ever had one of their own race come home from abroad playing a violin. See them looking proud at me and music over the heads of the white folks in the first rows, over the head of the white woman in the cheap coat and red hat who knows what music's all about. . . . Who are you, lady?

When the concert was over, even some of the white folks shook Roy's hand and said it was wonderful. The colored folks said, "Boy, you sure can play!" Roy was shaking a little and his eyes burned and he wanted terribly to cough. Pain shot across his shoulders. But he smiled his concert-jazz-band smile that the gold spending ladies of the European night clubs had liked so much. And he held out a feverish hand to everybody. The white woman in the red hat waited at the edge of the crowd.

When people thinned out a little from the pulpit, she came to Roy and shook his hand. She spoke of symphony concerts in St. Louis, of the fact that she was a teacher of music, of piano and violin, but that she had no pupils like Roy, that never in the town of Hopkinsville had anyone else played so beautifully. Roy looked into her thin, freckled face and was glad she knew what it was all about. He was glad she liked music.

"That's Miss Reese," his mother told him after she had gone. "An old maid musicianer at the white high school."

"Yes'm," said Roy. "She understands music."

VI

The next time he saw Miss Reese was at the white high school shortly after it opened the fall session. One morning a note had come asking him if he would play for her Senior class in music appreciation some day. She would accompany him if he would bring his music. It seems that one of Miss Reese's duties was the raising of musical standards in Hopkinsville; she had been telling her students about Bach and Mozart, and she would so appreciate it if Roy would visit the school and play those two great masters for her young people. She wrote him a nice note on clean white paper.

Roy went. His mother thought it was a great honor for the white high school to send for her colored son to play for them. "That Miss Reese's a right nice woman," Sister Williams said to her boy. "Sendin' for you to play up there at de school. First time I ever knowed 'em to have a Negro in there for anything but cleanin' up, and I been in Hopkinsville a long time. Go and play for 'em, son, to de glory of God!"

Roy played. But it was one of those days when his throat was hot and dry, and his eyes burned. He had been coughing all morning and, as he played, his breath left him and he stood covered with a damp sweat. He played badly.

But Miss Reese was more than kind to him. She accompanied him at the piano. And when he had finished, she turned to the assembled class of white kids sprawled in their seats and said, "This is art, my dear young people, this is true art!"

The students went home that afternoon and told their parents that a dressed-up nigger had come to school with a violin and played a lot of funny pieces nobody but Miss Reese liked. They went on to say that Miss Reese had grinned all over herself and cried, "Wonderful!" And had even bowed to the nigger when he went out!

Roy went home to bed. He was up and down these days, thinner and thinner all the time, weaker and weaker. Sometimes not practicing any more. Often not eating the food his mother cooked for him, or that his sister brought from where she worked. Sometimes being restless and hot in the night and getting up and dressing, even to spats and yellow gloves, and walking the streets of the little town at ten and eleven o'clock after nearly every one else had gone to bed. Midnight was late in Hopkinsville. But for years Roy had worked at night. It was hard for him to sleep before morning now.

But one night he walked out of the house for the last time. The moon had risen and Roy scarcely needed to light the oil lamp to dress by when he got up. The moon shone into his little room, across the white counterpane of his bed, down onto the bags with the bright stickers piled against the wall. It glistened on the array of medicine bottles on the side table. But Roy lighted the light, the better to see himself in the warped mirror of the dresser. Ashy pale his face was, that had once been brown. His cheeks were sunken. Trembling, he put on his suit and spats and his yellow gloves and soft felt hat. He got into an overcoat. He took a cane that he carried lately from weakness rather than from style. And he went out into the autumn moonlight.

Tiptoeing through the parlor, he heard his mother snoring on the couch there. (She had given up her room to him.) The front door was still unlocked. His brothers, Roy thought, were out with their girl friends. His sister had gone to bed.

In the streets it was very quiet. Misty with moonlight, the trees stood half clad in autumn leaves. Roy walked under the dry falling leaves toward the center of the town, breathing in the moonlight air and swinging his cane. Night and the streets always made him feel better. He remembered the boulevards of Paris and the Unter den Linden. He remembered Tauber singing *Wien, Du Stadt Meiner Traume*. His mind went back to the lights and the music of the cities of Europe. How like a dream that he had ever been in Europe at all, he thought. Ma never had any money. Her kids had barely managed to get through the grade school. There was no higher school for Negroes in Hopkinsville. For him there had been only a minstrel show to run away with for further education. Then that chance with a jazz band going to Berlin. And his violin for a mistress all the time—with the best teachers his earnings could pay for abroad. Jazz at night and the classics in the morning. Hard work and hard practice, until his violin sang like nobody's business. Music, real music! Then he began to cough in Berlin.

Roy was passing lots of people now in the brightness of the main street, but he saw none of them. He saw only dreams and memories, and heard music. Some of the people stopped to stare and grin at the flare of the European coat on his slender brown body. Spats and a cane on a young nigger in Hopkinsville, Missouri! What's the big idea, heh? A little white boy or two catcalled, "Hey, coon!" But everything might have been all right, folks might only have laughed or commented and cussed, had not a rather faded woman in a cheap coat and a red hat, a white woman, stepping out of the drug store just as Roy passed, bowed pleasantly to him, "Good evening."

Roy started, bowed, nodded, "Good evening, Miss Reese," and was glad to see her. Forgetting he wasn't in Europe, he took off his hat and his gloves, and held out his hand to this lady who understood music. They smiled at each other, the sick young colored man and the aging music teacher in the light of the main street. Then she asked him if he was still working on the Sarasate.

"Yes," Roy said. "It's lovely."

"And have you heard that marvellous Heifetz record of it?" Miss Reese inquired.

Roy opened his mouth to reply when he saw the woman's face suddenly grow pale with horror. Before he could turn around to learn what her eyes had seen, he felt a fist like a ton of bricks strike his jaw. There was a flash of lightning in his brain as his head hit the edge of the plate glass window of the drug store. Miss Reese screamed. The sidewalk filled with white young ruffians with red-necks, open sweaters, and fists doubled up to strike. The movies had just let out and the crowd, passing by and seeing, objected to a Negro talking to a white woman—insulting a White Woman—attacking a WHITE woman—RAPING A WHITE WOMAN. They saw Roy remove his gloves and bow. When Miss Reese screamed after Roy had been struck, they were sure he had been making love to her. And before the story got beyond the rim of the crowd, Roy had been trying to rape her, right there on the main street in front of the brightly-lighted windows of the drug store. Yes, he did, too! Yes, sir!

So they knocked Roy down. They trampled on his hat and cane and gloves as a dozen men tried to get to him to pick him up—so some one else could have the pleasure of knocking him down again. They struggled over the privilege of knocking him down.

Roy looked up from the sidewalk at the white mob around him. His mouth was full of blood and his eyes burned. His clothes were dirty. He wondered why Miss Reese had stopped to ask him about Sarasate. He knew he would never get home to his mother now.

Some one jerked him to his feet. Some one spat in his face. (It looked like his old playmate, Charlie Mumford.) Somebody cussed him for being a nigger, and another kicked him from behind. And all the men and boys in the lighted street began to yell and scream like mad people, and to snarl like dogs, and to pull at the little Negro in spats they were dragging through the town towards the woods.

The little Negro whose name was Roy Williams began to choke on the blood in his mouth. And the roar of their voices and the scuff of their feet were split by the moonlight into a thousand notes like a Beethoven sonata. And when the white folks left his brown body, stark naked, strung from a tree at the edge of town, it hung there all night, like a violin for the wind to play.

Passing

Chicago,
Sunday, Oct. 10.

Dear Ma,

I felt like a dog, passing you downtown last night and not speaking to you. You were great, though. Didn't give a sign that you even knew me, let alone I was your son. If I hadn't had the girl with me, Ma, we might have talked. I'm not as scared as I used to be about somebody taking me for colored any more just because I'm seen talking on the street to a Negro. I guess in looks I'm sort of suspect-proof, anyway. You remember what a hard time I used to have in school trying to convince teachers I was really colored. Sometimes, even after they met you, my mother, they wouldn't believe it. They just thought I had a mulatto mammy, I guess. Since I've begun to pass for white, nobody has ever doubted that I am a white man. Where I work, the boss is a Southerner and is always cussing out Negroes in my presence, not dreaming I'm one. It is to laugh!

Funny thing, though, Ma, how some white people certainly don't like colored people, do they? (If they did, then I wouldn't have to be passing to keep my good job.) They go out of their way sometimes to say bad things about colored folks, putting it out that all of us are thieves and liars, or else diseased—consumption and syphilis, and the like. No wonder it's hard for a black man to get a good job with that kind of false propaganda going around. I never knew they made a practice of saying such terrible things about us until I started passing and heard their conversations and lived their life.

But I don't mind being "white," Ma, and it was mighty generous of you to urge me to go ahead and make use of my light skin and good hair. It got me this job, Ma, where I still get $65 a week in spite of the depression. And I'm in line for promotion to the chief office secretary, if Mr. Weeks goes to Washington. When I look at the colored boy porter who sweeps out the office, I think that that's what I might be doing if I wasn't light-skinned enough to get by. No matter how smart that boy'd get to be, they wouldn't hire him for a clerk in the office, not if they knew it. Only for a porter. That's why I sometimes get a kick out of putting something over on the boss, who never dreams he's got a colored secretary.

But, Ma, I felt mighty bad about last night. The first time we'd met in public that way. That's the kind of thing that makes passing hard, having to deny your own family when you see them. Of course, I know you and I both realize it is all for the best, but anyhow it's terrible. I love you, Ma, and hate to do it, even if you say you don't mind.

But what did you think of the girl with me, Ma? She's the kid I'm going to marry. Pretty good looking, isn't she? Nice disposition. The parents are well fixed. Her folks are German-Americans and don't have much prejudice about them, either. I took her to see a colored revue last week and she thought it was great. She said, "Darkies are so graceful and gay." I wonder what she would have said if I'd told her *I* was colored, or half-colored—that my old man was white, but you weren't? But I guess I won't go into that. Since I've made up my mind to live in the white world, and have found my place in it (a good place), why think about race any more? I'm glad I don't have to, I know that much.

I hope Charlie and Gladys don't feel bad about me. It's funny I was the only one of the kids light enough to pass. Charlie's darker than you, even, Ma. I know he sort of resented it in school when the teachers used to take me for white, before they knew we were brothers. I used to feel bad about it, too, then. But now I'm glad you backed me up, and told me to go ahead and get all I could out of life. That's what I'm going to do, Ma. I'm going to marry white and live white, and if any of my kids are born dark I'll swear they aren't mine. I won't get caught in the mire of color again. Not me. I'm free, Ma, free!

I'd be glad, though, if I could get away from Chicago, transferred to the New York office, or the San Francisco branch of the firm—somewhere where what happened last night couldn't ever occur again. It was awful passing *you* and not speaking. And if Gladys or Charlie were to meet me in the street, they might not be as tactful as you were—because they don't seem to be very happy about my passing for white. I don't see why, though. I'm not hurting them any, and I send you money every week and help out just as much as they do, if not more. Tell them not to queer me, Ma, if they should ever run into me and the girl friend any place. Maybe it would have been better if you and they had stayed in Cincinnati and I'd come away alone when we decided to move after the old man died. Or at least, we should have gone to different towns, shouldn't we?

Gee, Ma, when I think of how papa left everything to his white family, and you couldn't legally do anything for us kids, my blood boils. You wouldn't have a chance in a Kentucky court, I know, but maybe if you'd tried anyway, his white children would have paid you something to shut up. Maybe they wouldn't want it known in the papers that they had colored brothers. But you was too proud, wasn't you, Ma? I wouldn't have been so proud.

Well, he did buy you a house and send all us kids through school. I'm glad I finished college in Pittsburgh before he died. It was too bad about Charlie and Glad having to drop out, but I hope Charlie gets something better to do than working in a garage. And from what you told me in your last letter about Gladys, I don't blame you for being worried about her—wanting to go in the chorus of one of those South Side cabarets. Lord! But I know it's really tough for girls to get any kind of a job during this depression, especially for colored girls, even if Gladys is high yellow, and smart. But I hope you can keep her home, and out of those South Side dumps. They're no place for a good girl.

Well, Ma, I will close because I promised to take my weakness to the movies this evening. Isn't she sweet to look at, all blonde and blue-eyed? We're making plans about our house when we get married. We're going to take a little apartment on the North Side, in a good neighborhood, out on one of those nice quiet side streets where there are trees. I will take a box at the Post Office for your mail. Anyhow, I'm glad there's nothing to stop letters from crossing the color-line. Even if we can't meet often, we can write, can't we, Ma?

> With love from your son,
> JACK.

V

A Good Job Gone

It was a good job. Best job I ever had. Got it my last year in high school and it took me damn near through college. I'm sure sorry it didn't last. I made good money, too. Made so much I changed from City College to Columbia my Sophomore year. Mr. Lloyd saw to it I got a good education. He had nothing against the Negro race, he said, and I don't believe he did. He certainly treated me swell from the time I met him till that high brown I'm gonna tell you about drove him crazy.

Now, Mr. Lloyd was a man like this: he had plenty of money, he liked his licker, and he liked his women. That was all. A damn nice guy— till he got hold of this jane from Harlem. Or till she got hold of him. My people—they won't do. They'd mess up the Lord if He got too intimate with 'em. Poor Negroes! I guess I was to blame. I should of told Mr. Lloyd she didn't mean him no good. But I was minding my own business, and I minded it too well.

That was one of the things Mr. Lloyd told me when I went to work there. He said, "Boy, you're working for me—nobody else. Keep your mouth shut about what goes on here, and I'll look out for you. You're in school, ain't you? Well, you won't have to worry about money to buy books and take your friends out—if you stay with me."

He paid me twenty-two dollars a week, and I ate and slept in. He had a four room apartment, as cozy a place as you'd want to see, looking right over Riverside Drive. Swell view. In the summer when Mr. Lloyd was in Paris, I didn't have a damn thing to do but eat and sleep, and air the furniture. I got so tired that I went to summer school.

"What you gonna be, boy?" he said.

I said, "A dentist, I reckon."

He said, "Go to it. They make a hell of a lot of money—if they got enough sex appeal."

He was always talking about sex appeal and lovin'. He knew more dirty stories, Mr. Lloyd did! And he liked his women young and pretty. That's about all I'd do, spend my time cleaning up after some woman he'd have around, or makin' sandwiches and drinks in the evenings. When I did something extra, he'd throw me a fiver any time. I made oodles o' money. Hell of a fine guy, Mr. Lloyd, with his 40-11 pretty gals—right out of the Scandals or the back pages of *Vanity Fair*—sweet and willing.[4]

His wife was paralyzed, so I guess he had to have a little outside fun. They lived together in White Plains. But he had a suite in the Hotel Roosevelt, and a office down on Broad. He says, when I got the job, "Boy, no matter what you find out about me, where I live, or where I work, don't *you* connect up with no place but here. No matter what happens on Riverside Drive, don't you take it no further."

"Yes, sir, Mr. Lloyd," I said, I knew where my bread was buttered. So I never went near the office or saw any of his other help but the chauffeur—and him a Jap.

Only thing I didn't like about the job, he used to bring some awfully cheap women there sometimes—big timers, but cheap inside. They didn't know how to treat a servant. One of 'em used to nigger and darkie me around, till I got her told right quietly one time, and Mr. Lloyd backed me up.

The boss said, "This is no ordinary boy, Lucille. True, he's my servant, but I've got him in Columbia studying to be a dentist, and he's just as white inside as he is black. Treat him right, or I'll see why." And it wasn't long before this Lucille dame was gone, and he had a little Irish girl with blue eyes he treated mean as hell.

Another thing I didn't like, though. Sometimes I used to have to drink a lot with him. When there was no women around, and Mr. Lloyd would get one of his blue spells and start talking about his wife, and how she hadn't walked for eighteen years, just laying flat on her back, after about an hour of this, he'd want me to start drinking with him. And when he felt good from licker he'd start talking about women in general, and he'd ask me what they were like in Harlem. Then he'd tell me what they were like in Montreal, and Havana, and Honolulu. He'd even had Gypsy women in Spain, Mr. Lloyd.

Then he would drink and drink, and make me drink with him. And we'd both be so drunk I couldn't go to classes the next morning, and he wouldn't go to the office all day. About four o'clock he'd send me for some clam broth and an American Mercury, so he could sober up on Mencken.[5] I'd give him an alcohol rub, then he'd go off to the Roosevelt and have dinner with the society folks he knew. I might not see him again for days. But he'd slip me a greenback usually.

"Boy, you'll never lose anything through sticking with me! Here," and it would be a fiver.

Sometimes I wouldn't see Mr. Lloyd for weeks. Then he'd show up late at night with a chippie, and I'd start making drinks and sandwiches and smoothing down the bed. Then there'd be a round o' women, six or eight different ones in a row, for days. And me working my hips off keeping 'em fed and lickered up. This would go on till he got tired, and had the blues again. Then he'd beat the hell out of one of 'em and send her off. Then we'd get drunk. When he sobered up he'd telephone for his chauffeur and drive to White Plains to see his old lady, or down to the hotel where he lived with a secretary. And that would be that.

He had so damn much money, Mr. Lloyd. I don't see where folks get so much cash. But I don't care so long as they're giving some of it to me. And if it hadn't been for this colored woman, boy, I'd still be sitting pretty.

I don't know where he got her. Out of one of the Harlem night clubs, I guess. They came bustin' in about four o'clock one morning. I heard a woman laughing in the living-room, and I knew it was a colored laugh— one of ours. So deep and pretty, it couldn't have been nothing else. I got up, of course, like I always did when I heard Mr. Lloyd come in. I broke some ice, and took 'em out some drinks.

Yep, she was colored, all right. One of those golden browns, like an Alabama moon. Swell looking kid. She had the old man standing on his ears. I never saw him looking so happy before. She kept him laughing till daylight, hugging and kissing. She had a hot line, that kid did, without seemin' serious. He fell for it. She hadn't worked in Harlem speakeasies for nothing. Jesus! She was like gin and vermouth mixed. You know!

We got on swell, too, that girl and I. "Hy, Pal," she said when she saw me bringing out the drinks. "If it ain't old Harlem, on the Drive."

She wasn't a bit hinkty[6] like so many folks when they're light-complexioned and up in the money. If she hadn't been the boss's girl, I'd have tried to make her myself. But she had a black boy friend—a number writer on 135th Street—so she didn't need me. She was in love with him. Used to call him up as soon as the boss got in the elevator bound for the office.

"Can I use this phone?" she asked me that very morning.

"Sure, Madam," I answered.

"Call me Pauline," she said, "I ain't white." And we got on swell. I cooked her some bacon and eggs while she called up her sweetie. She told him she'd hooked a new butter and egg man with bucks.

Well, the days went on. Each time, the boss would show up with Pauline. It looked like blondes didn't have a break—a sugar-brown had crowded the white babies out. But it was good for Mr. Lloyd. He didn't have the blues. And he stopped asking me to drink with him, thank God!

He was crazy about this Pauline. Didn't want no other woman. She kept him laughing all the time. She used to sing him bad songs that didn't seem bad when she was singing them, only seemed funny and good natured. She was nice, that girl. A gorgeous thing to have around the house.

But she knew what it was all about. Don't think she didn't. "You've got to kid white folks along," she said to me. "When you're depending on 'em for a living, make 'em *think* you like it."

"You said it," I agreed.

And she really put the bee on Mr. Lloyd. He bought her everything she wanted, and was as faithful to her as a husband. Used to ask me when she wasn't there, what I thought she needed. I don't know what got into him, he loved her like a dog.

She used to spend two or three nights a week with him—and the others with her boy-friend in Harlem. It was a hell of a long time before Mr. Lloyd found out about this colored fellow. When he did, it was pure accident. He saw Pauline going into the movies with him at the Capitol one night—a tall black good-looking guy with a diamond on his finger. And it made the old man sore.

That same night Mr. Lloyd got a ring-side table at the Cabin Club in Harlem. When Pauline came dancing out in the two o'clock revue, he called her, and told her to come there. He looked mad. Funny, boy, but that rich white man was jealous of the colored guy he had seen her with. Mr. Lloyd, jealous of a jig! Wouldn't that freeze you?

They had a hell of a quarrel that morning when they came to the apartment. First time I ever heard them quarrel. Pauline told him finally he could go to hell. She told him, yes, she loved that black boy, that he was the only boy she loved in the wide world, the only man she wanted.

They were all drunk, because between words they would drink licker. I'd left two bottles of Haig & Haig on the tray when I went to bed. I thought Pauline was stupid, talking like that, but I guess she was so drunk she didn't care.

"Yes, I love that colored boy," she hollered. "Yes, I love him. You don't think you're buying my heart, do you?"

And that hurt the boss. He'd always thought he was a great lover, and that women liked him for something else besides his money. (Because most of them wanted his money, nobody ever told him he wasn't so hot.

His girls all swore they loved him, even when he beat them. They all let
him put *them* out. They hung on till the last dollar.)

But that little yellow devil of a Pauline evidently didn't care what she
said. She began cussing the boss. Then Mr. Lloyd slapped her. I could
hear it way back in my bedroom where I was sleeping, with one eye open.

In a minute I heard a crash that brought me to my feet. I ran out,
through the kitchen, through the living-room, and opened Mr. Lloyd's
door. Pauline had thrown one of the whisky bottles at him. They were
battling like hell in the middle of the floor.

"Get out of here, boy!" Mr. Lloyd panted. So I got. But I stood
outside the door in case I was needed. A white man beating a Negro
woman wasn't so good. If she wanted help, I was there. But Pauline was
a pretty tough little scrapper herself. It sounded like the boss was getting
the worst of it. Finally, the tussling stopped. It was so quiet in there I
thought maybe one of them was knocked out, so I cracked the door to
see. The boss was kneeling at Pauline's feet, his arms around her knees.

"My God, Pauline, I love you!" I heard him say. "I want you, child.
Don't mind what I've done. Stay here with me. Stay, stay, stay."

"Lemme out of here!" said Pauline, kicking at Mr. Lloyd.

But the boss held her tighter. Then she grabbed the other whisky
bottle and hit him on the head. Of course, he fell out. I got a basin of
cold water and put him in bed with a cloth on his dome. Pauline took
off all the rings and things he'd given her and threw them at him, lying
there on the bed like a ghost.

"A white bastard!" she said. "Just because they pay you, they always
think they own you. No white man's gonna own me. I laugh with 'em
and they think I like 'em. Hell, I'm from Arkansas where the crackers
lynch niggers in the streets. How could *I* like 'em?"

She put on her coat and hat and went away.

When the boss came to, he told me to call his chauffeur. I thought he
was going to a doctor, because his head was bleeding. But the chauffeur
told me later he spent the whole day driving around Harlem trying to
find Pauline. He wanted to bring her back. But he never found her.

He had a lot of trouble with that head, too. Seems like a piece of glass
or something stuck in it. I didn't see him again for eight weeks. When
I did see him, he wasn't the same man. No, sir, boy, something had
happened to Mr. Lloyd. He didn't seem quite right in the head. I guess
Pauline dazed him for life, made a fool of him.

He drank more than ever and had me so high I didn't know B from
Bull's Foot. He had his white women around again, but he'd got the

idea from somewhere that he was the world's greatest lover, and that he didn't have to give them anything but himself—which wasn't so forty for them little Broadway gold diggers who wanted diamonds and greenbacks.

Women started to clearing out early when they discovered Mr. Lloyd had gone romantic—and cheap. There were scandals and fights and terrible goings on when the girls didn't get their presents and checks. But Mr. Lloyd just said, "To hell with them," and drank more than ever, and let the pretty girls go. He picked up women off the streets and then wouldn't pay them, cheap as they are. Late in the night he would start drinking and crying about Pauline. The sun would be rising over the Hudson before he'd stop his crazy carryings on—making me drink with him and listen to the nights he'd spent with Pauline.

"I loved her, boy! She thought I was trying to buy her. Some black buck had to come along and cut me out. But I'm just as good a lover as that black boy any day."

And he would begin to boast about the women he could have—without money, too. (Wrong, of course.) But he sent me to Harlem to find Pauline.

I couldn't find her. She'd gone away with her boy-friend. Some said they went to Memphis. Some said Chicago. Some said Los Angeles. Anyway, she was gone—that kid who looked like an Alabama moon.

I told Mr. Lloyd she was gone, so we got drunk again. For more'n a week, he made no move to go to the office. I began to be worried, cutting so many classes, staying up all night to drink with the old man, and hanging around most of the day. But if I left him alone, he acted like a fool. I was scared. He'd take out women's pictures and beat 'em and stamp on 'em and then make love to 'em and tear 'em up. Wouldn't eat. Didn't want to see anybody.

Then, one night, I knew he was crazy—so it was all up. He grabs the door like it was a woman, and starts to kiss it. I couldn't make him stop pawing at the door, so I telephoned his chauffeur. The chauffeur calls up one of Mr. Lloyd's broker friends. And they take him to the hospital.

That was last April. They've had him in the sanatorium ever since. The apartment's closed. His stuff's in storage, and I have no more job than a snake's got hips. Anyway, I went through college on it, but I don't know how the hell I'll get to dental school. I just wrote Ma down in Atlanta and told her times was hard. There ain't many Mr. Lloyd's, you can bet your life on that.

The chauffeur told me yesterday he's crazy as a loon now. Sometimes he thinks he's a stud-horse chasing a mare. Sometimes he's a lion. Poor man, in a padded cell! He was a swell guy when he had his right mind. But a yellow woman sure did drive him crazy. For me, well, it's just a good job gone!

Say, boy, gimme a smoke, will you? I hate to talk about it.

VI

Rejuvenation through Joy

Mr. Eugene Lesche in a morning coat, handsome beyond words, stood on the platform of the main ballroom of the big hotel facing Central Park at 59th Street, New York. He stood there speaking in a deep smooth voice, with a slight drawl, to a thousand well dressed women and some two or three hundred men who packed the place. His subject was "Motion and Joy," the last of his series of six Friday morning lectures, each of which had to do with something and Joy.

As the hour of his last lecture approached, expensive chauffeured motors turned off Fifth Avenue, circled around from the Park, drew up at the 59th Street entrance, discharged women. In the elevators leading to the level of the hotel ballroom, delicate foreign perfumes on the breasts of befurred ladies scented the bronze cars.

"I've just heard of it this week. Everybody's talking about him. Did you hear him before?"

"My dear, I shall have heard all six. . . . He sent me an announcement."

"Oh, why didn't I . . . ?"

"He's marvellous!"

"I simply can't tell you . . ."

The great Lesche speaking.

As he spoke, a thousand pairs of feminine eyes gazed as one. The men gazed, too. Hundreds of ears heard, entranced: Relax and be happy. Let Lesche tell you how to live. Lesche knows. Look at Lesche in a morning coat, strong and handsome, right here before you. Listen!

At $2.50 a seat (How little for his message!) they listened.

"Joy," said the great Lesche, "what is life without joy? . . . And how can we find joy? Not through sitting still with our world of troubles on our minds; not through taking thought—too often only another phrase for brooding; not by the sedentary study of books or pamphlets, of philosophies and creeds, of ancient lore; not through listening to *me* lecture or listening to any other person lecture," this was the *last* talk of his series, "but only through motion, through joyous motion; through life in motion! Lift up your arms to the sun," said Lesche. "Lift them up now! Right now," appealing to his audience. "Up, up, up!"

A thousand pairs of female arms, and some few hundred men's, were lifted up with great rustle and movement, then and there, toward the sun. They were really lifted up toward Lesche, because nobody knew quite where the sun was in the crowded ballroom—besides all eyes were on Lesche.

"Splendid," the big black-haired young man on the platform said, "beautiful and splendid! That's what life is, a movement up!" He paused. "But not always up. The trees point toward the sun, but they also sway in the wind, joyous in the wind. . . . Keep your hands skyward," said Lesche, "sway! Everybody sway! To the left, to the right, like trees in the wind, sway!" And the huge audience began, at Lesche's command, to sway. "Feet on the floor," said Lesche, "sway!"

He stood, swaying, too.

"Now," said Lesche suddenly, "stop!" "Try to move your hips! . . . Ah, you cannot! Seated as you are in chairs, you cannot! The life-center, the balance-point, cannot move in a chair. That is one of the great crimes of modern life, one of the murders of ourselves, we sit too much in chairs. We need to stand up—no, not now my friends." Some were already standing. "Not *just* when you are listening to *me*. I am speaking now of a way of life. We need to *live* up, point ourselves at the sun, sway in the wind of our rhythms, walk to an inner and outer music, put our balance-points in motion. (Do you not remember my talk on 'Music and Joy'?) Primitive man never sits in chairs. Look at the Indians! Look at the Negroes! They know how to move from the feet up, from the head down. Their centers live. They walk, they stand, they dance to their drum beats, their earth rhythms. They squat, they kneel, they lie—but they never, in their natural states, *never* sit in chairs. They do not mood and brood. No! They live through motion, through movement, through music, through joy! (Remember my lecture, 'Negroes and Joy'?) Ladies, and gentlemen, I offer you today—rejuvenation through joy."

Lesche bowed and bowed as he left the platform. With the greatest of grace he returned to bow again to applause that was thunderous. To a ballroom that was full of well-dressed women and cultured men, he bowed and bowed. Black-haired and handsome beyond words, he bowed. The people were loath to let him go.

Lesche had learned to bow that way in the circus. He used to drive the roan horses in the Great Roman Chariot Races—but nobody in the big ballroom of the hotel knew that. The women thought surely (to judge from their acclaim) that he had come fullblown right out of heaven to bring them joy.

Lesche knew what they thought, too, for within a month after the closing of his series of Friday Morning Lectures, they all received, at their town addresses, most beautifully written personal notes announcing the opening in Westchester of his Colony of Joy for the rebuilding of the mind, the body, and the soul.

Unfortunately, we did not hear Lesche's lecture on "Negroes and Joy" (the third in the series) but he said, in substance, that Negroes were the happiest people on earth. He said that they alone really knew the secret of rhythms and of movements. How futile, he said, to study Delsarte in this age! Go instead, he said, to Cab Calloway, Brick Top's,[7] and Bill Robinson! Move to music, he said, to the gaily primitive rhythms of the first man. Be Adam again, be Eve. Be not afraid of life, which is a garden. Be all this not by turning back time, but merely by living to the true rhythm of our own age, to music as modern as today, yet old as life, music that the primitive Negroes brought with their drums from Africa to America—that music, my friends, known to the vulgar as jazz, but which is so much *more* than jazz that we know not how to appreciate it; that music which is the Joy of Life.

His letter explained that these rhythms would play a great part in leading those—who would come—along the path to joy. And at Lesche's initial Westchester colony, the leader of the music would be none other than the famous Happy Lane (a *primitif de luxe*), direct from the Moon Club in Harlem, with the finest Negro band in America. To be both smart and modern in approaching the body and soul, was Lesche's aim. And to bring gaiety to a lot of people who had known nothing more joyous than Gurdjieff was his avowed intention—for those who could pay for it.

For Lesche's proposed path to life was not any less costly than that of the now famous masters at Fontainebleau. Indeed, it was even slightly more expensive. A great many ladies (and gentlemen, too) who received Lesche's beautifully written letter gasped when they learned the size of the initial check they would have to draw in order to enter, as a resident member, his Colony of Joy.

Some gasped and did *not* pay (because they could not), and so their lives went on without Joy. Others gasped, and paid. And several (enough to insure entirely Lesche's first season) paid without even gasping. These last were mostly old residents of Park Avenue or the better section of Germantown, ladies who had already tried everything looking toward happiness—now they wanted to try Joy, especially since it involved so new and novel a course as Lesche proposed—including the gaiety of Harlem Negroes, of which most of them knew nothing except through the rather remote chatter of the younger set who had probably been to the Cotton Club.

So Lesche opened up his house on an old estate in Westchester with a mansion and several cottages thereon that the crash let him lease for a little or nothing. (Or rather, Sol, his manager, did the leasing.) Instead of chairs, they bought African stools, low, narrow, and backless.

"I got the best decorator in town, too," said Sol, "to do it over primitive—modernistic—on a percentage of the profits, if there are any."

"It's got to be comfortable," said Lesche, "so people can relax after they get through enjoying themselves."

"It'll be," said Sol.

"We're admitting nobody west of Fifth Avenue," said Lesche.

"No Broadwayites," said Sol.

"Certainly not," said Lesche. "Only people with souls to save—and enough Harlemites to save 'em."

"Ha! Ha!" said Sol.

All the attendants were French—maids, butlers, and pages. Lesche's two assistants were a healthy and hard young woman, to whom he had once been married, a Hollywood Swede with Jean Harlow hair; and a young Yale man who hadn't graduated, but who read Ronald Firbank seriously, adored Louis Armstrong, worshipped Dwight Fisk, and had written Lesche's five hundred personal letters in a seven-lively-arts Gilbert Seldes style.[8]

Sol, of course, handled the money, with a staff of secretaries, book-keepers, and managers. And Happy Lane's African band, two tap dancers, and a real blues singer were contracted to spread joy, and act as the primordial pulse beat of the house. In other words, they were to furnish the primitive.

Within a month after the Colony opened in mid-January, its resident guests numbered thirty-five. Applications were legion. The demand for places was very great. The price went up.

"It's unbelievable how many people with money are unhappy," said Sol.

"It's unbelievable how they need what we got," drawled Lesche.

The press agents wrote marvellous stories about Lesche; how he had long been in his youth at Del Monte a student of the occult, how he had turned from that to the primitive and, through Africa, had discovered the curative values of Negro jazz.

The truth was quite otherwise.

Lesche had first worked in a circus. He rode a Roman chariot in the finale. All the way across the U. S. A. he rode twice daily, from Indianapolis where he got the job to Los Angeles where he quit, because nobody knew him there, and he liked the swimming at Santa Monica—and because he soon found a softer job posing for the members of a modernistic art colony who were modeling and painting away under a most expensive teacher at a nearby resort, saving their souls through art.

Lesche ate oranges and posed and swam all that summer and met a lot of nice, rich, and slightly faded women. New kind of people for him. Cultured people. He met, among others, Mrs. Oscar Willis of New Haven, one of the members of this colony of art expression. Her husband owned a railroad. She was very unhappy. She was lonely in her soul—and her pictures expressed that loneliness. She invited Lesche to tea at her bungalow near the beach.

Lesche taught her to swim. After that she was less unhappy. She began a new study in the painting class. She painted a circle and called it her impression of Lesche. It was hard to get it just right, so she asked him to do some extra posing for her in the late afternoons. And she paid him very well.

But summers end. Seasonal art classes too, and Mrs. Willis went back East.

Lesche worked in the movies as an extra. He played football for football pictures. Played gigolos for society films. Played a sailor, a cave man, a cop. He studied tap dancing. He did pretty well as far as earning money went, had lots of time for cocktails, parties, and books. Met lots of women.

He liked to read. He'd been a bright boy in high school back home in South Bend. And now at teas out Wilshire way he learned what one ought to read, and what one ought to have read. He spent money on books. Women spent money on him. He swam enough to keep a good body. Drank enough to be a good fellow, and acted well enough to have a job at the studios occasionally. He got married twice, but the other women were jealous, so divorces followed.

Then his friend Sol Blum had an idea. Sol ran a gym for the Hollywood elite. He had a newly opened swimming pool that wasn't doing so well. He asked Lesche if he would take charge of the lessons.

"Don't hurt yourself working, you know. Just swim around a little and show 'em that it looks easy. And be nice to the women," Sol said.

The swimming courses boomed. The fees went up. Sol and Lesche made money. (Lesche got a percentage cut.) He swam more and drank less. His body was swell, even if licker and women, parties and studio lights had made his face a little hard.

"But he's so damn nice," the women would say—who took swimming lessons for no good reason but to be held up by the black-haired Lesche.

Then one summer Lesche and Sol closed the gym and went to Paris. They drank an awful lot of licker at Harry's bar. And at Bricktop's they met an American woman who was giving a farewell party. She was Mrs. Oscar Willis, the artist—again—a long way from California.

"What's the idea?" said Lesche. "Are you committing suicide, Mrs. Willis, or going home, or what? Why a farewell party?"

"I am retiring from life," said Mrs. Willis, shouting above the frenzy of the Negro band. "I'm giving up art. I'm going to look for happiness. I'm going into the colony near Digne."

"Whose colony?" said Lesche. He remembered how much colonies cost, thinking of the art group.

"Mogador Bonatz's colony," said Mrs. Willis. "He's a very great Slav who can do so much for the soul. (Art does nothing.) Only one must agree to stay there six months when one goes."

"Is it expensive?" Lesche asked delicately. "I'm feeling awfully tired, too."

"Only $30 a day," said Mrs. Willis. "Have a drink?"

They drank a lot of champagne and said farewell to Mrs. Willis while the jazz band boomed and Bricktop shouted an occasional blues. Then Sol had an idea. After all, he was tired of gyms—why not start a colony? He mentioned it to Lesche when they got out into the open air.

"Hell, yes," said Lesche as they crossed Pigalle. "Let's start a colony."

From then on in Paris, Sol and Lesche studied soul cults. By night they went to Montmartre. By day they read occult books and thought how much people needed to retire and find beauty—and pay for it. By night they danced to the Negro jazz bands. And all the time they thought how greatly they needed a colony.

"You see how much people pay that guy Bonatz?" said Sol.

"Um-huh!" said Lesche, drinking from a tall glass at Josephine's. "And you see how much they'll spend on Harlem jazz, even in Paris?"

"Yeah," said Sol, "we're spending it ourselves. But what's that got to do with colonies?"

"Looks like to me," said Lesche, "a sure way to make money would be, combine a jazz band and a soul colony, and let it roll from there—black rhythm and happy souls."

"I see," said Sol. "That's not as silly as it sounds."

"Let 'em be mystic and have fun, too," said Lesche.

"What do you mean, mystic?" asked Sol.

"High brow fun," said Lesche. "Like they get from Bonatz. What do you suppose he's got we can't get?"

"Nothing," said Sol, who learned to sell ideas in Hollywood. "Now, you got the personality. With me for manager, a jazz band for background, and a little showmanship, it could be a riot."

"A riot is right," said Lesche.

When they returned to America, they stayed in New York. Sol got hold of a secretary who knew a lot of rich addresses and some rich people. Together they got hold of a smart young man from Yale who prepared a program of action for a high brow cult of joy—featuring the primitive. Then they got ready to open a Colony.

They cabled Mrs. Willis at Digne for the names of some of her friends who might need their souls fixed up—in America. They sent out a little folder. And they had the young Yale man write a few articles on *Contentment and Aboriginal Rhythms* for Lesche to try on the high brow magazines.

They really had a lot of nerve.

Lesche learned his lectures by heart that the college boy wrote. Then, he improvised, added variations of his own, made them personal, and bought a morning coat. Nightly he went to Harlem, brushing up on the newer rhythms. In November, they opened cold in the grand ballroom of the hotel facing the Park, without even a try-out elsewhere: Six lectures by Eugene Lesche on Joy in Relation to the Mind, Body, and Soul.

"Might as well take a big chance," said Sol. "Win or lose."

They won. In Sol's language, they wowed 'em. When the Friday Morning Series began, the ballroom was half full. When it ended, it was crowded and Sol had already signed the lease for the old Westchester estate.

So many people were in need of rejuvenating their souls and could seemingly still afford to pay for it that Sol gave up the idea for returning immediately to his gym in Hollywood. Souls seemed more important than bodies.

"How about it, Lesche?"

The intelligentsia dubbed their highly publicized efforts neo-paganism; others called it one more return to the primitive; others said out loud, it was a gyp game. Some said the world was turning passionate and spiritual; some said it was merely a sign of the decadence of the times. But everybody talked about it. The papers began to write about it. And the magazines that winter, from the *Junior League Bulletin* to the *Nation,* even the *New Masses,* remarked—usually snootily—but nevertheless remarked—about this Cult of Joy. (Harlem Hedonism, the *Forum* called it.) Lesche's publicity men who'd started it all, demanded higher wages, so Sol fired them. The thing went rolling of its own accord. The world was aware—of Joy! The Westchester Colony prospered.

Ten days before the January opening of the Colony, the huge mansion of the once aristocratic estate hummed with activity. It looked like a Broadway theatre before a première. Decorators were working for big effects. (They hoped *House and Garden, Vogue,* or *Vanity Fair* would picturize their super-modernistic results.) The house manager, a former hotel-head out of work, was busy getting his staff together—trying to keep them French—for the swank of it.

The bed-rooms were receiving special attention. At Lesche's, sleep also was to be a joy. And each private bathroom was being fitted with those special apparatus at colonies necessary for the cleansing of the body—for Sol and Lesche had hired a doctor to tell them what the best cults used.

"Body and soul," said Sol. "Body and soul."

"Gimme the body," said Lesche, "and let the Yale man take care of the soul."

Occult assistants, chefs and waitresses, *masseurs* and hairdressers, began to arrive—for the house was to be fully staffed. And there were plenty of first-class people out of work and willing to take a chance, too.

Upstairs in a third floor room, Lesche, like an actor preparing for a role, studied his lectures word for word. His former wife listened to him daily, reciting them by heart, puzzling over their allusions.

In another room, the Yale man, surrounded by books on primitive art, spiritual guidance, Negro jazz, German eurythmics, psychoanalysis, Yogi philosophy, all of Krishnamurti, half of Havelock Ellis, and most of Freud, besides piles of spirituals, jazz records, Paul Robeson, and Ethel Waters, and in the midst of all this—a typewriter. There sat the Yale man creating lectures—preparing, for a month in advance, twenty-minute daily talks for the great Lesche.

On the day when the Negroes arrived for their rehearsals, just prior to the opening of the place, Sol gave them a lecture. "Fellows," he said, addressing the band, "and Miss Lucas," to the blues-singing little coal-black dancer, "listen! Now I want to tell you about this place. This will not be no night club. Nor will it be a dance hall. This place is more like a church. It's for the rebuilding of souls—and bodies. It's for helping people. People who are wore out and tired, sick and bored, *ennui-ed* in other words, will come here for treatments, the kind of treatments, that Mr. Lesche and I have devised, which includes music, the best music, jazz, real primitive jazz out of Africa (you know, Harlem) to help 'em learn to move, to walk, to live in harmony with their times and themselves. Now, I want you all to be ladies and gentlemen (I know you are), to play with abandon, to give 'em all you got, but don't treat this like a rough house, nor like the Moon Club either. We allow only champagne drinkers here, cultured ladies, nice gentlemen, the best, the very best. Park Avenue. You know what I mean. . . . Now this is the order of the day. In the morning at eleven, Mr. Lesche will lecture in the Palm Garden, glass-enclosed, on the Art of Motion and Rhythm. You, Miss Tulane Lucas, and you two tap dancers there, will illustrate. You will show grace in modern movements, aliveness, the beat of Africa as expressed through the body. Mr. Lesche will illustrate, too. He's one of Bill Robinson's disciples, you know! You all know how tap-dancing has preserved Bill. A man of his age, past fifty! Well, we want to show our clients how it can preserve them. But don't do no stunts now, just easy rhythm stuff. We got to start 'em off slow. Some of 'em is old. And I expect some is Christian Scientists. . . . Then in the late afternoon, we will have tea-dancing, just for pleasure. We want to give 'em plenty of exercise, so they won't be bored. And so they will eat. We expect to make money on our table, and on massages, too. In the evening for one hour, put on the best show you got, singing and dancing—every week we gonna bring up new specialities—send 'em to bed feeling happy, before Mr. Lesche gives his goodnight and sweet dreams talk. . . . Now, you boys understand, you'll be off early here, by ten or eleven. Not like at the Club. You got your own cottage here on the estate to live in, you got your cars. Don't mind you driving to town, if you want to, but I want you back here for the eleven o'clock services in the morning. And I don't want you sleepy, either. This house is dedicated to Joy, and all who work here have got to be bright and snappy. That's what our people are paying for. . . . Lesche! Where is Lesche, Miss Boxall?"

The secretary looked startled. "He was in the halls talking to the new French maids."

"Well, get him in here. Tell him to explain to these boys how he wants to fix up his routine for his lectures. Let's get down to business now."

"What kind of clothes you want us to wear?" Happy Lane, the Negro leader, asked.

"Red," said Sol. "Red is the color of Joy."

"Lord!" said the blues singer, "I'm too dark to wear red!"

"That's what we want," said Sol, "darkness and light! We want to show 'em how much light there is in darkness."

"Now, here!" said the blues singer to herself, "I don't like no white folks talkin' 'bout me being dark."

"Lesche," Sol called to his partner strolling in through the door, "let's get going."

"O.K.," Lesche said. "Where's my boy?" meaning the Yale man.

"Right here, Gene."

"Now, how does that first lecture go?"

"My Gawd!" said Sol.

The Yale man referred to his notes. "*Joy,*" he read, "*Joy, springing from the dark rhythm of the primitive. . . .*"

"Oh, yes," said Lesche, turning to the band. "Now for that, give me *Mood Indigo,* you know, soft and syncopated, moan it soft and low. Then you, Miss Lucas," to the dancer, "you come gliding on. Give it plenty hip movement. I want 'em to learn to use their life-center. Then I'm gonna say . . . what's that boy-friend?" to the Yale man.

"*See how the . . .*"

"Oh, yes . . . *See how the Negroes live, dark as the earth, the primitive earth, swaying like trees, rooted in the deepest source of life. . . .* Then I'm gonna have 'em all rise and sway, like Miss Lucas here. . . . That ought to keep 'em from being bored until lunch time."

"Lawd," said Miss Lucas, muttering to herself, "what is this, a dancing school or a Sunday school?" And louder, "All right, Mr. Lesche, sounds like it might be a good act."

"Act, nothing," said Sol. "This is the art of life."

"Must be, if you say so," said Miss Lucas.

"Well, let's go," commanded the great Lesche. "Let's rehearse this first lecture now. Come on, boys."

The jazz band began to cry *Mood Indigo* in the best manner of the immortal Duke Ellington. Lesche began to speak in his great soft voice. Bushy-haired Tulane Lucas began to glide across the floor.

"Goddamn!" said Sol, "It's worth the money!"

"Hey! Hey!" said Miss Lucas.

"Sh-ss-ss-s!" said Lesche. "Be dignified . . . *rooted in the deepest source of life . . .* er-r-r?"

" . . . *O, early soul in motion* . . ." prompted the Yale man.

"*O, early soul* . . ." intoned Lesche.

The amazing collection of people gathered together in the Colony of Joy astounded even Lesche, whose very blasé-ness was what really made him appear so fresh. His thirty-seven clients in residence came almost all from families high in the Social Register, and equally high in the financial world. When Mrs. Carlos Gleed's check of entrance came in, Sol said, "Boy, we're made" . . . for of society there could be no higher—blue blood straight out of Back Bay.

The opening of the Colony created a furor among all the smart neurasthenics from Park Avenue right on up to New England. Dozens applied too late, and failed to get in. Others drove up daily for the lectures.

Of those who came, some had belonged formerly to the self-denial cults; others to Gurdjieff; others had been analyzed in Paris, Berlin, Vienna; had consulted Adler, Hirschfeld, Freud. Some had studied *under* famous Yogi. Others had been at Nyack. Now they had come to the Colony of Joy.

Up and down Park Avenue miraculous gossip flew.

Why, Mrs. Charles Duveen Althouse of Newport and Paris—feeling bad for years—is said to look like a cherub since she's gone into the Colony. . . . My dear, the famous Oriental fan-painter, Vankulmer Jones—he's *another* man these days. The rhythms, he says, the rhythms have worked wonders! And just the very presence of Lesche . . . Nothing America has ever known—rumor flew about the penthouses of the East River—nothing is equal to it. . . . The Baroness Langstrund gasped in a letter to a talkative friend, "My God, it's marvellous!"

Far better than Indian thought, Miss Joan Reeves, the heiress of Meadow Brook, was said to have said by her best friends. "The movement is amazing."

Almost all of them had belonged to cults before—cults that had never satisfied. Some had even been injured by them. To a cult that based the soul-search on self-denial—deny what you like best, have it around you all the time, but never touch it, *never*—then you will be strong—Mrs. Duveen Althouse had belonged. She denied chocolates for a whole year; kept fresh candy sitting in each corner of her boudoir—resisted with all her soul—and at the end of a year was a wreck.

Mr. Jones, the fan-painter, had belonged to a group on Cape Cod that believed in change through change: that is, whatever you want to be, you can. And all the members, after they had paid their fees, were told by the Mystic Master to change their names to whatever they most wished to be, or whoever, past or present, they admired. Some, without much depth, chose Napoleon or Cleopatra. But others, Daphne or Zeus or Merry del Val.[9] Mr. Jones chose Horse. He'd always wanted to be an animal, to possess their strength and calm, their vigor, their ways. But after a whole summer at the Cape he was even less of a horse than before. And greatly mosquito bitten.

Mrs. Ken Prather, II, a member of Lesche's group, had once spent months entire kneeling holding her big toes behind her, deep in contemplation. A most handsome Indian came once a week to her home on East 64th, for an enormous consideration, and gave her lessons in silence, and in positions of thought. But finally she just couldn't stand it any more.

Others of the Colony of Joy had been Scientists in their youth. Others had wandered, disappointed, the ways of spiritualism, never finding soulmates; still others had gazed solemnly into crystals, but had seen nothing but darkness; now, they had come to Joy!

How did it happen that nobody before had ever offered them Rejuvenation through Joy? Why, that was what they had been looking for all these years! And who would have thought it might come through the amusing and delightful rhythms of Negroes?

Nobody but Lesche.

In the warm glass-enclosed Palm Garden that winter, where the cupid fountain had been replaced by an enlargement of an African plastic and where a jazz band played soft and low behind the hedges, they felt (those who were there by virtue of their check books) all a-tremble in the depths of their souls after they had done their African exercises looking at Lesche—those slow, slightly grotesque, center-swaying exercises that he and Tulane Lucas from the Moon Club had devised. When they had finished, the movement, the music, and Lesche's voice, made them feel all warm and close to the earth, and as though they never wanted to leave the Colony of Joy or to be away from their great leader again.

Of course, there were a few who left, but their places were soon filled by others more truly mystic in the primitive sense than those whose arteries had already hardened, and who somehow couldn't follow a modern path to happiness, or sit on African stools. Clarence Lochard, for one, with *his* spine, had needed actual medical treatment not to be found at the Colony of Joy. And Mrs. J. Northcliff Hill, in the seventies, was a little too old for even the simple exercises that led to center-swaying. But for the two or three who went away, four or five came. And the house was full of life and soul. Every morning, *ensemble,* they lifted up their hands to the sun when the earth-drums rang out—and the sun was Lesche, standing right there.

Lesche was called the New Leader. The Negro bandmaster was known as Happy Man. The dancers were called the Primitives. The drummer was ritualized as Earth-Drummer. And the devotees were called New Men, New Women—for the Yale man had written in one of the lectures, "*and the age-old rhythm of the earth as expressed by the drums is also the ever new rhythm of life. And all you who walk to it, dance to it, live to it, are New Men and New Women. You shall call one another, not by the old names but only New Man, New Woman, New One, forgetting the past.*"

They called Lesche, Dear New Leader.

"*For,*" continued the gist of that particular lecture, "*newness, eternal renewal, is the source of all growth, all life, and as we grow from day to day here in this colony, we shall be ever new, ever joyous and new.*"

"Gimme sweet jazz on that line," Lesche had instructed at rehearsals. So on the thrilling morning of that lecture, the saxophones and clarinets moaned so beautiful and low, the drum beats called behind the palms with such wistful syncopation, that everybody felt impelled to move a new way as Lesche said, "Let us rise this morning and do a new dance, the dance of our new selves." And thirty-nine life-centers began to sway with the greatest of confidence in the palm court, for by now many inhibitions had fallen away, and the first exercise had been learned perfectly.

Who knows how long all might have gone on splendidly with Lesche and Sol and their Colony of Joy had not a most unhappy monster entered in to plague them. "The monster that's in every man," wrote the Yale man later in his diary, "the monster of jealousy—came to break down joy."

For the various New Ones became jealous of Lesche.

"It's your fault," stormed Sol. "Your fault. I told you to treat 'em all the same. I told you if you had to walk in the snow by moonlight, walk with your used-to-be wife, and leave the rest of these ladies alone. You know how women are. I told you not to start that Private Hour in the afternoon. I knew it would make trouble, create jealousy."

For out of the Private Hour devoted to the problems of each New One once a fortnight, where Lesche never advised (he couldn't) but merely received alone in confidence their troubles for contemplation, out of this private hour erelong, howls, screams, and recriminations were heard to issue almost daily. And in late March, New Woman Althouse was known to have thrown an African mask at New Leader Lesche because he kept her waiting a whole hour overtime while he devoted his attentions to the Meadow Brook heiress, New Woman Reeves.

"My Gawd!" said Sol, "the house is buzzing with scandal—I heard it all from Vankulmer Jones."

"These damn women," said Lesche, "I got to get rid of some of these women."

"You can't," said Sol. "They've all paid."

"Well, I will," said Lesche, "I'm tired! Why even my divorced wife's in love with me again. Fire her, will you?"

"Don't be foolish," said Sol, "she's a good secretary."

"Well, I'm gonna quit," said Lesche.

"You can't," said Sol. "I got you under contract."

"Oh, yeah?" said Lesche. "Too much is enough! And sometimes enough is too much! I'm tired, I tell you."

So they fell out. But Lesche didn't quit. It might have been better if he had, for Spring that year was all too sudden and full of implications. The very earth seemed to moan with excess of joy. Life was just too much to bear alone. It needed to be shared, its beauty given to others, taken in return. Its eternal newness united.

To the Colony, Lesche was their Leader, their life. And they wanted him, each one, alone. In desperation, he abolished the Private Hour. But that didn't help any. Mrs. Duveen Althouse was desperately in love with him now. (She called him Pan.) Miss Joan Reeves could not turn her eyes away. (He was her god.) Mrs. Carlos Gleed insisted that he summer at her island place in Maine. Baroness Langstrund announced quite definitely she intended to marry him—whereupon Mrs. Althouse, who had thrown the mask, threatened, without ceremony, to wring at once the Baroness' neck. Several other New Ones stopped speaking to each other over Lesche. Even the men members were taking sides for or against Lesche, or against each other. That dear soul Vankulmer Jones said he simply couldn't stand it any more—and left.

In the city, the Broadway gossip columns got hold of it—this excitement over Joy—and began to wise-crack. Then suddenly a minister started a crusade against the doings of the rich at the Colony and the tabloids sent men up to get pictures. Blackmailers, scenting scandal, began to blackmail. The righteous and the racketeers both sprang into action. And violets bloomed in April.

Sol tore his hair. "We're ruined!"

"Who cares?" said Lesche, "let's go back to the Hollywood gym. We made plenty on this. And I've still got the Hispano Mrs. Hancock donated."

"But we could've made millions."

"We'll come back to it next year," said Lesche. "And get some fresh New Ones. I'm damn tired of these old ones." And so they bickered.

But the final fireworks were set off by Miss Tulane Lucas, the dusky female of the Primitives. They began over the Earth-Drummer, and really had nothing to do with the Colony. But fire, once started, often spreads beyond control.

The drummer belonged to Miss Lucas. But when Spring came, he got a bad habit of driving down to New York after work every night and not getting back till morning.

"Another woman," said Tulane to herself, "after all I've done." She warned him, but he paid her no mind.

One April morning, just in time to play for the eleven o'clock lecture, with Lesche already on the platform, the little colored drummer arrived late and, without even having gone by the cottage to greet Tulane—rushed into the palm court and took his place at the earth-drums.

"Oh, no!" said Tulane suddenly from among the palms while all the New Ones, contemplating on their African stools, started at the unwonted sound. "Oh, no, you don't," she said. "You have drummed for your last time." And she took a pistol from her bosom and shot.

Bang! . . . Bang! . . . Bang!

Screams rent the palm court. As the drummer fled, bang! a bullet hit somewhere near his life-center, but he kept on. Pandemonium broke out.

"My Gawd!" said Sol. "Somebody grab that gun." But Mrs. Duveen Althouse beat him to it. From Tulane, she snatched the weapon for herself and approached the great Lesche.

"How right to shoot the one you love!" she cried. "How primitive, how just!" And she pointed the gun directly at their dear Leader.

Again shots rang out. One struck the brass curve of the bass horn, glanced upward toward the ceiling, and crashed through the glass of the sun court, showering slivers on everybody.

But by that time, Baroness Langstrund had thrown herself on Duveen Althouse. "Aw-oo!" she screamed. "You wretch, shooting the man I love." Her fingers sought the other's hair, her nails tore at her eyes. Meanwhile, Mrs. Carlos Gleed threw an African stool.

Mrs. Althouse fired once more—but Lesche had gone. The final bullet hit only the marble floor, flew upward through the piano, and sounded a futile chord.

By this time, Sol had grabbed the gun. The screams died. Somebody separated the two women. Little French maids came running with water for the fainting. Happy Lane emerged from behind the bass-viol, pale as an African ghost—but nobody knew where the rest of the jazz band had disappeared, nor Lesche either. They were long gone.

There was no lecture that morning. Indeed, there were never any more lectures. That was the end of the Colony of Joy.

The newspapers laughed about it for weeks, published pictures and names of the wealthy inmates; the columnists wisecracked. It was all very terrible! As a final touch, one of the tabloids claimed to have discovered that the great Lesche was a Negro—passing for white!

VII

The Blues I'm Playing

Oceola Jones, pianist, studied under Philippe in Paris. Mrs. Dora Ellsworth paid her bills. The bills included a little apartment on the Left Bank and a grand piano. Twice a year Mrs. Ellsworth came over from New York and spent part of her time with Oceola in the little apartment. The rest of her time abroad she usually spent at Biarritz or Juan les Pins, where she would see the new canvases of Antonio Bas, young Spanish painter who also enjoyed the patronage of Mrs. Ellsworth. Bas and Oceola, the woman thought, both had genius. And whether they had genius or not, she loved them, and took good care of them.

Poor dear lady, she had no children of her own. Her husband was dead. And she had no interest in life now save art, and the young people who created art. She was very rich, and it gave her pleasure to share her richness with beauty. Except that she was sometimes confused as to where beauty lay—in the youngsters or in what they made, in the creators or the creation. Mrs. Ellsworth had been known to help charming young people who wrote terrible poems, blue-eyed young men who painted awful pictures. And she once turned down a garlic-smelling soprano-singing girl who, a few years later, had all the critics in New York at her feet. The girl was so sallow. And she really needed a bath, or at least a mouth wash, on the day when Mrs. Ellsworth went to hear her sing at an East Side settlement house. Mrs. Ellsworth had sent a small check and let it go at that—since, however, living to regret bitterly her lack of musical acumen in the face of garlic.

About Oceola, though, there had been no doubt. The Negro girl had been highly recommended to her by Ormond Hunter, the music critic, who often went to Harlem to hear the church concerts there, and had thus listened twice to Oceola's playing.

"A most amazing tone," he had told Mrs. Ellsworth, knowing her interest in the young and unusual. "A flare for the piano such as I have seldom encountered. All she needs is training—finish, polish, a repertoire."

"Where is she?" asked Mrs. Ellsworth at once. "I will hear her play."

By the hardest, Oceola was found. By the hardest, an appointment was made for her to come to East 63rd Street and play for Mrs. Ellsworth.

Oceola had said she was busy every day. It seemed that she had pupils, rehearsed a church choir, and played almost nightly for colored house parties or dances. She made quite a good deal of money. She wasn't tremendously interested, it seemed, in going way downtown to play for some elderly lady she had never heard of, even if the request did come from the white critic, Ormond Hunter, via the pastor of the church whose choir she rehearsed, and to which Mr. Hunter's maid belonged.

It was finally arranged, however. And one afternoon, promptly on time, black Miss Oceola Jones rang the door bell of white Mrs. Dora Ellsworth's grey stone house just off Madison. A butler who actually wore brass buttons opened the door, and she was shown upstairs to the music room. (The butler had been warned of her coming.) Ormond Hunter was already there, and they shook hands. In a moment, Mrs. Ellsworth came in, a tall stately grey-haired lady in black with a scarf that sort of floated behind her. She was tremendously intrigued at meeting Oceola, never having had before amongst all her artists a black one. And she was greatly impressed that Ormond Hunter should have recommended the girl. She began right away, treating her as a protegee; that is, she began asking her a great many questions she would not dare ask anyone else at first meeting, except a protegee. She asked her how old she was and where her mother and father were and how she made her living and whose music she liked best to play and was she married and would she take one lump or two in her tea, with lemon or cream?

After tea, Oceola played. She played the Rachmaninoff *Prelude in C Sharp Minor.* She played from the Liszt *Études.* She played the *St. Louis Blues.* She played Ravel's *Pavanne pour une Enfante Défunte.* And then she said she had to go. She was playing that night for a dance in Brooklyn for the benefit of the Urban League.

Mrs. Ellsworth and Ormond Hunter breathed, "How lovely!"

Mrs. Ellsworth said, "I am quite overcome, my dear. You play so beautifully." She went on further to say, "You must let me help you. Who is your teacher?"

"I have none now," Oceola replied. "I teach pupils myself. Don't have time any more to study—nor money either."

"But you must have time," said Mrs. Ellsworth, "and money, also. Come back to see me on Tuesday. We will arrange it, my dear."

And when the girl had gone, she turned to Ormond Hunter for advice on piano teachers to instruct those who already had genius, and need only to be developed.

II

Then began one of the most interesting periods in Mrs. Ellsworth's whole experience in aiding the arts. The period of Oceola. For the Negro girl, as time went on, began to occupy a greater and greater place in Mrs. Ellsworth's interests, to take up more and more of her time, and to use up more and more of her money. Not that Oceola ever asked for money, but Mrs. Ellsworth herself seemed to keep thinking of so much more Oceola needed.

At first it was hard to get Oceola to need anything. Mrs. Ellsworth had the feeling that the girl mistrusted her generosity, and Oceola did—for she had never met anybody interested in pure art before. Just to be given things for *art's sake* seemed suspicious to Oceola.

That first Tuesday, when the colored girl came back at Mrs. Ellsworth's request, she answered the white woman's questions with a why-look in her eyes.

"Don't think I'm being personal, dear," said Mrs. Ellsworth, "but I must know your background in order to help you. Now, tell me . . ."

Oceola wondered why on earth the woman wanted to help her. However, since Mrs. Ellsworth seemed interested in her life's history, she brought it forth so as not to hinder the progress of the afternoon, for she wanted to get back to Harlem by six o'clock.

Born in Mobile in 1903. Yes, m'am, she was older than she looked. Papa had a band, that is her stepfather. Used to play for all the lodge turn-outs, picnics, dances, barbecues. You could get the best roast pig in the world in Mobile. Her mother used to play the organ in church, and when the deacons bought a piano after the big revival, her mama played that, too. Oceola played by ear for a long while until her mother taught her notes. Oceola played an organ, also, and a cornet.

"My, my," said Mrs. Ellsworth.

"Yes, m'am," said Oceola. She had played and practiced on lots of instruments in the South before her step-father died. She always went to band rehearsals with him.

"And where was your father, dear?" asked Mrs. Ellsworth.

"My step-father had the band," replied Oceola. Her mother left off playing in the church to go with him traveling in Billy Kersands' Minstrels. He had the biggest mouth in the world, Kersands did, and used to let Oceola put both her hands in it at a time and stretch it. Well, she and her mama and step-papa settled down in Houston. Sometimes her parents had jobs and sometimes they didn't. Often they were hungry, but

Oceola went to school and had a regular piano-teacher, an old German woman, who gave her what technique she had today.

"A fine old teacher," said Oceola. "She used to teach me half the time for nothing. God bless her."

"Yes," said Mrs. Ellsworth. "She gave you an excellent foundation."

"Sure did. But my step-papa died, got cut, and after that Mama didn't have no more use for Houston so we moved to St. Louis. Mama got a job playing for the movies in a Market Street theater, and I played for a church choir, and saved some money and went to Wilberforce. Studied piano there, too. Played for all the college dances. Graduated. Came to New York and heard Rachmaninoff and was crazy about him. Then Mama died, so I'm keeping the little flat myself. One room is rented out."

"Is she nice?" asked Mrs. Ellsworth, "your roomer?"

"It's not a she," said Oceola. "He's a man. I hate women roomers."

"Oh!" said Mrs. Ellsworth. "I should think all roomers would be terrible."

"He's right nice," said Oceola. "Name's Pete Williams."

"What does he do?" asked Mrs. Ellsworth.

"A Pullman porter," replied Oceola, "but he's saving money to go to Med school. He's a smart fellow."

But it turned out later that he wasn't paying Oceola any rent.

That afternoon, when Mrs. Ellsworth announced that she had made her an appointment with one of the best piano teachers in New York, the black girl seemed pleased. She recognized the name. But how, she wondered, would she find time for study, with her pupils and her choir, and all. When Mrs. Ellsworth said that she would cover her *entire* living expenses, Oceola's eyes were full of that why-look, as though she didn't believe it.

"I have faith in your art, dear," said Mrs. Ellsworth, at parting. But to prove it quickly, she sat down that very evening and sent Oceola the first monthly check so that she would no longer have to take in pupils or drill choirs or play at house parties. And so Oceola would have faith in art, too.

That night Mrs. Ellsworth called up Ormond Hunter and told him what she had done. And she asked if Mr. Hunter's maid knew Oceola, and if she supposed that that man rooming with her were anything to her. Ormond Hunter said he would inquire.

Before going to bed, Mrs. Ellsworth told her housekeeper to order a book called "Nigger Heaven" on the morrow, and also anything else

Brentano's had about Harlem. She made a mental note that she must go up there sometime, for she had never yet seen that dark section of New York; and now that she had a Negro protegee, she really ought to know something about it. Mrs. Ellsworth couldn't recall ever having known a single Negro before in her whole life, so she found Oceola fascinating. And just as black as she herself was white.

Mrs. Ellsworth began to think in bed about what gowns would look best on Oceola. Her protegee would have to be well-dressed. She wondered, too, what sort of a place the girl lived in. And who that man was who lived with her. She began to think that really Oceola ought to have a place to herself. It didn't seem quite respectable. . . .

When she woke up in the morning, she called her car and went by her dressmaker's. She asked the good woman what kind of colors looked well with black; not black fabrics, but a black skin.

"I have a little friend to fit out," she said.

"A *black* friend?" said the dressmaker.

"A black friend," said Mrs. Ellsworth.

III

Some days later Ormond Hunter reported on what his maid knew about Oceola. It seemed that the two belonged to the same church, and although the maid did not know Oceola very well, she knew what everybody said about her in the church. Yes, indeedy! Oceola were a right nice girl, for sure, but it certainly were a shame she were giving all her money to that man what stayed with her and what she was practically putting through college so he could be a doctor.

"Why," gasped Mrs. Ellsworth, "the poor child is being preyed upon."

"It seems to me so," said Ormond Hunter.

"I must get her out of Harlem," said Mrs. Ellsworth, "at once. I believe it's worse than Chinatown."

"She might be in a more artistic atmosphere," agreed Ormond Hunter. "And with her career launched, she probably won't want that man anyhow."

"She won't need him," said Mrs. Ellsworth. "She will have her art."

But Mrs. Ellsworth decided that in order to increase the rapprochement between art and Oceola, something should be done now, at once. She asked the girl to come down to see her the next day, and when it was time to go home, the white woman said, "I have a half-hour before dinner. I'll drive you up. You know I've never been to Harlem."

"All right," said Oceola. "That's nice of you."

But she didn't suggest the white lady's coming in, when they drew up before a rather sad-looking apartment house in 134th Street. Mrs. Ellsworth had to ask could she come in.

"I live on the fifth floor," said Oceola, "and there isn't any elevator."

"It doesn't matter, dear," said the white woman, for she meant to see the inside of this girl's life, elevator or no elevator.

The apartment was just as she thought it would be. After all, she had read Thomas Burke on Limehouse. And here was just one more of those holes in the wall, even if it was five stories high. The windows looked down on slums. There were only four rooms, small as maids' rooms, all of them. An upright piano almost filled the parlor. Oceola slept in the dining-room. The roomer slept in the bed-chamber beyond the kitchen.

"Where is he, darling?"

"He runs on the road all summer," said the girl. "He's in and out."

"But how do you breathe in here?" asked Mrs. Ellsworth. "It's so small. You must have more space for your soul, dear. And for a grand piano. Now, in the Village . . ."

"I do right well here," said Oceola.

"But in the Village where so many nice artists live we can get . . ."

"But I don't want to move yet. I promised my roomer he could stay till fall."

"Why till fall?"

"He's going to Meharry then."

"To marry?"

"Meharry, yes m'am. That's a colored Medicine school in Nashville."

"Colored? Is it good?"

"Well, it's cheap," said Oceola. "After he goes, I don't mind moving."

"But I wanted to see you settled before I go away for the summer."

"When you come back is all right. I can do till then."

"Art is long," reminded Mrs. Ellsworth, "and time is fleeting, my dear."

"Yes, m'am," said Oceola, "but I gets nervous if I start worrying about time."

So Mrs. Ellsworth went off to Bar Harbor for the season, and left the man with Oceola.

IV

That was some years ago. Eventually art and Mrs. Ellsworth triumphed. Oceola moved out of Harlem. She lived in Gay Street west of Washington

Square where she met Genevieve Taggard, and Ernestine Evans, and two or three sculptors, and a cat-painter who was also a protegee of Mrs. Ellsworth. She spent her days practicing, playing for friends of her patron, going to concerts, and reading books about music. She no longer had pupils or rehearsed the choir, but she still loved to play for Harlem house parties—for nothing—now that she no longer needed the money, out of sheer love of jazz. This rather disturbed Mrs. Ellsworth, who still believed in art of the old school, portraits that really and truly looked like people, poems about nature, music that had soul in it, not syncopation. And she felt the dignity of art. Was it in keeping with genius, she wondered, for Oceola to have a studio full of white and colored people every Saturday night (some of them actually drinking gin *from bottles*) and dancing to the most tomtom-like music she had ever heard coming out of a grand piano? She wished she could lift Oceola up bodily and take her away from all that, for art's sake.

So in the spring, Mrs. Ellsworth organized weekends in the up-state mountains where she had a little lodge and where Oceola could look from the high places at the stars, and fill her soul with the vastness of the eternal, and forget about jazz. Mrs. Ellsworth really began to hate jazz—especially on a grand piano.

If there were a lot of guests at the lodge, as there sometimes were, Mrs. Ellsworth might share the bed with Oceola. Then she would read aloud Tennyson or Browning before turning out the light, aware all the time of the electric strength of that brown-black body beside her, and of the deep drowsy voice asking what the poems were about. And then Mrs. Ellsworth would feel very motherly toward this dark girl whom she had taken under her wing on the wonderful road of art, to nurture and love until she became a great interpreter of the piano. At such times the elderly white woman was glad her late husband's money, so well invested, furnished her with a large surplus to devote to the needs of her protegees, especially to Oceola, the blackest—and most interesting of all.

Why the most interesting?

Mrs. Ellsworth didn't know, unless it was that Oceola really was talented, terribly alive, and that she looked like nothing Mrs. Ellsworth had ever been near before. Such a rich velvet black, and such a hard young body! The teacher of the piano raved about her strength.

"She can stand a great career," the teacher said. "She has everything for it."

"Yes," agreed Mrs. Ellsworth, thinking, however, of the Pullman porter at Meharry, "but she must learn to sublimate her soul."

So for two years then, Oceola lived abroad at Mrs. Ellsworth's expense. She studied with Philippe, had the little apartment on the Left Bank, and learned about Debussy's African background. She met many black Algerian and French West Indian students, too, and listened to their interminable arguments ranging from Garvey to Picasso to Spengler to Jean Cocteau, and thought they all must be crazy. Why did they or anybody argue so much about life or art? Oceola merely lived—and loved it. Only the Marxian students seemed sound to her for they, at least, wanted people to have enough to eat. That was important, Oceola thought, remembering, as she did, her own sometimes hungry years. But the rest of the controversies, as far as she could fathom, were based on air.

Oceola hated most artists, too, and the word *art* in French or English. If you wanted to play the piano or paint pictures or write books, go ahead! But why talk so much about it? Montparnasse was worse in that respect than the Village. And as for the cultured Negroes who were always saying art would break down color lines, art could save the race and prevent lynchings! "Bunk!" said Oceola. "My ma and pa were both artists when it came to making music, and the white folks ran them out of town for being dressed up in Alabama. And look at the Jews! Every other artist in the world's a Jew, and still folks hate them."

She thought of Mrs. Ellsworth (dear soul in New York), who never made uncomplimentary remarks about Negroes, but frequently did about Jews. Of little Menuhin she would say, for instance, "He's a *genius*—not a Jew," hating to admit his ancestry.

In Paris, Oceola especially loved the West Indian ball rooms where the black colonials danced the beguin. And she liked the entertainers at Bricktop's. Sometimes late at night there, Oceola would take the piano and beat out a blues for Brick and the assembled guests. In her playing of Negro folk music, Oceola never doctored it up, or filled it full of classical runs, or fancy falsities. In the blues she made the bass notes throb like tom-toms, the trebles cry like little flutes, so deep in the earth and so high in the sky that they understood everything. And when the night club crowd would get up and dance to her blues, and Bricktop would yell, "Hey! Hey!" Oceola felt as happy as if she were performing a Chopin étude for the nicely gloved Oh's and Ah-ers in a Crillon salon.

Music, to Oceola, demanded movement and expression, dancing and living to go with it. She liked to teach, when she had the choir, the singing of those rhythmical Negro spirituals that possessed the power to pull colored folks out of their seats in the amen corner and make them prance and shout in the aisles for Jesus. She never liked those fashionable colored churches where shouting and movement were discouraged and looked down upon, and where New England hymns instead of spirituals were sung. Oceola's background was too well-grounded in Mobile, and Billy Kersands' Minstrels, and the Sanctified churches where religion was a joy, to stare mystically over the top of a grand piano like white folks and imagine that Beethoven had nothing to do with life, or that Schubert's love songs were only sublimations.

Whenever Mrs. Ellsworth came to Paris, she and Oceola spent hours listening to symphonies and string quartettes and pianists. Oceola enjoyed concerts, but seldom felt, like her patron, that she was floating on clouds of bliss. Mrs. Ellsworth insisted, however, that Oceola's spirit was too moved for words at such times—therefore she understood why the dear child kept quiet. Mrs. Ellsworth herself was often too moved for words, but never by pieces like Ravel's *Bolero* (which Oceola played on the phonograph as a dance record) or any of the compositions of *les Six*.

What Oceola really enjoyed most with Mrs. Ellsworth was not going to concerts, but going for trips on the little river boats in the Seine; or riding out to old chateaux in her patron's hired Renault; or to Versailles, and listening to the aging white lady talk about the romantic history of France, the wars and uprising, the loves and intrigues of princes and kings and queens, about guillotines and lace handkerchiefs, snuff boxes and daggers. For Mrs. Ellsworth had loved France as a girl, and had made a study of its life and lore. Once she used to sing simple little French songs rather well, too. And she always regretted that her husband never understood the lovely words—or even tried to understand them.

Oceola learned the accompaniments for all the songs Mrs. Ellsworth knew and sometimes they tried them over together. The middle-aged white woman loved to sing when the colored girl played, and she even tried spirituals. Often, when she stayed at the little Paris apartment, Oceola would go into the kitchen and cook something good for late supper, maybe an oyster soup, or fried apples and bacon. And sometimes Oceola had pigs' feet.

"There's nothing quite so good as a pig's foot," said Oceola, "after playing all day."

"Then you must have pigs' feet," agreed Mrs. Ellsworth.

And all this while Oceola's development at the piano blossomed into perfection. Her tone became a singing wonder and her interpretations warm and individual. She gave a concert in Paris, one in Brussels, and another in Berlin. She got the press notices all pianists crave. She had her picture in lots of European papers. And she came home to New York a year after the stock market crashed and nobody had any money—except folks like Mrs. Ellsworth who had so much it would be hard to ever lose it all.

Oceola's one time Pullman porter, now a coming doctor, was graduating from Meharry that spring. Mrs. Ellsworth saw her dark protegee go South to attend his graduation with tears in her eyes. She thought that by now music would be enough, after all those years under the best teachers, but alas, Oceola was not yet sublimated, even by Philippe. She wanted to see Pete.

Oceola returned North to prepare for her New York concert in the fall. She wrote Mrs. Ellsworth at Bar Harbor that her doctor boy-friend was putting in one more summer on the railroad, then in the autumn he would intern at Atlanta. And Oceola said that he had asked her to marry him. Lord, she was happy!

It was a long time before she heard from Mrs. Ellsworth. When the letter came, it was full of long paragraphs about the beautiful music Oceola had within her power to give the world. Instead, she wanted to marry and be burdened with children! Oh, my dear, my dear!

Oceola, when she read it, thought she had done pretty well knowing Pete this long and not having children. But she wrote back that she didn't see why children and music couldn't go together. Anyway, during the present depression, it was pretty hard for a beginning artist like herself to book a concert tour—so she might just as well be married awhile. Pete, on his last run in from St. Louis, had suggested that they have the wedding Christmas in the South. "And he's impatient, at that. He needs me."

This time Mrs. Ellsworth didn't answer by letter at all. She was back in town in late September. In November, Oceola played at Town Hall. The critics were kind, but they didn't go wild. Mrs. Ellsworth swore it was because of Pete's influence on her protegee.

"But he was in Atlanta," Oceola said.

"His spirit was here," Mrs. Ellsworth insisted. "All the time you were playing on that stage, he was here, the monster! Taking you out of yourself, taking you away from the piano."

"Why, he wasn't," said Oceola. "He was watching an operation in Atlanta."

But from then on, things didn't go well between her and her patron. The white lady grew distinctly cold when she received Oceola in her beautiful drawing room among the jade vases and amber cups worth thousands of dollars. When Oceola would have to wait there for Mrs.

Ellsworth, she was afraid to move for fear she might knock something over—that would take ten years of a Harlemite's wages to replace, if broken.

Over the tea cups, the aging Mrs. Ellsworth did not talk any longer about the concert tour she had once thought she might finance for Oceola, if no recognized bureau took it up. Instead, she spoke of that something she believed Oceola's fingers had lost since her return from Europe. And she wondered why any one insisted on living in Harlem.

"I've been away from my own people so long," said the girl, "I want to live right in the middle of them again."

Why, Mrs. Ellsworth wondered farther, did Oceola, at her last concert in a Harlem church, not stick to the classical items listed on the program. Why did she insert one of her own variations on the spirituals, a syncopated variation from the Sanctified Church, that made an old colored lady rise up and cry out from her pew, "Glory to God this evenin'! Yes! Hallelujah! Whooo-oo!" right at the concert? Which seemed most undignified to Mrs. Ellsworth, and unworthy of the teachings of Philippe. And furthermore, why was Pete coming up to New York for Thanksgiving? And who had sent him the money to come?

"Me," said Oceola. "He doesn't make anything interning."

"Well," said Mrs. Ellsworth, "I don't think much of him." But Oceola didn't seem to care what Mrs. Ellsworth thought, for she made no defense.

Thanksgiving evening, in bed, together in a Harlem apartment, Pete and Oceola talked about their wedding to come. They would have a big one in a church with lots of music. And Pete would give her a ring. And she would have on a white dress, light and fluffy, not silk. "I hate silk," she said. "I hate expensive things." (She thought of her mother being buried in a cotton dress, for they were all broke when she died. Mother would have been glad about her marriage.) "Pete," Oceola said, hugging him in the dark, "let's live in Atlanta, where there are lots of colored people, like us."

"What about Mrs. Ellsworth?" Pete asked. "She coming down to Atlanta for our wedding?"

"I don't know," said Oceola.

"I hope not, 'cause if she stops at one of them big hotels. I won't have you going to the back door to see her. That's one thing I hate about the South—where there're white people, you have to go to the back door."

"Maybe she can stay with us," said Oceola. "I wouldn't mind."

"I'll be damned," said Pete. "You want to get lynched?"

But it happened that Mrs. Ellsworth didn't care to attend the wedding, anyway. When she saw how love had triumphed over art, she decided she could no longer influence Oceola's life. The period of Oceola was over. She would send checks, occasionally, if the girl needed them, besides, of course, something beautiful for the wedding, but that would be all. These things she told her the week after Thanksgiving.

"And Oceola, my dear, I've decided to spend the whole winter in Europe. I sail on December eighteenth. Christmas—while you are marrying —I shall be in Paris with my precious Antonio Bas. In January, he has an exhibition of oils in Madrid. And in the spring, a new young poet is coming over whom I want to visit Florence, to really know Florence. A charming white-haired boy from Omaha whose soul has been crushed in the West. I want to try to help him. He, my dear, is one of the few people who live for their art—and nothing else. . . . Ah, such a beautiful life! . . . You will come and play for me once before I sail?"

"Yes, Mrs. Ellsworth," said Oceola, genuinely sorry that the end had come. Why did white folks think you could live on nothing but art? Strange! Too strange! Too strange!

V

The Persian vases in the music room were filled with long-stemmed lilies that night when Oceola Jones came down from Harlem for the last time to play for Mrs. Dora Ellsworth. Mrs. Ellsworth had on a gown of black velvet, and a collar of pearls about her neck. She was very kind and gentle to Oceola, as one would be to a child who has done a great wrong but doesn't know any better. But to the black girl from Harlem, she looked very cold and white, and her grand piano seemed like the biggest and heaviest in the world—as Oceola sat down to play it with the technique for which Mrs. Ellsworth had paid.

As the rich and aging white woman listened to the great roll of Beethoven sonatas and to the sea and moonlight of the Chopin nocturnes, as she watched the swaying dark strong shoulders of Oceola Jones, she began to reproach the girl aloud for running away from art and music, for burying herself in Atlanta and love—love for a man unworthy of lacing up her boot straps, as Mrs. Ellsworth put it.

"You could shake the stars with your music, Oceola. Depression or no depression, I could make you great. And yet you propose to dig a grave for yourself. Art is bigger than love."

"I believe you, Mrs. Ellsworth," said Oceola, not turning away from the piano. "But being married won't keep me from making tours, or being an artist."

"Yes, it will," said Mrs. Ellsworth. "He'll take all the music out of you."

"No, he won't," said Oceola.

"You don't know, child," said Mrs. Ellsworth, "what men are like."

"Yes, I do," said Oceola simply. And her fingers began to wander slowly up and down the keyboard, flowing into the soft and lazy syncopation of a Negro blues, a blues that deepened and grew into rollicking jazz, then into an earth-throbbing rhythm that shook the lilies in the Persian vases of Mrs. Ellsworth's music room. Louder than the voice of the white woman who cried that Oceola was deserting beauty, deserting her real self, deserting her hope in life, the flood of wild syncopation filled the house, then sank into the slow and singing blues with which it had begun.

The girl at the piano heard the white woman saying, "Is this what I spent thousands of dollars to teach you?"

"No," said Oceola simply. "This is mine. . . . Listen! . . . How sad and gay it is. Blue and happy—laughing and crying. . . . How white like you and black like me. . . . How much like a man. . . . And how like a woman. . . . Warm as Pete's mouth. . . . These are the blues. . . . I'm playing."

Mrs. Ellsworth sat very still in her chair looking at the lilies trembling delicately in the priceless Persian vases, while Oceola made the bass notes throb like tomtoms deep in the earth.

> *O, if I could holler*

sang the blues,

> *Like a mountain jack,*
> *I'd go up on de mountain*

sang the blues,

> *And call my baby back.*

"And I," said Mrs. Ellsworth rising from her chair, "would stand looking at the stars."

VIII

Red-Headed Baby

"Dead, dead as hell, these little burgs on the Florida coast. Lot of half-built skeleton houses left over from the boom. Never finished. Never will be finished. Mosquitoes, sand, niggers. Christ, I ought to break away from it. Stuck five years on same boat and still nothin' but a third mate puttin' in at dumps like this on a damned coast-wise tramp. Not even a good time to be had. Norfolk, Savannah, Jacksonville, ain't bad. Ain't bad. But what the hell kind of port's this? What the hell is there to do except get drunk and go out and sleep with niggers? Hell!"

Feet in the sand. Head under palms, magnolias, stars. Lights and the kid-cries of a sleepy town. Mosquitoes to slap at with hairy freckled hands and a dead hot breeze, when there is any breeze.

"What the hell am I walkin' way out here for? She wasn't nothin' to get excited over—last time I saw her. And that must a been a full three years ago. She acted like she was a virgin then. Name was Betsy. Sure ain't a virgin now, I know that. Not after we'd been anchored here damn near a month, the old man mixed up in some kind of law suit over some rich guy's yacht we rammed in a midnight squall off the bar. Damn good thing I wasn't on the bridge then. And this damn yellow gal, said she never had nothing to do with a seaman before. Lyin' I guess. Three years ago. She's probably on the crib-line now. Hell, how far was that house?"

Crossing the railroad track at the edge of town. Green lights. Sand in the road, seeping into oxfords and the cuffs of dungarees. Surf sounds, mosquito sounds, nigger-cries in the night. No street lights out here. There never is where niggers live. Rickety run-down huts, under palm trees. Flowers and vines all over. Always growing, always climbing. Never finished. Never will be finished climbing, growing. Hell of a lot of stars these Florida nights.

"Say, this ought to be the house. No light in it. Well, I remember this half-fallin'-down gate. Still fallin' down. Hell, why don't it go on and fall? Two or three years, and ain't fell yet. Guess *she's* fell a hell of a lot, though. It don't take them yellow janes long to get old and ugly. Said she was seventeen then. A wonder her old woman let me come in the house that night. They acted like it was the first time a white man had ever come in the house. They acted scared. But she was worth the money that time all right. She played like a kid. Said she liked my red hair. Said she'd never had a white man before. . . . Holy Jesus, the yellow wenches I've had, though. . . . Well, it's the same old gate. Be funny if she had another mule in my stall, now wouldn't it? . . . Say, anybody home there?"

"Yes, suh! Yes, suh! Come right in!"

"Hell, I know they can't recognize my voice. . . . It's the old woman, sure as a yard arm's long. . . . Hello! Where's Betsy?"

"Yes, suh, right here, suh. In de kitchen. Wait till I lights de light. Come in. Come in, young gentleman."

"Hell, I can't see to come in."

Little flare of oil light.

"Howdy! Howdy do, suh! Howdy, if 'tain't Mister Clarence, now, 'pon my word! Howdy, Mister Clarence, howdy! Howdy! After sich a long time."

"You must-a knowed my voice."

"No, suh, ain't recollected, suh. No, suh, but I knowed you was some white man comin' up de walk. Yes, indeedy! Set down, set down. Betsy be here directly. Set *right* down. Lemme call her. She's in de kitchen. . . . You Betsy!"

"Same old woman, wrinkled as hell, and still don't care where the money comes from. Still talkin' loud. . . . She knew it was some white man comin' up the walk, heh? There must be plenty of 'em, then, comin' here now. She knew it was some white man, heh! . . . What yuh sayin', Betsy, old gal? Damn if yuh ain't just as plump as ever. Them same damn moles on your cheek! Com'ere, lemme feel 'em."

Young yellow girl in a white house dress. Oiled hair. Skin like an autumn moon. Gold-ripe young yellow girl with a white house dress to her knees. Soft plump bare legs, color of the moon. Barefooted.

"Say, Betsy, here is Mister Clarence come back."

"Sure is! Claren—Mister Clarence! Ma, give him a drink."

"Keepin' licker in the house, now, heh? Yes? I thought you was church members last time I saw yuh? You always had to send out and get licker then."

"Well, we's expectin' company some of the times these days," smiling teeth like bright-white rays of moon, Betsy, nearly twenty, and still pretty.

"You usin' rouge, too, ain't yuh?"

"Sweet rouge."

"Yal?"

"Yeah, man, sweet and red like your hair."

"Yal?"

No such wise cracking three years ago. Too young and dumb for flirtation then: Betsy. Never like the old woman, talkative, "This here rum come right off de boats from Bermudy. Taste it, Mister Clarence. Strong enough to knock a mule down. Have a glass."

"Here's to you, Mister Clarence."

"Drinkin' licker, too, heh? Hell of a baby, ain't yuh? Yuh wouldn't even do that last time I saw yuh."

"Sure wouldn't, Mister Clarence, but three years a long time."

"Don't Mister Clarence *me* so much. Yuh know I christened yuh. . . . Auntie, yuh right about this bein' good licker."

"Yes, suh, I knowed you'd like it. It's strong."

"Sit on my lap, kid."

"Sure. . . ."

Soft heavy hips. Hot and browner than the moon—good licker. Drinking it down in little nigger house Florida coast palm fronds scratching roof hum mosquitoes night bugs flies ain't loud enough to keep a man named Clarence girl named Betsy old woman named Auntie from talking and drinking in a little nigger house on Florida coast dead warm night with the licker browner and more fiery than the moon. Yeah, man! A blanket of stars in the Florida sky—outside. In oil-lamp house you don't see no stars. Only a white man with red hair—third mate on a lousy tramp, a nigger girl, and Auntie wrinkled as an alligator bringing the fourth bottle of licker and everybody drinking—when the door . . . slowly . . . opens.

"Say, what the hell? Who's openin' that room door, peepin' in here? It can't be openin' itself?"

The white man stares intently, looking across the table, past the lamp, the licker bottles, the glasses and the old woman, way past the girl. Standing the door from the kitchen—Look! a damn red-headed baby. Standing not saying a damn word, a damn runt of a red-headed baby.

"What the hell?"

"You Clar—— . . . Mister Clarence, 'cuse me! . . . You hatian, you, get back to you' bed this minute—fo' I tan you in a inch o' yo' life!"

"Ma, let him stay."

Betsy's red-headed child stands in the door looking like one of those goggly-eyed dolls you hit with a ball at the County Fair. The child's face got no change in it. Never changes. Looks like never will change. Just staring—blue-eyed. Hell! God damn! A red-headed blue-eyed yellow-skinned baby!

"You Clarence! . . .'Cuse me, Mister Clarence. I ain't talkin' to you suh. . . . You, Clarence, go to bed. . . . That chile near 'bout worries de soul-case out o' me. Betsy spiles him, that's why. De po' little thing can't hear, nohow. Just deaf as a post. And over two years old and can't even say, 'Da!' No, suh, can't say, 'Da!' "

"Anyhow, Ma, my child ain't blind."

"Might just as well be blind fo' all de good his eyesight do him. I show him a switch and he don't pay it no mind—'less'n I hit him."

"He's mighty damn white for a nigger child."

"Yes, suh, Mister Clarence. He really ain't got much colored blood in him, a-tall. Betsy's papa, Mister Clarence, now he were a white man, too. . . . Here, lemme pour you some licker. Drink, Mister Clarence, drink."

Damn little red-headed stupid-faced runt of a child, named Clarence. Bow-legged as hell, too. Three shots for a quarter like a loaded doll in a County Fair. Anybody take a chance. For Christ's sake, stop him from walking across the floor! Will yuh?

"Hey! Take your hands off my legs, you lousy little bastard!"

"He can't hear you, Mister Clarence."

"Tell him to stop crawlin' around then under the table before I knock his block off."

"You varmint. . . ."

"Hey! Take him up from there, will you?"

"Yes, suh, Mister Clarence."

"Hey!"

"You little . . ."

"Hurry! Go on! Get him out then! What's he doin' crawlin' round dumb as hell lookin' at me up at me. I said, *me*. Get him the hell out of here! Hey, Betsy, get him out!"

A red-headed baby. Moonlight-gone baby. No kind of yellow-white bow-legged goggled-eyed County Fair baseball baby. Get him the hell out of here pulling at my legs looking like me at me like me at myself like me red-headed as me.

"Christ!"

"Christ!"

Knocking over glasses by the oil lamp on the table where the night flies flutter Florida where skeleton houses left over from boom sand in the road and no lights in the nigger section across the railroad's knocking over glasses at edge of town where a moon-colored girl's got a red-headed baby deaf as a post like the dolls you wham at three shots for a quarter in the County Fair half full of licker and can't hit nothing.

"Lemme pay for those drinks, will yuh? How much is it?"

"Ain't you gonna stay, Mister Clarence?"

"Lemme pay for my licker, I said."

"Ain't you gonna stay all night?"

"Lemme pay for that licker."

"Why, Mister Clarence? You stayed before."

"How much is the licker?"

"Two dollars, Mister Clarence."

"Here."

"Thank you, Mister Clarence."

"Go'bye!"

"Go'bye."

IX

Poor Little Black Fellow

Amanda Lee had been a perfect servant. And her husband Arnold likewise. That the Lord had taken them both so soon was a little beyond understanding. But then, of course, the Lord was just. And He had left the Pembertons poor little black Arnie as their Christian duty. There was no other way to consider the little colored boy whom they were raising as their own, *their very own,* except as a Christian duty. After all, they were white. It was no easy thing to raise a white child, even when it belonged to one, whereas this child was black, and had belonged to their servants, Amanda and Arnold.

But the Pembertons were never known to shirk a duty. They were one of New England's oldest families, one of the finest. They were wealthy. They had a family tree. They had a house in a charming maple-shaded town a few hours from Boston, a cottage at the beach, and four servants. On Tuesdays and Fridays Mr. Pemberton went to town. He had an office of some sort there. But the ladies, Grace Pemberton and her sister, sat on the wide porch at home and crocheted. Or maybe they let James take them for a drive in the car. One of them sang in the choir.

Sometimes they spoke about the two beautiful Negro servants they once had, Amanda and Arnold. They liked to tell poor little Arnie how faithful and lovely his parents had been in life. It would encourage the boy. At present, of course, all their servants were white. Negroes were getting so unsteady. You couldn't keep them in the villages any more. In fact, there were none in Mapleton now. They all went running off to Boston or New York, sporting their money away in the towns. Well, Amanda and Arnold were never like that. They had been simple, true, honest, hard-working. Their qualities had caused the Pembertons to give, over a space of time, more than ten thousand dollars to a school for Negroes at Hampton, Va. Because they thought they saw in Amanda and Arnold the real qualities of an humble and gentle race. That, too, was why they had decided to keep Arnie, poor little black fellow.

The Pembertons had lost nobody in the war except Arnold, their black stable man, but it had been almost like a personal loss. Indeed, after his death, they had kept horses no longer. And the stable had been turned into a garage.

Amanda, his wife, had grieved terribly, too. She had been all wrapped up in Arnold, and in her work with the Pembertons (she was their house-keeper) and in her little dark baby, Arnold, Junior. The child was five when his father went to war; and six when Amanda died of pneumonia a few weeks after they learned Arnold had been killed in the Argonne. The Pembertons were proud of him. A Negro who died for his country. But when that awful Winter of 1919 ended (the Pembertons judged it must have been awful from what they read), when that Winter ended the family was minus two perfect servants who could never come back. And they had on their hands an orphan.

"Poor little black fellow," said Grace Pemberton to her husband and her sister. "In memory of Arnold and Amanda, I think it is our Christian duty to keep it, and raise it up in the way it should go." Somehow, for a long time she called Arnie "it."

"We can raise it, without keeping it," said her husband. "Why not send it to Hampton?"

"Too young for that," said Emily, Mrs. Pemberton's sister. "I have been to Hampton, and they don't take them under twelve there."

So it was decided to keep the little black boy right in Mapleton, to send him to the village school, and to raise him up a good Christian and a good worker. And, it must be admitted, things went pretty well for some years. The white servants were kind to Arnie. The new housekeeper, a big-bosomed Irish woman who came after Amanda's death, treated him as though he were her very own, washed him and fed him. Indeed, they all treated him as if he were their very own.

II

Mr. Pemberton took Arnie to Boston once a season and bought him clothes. On his birthday, they gave him a party—on the lawn—because, after all, his birthday came in the Spring, and there was no need of filling the living-room with children. There was much more room on the lawn. In Summer Arnie went to the sea-shore with the rest of the family.

And Arnie, dark as he was, thrived. He grew up. He did well in his classes. He did well at home, helped with the chores about the house, raked the yard in the Fall, and shoveled snow when the long Winters set in. On Sundays he went to church with the family, listened to a dry and intelligent sermon, chanted the long hymns, and loved the anthems in which Miss Emily sang the solo parts.

Arnie, in church, a little black spot in a forest of white heads above stiff pews. Arnie, out of church, a symbol of how Christian charity should really be administered in the true spirit of the human brotherhood.

The church and the Pembertons were really a little proud of Arnie. Did they not all accept him as their own? And did they not go out of their way to be nice to him—a poor little black fellow whom they, through Christ, had taken in? Throughout the years the whole of Mapleton began to preen itself on its charity and kindness to Arnie. One would think that nobody in the town need ever again do a good deed: that this acceptance of a black boy was quite enough.

Arnie realized how they felt, but he didn't know what to do about it. He kept himself quiet and inconspicuous, and studied hard. He was very grateful, and very lonely. There were no other colored children in the town. But all the grown-up white people made their children be very nice to him, always very nice. "Poor little black boy," they said. "An orphan, and colored. And the Pembertons are so good to him. You be nice to him, too, do you hear? Share your lunch with him. And don't fight him. Or hurt his feelings. He's only a poor little Negro who has no parents." So even the children were over-kind to Arnie.

Everything might have been all right forever had not Arnie begun to grow up. The other children began to grow up, too. Adolescence. The boys had girls. They played kissing games, and learned to dance. There were parties to which Arnie was not invited—really couldn't be invited—with the girls and all. And after generations of peace the village of Mapleton, and the Pembertons, found themselves beset with a Negro problem. Everyone was a little baffled and a little ashamed.

To tell the truth, everybody had got so used to Arnie that nobody really thought of him as a Negro—until he put on long trousers and went to high-school. Now they noticed that he was truly very black. And his voice suddenly became deep and mannish, even before the white boys in Arnie's class talked in the cracks and squeaks of coming manhood.

Then there had arisen that problem of the Boy Scouts. When Arnie was sixteen the Pembertons applied for him to be admitted to a Summer camp for the Scouts at Barrow Beach, and the camp had refused. In a personal letter to Mr. Pemberton, they said they simply could not admit Negroes. Too many parents would object. So several of Arnie's friends and classmates went off to camp in June, and Arnie could not go. The village of Mapleton and the Pembertons felt awfully apologetic for American democracy's attitude to Arnie, whose father had died in the War. But, after all, they couldn't control the Boy Scout Camp. It was a semi-private institution. They were extra nice to Arnie, though—everybody.

That Summer, the Pembertons bought him a bicycle. And toward the end of the Summer (because they thought it was dull for him at the bungalow) they sent him to a Negro charity camp near Boston. It would be nice for him to come to know some of his own people. But Arnie hated it. He stayed a week and came home. The charity camp was full of black kids from the slums of Boston who cussed and fought and made fun of him because he didn't know how to play the dozens. So Arnie, to whom Negroes were a new nation, even if he was black, was amazed and bewildered, and came home. The Pembertons were embarrassed to find him alone in his attic room in the big empty house when they and the servants returned from the beach.

But they wanted so to be nice to him. They asked him if he'd met any friends he'd like to ask down for a week-end. They thought they would give him the whole top floor of the garage that year for a little apartment of his own and he could have his colored friends there. But Arnie hadn't met anyone he wanted to have. He had no colored friends.

The Pembertons knew that he couldn't move in the social world of Mapleton much longer. He was too big. But, really, what could they do? Grace Pemberton prayed. Emily talked it over with the mission board at church, and Mr. Pemberton spoke to the Urban League in Boston. Why not send him to Hampton now?

Arnie had only one more year in the high-school. Then, of course, he would go to college. But to one of the nicer Negro colleges like Fisk, they decided, where those dear Jubilee singers sang so beautifully, and where he would be with his own people, and wouldn't be embarrassed. No, Fisk wasn't as good as Harvard, they knew, but then Arnie had to find his own world after all. They'd have to let him go, poor black fellow! Certainly, he was their very own! But in Mapleton, what could he do, how could he live, whom could he marry? The Pembertons were a bit worried, even, about this one more year. So they decided to be extra nice to him. Indeed, everybody in Mapleton decided to be extra nice to him.

The two rooms over the garage made a fine apartment for a growing boy. His pennants and books and skis were there. Sometimes the white boys came in the evenings and played checkers and smoked forbidden cigarettes. Sometimes they walked out and met the girls at the soda-fountain in Dr. Jourdain's drug-store, and Arnie had a soda with the group. But he always came away alone, while the others went off in pairs. When the Christmas parties were being given, many of the girls were lovely in dresses that looked almost like real evening gowns, but Arnie wasn't invited anywhere but to the Allens'. (And they really didn't count in Mapleton—they were very poor white folks.)

The Pembertons were awfully sorry, of course. They were one of New England's oldest families, and they were raising Arnie as their son. But he was an African, a nice Christian African, and he ought to move among his own people. There he could be a good influence and have a place. The Pembertons couldn't help it that there were no Negroes in Mapleton. Once there had been some, but now they had all moved away. It was more fashionable to have white help. And even as a servant in Mapleton, Arnie would have been a little out of place. But he was smart in school, and a good clean boy. He sang well. (All Negroes were musical.) He skated and swam and played ball. He loved and obeyed the Pembertons. They wanted him to find his place in the world, poor fine little black fellow. Poor dear Arnie.

So it was decided that he would go to Fisk next year. When Arnie agreed, the Pembertons breathed a sort of sigh of joy. They thought he might remember the camp at Boston, and not want to go to a Negro college.

III

And now the Summer presented itself, the last Summer before they let Arnie go away—the boy whom they'd raised as their own. They didn't want that last Summer spoiled for him. Or for them. They wanted no such incidents as the Boy Scout business. The Pembertons were kind people. They wanted Arnie to remember with pleasure his life with them.

Maybe it would be nice to take him to Europe. They themselves had not been abroad for a long time. Arnie could see Paris and his father's grave and the Tower of London. The Pembertons would enjoy the trip, too. And on their return, Arnie could go directly to Fisk, where his life at college, and in the grown-up world, would begin. Maybe he'd marry one of those lovely brown girls who sang spirituals so beautifully, and live a good Christian man—occasionally visiting the Pembertons, and telling them about his influence on the poor black people of the South.

Graduation came. Arnie took high honors in the class, and spoke on the program. He went to the senior prom, but he didn't dance with any of the girls. He just sort of stood around the punch-bowl, and joked with the fellows. So nobody was embarrassed, and everyone was glad to see him there. The one dark spot in a world of whiteness. It was too bad he didn't have a partner to stand with him when they sang the Alma Mater after the final dance. But he was a lucky chap to be going to Europe. Not many youngsters from Mapleton had been. The Pembertons were doing well by him, everybody said aloud, and the church board had got him into Fisk.

But with all their careful planning, things weren't going so well about the European trip. When the steamship company saw the passports, they cancelled the cabin that had been engaged for Arnie. Servants always went second class, they wrote. That Arnie wasn't a servant, it was revealed ultimately, made no difference. He was a Negro, wasn't he?

So it ended with the Pembertons going first, and Arnie second class on the same boat. They would have all gone second, out of sympathy for Arnie, except that accommodations in that class had been completely booked for months ahead. Only as a great favor to first-class passengers had the steamship company managed to find a place for Arnie at all. The Pembertons and their boy had a cross to bear, but they bore it like Christians. At Cherbourg they met the little black fellow again on an equal footing. The evening found them in Paris.

Paris, loveliest of cities, where at dusk the lights are a great necklace among the trees of the Champs Elysées. Paris, song-city of the world. Paris, with the lips of a lovely woman kissing without fear. June, in Paris.

The Pembertons stopped at one of the best hotels. They had a suite which included a room for Arnie. Everything was very nice. The Louvre and the Eiffel Tower and the Café de la Paix were very nice. All with Arnie. Very nice. Everything would have gone on perfectly, surely; and there would have been no story, and Arnie and the Pembertons would have continued in Christian love forever—Arnie at Fisk, of course, and the Pembertons at Mapleton, then Arnie married and the Pembertons growing old, and so on and on—had not Claudina Lawrence moved into the very hotel where the Pembertons were staying. Claudina Lawrence! My God!

True, they had all seen dark faces on the boulevards, and a Negro quartet at the Olympia, but only very good Americans and very high English people were staying at this hotel with the Pembertons. Then Claudina Lawrence moved in—the Claudina who had come from Atlanta, Georgia, to startle the Old World with the new beauty of brown flesh behind footlights. That Claudina who sang divinely and danced like a dryad and had amassed a terrible amount of fame and money in five years. Even the Pembertons had heard of Claudina Lawrence in the quiet and sedate village of Mapleton. Even Arnie had heard of her. And Arnie had been a little bit proud. She was a Negro.

But why did she have to move next door to the Pembertons in this hotel? "Why, Lord, oh, why?" said Grace Pemberton. "For the sake of Arnie, why?" But here the tale begins.

IV

A lot of young Negroes, men and women, shiny and well-dressed, with good and sophisticated manners, came at all hours to see Claudina. Arnie and the Pembertons would meet them in the hall. They were a little too well dressed to suit the Pembertons. They came with white people among them, too—very pretty French girls. And they were terribly lively and gay and didn't seem dependent on anybody. Their music floated out of the windows on the Summer night. The Pembertons hoped they wouldn't get hold of Arnie. They would be a bad influence.

But they did get hold of Arnie.

One morning, as he came out to descend to the lobby to buy post-cards, Claudina herself stepped into the hall at the same time. They met at the elevator. She was the loveliest creature Arnie had ever seen. In pink, all tan and glowing. And she was colored.

"Hello," she said to the young black boy who looked old enough to be less shy. "You look like a home-towner."

"I'm from Mapleton," Arnie stuttered.

"You sound like you're from London," said Claudina, noting his New England accent and confusing it with Mayfair. "But your face says Alabama."

"Oh, I'm colored all right," said Arnie, happy to be recognized by one of his own. "And I'm glad to know you."

"Having a good time?" asked Claudina, as the elevator came.

"No," Arnie said, suddenly truthful. "I don't know anybody."

"Jesus!" said Claudina, sincerely. "That's a shame. A lot of boys and girls are always gathering in my place. Knock on the door some time. I can't see one of my down-home boys getting the blues in Paris. Some of the fellows in my band'll take you around a bit, maybe. They know all the holes and corners. Come in later."

"Thanks awfully," said Arnie.

Claudina left him half-dazed in the lobby. He saw her get into her car at the curb, saw the chauffeur tip his hat, and then drive away. For the first time in his life Arnie was really happy. Somebody had offered him something without charity, without condescension, without prayer, without distance, and without being nice.

All the pictures in the Luxembourg blurred before his eyes that afternoon, and Miss Emily's explanations went in one ear and out the other. He was thinking about Claudina and the friends he might meet in her rooms, the gay and well-dressed Negroes he had seen in the hall, the Paris they could show him, the girls they would be sure to know.

That night he went to see Claudina. He told the Pembertons he didn't care about going to the Odéon, so they went without him, a little reluctantly—because they didn't care about going either, really. They had been sticking rather strenuously to their program of cultural Paris. They were tired. Still, the Pembertons went to the Odéon—it was a play they really should see—and Arnie went next door to Claudina's. But only after he was sure the Pembertons were sitting in the theatre.

Claudina was playing whist. A young English man was her partner. Two sleek young colored men were their opponents. "Sit down, honey," Claudina said as if she had known Arnie for years. "You can take a hand in a minute, if you'd like to play. Meet Mr. So and so and so. . . ." She introduced him to the group. "It's kinda early yet. Most of our gang are at work. The theatres aren't out. . . . Marie, bring him a drink." And the French maid poured a cocktail.

A knock, and a rather portly brown-skinned woman, beautifully dressed, entered. "Hello! Who's holding all the trump cards? Glad to meet you, Mr. Arnie. From Boston, you say? My old stamping-ground. Do you know the Roundtrees there?"

"No'm," Arnie said.

"Well, I used to study at the Conservatory and knew all the big shots," the brown-skin woman went on. "Did you just come over? Tourist, heh? Well, what's new in the States now? I haven't been home for three years. Don't intend to go soon. The color-line's a little too much for me. What are they dancing now-a-days? You must've brought a few of the latest steps with you. Can you do the Lindy Hop?"

"No'm," said Arnie.

"Well, I'm gonna see," said the brown-skin lady. She put a record on the victrola, and took Arnie in her arms. Even if he couldn't do the Lindy Hop, he enjoyed dancing with her and they got along famously. Several more people came in, a swell-looking yellow girl, some rather elderly musicians, in spats, and a young colored art student named Harry Jones. Cocktails went around.

"I'm from Chicago," Harry said eventually. "Been over here about a year and like it a hell of a lot. You will, too, soon as you get to know a few folks."

Gradually the room took on the life and gaiety of a party. Somebody sat down at a piano in the alcove, and started a liquid ripple of jazz. Three or four couples began to dance. Arnie and the lovely yellow girl got together. They danced a long time, and then they drank cocktails. Arnie forgot about the clock. It was long after midnight.

Somebody suggested that they all go to the opening of a new Martinique ballroom where a native orchestra would play rattles and drums.

"Come on, Arnie," Harry Jones said. "You might as well make a night of it. Tomorrow's Sunday."

"I start rehearsals tomorrow," Claudina said, "so I can't go. But listen here," she warned. "Don't you-all take Arnie out of here and lose him. Some of these little French girls are liable to put him in their pockets, crazy as they are about chocolate."

Arnie hoped he wouldn't meet the Pembertons in the hall. He didn't. They were long since in bed. And when Arnie came in at dawn, his head was swimming with the grandest night he'd ever known.

At the Martinique ball he'd met dozens of nice girls: white girls and brown girls, and yellow girls, artists and students and dancers and models and tourists. Harry knew everybody. And everybody was gay and friendly. Paris and music and cocktails made you forget what color people were—and what color you were yourself. Here it didn't matter—color.

Arnie went to sleep dreaming about a little Rumanian girl named Vivi.[10] Harry said she was a music student. But Arnie didn't care what she was, she had such soft black hair and bright grey eyes. How she could dance! And she knew quite a little English. He'd taken her address. Tomorrow he would go to see her. Aw, hell, tomorrow the Pembertons wanted to go to Versailles!

V

When Arnie woke up it was three o'clock. This time Grace Pemberton had actually banged on the door. Arnie was frightened. He'd never slept so late before. What would the Pembertons think?

"What ever is the matter, Arnold?" Mrs. Pemberton called. Only when she was put out did she call him Arnold.

"Up late reading," Arnie muttered through the closed door. "I was up late reading." And then was promptly ashamed of himself for having lied.

"Well, hurry up," Mrs. Pemberton said. "We're about to start for Versailles."

"I don't want to go," said Arnie.

"What ever is the matter with you, boy?" gasped Grace Pemberton.

Arnie had slipped on a bathrobe, so he opened the door.

"Good morning," he said. "I've met some friends. I want to go out with them."

The contrariness of late adolescence was asserting itself. He felt stubborn and mean.

"Friends?" said Grace Pemberton. "What friends, may I ask?"

"A colored student and some others."

"Where did you meet them?"

"Next door, at Miss Lawrence's."

Grace Pemberton stiffened like a bolt. "Get ready, young man," she said, "and come with us to Versailles." She left the room. The young man got ready.

Arnie pouted, but he went with the Pembertons. The sun gave him a headache, and he didn't give a damn about Versailles. That evening, after a private lecture by Mr. Pemberton on the evils of Paris (Grace and Emily had spoken about the beauty of the city), he went to bed feeling very black and sick.

For several days, he wasn't himself at all, what with constant excursions to museums and villages and chateaux, when he wanted to be with Vivi and Harry and Claudina. (Once he did sneak away with Harry to meet Vivi.) Meanwhile, the Pembertons lectured him on his surliness. They were inclined to be dignified and distant to the poor little black fellow now. After all, it had cost them quite a lot to bring him to Paris. Didn't he appreciate what they were doing for him? They had raised him. Had they then no right to forbid him going about with a crowd of Negroes from the theatres?

"He's a black devil," said Mr. Pemberton.

"Poor little fellow," said Grace. She was a little sorry for him.

"After all, he doesn't know. He's young. Let us just try loving him, and being very nice to him."

So once again the Pembertons turned loose on Arnie their niceness. They took him to the races, and they bought him half a dozen French ties from a good shop, and they treated him better than if he were their own.

But Arnie was worse than ever. He stayed out all night one night. Grace knew, because she knocked on his door at two o'clock. And the Negroes next door, how they laughed! How they danced! How the music drifted through the windows. It seemed as if the actual Devil had got into Arnie. Was he going to the dogs before their very eyes? Grace Pemberton was worried. After all, he *was* the nearest thing she'd ever had to a son. She was really fond of him.

As for Arnie, it wasn't the Devil at all that had got him. It wasn't even Claudina. It was Vivi, the little girl he'd met through Harry at the Martinique ball. The girl who played Chopin on the piano, and had grey eyes and black hair and came from Rumania. By himself, Arnie had managed to find, from the address she had given him, the tall house near the Parc Monceau where she lived in an attic room. Up six flights of stairs he walked. He found her with big books on theory in front of her and blank music pages, working out some sort of exercise in harmony. Her little face was very white, her grey eyes very big, and her black hair all fluffy around her head. Arnie didn't know why he had come to see her except that he liked her very much.

They talked all afternoon and Arnie told her about his life at home, how white people had raised him, and how hard it was to be black in America. Vivi said it didn't make any difference in Rumania, or in Paris either, about being black.

"Here it's only hard to be poor," Vivi said.

But Arnie thought he wouldn't mind being poor in a land where it didn't matter what color you were.

"Yes, you would mind," Vivi said.

"Being poor's not easy anywhere. But then," and her eyes grew bigger, "by and by the Revolution will come. In Rumania the Revolution will come. In France, too. Everywhere poor people are tired of being poor."

"What Revolution?" Arnie asked, for he hadn't heard about it in Mapleton.

Vivi told him.

"Where we live, it's quiet," he said. "My folks come from Massachusetts."

VI

And then the devil whispered to Arnie. Maybe Vivi would like to meet some real Americans. Anyway, he would like the Pembertons to meet her.

He'd like to show them that there actually was a young white girl in the world who didn't care about color. They were always educating him. He would educate them a bit. So Arnie invited Vivi to dinner at the hotel that very night.

The Pembertons had finished their soup when he entered the sparkling dining-room of the hotel. He made straight for their table. The orchestra was playing Strauss. Gentlemen in evening clothes and ladies in diamonds scanned a long and expensive menu. The Pembertons looked up and saw Arnie coming, guiding Vivi by the hand. Grace Pemberton gasped and put her spoon back in the soup. Emily went pale. Mr. Pemberton's mouth opened. All the Americans stared. Such a white, white girl and such a black, black boy coming across the dining-room floor! The girl had a red mouth and grey eyes.

The Pembertons had been waiting for Arnie since four o'clock. Today a charming Indian mystic, Nadjuti, had come to tea with them, especially to see the young Negro student they had raised in America. The Pembertons were not pleased that Arnie had not been there.

"This is my friend," Arnie said. "I've brought her to dinner."

Vivi smiled and held out her hand, but the Pembertons bowed in their stiffest fashion. Nobody noticed her hand.

"I'm sorry," said Grace Pemberton, "but there's room for only four at our table."

"Oh," said Arnie. He hadn't thought they'd be rude. Polite and formal, maybe, but not rude. "Oh! Don't mind us then. Come on, Vivi." His eyes were red as he led her away to a vacant table by the fountain. A waiter came and took their orders with the same deference he showed everyone else. The Pembertons looked and could not eat.

"Where ever did he get her?" whispered Emily in her thin New England voice, as her cheeks burned. "Is she a woman from the streets?" The Pembertons couldn't imagine that so lovely a white girl would go out with a strange Negro unless she were a prostitute. They were terribly mortified. What would he do next?

"But maybe he doesn't know. Did you warn him, John?" Grace Pemberton addressed her husband.

"I did," replied Mr. Pemberton shortly.

"A scarlet woman," said Emily faintly. "A scarlet . . . I think I shall go to my room. All the Americans in the dining-room must have seen." She was white as she rose. "We've been talked about enough as it is— travelling with a colored boy. For our sakes, he might have been careful."

The Pembertons left the dining-room. But Grace Pemberton was afraid for Arnie. Near the door, she turned and came over to the table by the fountain. "Please, Arnold, come to my room before you go."

"Yes, Miss Grace, I'll come," he said.

"You mustn't mind." Vivi patted his arm. The orchestra was playing "The Song of India." "All old people are the same."

As they ate, Vivi and Arnie talked about parents. Vivi told him how her folks hadn't allowed her to come away to study music, how they'd even tried to stop her at the station. "Most elderly people are terrible," she said, "especially parents."

"But they're not my parents," Arnie said. "They are white people."

When he took Vivi home, he kissed her. Then he came back and knocked on the living-room door.

VII

"Come in," Grace Pemberton said. "Come in, Arnie, I want to talk to you." She was sitting there alone, very straight with her iron-grey hair low on her neck. "Poor little black fellow," she said, as through Arnie had done a great and careless wrong. "Come here."

When Arnie saw her pale white face from the door, he was a little sad and ashamed that he might have done something to hurt her. But when she began to pity him, "poor little black fellow," a sudden anger shook him from head to foot. His eyes grew sultry and red, his spirit stubborn.

"Arnold," she said, "I think we'd better go home, back to America."

"I don't want to go," he replied.

"But you don't seem to appreciate what we are doing for you here," she said, "at all."

"I don't," Arnie answered.

"You don't!" Grace Pemberton's throat went dry. "You don't? We're showing you the best of Paris, and you don't? Why, we've done all we could for you always, Arnie boy. We've raised you as our own. And we want to do more. We're going to send you to college, of course, to Fisk this Fall."

"I don't want to go to Fisk," Arnie said.

"What?"

"No," said Arnie. "I don't want to go. It'll be like that camp in Boston. Everything in America's like that camp in Boston." His eyes grew redder.

"Separate, segregated, shut-off! Black people kept away from everybody else. I go to Fisk; my classmates, Harvard and Amherst and Yale . . . I sleep in the garage, you sleep in the house."

"Oh," Grace Pemberton said. "We didn't mean it like that!"

Arnie was being cruel, just cruel. She began, in spite of herself, to cry.

"I don't want to go back home," Arnie went on. "I hate America."

"But your father *died* for America," Grace Pemberton cried.

"I guess he was a fool," said Arnie.

The hall door opened. Mr. Pemberton and his sister-in-law came in from a walk through the park.

They saw Mrs. Pemberton's eyes wet, and Arnie's sultry face. Mrs. Pemberton told them what he'd said.

"So you want to stay here," said Mr. Pemberton, trying to hold his temper. "Well, stay. Take your things and stay. Stay now. Get out! Go!"

Anger possessed him, fury against this ungrateful black boy who made his wife cry. Grace Pemberton never cried over anything Mr. Pemberton did. And now, she was crying over this . . . this . . . In the back of his mind was the word *nigger.* Arnold felt it.

"I want to go," said Arnie. "I've always wanted to go."

"You little black fool!" said Emily.

"Where will you go?" Grace Pemberton asked. Why, oh why, didn't Arnie say he was sorry, beg their pardon, and stay? He knew he could if he wanted to.

"I'll go to Vivi," Arnie said.

"Vivi?" a weak voice gasped.

"Yes, marry Vivi!"

"Marry white, eh?" said Mr. Pemberton. Emily laughed drily. But Grace Pemberton fainted.

Next door, just then, the piano was louder than ever. Somebody was doing a tap dance. The dancing and the music floated through the windows on the soft Paris air. Outside, the lights were a necklace of gold over the Champs Elysées. Autos honked. Trees rustled. People passed.

Arnie went out.

X

Little Dog

Miss Briggs had a little apartment all alone in a four story block just where Oakwood Drive curved past the park and the lake. Across the street, beneath her window, kids skated in winter, and in the spring the grass grew green. In summer, lovers walked and necked by the lake in the moonlight. In fall brown and red-gold leaves went skithering into the water when the wind blew.

Miss Briggs came home from work every night at eight, unless she went to the movies or the Women's Civics Club. On Sunday evenings she sometimes went to a lecture on Theosophy. But she was never one to gad about, Miss Briggs. Besides she worked too hard. She was the head bookkeeper for the firm of Wilkins and Bryant, Wood, Coal and Coke. And since 1930, when they had cut down the staff, she had only one assistant. Just two of them now to take care of the books, bills, and everything. But Miss Briggs was very efficient. She had been head bookkeeper for twenty-one years. Wilkins and Bryant didn't know what they would do without her.

Miss Briggs was proud of her record as a bookkeeper. Once the City Hall had tried to get her, but Wilkins and Bryant said, "No, indeed. We can pay as much as the city, if not more. You stay right here with us." Miss Briggs stayed. She was never a person to move about much or change jobs.

As a young girl she had studied very hard in business school. She never had much time to go out. A widowed mother, more or less dependent on her then, later became completely dependent—paralyzed. Her mother had been dead for six years now.

Perhaps it was the old woman's long illness that had got Miss Briggs in the habit of staying home every night in her youth, instead of going out to the theatre or to parties. They had never been able to afford a maid even after Miss Briggs became so well paid—for doctors' bills were such a drain, and in those last months a trained nurse was needed for her mother—God rest her soul.

Now, alone, Miss Briggs usually ate her dinner in the Rose Bud Tea Shoppe. A number of genteel business women ate there, and the colored waiters were so nice. She had been served by Joe or Perry, flat-footed old Negro gentlemen, for three or four years now. They knew her tastes, and would get the cook to make little special dishes for her if she wasn't feeling very well.

After dinner, with a walk of five or six blocks from the Rose Bud, the park would come into view with its trees and lights. The Lyle Apartments loomed up. A pretty place to live, facing the park. Miss Briggs had moved there after her mother died. Trying to keep house alone was just a little too much. And there was no man in view to marry. Most of them would want her only for her money now, at her age, anyway. To move with another woman, Miss Briggs thought, would be a sort of sacrilege so soon after her mother's death. Besides, she really didn't know any other woman who, like herself, was without connections. Almost everybody had somebody, Miss Briggs reflected. Every woman she knew had either a husband, or sisters, or a friend of long standing with whom she resided. But Miss Briggs had nobody at all. Nobody.

Not that she thought about it very much. Miss Briggs was too used to facing the world alone, minding her own business, and going her own way. But one summer, while returning from Michigan where she had taken her two weeks' rest, as she came through Cleveland, on her way from the boat to the station there, she happened to pass a dog shop with a window full of fuzzy little white dogs. Miss Briggs called to the taxi man to stop. She got out and went in. When she came back to the taxi, she carried a little white dog named Flips. At least, the dealer said he had been calling it Flips because its ears were so floppy.

"They just flip and flop," the man said, smiling at the tall middle-aged woman.

"How much is he?" Miss Briggs asked, holding the puppy up.

"I'll let you have him for twenty-five dollars," the man said.

Miss Briggs put the puppy down. She thought that was a pretty steep price. But there was something about Flips that she liked, so she picked him up again and took him with her. After all, she allowed herself very few indulgences. And somehow, this summer, Miss Briggs sort of hated going back to an empty flat—even if it did overlook the park.

Or maybe it was because it overlooked the park that had made it so terrible a place to live lately. Miss Briggs had never felt lonely, not *very* lonely, in the old house after her mother died. Only when she moved to the flat, did her loneliness really come down on her. There were some nights there, especially summer nights, when she thought she couldn't stand it, to sit in her window and see so many people going by, couple by couple, arms locked; or else in groups, laughing and talking.

Miss Briggs wondered why she knew no one, male or female, to walk out with, laughing and talking. She knew only the employees where she worked, and with whom she associated but little (for she hated to have people know her business). She knew, of course, the members of the Women's Civics Club, but in a cultural sort of way. The warmth of friendship seldom mellowed her contacts there. Only one or two of the club women had ever called on her. Miss Briggs always believed in keeping her distance, too. Her mother used to say she'd been born poor but proud, and would stay that way.

"Folks have to amount to something before Clara takes up with them," old Mrs. Briggs always said. "Men'll have a hard time getting Clara."

Men did. Now, with no especial attractions to make them keep trying, Miss Briggs, tall and rail-like, found herself left husbandless at an age when youth had gone.

So, in her forty-fifth year, coming back from a summer boarding house in Michigan, Miss Briggs bought herself a little white dog. When she got home, she called on the janitor and asked him to bring her up a small box for Flips. The janitor, a tow-headed young Swede, brought her a grapefruit crate from the A & P. Miss Briggs put it in the kitchen for Flips.

She told the janitor to bring her, too, three times a week, a dime's worth of dog meat or bones, and leave it on the back porch where she could find it when she came home. On other nights, Flips ate dog biscuits.

Flips and Miss Briggs soon settled on a routine. Each evening when she got home she would feed him. Then she would take him for a walk. This gave Miss Briggs an excuse for getting out, too. In warm weather she would walk around the little lake fronting her apartment with Flips on a string. Sometimes she would even smile at other people walking around the lake with dogs at night. It was nice the way dogs made things friendly. It was nice the way people with dogs smiled at her occasionally because she had a dog, too. But whenever (as seldom happened) someone in the park, dog or no dog, tried to draw her into conversation, Miss Briggs would move on as quickly as she could without being rude. You could never tell just who people were, Miss Briggs thought, or what they might have in their minds. No, you shouldn't think of taking up with strange people in parks. Besides, she was head bookkeeper for Wilkins and Bryant, and in these days of robberies and kidnappings maybe they just wanted to find out when she went for the pay roll, and how much cash the firm kept on hand. Miss Briggs didn't trust people.

Always, by ten o'clock, she was back with Flips in her flat. A cup of hot milk then maybe, with a little in a saucer for Flips, and to bed. In the morning she would let Flips run down the back steps for a few minutes, then she gave him more milk, left a pan of water, and went to work. A regular routine, for Miss Briggs took care of Flips with great seriousness. At night when she got back from the Rose Bud Tea Shoppe, she fed him biscuits; or if it were dog meat night, she looked out on the back porch for the package the janitor was paid to leave. (That is, Miss Briggs allowed the Swede fifty cents a week to buy bones. He could keep the change.)

But one night, the meat was not there. Miss Briggs thought perhaps he had forgotten. Still he had been bringing it regularly for nearly two years. Maybe the warm spring this year made the young janitor listless, Miss Briggs mused. She fed Flips biscuits.

But two days later, another dog meat night, the package was not there either. "This is too much!" thought Miss Briggs. "Come on, Flipsy, let's go downstairs and see. I'm sure I gave him fifty cents this week to buy your bones."

Miss Briggs and the little white beast went downstairs to ask why there was no meat for her dog to eat. When they got to the janitor's quarters in the basement, they heard a mighty lot of happy laughter and kids squalling, and people moving. They didn't sound like Swedes, either. Miss Briggs was a bit timid about knocking, but she finally mustered up courage with Flips there beside her. A sudden silence fell inside.

"You Leroy," a voice said. "Go to de door."

A child's feet came running. The door opened like a flash and a small colored boy stood there grinning.

"Where—where is the janitor?" Miss Briggs said, taken aback.

"You mean my papa?" asked the child, looking at the gaunt white lady. "He's here." And off he went to call his father.

Surrounded by children, a tall broad-shouldered Negro of perhaps forty, gentle of face and a little stooped, came to the door.

"Good evenin'," he said pleasantly.

"Why, are you the janitor?" stammered Miss Briggs. Flips had already begun to jump up on him with friendly mien.

"Yes'm, I'm the new janitor," said the Negro in a softly beautiful voice, kids all around him. "Is there something I can help you to do?"

"Well," said Miss Briggs, "I'd like some bones for my little dog. He's missed his meat two times now. Can you get him some?"

"Yes'm, sure can," said the new janitor, "if all the stores ain't closed." He was so much taller than Miss Briggs that she had to look up at him.

"I'd appreciate it," said Miss Briggs, "please."

As she went back upstairs she heard the new janitor calling in his rich voice, "Lora, you reckon that meat store's still open?" And a woman's voice and a lot of children answered him.

It turned out that the store was closed. So Miss Briggs gave the Negro janitor ten cents and told him to have the meat there the next night when she came home.

"Flips, you shan't starve," she said to the little white dog, "new janitor or no new janitor."

"Wruff!" said Flips.

But the next day when she came home there was no meat on the back porch either. Miss Briggs was puzzled, and a little hurt. Had the Negro forgotten?

Scarcely had she left the kitchen, however, when someone knocked on the back door and there stood the colored man with the meat. He was almost as old as Miss Briggs, she was certain of it, looking at him. Not a young man at all, but he was awfully big and brown and kind looking. So sort of sure about life as he handed her the package.

"I thought some other dog might get it if I left it on the porch," said the colored man. "So I kept it downstairs till you come."

Miss Briggs was touched. "Well, thank you very much," she said.

When the man had gone, she remembered that she had not told him how often to get meat for the dog.

The next night he came again with bones, and every night from then on. Miss Briggs did not stop him, or limit him to three nights a week. Just after eight, whenever she got home, up the back porch steps the Negro would come with the dog meat. Sometimes there would be two or three kids with him. Pretty little brown-black rather dirty kids, Miss Briggs thought, who were shy in front of her, but nice.

Once or twice during the spring, the janitor's wife, instead, brought the dog meat up on Saturday nights. Flips barked rudely at her. Miss Briggs didn't take to the creature, either. She was fat and yellow, and certainly too old to just keep on having children as she evidently did. The janitor himself was so solid and big and strong! Miss Briggs felt better when he brought her the bones for her dog. She didn't like his wife.

That June, on warm nights, as soon as she got home, Miss Briggs would open the back door and let the draft blow through. She could hear the janitor better coming up the rear stairs when he brought the bones. And, of course, she never said more than good-evening to him and thank you. Or here's a dollar for the week. Keep the change.

Flips ate an awful lot of meat that spring. "Your little dog's a regular meat-hound," the janitor said one night as he handed her the bones; and Miss Briggs blushed, for no good reason.

"He does eat a lot," she said. "Goodnight."

As she spread the bones out on paper for the dog, she felt that her hands were trembling. She left Flips eating and went into the parlor, but found that she could not keep her mind on the book she was reading. She kept looking at the big kind face of the janitor in her mind, perturbed that it was a Negro face, and that it stayed with her so.

The next night, she found herself waiting for the dog meat to arrive with more anxiety than Flips himself. When the colored man handed it to her, she quickly closed the door, before her face got red again.

"Funny old white lady," thought the janitor as he went back downstairs to his basement full of kids. "Just crazy about that dog," he added to his wife. "I ought to tell her it ain't good to feed a dog so much meat."

"What do you care, long as she wants to?" asked his wife.

The next day in the office Miss Briggs found herself making errors over the books. That night she hurried home to be sure and be there on time when he brought the dog meat up, in case he came early.

"What's the matter with me," she said sharply to herself, "rushing this way just to feed Flips? Whatever is the matter with me?" But all the way through the warm dusky streets, she seemed to hear the janitor's deep voice saying, "Good evenin'," to her.

Then, when the Negro really knocked on the door with the meat, she was trembling so that she could not go to the kitchen to get it. "Leave it right there by the sink," she managed to call out. "Thank you, Joe."

She heard the man going back downstairs sort of humming to himself, a kid or so following him. Miss Briggs felt as if she were going to faint, but Flips kept jumping up on her, barking for his meat.

"Oh, Flips," she said, "I'm so hungry." She meant to say, "*You're* so hungry." So she repeated it. "You're so hungry! Heh, Flipsy, dog?"

And from the way the little dog barked, he must have been hungry. He loved meat.

The next evening, Miss Briggs was standing in the kitchen when the colored man came with the bones.

"Lay them down," she said, "thank you," trying not to look at him.

But as he went downstairs, she watched through the window his beautifully heavy body finding the rhythm of the steps, his big brown neck moving just a little.

"Get down!" she said sharply to Flips barking for his dinner.

To herself she said earnestly, "I've got to move. I can't be worried being so far from a meat shop, or from where I eat my dinner. I think I'll move downtown where the shops are open at night. I can't stand this. Most of my friends live downtown anyway."

But even as she said it, she wondered what friends she meant. She had a little white dog named Flips, that was all. And she was acquainted with other people who worked at Wilkins and Bryant, but she had nothing to do with them. She was the head bookkeeper. She knew a few women in the Civics Club fairly well. And the Negro waiters at the Rose Bud Shoppe. And this janitor!

Miss Briggs decided that she could not bear to have this janitor come upstairs with a package of bones for Flips again. She was sure he was happy down there with his portly yellow wife and his house full of children. Let him stay in the basement, then, where he belonged. She never wanted to see him again, never.

The next night, Miss Briggs made herself go to a movie before coming home. And when she got home, she fed Flips dog biscuits. That week she began looking for a new apartment, a small one for two, her and the dog. Fortunately there were plenty to be had, what with people turned out for not being able to pay their rent—which would never happen to her, thank God! She had saved her money. When she found an apartment, she deposited the first month's rent at once. On her coming Saturday afternoon off, she planned to move.

Friday night, when the janitor came up with the bones, she decided to be just a little pleasant to him. Probably she would never see him again. Perhaps she would give him a dollar for a tip, then. Something to remember her by.

When he came upstairs, she was aware a long time of his feet approaching. Coming up, up, up, bringing bones for her dog. Flips began to bark. Miss Briggs went to the door. She took the package in one hand. With the other she offered the bill.

"Thank you so much for buying bones for my little dog," she said. "Here, here is a dollar for your trouble. You keep it all."

"Much obliged, m'am," said the astonished janitor. He had never seen Miss Briggs so generous before. "Thank you, m'am! He sure do eat a heap o' bones, your little dog."

"He almost keeps me broke buying bones," Miss Briggs said, holding the door.

"True," said the janitor. "But I reckon you don't have much other expenses on hand, do you? No family and all like me?"

"You're right," answered Miss Briggs. "But a little dog is so much company, too."

"Guess they are, m'am," said the janitor, turning to go. "Well, goodnight, Miss Briggs. I'm much obliged."

"Goodnight, Joe."

As his broad shoulders and tall brown body disappeared down the stairs, Miss Briggs slowly turned her back, shut the door, and put the bones on the floor for Flipsy. Then suddenly she began to cry.

The next day she moved away as she had planned to do. The janitor never saw her any more. For a few days, the walkers in the park beside the lake wondered where a rather gaunt middle-aged woman who used to come out at night with a little white dog had gone. But in a very short while the neighborhood had completely forgotten her.

XI

Berry

When the boy arrived on the four o'clock train, lo and behold, he turned out to be colored! Mrs. Osborn saw him the minute he got out of the station wagon, but certainly there was nothing to be done about it that night—with no trains back to the city before morning—so she set him to washing dishes. Lord knows there were a plenty. The Scandinavian kitchen boy had left right after breakfast, giving no notice, leaving her and the cook to do everything. Her wire to the employment office in Jersey City brought results—but dark ones. The card said his name was Milberry Jones.

Well, where was he to sleep? Heretofore, the kitchen boy and the handy-man gardener-chauffeur shared the same quarters. But Mrs. Osborn had no idea how the handy-man might like Negroes. Help were so touchy, and it was hard keeping good servants in the country. So right after dinner, leaving Milberry with his arms in the dish water, Mrs. Osborn made a bee line across the side lawn for Dr. Renfield's cottage.

She heard the kids laughing and playing on the big screened-in front porch of the sanatorium. She heard one of the nurses say to a child, "Behave, Billy!" as she went across the yard under the pine and maple trees. Mrs. Osborn hoped Dr. Renfield would be on his porch. She hated to knock at the door and perhaps be faced with his wife. The gossip among the nurses and help at Dr. Renfield's Summer Home for Crippled Children had it that Mrs. Osborn was in love with Dr. Renfield, that she just worshipped him, that she followed him with her eyes every chance she got—and not only with her eyes.

Of course, there wasn't a word of truth in it, Mrs. Osborn said to herself, admitting at the same time that that Martha Renfield, his wife, was certainly not good enough for the doctor. Anyway tonight, she was not bound on any frivolous errand toward the Doctor's cottage. She had to see him about this Negro in their midst. At least, they'd have to keep him there overnight, or until they got somebody else to help in the kitchen. However, he looked like a decent boy.

Dr. Renfield was not at home. His wife came to the door, spoke most coldly, and said that she presumed, as usual, the Doctor would make his rounds of the Home at eight. She hoped Mrs. Osborn could wait until then to see him.

"Good evening!"

Mrs. Osborn went back across the dusk-dark yard. She heard the surf rushing at the beach below, and saw the new young moon rising. She thought maybe the Doctor was walking along the sea in the twilight alone. Ah, Dr. Renfield, Dr. Ren. . . .

When he made the usual rounds at eight he came, for a moment, by Mrs. Osborn's little office where the housekeeper held forth over her linens and her accounts. He turned his young but bearded face toward Mrs. Osborn, cast his great dark eyes upon her, and said, "I hear you've asked to see me?"

"Yes, indeed, Dr. Renfield," Mrs. Osborn bubbled and gurgled. "We have a problem on our hands. You know the kitchen man left this morning so I sent a wire to the High Class Help Agency in the city for somebody right away by the four o'clock train—and they sent us a Negro! He seems to be a nice boy, and all that, but I just don't know how he would fit in our Home. Now what do you think?"

The doctor looked at her with great seriousness. He thought. Then he answered with a question, "Do the other servants mind?"

"Well, I can't say they do. They got along all right tonight during dinner. But the problem is, where would he sleep?"

"Oh, yes," said Dr. Renfield, pursing his lips.

"And whether we should plan to keep him all summer, or just till we get someone else?"

"I see," said Dr. Renfield.

And again he thought. "You say he can do the work? . . . How about the attic in this building? It's not in use. . . . And by the way, how much did we pay the other fellow?"

"Ten dollars a week," said Mrs. Osborn raising her eyes.

"Well, pay the darkie eight," said Dr. Renfield, "and keep him." And for a moment he gazed deep into Mrs. Osborn's eyes. "Goodnight." Then turned and left her. Left her. Left her.

So it was that Milberry entered into service at Dr. Renfield's Summer Home for Crippled Children.

Milberry was a nice black boy, big, good natured and strong—like what Paul Robeson must have been at twenty. Except that he wasn't educated. He was from Georgia, where they don't have many schools for Negroes. And he hadn't been North long. He was glad to have a job, even if it was at a home for Crippled Children way out in the country on a beach five miles from the nearest railroad. Milberry had been hungry for weeks in Newark and Jersey City. He needed work and food.

And even if he wasn't educated, he had plenty of mother wit and lots of intuition about people and places. It didn't take him long to realize that he was doing far too much work for the Home's eight dollars a week, and that everybody was imposing on him in that taken-for-granted way white folks do with Negro help.

Milberry got up at 5:30 in the mornings, made the fire for the cook, set the water to boiling for the head nurse's coffee, started peeling potatoes, onions, and apples. After breakfast he washed up all the dishes, scoured the pots and pans, scrubbed the floors, and carried in wood for the fireplace in the front room (which really wasn't his job at all, but the handy-man's who had put it off on Milberry). The waitresses, too, got in the habit of asking him to polish their silver, and ice their water. And Mrs. Osborn always had something extra that needed to be done (not kitchen-boy work), a cellar to be cleaned out, or the linen in her closet reshelved, or the dining-room windows washed. Milberry knew they took him for a work horse, a fool—and a nigger. Still he did everything, and didn't look mad—jobs were too hard to get, and he had been hungry too long in town.

"Besides," Milberry said to himself, "the ways of white folks, I mean some white folks, is too much for me. I reckon they must be a few good ones, but most of 'em ain't good—leastwise they don't treat me good. And Lawd knows, I ain't never done nothin' to 'em, nothin' a-tall."

But at the Home it wasn't the work that really troubled him, or the fact that nobody ever said anything about a day off or a little extra pay. No, he'd had many jobs like this one before, where they worked you to death. But what really worried Milberry at this place was that he seemed to sense something wrong—something phoney about the whole house—except the little crippled kids there like himself because they couldn't help it. Maybe it was the lonesomeness of that part of the Jersey coast with its pines and scrubs and sand. But, more nearly, Milberry thought it was that there doctor with the movie beard and the woman's eyes at the head of the home. And it was the cranky nurses always complaining about food and the little brats under them. And the constant talk of who was having an affair with Dr. Renfield. And Mrs. Osborn's grand manner to everybody but the doctor. And all the white help kicking about their pay, and how far it was from town, and how no-good the doctor was, or the head nurse, or the cook, or Mrs. Osborn.

"It's sho a phoney, this here place," Milberry said to himself. "Funny how the food ain't nearly so good 'cept when some ma or pa of some chile is visitin' here—then when they gone, it drops right back down again. This here hang-out is jest Doc Renfield's own private gyp game. Po' little children."

The Negro was right. The Summer Home was run for profits from the care of permanently deformed children of middle class parents who couldn't afford to pay too much, but who still paid well—too well for what their children got in return. Milberry worked in the kitchen and saw the good cans opened for company, and the cheap cans opened for the kids. Somehow he didn't like such dishonesty. Somehow, he thought he wouldn't even stay there and work if it wasn't for the kids.

For the children grew terribly to like Milberry.

One afternoon, during his short period of rest between meals, he had walked down to the beach where those youngsters who could drag themselves about were playing, and others were sitting in their wheel chairs watching. The sky was only a little cloudy, and the sand was grey. But quite all of a sudden it began to rain. The nurses saw Milberry and called him to help them get the young ones quickly back to the house. Some of the children were too heavy for a nurse to lift easily into a wheel chair. Some couldn't run at all. The handy-man helper wasn't around. So Milberry picked up child after child, sometimes two at once, and carried them up to the broad screened-in porch of the Home like a big gentle horse. The children loved it, riding on his broad back, or riding in his arms in the soft gentle rain.

"Come and play with us sometimes," one of them called as Milberry left them all on the safe dry porch with their nurses.

"Sure, come back and play," another said.

So Milberry, the next day, went down to the beach again in the afternoon and played with the crippled children. At first the nurses, Miss Baxter and Mrs. Hill, didn't know whether to let him stay or not, but their charges seemed to enjoy it. Then when the time came to go in for rest before dinner, Milberry helped push the wheel chairs, a task which the nurses hated. And he held the hands of those kids with braces and twisted limbs as they hobbled along. He told them stories, and he made up jokes in the sun on the beach. And one rainy afternoon on the porch he sang songs, old southern Negro songs, funny ones that the children loved.

Almost every afternoon then, Milberry came to the beach after the luncheon dishes were done, and he had washed himself—except those afternoons when Mrs. Osborn found something else for him to do—

vases to be emptied or bath tubs scoured. The children became Milberry's friends. They adored him and he them. They called him Berry. They put their arms about him.

The grown-up white folks only spoke to him when they had some job for him to do, or when they were kidding him about being dark, and talking flat and Southern, and mispronouncing words. But the kids didn't care how he talked. They loved his songs and his stories.

And he made up stories out of his own head just for them—po' little crippled-up things that they were—for Berry loved them, too.

So the summer wore on. August came. In September the Home would close. But disaster overtook Milberry before then.

At the end of August a week of rain fell, and the children could not leave the porch. Then, one afternoon, the sun suddenly came out bright and warm. The sea water was blue again and the sand on the beach glistened. Miss Baxter (who by now had got the idea it was part of Milberry's job to help her with the children) went to the kitchen and called him while he was still washing luncheon dishes.

"Berry, we're going to take the children down to the beach. Come on and help us with the chairs as soon as you get through."

"Yes, m'am," said Berry.

When he came out on the porch, the kids were all excited about playing in the sun once more. Little hunchbacks jumped and cried and clapped their hands, and little paralytics laughed in their wheel chairs. And some with braces on had already hobbled out the screen door and were gathered on the walk.

"Hello, Berry," the children called.

"Hey, Berry," they cried to the black boy.

Berry grinned.

It was a few hundred yards to the beach. On the cement walk, you could push a couple of wheel chairs at a time to the sand's edge. Some of the children propelled their own. Besides the nurses, today the handyman was helping for the sun might not last long.

"Take me," a little boy called from his wheel chair, "Berry, take me."

"Sho, I will," the young Negro said gently.

But when Berry started to push the chair down from the porch to the walk, the child, through excess of joy, suddenly leaned forward laughing, and suddenly lost his balance. Berry saw that he was going to fall. To try to catch the boy, the young Negro let the chair go. But quick as a wink, the child had fallen one way onto the lawn, the chair the other onto the cement walk. The back of the chair was broken, snapped off, except for the wicker. The little boy lay squalling on the ground in the grass.

Lord have mercy!

All the nurses came running, the handy-man, and Mrs. Osborn, too. Berry picked up the boy, who clung to his neck sobbing, more frightened, it seemed, than hurt.

"Po' little chile," Berry kept saying. "Is you hurt much? I's so sorry."

But the nurses were very angry, for they were responsible. And Mrs. Osborn—well, she lit out for Dr. Renfield.

The little boy still clung to Berry, and wouldn't let the nurses take him at all. He had stopped crying when Dr. Renfield arrived, but was still sniffling. He had his arms tight around the black boy's neck.

"Give that child to me," Dr. Renfield said, his brown beard pointing straight at Berry, his mind visualizing irate parents and a big damage suit, and bad publicity for the Home.

But when the doctor tried to take the child, the little boy wriggled and cried and wouldn't let go of Berry. With what strength he had in his crooked braced limbs, he kicked at the doctor.

"Give me that child!" Dr. Renfield shouted at Berry. "Bring him into my office and lay him down." He put on his nose glasses. "You careless black rascal! And you, Miss Baxter—" the doctor shriveled her with a look. "I want to see you."

In the clinic, it turned out that the child wasn't really hurt, though. His legs had been, from birth, twisted and deformed. Nothing could injure them much further. And fortunately his spine wasn't weak.

But the doctor kept saying, "Criminal carelessness! Criminal carelessness!" Mrs. Osborn kept agreeing with him, "Yes, it is! Indeed, it is!" Milberry was to blame.

The black boy felt terrible. But nobody else among the grown-ups seemed to care how he felt. They all said: What dumbness! he had let that child fall!

"Get rid of him," Dr. Renfield said to the housekeeper, "today. The fool nigger! And deduct ten dollars for that broken chair."

"We don't pay him but eight," Mrs. Osborn said.

"Well, deduct that," said the doctor.

So, without his last week's wages, Milberry went to Jersey City.

XII

Mother and Child

"Ain't nobody seen it," said old lady Lucy Doves. "Ain't nobody seen it, but the midwife and the doctor, and her husband, I reckon. They say she won't let a soul come in the room. But it's still living, 'cause Mollie Ransom heard it crying. And the woman from Downsville what attended the delivery says it's as healthy a child as she ever seed, indeed she did."

"Well, it's a shame," said Sister Wiggins, "it's here. I been living in Boyd's Center for twenty-two years, at peace with these white folks, ain't had no trouble yet, till this child was born—now look at 'em. Just look what's goin' on! People acting like a pack o' wolves."

"Poor little brat! He ain't been in the world a week yet," said Mrs. Sam Jones, taking off her hat, "and done caused more trouble than all the rest of us in a life time. I was born here, and I ain't never seen the white folks up in arms like they are today. But they don't need to think they can walk over Sam and me—for we owns our land, it's bought and paid for, and we sends our children to school. Thank God, this is Ohio. It ain't Mississippi."

"White folks is white folks, honey, South or North, North or South," said Lucy Doves. "I's lived both places and I know."

"Yes, but in Mississippi they'd lynched Douglass by now."

"Where is Douglass?" asked Mattis Crane. "You all know I don't know much about this mess. Way back yonder on that farm where I lives, you don't get nothing straight. Where is Douglass?"

"Douglass is here! Saw him just now out in de field doin' his spring plowin' when I drive down de road, as stubborn and bold-faced as he can be. We told him he ought to leave here."

"Well, I wish he'd go on and get out," said Sister Wiggins. "If that would help any. His brother's got more sense than he has, even if he is a seventeen-year-old child. Clarence left here yesterday and went to Cleveland. But their ma, poor Sister Carter, she's still trying to battle it out. She told me last night, though, she thinks she have to leave. They won't let her have no more provisions at de general store. And they ain't got their spring seed yet. And they can't pay cash for 'em."

"Don't need to tell me! Old man Hartman's got evil as de rest of de white folks. Didn't he tell ma husband Saturday night he'd have to pay up every cent of his back bill, or he couldn't take nothing out of that store. And we been trading there for years."

"That's their way o' striking back at us niggers."

"Yes, but Lord knows my husband ain't de father o' that child."

"Nor mine."

"Jim's got too much pride to go foolin' round any old loose white woman."

"Child, you can't tell about men."

"I knowed a case once in Detroit where a nigger lived ten years with a white woman, and her husband didn't know it. He was their chauffeur."

"That's all right in the city, but please don't come bringing it out here to Boyd's Center where they ain't but a handful o' us colored—and we has a hard enough time as it is."

"You right! This sure has brought de hammer down on our heads."

"Lawd knows we's law-biding people, ain't harmed a soul, yet some o' these white folks talking 'bout trying to run all de colored folks out o' de country on account o' Douglass."

"They'll never run me," said Mrs. Sam Jones.

"Don't say what they *won't* do," said Lucy Doves, "cause they might."

"Howdy, Sister Jenkins."

"Howdy!"

"Good evenin'."

"Yes, de meetin' due to start directly."

"Soon as Madam President arrives. Reckon she's having trouble gettin' over that road from High Creek."

"Sit down and tell us what you's heard, Sister Jenkins."

"About Douglass?"

"Course 'bout Douglass. What else is anybody talkin' 'bout nowadays?"

"Well, my daughter told me Douglass' sister say they was in love."

"Him and that white woman?"

"Yes. Douglass' sister say it's been going on 'fore de woman got married."

"Un-huh! Then why didn't he stop foolin' with her after she got married? Bad enough, colored boy foolin' 'round a unmarried white woman, let alone a married one."

"Douglass' sister say they was in love."

"Well, why did she marry the *white* man, then?"

"She's white, ain't she? And who wouldn't marry a rich white man?

Got his own farm, money and all, even if he were a widower with grown children gone to town. He give her everything she wanted, didn't he?"

"Everything but the right thing."

"Well, she must not o' loved him, sneaking 'round meeting Douglass in de woods."

"True."

"But what you reckon she went on and had that colored baby for?"

"She must a thought it was the old man's baby."

"She don't think so now! Mattie say when the doctor left and they brought the child in to show her, she like to went blind. It were near black as me."

"Do tell!"

"And what did her husband say?"

"Don't know. Don't know."

"He must a fainted."

"That old white woman lives across the crick from us said he's gonna put her out soon's she's able to walk."

"Ought to put her out!"

"Maybe that's what Douglass waitin' for."

"I heard he wants to take her away."

"He better take his fool self away, 'fore these white folks get madder. Ain't nobody heard it was a black baby till day before yesterday. Then it leaked out. And now de white folks are rarin' to kill Douglass!"

"I sure am scared!"

"And how come they all said right away it were Douglass?"

"Honey, don't you know? Colored folks knowed Douglass been eyeing that woman since God knows when, and she been eyeing back at him. You ought to seed 'em when they meet in de store. Course they didn't speak no more 'n Howdy, but their eyes followed one another 'round just like dogs."

"They was in love, I tell you. Been in love."

"Mighty funny kind o' love. Everybody knows can't no good come out o' white and colored love. Everybody knows that. And Douglass ain't no child. He's twenty-six years old, ain't he? And Sister Carter sure did try to raise her three chillun right. You can't blame her."

"Blame that fool boy, that's who, and that woman. Plenty colored girls in Camden he could of courted ten miles up de road. One or two right here. I got a daughter myself."

"No, he had to go foolin' round with a white woman."

"Yes, a white woman."

"They say he loved her."

"What do Douglass say, since it happened?"

"He don't say nothing."

"What could he say?"

"Well, he needn't think he's gonna keep his young mouth shut and let de white folks take it out on us. Down yonder at de school today, my Dorabella says they talkin' 'bout separatin' de colored from de white and makin' all de colored children go in a nigger room next term."

"Ain't nothing like that ever happened in Boyd's Center long as I been here—these twenty-two years."

"White folks is mad now, child, mad clean through."

"Wonder they ain't grabbed Douglass and lynched him."

"It's a wonder!"

"And him calmly out yonder plowin' de field this afternoon."

"He sure is brave."

"Woman's husband's liable to kill him."

"Her brother's done said he's gunning for him."

"They liable to burn Negroes' houses down."

"Anything's liable to happen. Lawd, I'm nervous as I can be."

"You can't tell about white folks."

"I ain't nervous. I'm *scared*."

"Don't say a word!"

"Why don't Sister Carter make him leave here?"

"I wish I knew."

"She told me she were nearly crazy."

"And she can't get Douglass to say nothin', one way or another—if he go, or if he stay. . . . Howdy, Madam President."

"Good evenin', Madam President."

"I done told you Douglass loves her."

"He wants to see that white woman, once more again, that's what he wants."

"A white hussy!"

"He's foolin' with fire."

"Poor Mis' Carter. I'm sorry for his mother."

"Poor Mis' Carter."

"Why don't you all say poor Douglass? Poor white woman? Poor child?"

"Madam President's startin' de meetin'."

"Is it boy or girl?"

"Sh-s-s-s! There's de bell."

"I hear it's a boy."

"Thank God, ain't a girl then."

"I hope it looks like Douglass, cause Douglass a fine-looking nigger."

"He's too bold, too bold."

"Shame he's got us all in this mess."

"Shame, shame, shame!"

"Sh-sss-sss!"

"Yes, indeedy!"

"Sisters, can't you hear this bell?"

"Shame!"

"Sh-sss!"

"Madam Secretary, take your chair."

"Shame!"

"The March meeting of the Salvation Rock Ladies' Missionary Society for the Rescue o' the African Heathen is hereby called to order. . . . Sister Burns, raise a hymn. . . . Will you-all ladies *please* be quiet? What are you talking 'bout back there anyhow?"

> *Ring a golden bell,*

"Heathens, daughter, heathens."

> *Aw, ring a golden bell,*

"They ain't in Africa neither!"

> *Ring a golden bell for me.*
> *Ring a golden bell,*
> *Aw, ring a golden bell,*
> *My Lawd's done set me free!*
>
> *I was a sinner*
> *Lost and lone,*
> *Till Jesus claimed me*
> *For His own.*
> *Ring a golden bell,*
> *Ring a golden bell,*
> *Aw, ring a golden bell for me. . . .*

XIII

One Christmas Eve

Standing over the hot stove cooking supper, the colored maid, Arcie, was very tired. Between meals today, she had cleaned the whole house for the white family she worked for, getting ready for Christmas tomorrow. Now her back ached and her head felt faint from sheer fatigue. Well, she would be off in a little while, if only the Missus and her children would come on home to dinner. They were out shopping for more things for the tree which stood all ready, tinsel-hung and lovely in the living-room, waiting for its candles to be lighted.

Arcie wished she could afford a tree for Joe. He'd never had one yet, and it's nice to have such things when you're little. Joe was five, going on six. Arcie, looking at the roast in the white folks' oven, wondered how much she could afford to spend tonight on toys. She only got seven dollars a week, and four of that went for her room and the landlady's daily looking after Joe while Arcie was at work.

"Lord, it's more'n a notion raisin' a child," she thought.

She looked at the clock on the kitchen table. After seven. What made white folks so darned inconsiderate? Why didn't they come on home here to supper? They knew she wanted to get off before all the stores closed. She wouldn't have time to buy Joe nothin' if they didn't hurry. And her landlady probably wanting to go out and shop, too, and not be bothered with little Joe.

"Dog gone it!" Arcie said to herself. "If I just had my money, I might leave the supper on the stove for 'em. I just got to get to the stores fo' they close." But she hadn't been paid for the week yet. The Missus had promised to pay her Christmas Eve, a day or so ahead of time.

Arcie heard a door slam and talking and laughter in the front of the house. She went in and saw the Missus and her kids shaking snow off their coats.

"Umm-mm! It's swell for Christmas Eve," one of the kids said to Arcie. "It's snowin' like the deuce, and mother came near driving through a stop light. Can't hardly see for the snow. It's swell!"

"Supper's ready," Arcie said. She was thinking how her shoes weren't very good for walking in snow.

It seemed like the white folks took as long as they could to eat that evening. While Arcie was washing dishes, the Missus came out with her money.

"Arcie," the Missus said, "I'm so sorry, but would you mind if I just gave you five dollars tonight? The children have made me run short of change, buying presents and all."

"I'd like to have seven," Arcie said. "I needs it."

"Well, I just haven't got seven," the Missus said. "I didn't know you'd want all your money before the end of the week, anyhow. I just haven't got it to spare."

Arcie took five. Coming out of the hot kitchen, she wrapped up as well as she could and hurried by the house where she roomed to get little Joe. At least he could look at the Christmas trees in the windows downtown.

The landlady, a big light yellow woman, was in a bad humor. She said to Arcie, "I thought you was comin' home early and get this child. I guess you know I want to go out, too, once in awhile."

Arcie didn't say anything for, if she had, she knew the landlady would probably throw it up to her that she wasn't getting paid to look after a child both night and day.

"Come on, Joe," Arcie said to her son, "let's us go in the street."

"I hears they got a Santa Claus down town," Joe said, wriggling into his worn little coat. "I wants to see him."

"Don't know 'bout that," his mother said, "but hurry up and get your rubbers on. Stores'll all be closed directly."

It was six or eight blocks downtown. They trudged along through the falling snow, both of them a little cold. But the snow was pretty!

The main street was hung with bright red and blue lights. In front of the City Hall there was a Christmas tree—but it didn't have no presents on it, only lights. In the store windows there were lots of toys—for sale.

Joe kept on saying, "Mama, I want . . ."

But mama kept walking ahead. It was nearly ten, when the stores were due to close, and Arcie wanted to get Joe some cheap gloves and something to keep him warm, as well as a toy or two. She thought she might come across a rummage sale where they had children's clothes. And in the ten-cent store, she could get some toys.

"O-oo! Lookee . . . ," little Joe kept saying, and pointing at things in the windows. How warm and pretty the lights were, and the shops, and the electric signs through the snow.

It took Arcie more than a dollar to get Joe's mittens and things he needed. In the A & P Arcie bought a big box of hard candies for 49¢. And then she guided Joe through the crowd on the street until they came to the dime store. Near the ten-cent store they passed a moving picture theatre. Joe said he wanted to go in and see the movies.

Arcie said, "Ump-un! No, child! This ain't Baltimore where they have shows for colored, too. In these here small towns, they don't let colored folks in. We can't go in there."

"Oh," said little Joe.

In the ten-cent store, there was an awful crowd. Arcie told Joe to stand outside and wait for her. Keeping hold of him in the crowded store would be a job. Besides she didn't want him to see what toys she was buying. They were to be a surprise from Santa Claus tomorrow.

Little Joe stood outside the ten-cent store in the light, and the snow, and people passing. Gee, Christmas was pretty. All tinsel and stars and cotton. And Santa Claus a-coming from somewhere, dropping things in stockings. And all the people in the streets were carrying things, and the kids looked happy.

But Joe soon got tired of just standing and thinking and waiting in front of the ten-cent store. There were so many things to look at in the other windows. He moved along up the block a little, and then a little more, walking and looking. In fact, he moved until he came to the white folks' picture show.

In the lobby of the moving picture show, behind the plate glass doors, it was all warm and glowing and awful pretty. Joe stood looking in, and as he looked his eyes began to make out, in there blazing beneath holly and colored streamers and the electric stars of the lobby, a marvellous Christmas tree. A group of children and grown-ups, white, of course, were standing around a big jovial man in red beside the tree. Or was it a man? Little Joe's eyes opened wide. No, it was not a man at all. It was Santa Claus!

Little Joe pushed open one of the glass doors and ran into the lobby of the white moving picture show. Little Joe went right through the crowd and up to where he could get a good look at Santa Claus. And Santa Claus was giving away gifts, little presents for children, little boxes of animal crackers and stick-candy canes. And behind him on the tree was a big sign (which little Joe didn't know how to read). It said, to those who understood, MERRY XMAS FROM SANTA CLAUS TO OUR YOUNG PATRONS.

Around the lobby, other signs said, WHEN YOU COME OUT OF THE SHOW STOP WITH YOUR CHILDREN AND SEE OUR SANTA CLAUS. And another announced, GEM THEATRE MAKES ITS CUSTOMERS HAPPY—SEE OUR SANTA.

And there was Santa Claus in a red suit and a white beard all sprinkled with tinsel snow. Around him were rattles and drums and rocking horses which he was not giving away. But the signs on them said (could little Joe have read) that they would be presented from the stage on Christmas Day to the holders of the lucky numbers. Tonight, Santa Claus was only giving away candy, and stick-candy canes, and animal crackers to the kids.

Joe would have liked terribly to have a stick-candy cane. He came a little closer to Santa Claus, until he was right in the front of the crowd. And then Santa Claus saw Joe.

Why is it that lots of white people always grin when they see a Negro child? Santa Claus grinned. Everybody else grinned, too, looking at little black Joe—who had no business in the lobby of a white theatre. Then Santa Claus stooped down and slyly picked up one of his lucky number rattles, a great big loud tin-pan rattle such as they use in cabarets. And he shook it fiercely right at Joe. That was funny. The white people laughed, kids and all. But little Joe didn't laugh. He was scared. To the shaking of the big rattle, he turned and fled out of the warm lobby of the theatre, out into the street where the snow was and the people. Frightened by laughter, he had begun to cry. He went looking for his mama. In his heart he never thought Santa Claus shook great rattles at children like that—and then laughed.

In the crowd on the street he went the wrong way. He couldn't find the ten-cent store or his mother. There were too many people, all white people, moving like white shadows in the snow, a world of white people.

It seemed to Joe an awfully long time till he suddenly saw Arcie, dark and worried-looking, cut across the side-walk through the passing crowd and grab him. Although her arms were full of packages, she still managed with one free hand to shake him until his teeth rattled.

"Why didn't you stand where I left you?" Arcie demanded loudly. "Tired as I am, I got to run all over the streets in the night lookin' for you. I'm a great mind to wear you out."

When little Joe got his breath back, on the way home, he told his mama he had been in the moving picture show.

"But Santa Claus didn't give me nothin'," Joe said tearfully. "He made a big noise at me and I runned out."

"Serves you right," said Arcie, trudging through the snow. "You had no business in there. I told you to stay where I left you."

"But I seed Santa Claus in there," little Joe said, "so I went in."

"Huh! That wasn't no Santa Claus," Arcie explained. "If it was, he wouldn't a-treated you like that. That's a theatre for white folks—I told you once—and he's just a old white man."

"Oh . . . ," said little Joe.

XIV

Father and Son

Colonel Thomas Norwood stood in his doorway at the Big House looking down the dusty plantation road. Today his youngest son was coming home. A heavy Georgia spring filled the morning air with sunshine and earth-perfumes. It made the old man feel strangely young again. Bert was coming home.

Twenty years ago he had begotten him.

This boy, however, was not his real son, for Colonel Thomas Norwood had no real son, no white and legal heir to carry on the Norwood name; this boy was a son by his Negro mistress, Coralee Lewis, who kept his house and had borne him all his children.

Colonel Norwood never would have admitted, even to himself, that he was standing in his doorway waiting for this half-Negro son to come home. But in truth that is what he was doing. He was curious about this boy. How would he look after all these years away at school? Six or seven surely, for not once in that long time had he been allowed to come back to Big House Plantation. The Colonel had said then that never did he want to see the boy. But in truth he did—for this boy had been, after all, the most beautiful of the lot, the brightest and the baddest of the Colonel's five children, lording it over the other children, and sassing not only his colored mother, but his white father, as well. Handsome and mischievous, favoring too much the Colonel in looks and ways, this boy Bert, at fourteen, had got himself sent off to school to stay. Now a student in college (or what they call a college in Negro terms in Georgia) he was coming home for the summer vacation.

Today his brother, Willie, had been sent to the station to meet him in the new Ford. The ten o'clock train must have reached the Junction by now, thought the Colonel, standing in the door. Soon the Ford would be shooting back down the road in a cloud of dust, curving past the tall white pillars of the front porch, and around to the kitchen stoop where Cora would greet her child.

Thinking thus, Colonel Norwood came inside the house, closed the screen, and pulled at a bellcord hanging from the wall of the great dark living-room with its dignified but shabby horse hair furniture of the nineties. By and by, an old Negro servant, whose name was Sam and who wore a kind of old-fashioned butler's coat, came and brought the Colonel a drink.

"I'm going in my library where I don't want to be disturbed."

"Yes, suh," said the Negro servant.

"You hear me?"

"Yes, suh," said the servant, knowing that when Colonel Norwood said "library," he meant he did not want to be disturbed.

The Colonel entered the small room where he kept his books and papers of both a literary and a business nature. He closed the door. He did this deliberately, intending to let all the Negroes in the house know that he had no interest whatsoever in the homecoming about to take place. He intended to remain in the library several hours after Bert's arrival. Yet, as he bent over his desk peering at accounts his store-keeper had brought him, his head kept turning toward the window that gave on the yard and the road, kept looking to see if a car were coming in a cloud of dust.

An hour or so later, when shouts of welcome, loud warm Negro-cries, laughter, and the blowing of an auto horn filled the Georgia sunlight outside, the Colonel bent more closely over his ledgers—but he did turn his eyes a little to catch the dust sifting in the sunny air above the road where the car had passed. And his mind went back to that little olive-colored kid he had beaten one day in the stables years ago—the kid grown up now, and just come home.

He had always been a little ashamed of that particular beating he had given the boy. But his temper had got the best of him. That child, Bert, looking almost like a white child (a hell of a lot favoring the Colonel), had come running out to the stables one afternoon when he was showing his horses to some guests from in town. The boy had come up to him crying, "Papa!" (He knew better, right in front of company.) "Papa, Ma says she's got dinner ready."

The Colonel had knocked him down under the feet of the horses right there in front of the guests. And afterwards he had locked him in the stable and beaten him severely. The boy had to learn not to call him papa, and certainly not in front of white people from the town.

But it had been hard to teach Bert anything, the Colonel ruminated. Trouble was, the boy was too smart. There were other unpleasant memories of that same saucy ivory-skinned youngster playing about the front yard, even running through the Big House, in spite of orders that

Coralee's children and all other pickaninnies keep to the back of the house, or down in the Quarters. But as a child, Bert had never learned his place.

"He's too damn much like me," the Colonel thought. "Quick as hell. Cora's been telling me he's leading his class at the Institute, and a football captain. . . . H-m-m-m, so they waste their time playing football at these darkie colleges. . . . Well, anyway, he must be a smart darkie. Got my blood in him."

The Colonel had Sam bring some food into the library. He pretended to be extremely busy, and did not give the old Negro, bursting with news, a chance to speak. The Colonel acted as though he were unaware of the presence of the newly arrived boy on the plantation; or if he were aware, completely uninterested, and completely occupied.

But in the late afternoon, the Colonel got up from his desk, went out into the parlor, picked up an old straw hat, and strolled through the front door, across the wide-porticoed porch with its white pillars, and down the road toward the South Field. The Colonel saw the brown backs of his Negroes in the green cotton. He smelt the earth-scent of a day that had been long and hot. He turned off by the edge of a field, went down to the creek, and back toward the house along a path that took him through a grove of pecan trees skirting the old slave quarters, to the back door of the Big House.

Long before he approached the Big House, he could hear Negroes' voices, musical and laughing. Then he could see a small group of dark bare arms and faces about the kitchen stoop. Cora was sitting on a stool in the yard, probably washing fruit for jelly. Livonia, the fat old cook, was on the porch shelling peas for dinner. Seated on the stoop, and on the ground, and standing around, were colored persons the Colonel knew had no good reason to be there at that time of day. Some of them, when they saw the Colonel coming, began to move away, back toward the barns, or whatever work they were doing.

He was aware, too, standing in the midst of this group, of a tall young man in sporty white trousers, black-and-white oxfords, and a blue shirt. He looked very clean and well-dressed, like a white man. The Colonel took this to be his son, and a certain vibration shook him from head to foot. Across the wide dusty yard, their eyes met. The Colonel's brows came together, his shoulders lifted and went back as though faced by an indignity just suffered. His chin went up. And he began to think, on the way toward them, how he would walk through this group like a white man. The Negroes, of course, would be respectful and afraid, as usual.

He would say merely, "Good evening, Bert," to this boy, his son, then wait a moment, perhaps, and see what the boy said before passing on into the house.

Laughter died and dripped and trickled away, and talk quieted, and silence fell degree by degree, each step the white man approached. A strange sort of stiffness like steel nearing steel grew and straightened between the colored boy in the black-and-white shoes and the old Colonel who had just come from looking at his fields and his Negroes working.

"Good evening, Bert," the Colonel said.

"Good evening, Colonel Tom," the boy replied quickly, politely, almost eagerly. And then, like a puppet pulled by some perverse string, the boy offered his hand.

The Colonel looked at the strong young near-white hand held out toward him, and made no effort to take it. His eyes lifted to the eyes of the boy, his son, in front of him. The boy's eyes did not fall. But a slow flush reddened the olive of his skin as the old man turned without a word toward the stoop and into the house. The boy's hand went to his side again. A hum of dark voices broke the silence.

This happened between father and son. The mother, sitting there washing plums in a pail, did not understand what had happened. But the water from which she took the plums felt cool to her hands that were suddenly burning hot.

II

Coralee Lewis, sitting washing plums, had been Colonel Norwood's mistress for thirty years. She had lived in the Big House, supervised his life, given him children, and loved him. In his turn, he felt something very like love for her. Now, in his sixties, without Cora he would have been lost, but of course he did not realize that—consciously.

The history of their liaison, like that of so many between Negro women and white men in the South, began without love, at least on his part. For a long while its motif was lust—whose sweeter name, perhaps, is passion.

The Colonel had really known Cora all her life. As a half-grown boy, he had teased her as a baby, pulling her kinky braids and laughing at the way she rolled in the dust with the other pickaninnies born to the black servants and share-croppers on his father's plantation. He had seen her as a girl, barefooted and shy, brown face shining, bringing milk to the

Big House night and morning, for her father took care of the cows. Her mother worked sometimes in the house but mostly in the fields. And Cora knew early how to pick cotton, too.

Then there came years when young Norwood had no contact with Cora: years when he had been away at Military School; those first few years when he had come back from Macon with his new bride; those years of love and worry with the delicate and lovely woman he had wedded. During his early married life the Colonel could not truthfully remember ever having laid eyes on Cora, although she was about the place surely.

But Cora remembered often seeing the Colonel. Young and handsome, tall and straight, he drove over the plantation roads with the wisp of a pretty little lady he had married. She remembered him particularly well the day of his father's funeral, when he came back from the burial—he and his wife, master and mistress of the Big House now. How sad and worried young Colonel Norwood looked that day descending from the carriage.

And as the months went by, he began to look more and more worried and weary. Servants' gossip from the Big House, drifting down to the humbler Negroes in the cabins, said that a wall had grown up between the young Colonel and his little wife, who seemed to be wasting away day by day. A wall like a mist. And the Negroes began to laugh that there were never no children born to Mister and Missus. Then gossip began to say that the young Colonel had taken up with the cook's daughter, black but comely Livonia, who worked in the pantry. Then the Quarters laughed all the more—for Livonia had four or five Negro lovers, too. And she wasn't faithful to anybody—just liked to love.

Cora heard all this and in her mind a certain envy sprang up. Livonia! Huh! Cora began to look more carefully into the cracked mirror in her mother's cabin. She combed her hair and oiled it better than before. She was seventeen then.

"Time you was takin' some pride about yo'self," said her mother, noting the change.

"Yes'm," said Cora. And when she took milk to the Big House now, she tried to look her best.

One night, there was a party there. A great many people came from the Junction, and even seventy miles off from in town, by horse and by carriage, by train, and even some by that new-fangled autobuggy that most of the plantation hands had never seen before. The Negroes were all excited at having so many white folks around. It was the Missus' birthday. There were great doings at Big House Plantation.

The first evening, the party went on until late in the night. Some people left at dawn. Others slept awhile and left in the afternoon. Some were house guests, and on the second night there was a party again. But that night everybody was pretty tired. And got pretty drunk, too, mostly. The Colonel was very gay and very drunk; but his little wife cried, and went to bed. She was mighty touchy, all the Negroes knew. Always poutin' and spattin' and actin' funny with the Colonel.

Wonder why? Wonder why?

There was a party in the Quarters among the Negroes, too, that second night. Livonia was there, dancing fit to kill. And the music was wild. In the heat of the night, Cora went out of the barn where the party was, out into the moonlight, and looked up at the lights of the Big House on the rise. She stretched, and breathed in the warm night air, and walked through the trees toward the road that ran to town. She made a big circle about the Big House, wondering a little what was going on there. When she got to the road, she sat down under a huge live oak tree. She could hear the laughter and clapping of the Negroes down on the edge of the cotton fields. But in the Big House, where it should have been gay, too, it was mighty quiet. Sometimes a loud and quarrelsome voice could be heard. Probably the men were gambling, and the ladies gone to bed.

The trees cast great shadows across the road in the warm light of the moon. Cora stretched, breathed deeply again, and got up to go, when she saw very near her a figure walking in the silvery dusk, a tall thin young white man walking in the cotton. Suddenly he called her.

"Who're you?" It was young Norwood speaking.

"I's Coralee Lewis, Aunt Tobie Lewis' daughter."

The white man came up to her, took her brown face in his hands and lifted it at the moon. "You're out mighty late," he said.

Cora's body trembled. Her mouth opened. In the shadow of the live oak tree there by the road, thirty years ago, in a night of moon. . . .

III

When the first child, Willie, was in her, she told her mother all about it. The old woman was glad. "It's better'n slavin' in the cotton fields," she said. "I's known colored women what's wore silk dresses and lived like queens on plantations right here in Georgy. . . ."

Even before the young Mrs. Norwood died (she did die—and child-less) Cora was working in the Big House. And after Mrs. Norwood's death, Cora came there to sleep.

Now the water where the plums were felt cool to her hands this spring afternoon many years later as the Colonel went into the house leaving their youngest boy dazed in front of her; and the nigger-voices all around her humming and chattering into loudness and laughter.

IV

"Listen hyar," brother Willie said to Bert on the way from the Junction to the plantation that morning his brother arrived. "Listen hyar, I hopes you don't expect to go around all dressed up like you is now after you gets out to de place, 'cause de Colonel won't 'low it. He made Sis put away all them fine clothes she brought hyar last year—till she left."

"Tell him to kiss my behind," Bert said.

Willie bucked his eyes, stuttered, then kept quiet. His brother was the same Bert as he had been as a child. Crazy! Trouble coming. William made up his mind not to be in it, himself, one way or another. Though he was eight years older, he had always been afraid of Bert with a fear worse than physical, afraid of the things that happened around Bert.

From the new Ford, Bert looked out at the straggling streets of the village of the Junction, at the Negroes lounging in front of stores, at the rednecked crackers, at the unkempt women. He heard the departing train whistle as it went deeper into Georgia, into Alabama. As they rode, he looked at the wide fields of young cotton stretching on either side, at the cabins of the share croppers, at the occasional house of a white owner or overseer. Then he saw the gradual rise of the Norwood plantation, the famous Big House, surrounded by its live oaks and magnolias and maples, and its many acres of cotton. And he knew he was nearing home.

Six years away. Kid of fourteen when he left, wearing his first long trousers bought in the commissary store, feeling funny out of overalls, feeling very proud going away to school. Only the Lewis niggers (old man Norwood's kids by Cora) went away to school in these parts. And with the going of Sallie, the youngest, the little county school at Norwood's Crossroads closed up, and didn't open any more. Sallie was the *Colonel's* last child—no other niggers needed a school.

Old Aunt Tobie, the grandma, before she died, used to keep on saying that the Lewis young 'uns ought to appreciate what the Colonel was doing for 'em. No white man she ever heard of cared anything 'bout educatin' his tar-brush chillun. But the Colonel did. Somehow 'nother Cora was able to put it in the Colonel's mind and keep it there until the last child, Sallie, got sent off to Atlanta.

In Atlanta, Bert had entered the same run-down Negro boarding school, the Institute, that brother Willie and his oldest sister, Bertha, had attended. But Willie, several years before, hadn't stayed there long, being a dumb boy who liked the plantation better. Bertha had gone up North once with the Spiritual Jubilee Singers, and liked it so well that she remained to work in Chicago. Now, little sister Sallie, seventeen, went to the Institute also, but had come home this spring ahead of Bert, who fooled around Atlanta a week or so before leaving, not wanting to come home really.

"Home, hell!"

Bert didn't want to come home. He felt he had no home. A brown mother, and a white father; bed for him in a nigger cabin down on the edge of the cotton fields. Soon as Cora's kids stopped nursing they went to live outside the Big House. Aunt Tobie, the grandmother, had really raised them, until she died. Then a cousin of Cora's brought up Sallie.

"Hell of a way to live," Bert thought, the night before his arrival, sitting in the Jim Crow car bound for south Georgia. During the long ride, he had turned over in his mind incidents of his childhood on the Big House Plantation. Sitting in the smoky half-coach allotted to Negroes (the other half being a baggage car) he thought of what it meant growing up as one of Colonel Norwood's yard-niggers (a term used by field hands for the mulatto children of a white planter).

"It's hell," Bert thought.

Not that Cora's other kids had found it hell. Only he had found it so, strangely enough. "The rest of 'em are too dumb, except little Sallie, and she don't say nothing—but it's hell to her, too, I reckon," the boy thought to himself as the train rocked and rumbled over the road. "Willie don't give a damn so long as his belly's full. And Bertha's got up North away from it all. I don't know what she really thought. . . . But I wish it hadn't happened to me."

With the self-pity of bewildered youth, he began to think about himself. Always, he had known the Colonel was his father, from the earliest he could remember. For one thing, Bert had been lighter than any of the other colored children on the plantation—a sort of ivory white. And as a small child, his hair had been straight and brown, his eyes grey, like Norwood's. His grandma, old Aunt Tobie, used to refer to them all, Willie and Bertha and Bert and Sallie, not without pride, as Colonel Tom's children. (There had been another brother who died.) Bert noticed early in life that all the other kids in the Quarters were named after their fathers, whereas he and his brother and sisters bore the mother's name, Lewis. He was Bert Lewis—not Bert Norwood. His mother slept in the Big House—but the children lived outside with Aunt Tobie or Cousin Betty. Those things puzzled little Bert.

As he grew up, he used to hear folks remarking on how much he looked like Colonel Tom, and how little like Cora. Nearly light enough to pass for white, folks said, spittin' image of his father, too. Bert had a temper and ways like white folks, too. Indeed, "You needn't act so much like quality with me," was one of Aunt Tobie's favorite ways of reprimanding him when she wanted to take him down a peg or two.

He was always getting into mischief, playing pranks and worrying his mother at the backdoor of the Big House. There was a time once when the Colonel seemed to get pleasure out of letting little Bert trail around at his heels, but that period didn't last very long, for young Bert sassed the Colonel, too, just as though he were colored. And somehow, he had acquired that way of referring to Norwood as papa. The Colonel told him, sternly and seriously, "Boy, don't *you* use that word to me." But still, forgetful little devil that he was, he had come running up to the Colonel that day in the stables yelling, "Papa, dinner's ready."

The slap that he received made him see stars and darkness, Bert remembered. As though he were brushing a fly out of the way, the Colonel had knocked him down under the feet of the horses, and went on talking to his guests. After the guests had gone, he switched Bert mercilessly.

"Can't nobody teach you nothin' but a switch, nohow," said old Aunt Tobie afterwards. "I tole you 'bout gittin' familiar wid that white man."

"But he didn't need to scar him all up," Bert remembered Cora's saying when she saw the black and blue marks on his back. "I ain't bearin' him children for to beat 'em to death. . . . You stay way from him, son, you hear?"

From that time on, between Bert and the Colonel, there had been a barrier of fear—a fear that held a certain mysterious fascination for Bert's sense of defiance, a fear that Bert from afar was continually taunting and baiting. For instance, the Colonel had a complex, Bert recalled, that all the Negroes knew, about the front door of the Big House. His orders were that no Negroes go in and out of that door, or cross his front porch.

When the old house-man, Sam, wanted to sweep off the porch, he would have to go out the back and come all the way around. It was as absurd as that. Yet Bert, as a child, in the Big House visiting or helping Cora, would often dart out the front way when he thought the Colonel was in town or down in the South Field, or asleep in his library. Cora used to spank him for it, but it was a habit he kept up until he went away, a big boy, to Atlanta.

Bert, home-bound now, smiled to himself in the stuffy Jim Crow car, and wondered if the Colonel were still as tall and stern and stiff-fronted as he used to be. No wonder his young white wife had died years ago—having to live with him—although, according to Aunt Tobie's version, the Colonel had humored her in every way. He really loved her, folks said, and had sworn after her death that he would never marry again. He hadn't—he had taken Cora.

And here Bert's mind balked and veered away from speculating about the intimate life of this old man and his mother. Bert knew that in a sense the white man had been kind to her. He remembered as a child the extra little delicacies that came down to Aunt Tobie and Cousin Betty and Cora's other relatives in the Quarters, especially at Christmas. He remembered how he had always known that the little colored school had not been there before Cora's children were born, and that it was no longer at the Cross Roads now. (For the Colonel and Mr. Higgins, being political powers in the county, were in charge of education, and their policy was to let Negroes remain unlettered. They worked better.) Bert knew, too, that it was his mother's influence that had got her children sent off to the Institute in Atlanta. But it was the *Colonel's* dislike of Bert that had kept him there, summer and winter, until now. Not that Bert minded. Summer school was fun, too. And tennis. And the pleasures of the town. And he was never homesick for the plantation—but he did wish sometimes that he had a home, and that the Colonel would treat him like a son.

Tall and light and good-looking, as Bert was now at twenty, he could have a very good time in Atlanta. Colored society had taken him up. He went around with the sons and daughters of Negro doctors and dentists and insurance brokers and professors. He had his hands full of pretty girls. Lots of cream-colored girls, chocolate brown girls, velvet-soft night-shade girls all liked Bert. And already he had been involved in a scandal with a doctor's wife.

To add to his good looks, Bert was an excellent athlete. He had been as far north as Washington with Institute teams, and had seen colored people at the Capitol riding in street cars where there had been no Jim Crow signs, and getting on trains that had no coaches especially for Negroes. Bert made up his mind to come North to live, as soon as he finished school. He had one more year. And this last summer, Cora wanted him to spend with her—because she sensed he might never come back to the plantation again.

Sallie, his sister, three classes behind him at the Institute, was frankly worried about his going home. She was afraid. "Colonel Tom's getting old. He ain't nice a-tall like he kinder used to be. He's getting more and more touchy," Sallie said to her brother. "And I know he ain't gonna like the looks of you. You don't look a bit like a Georgia boy any more."

"To hell with him," said Bert.

"I wouldn't even know you and Willie were brothers," Sallie said. For Sallie went home every summer and worked in the Big House with her mother, and saw Willie, and knew how things were on the plantation. Willie and the Colonel got along fine, because Willie was docile and good-natured and nigger-like,[11] bowing and scraping and treating white folks like they expected to be treated. "But Bert, you ain't a bit like that."

"Why should I be?" Bert asked. "I'm the old man's son, ain't I? Got white blood in me, too."

"Yes, but . . ."

"But what?" Bert said. "Let old knotty-headed[12] Willie go on being a white-folks' nigger if he wants to, I won't!"

And that's the way it was when he came home.

V

There are people (you've probably noted it also) who have the unconscious faculty of making the world spin around themselves, throb and expand, contract and go dizzy. Then, when they are gone away, you feel sick and lonesome and meaningless.

In the chemistry lab at school, did you ever hold a test tube, pouring in liquids and powders and seeing nothing happen until a *certain* liquid or a *certain* powder is poured in and then everything begins to smoke and fume, bubble and boil, hiss to foam, and sometimes even explode? The tube is suddenly full of action and movement and life. Well, there are people like those certain liquids or powders; at a given moment they come into a room, or into a town, even into a country—and the place is never the same again. Things bubble, boil, change. Sometimes the whole world is changed. Alexander came. Christ. Marconi.[13] A Russian named Lenin.

Not that there is any comparing Bert to Christ or Lenin. But after he returned to the Big House Plantation that summer, life was never the same. From Bert's very first day on the place something was broken, something went dizzy. The world began to spin, to ferment, and move into a new action.

Not to be a *white folks' nigger*—Bert had come home with that idea in his head.

The Colonel sensed it in his out-stretched hand and his tall young body—and had turned his back and walked into the house. Cora with her hands in the cool water where the plums were, suddenly knew in her innermost soul a period of time had closed for her. That first night she prayed, cried in her room, asked the Lord why she had ever let her son come home. In his cabin Willie prayed, too, humble, Lord, humble. The Colonel rocked alone on his front porch sucking a black cigar and cussing bitterly at he knew not what. The hum and laughter of the Negro voices went on as usual on the vast plantation down to the last share-cropper's cabin, but not quite, not *quite* the same as they had been in the morning. And never to be the same again.

"Is you heard about Bert?"

Not to be a *white folks' nigger*!

Bow down and pray in fear and trembling, go way back in the dark afraid; or work harder and harder; or stumble and learn; or raise up your fist and strike—but once the idea comes into your head you'll never be the same again. Oh, test tube of life! Crucible of the South, find the right powder and you'll never be the same again—the cotton will blaze and the cabins will burn and the chains will be broken and men, all of a sudden, will shake hands, black men and white men, like steel meeting steel!

"The bastard," Bert said. "Why couldn't he shake hands with me? I'm a Norwood, too."

"Hush, son," said Cora with the cool water from the plums on her hands.

And the hum of the black voices that afternoon spread to the cabins, to the cotton fields, to the dark streets of the Junction, what Bert had said—Bert with the ivory-yellow skin and the tall proud young body, Bert come home not to be a white folks' nigger.

"Lawd, chile, Bert's come home. . . ."

"Lawd, chile, and he said . . ."

"Lawd, chile, he said . . ."
"Lawd, chile . . ."
"Lawd . . ."

VI

July passed, and August. The hot summer sun marched across the skies. The Colonel ordered Bert to work in the fields. Bert had not done so. Talbot, the white foreman, washed his hands of it, saying that if he had his way, "that nigger would be run off the place."

For the Colonel, the summer was hectic enough, what with cotton prices dropping on the market; share-croppers restless and moving; one black fieldhand beaten half to death by Talbot and the storekeeper because he "talked high" to a neighboring white planter; news of the Scottsboro trials and the Camp Hill shootings exciting black labor.[14]

Colonel Norwood ordered the colored rural Baptist minister to start a revival and keep it going until he said stop. Let the Negroes sing and shout their troubles away, as in the past. White folks had always found revivals a useful outlet for sullen overworked darkies. As long as they were singing and praying, they forgot about the troubles of this world. In a frenzy of rhythm and religion, they laid their cross at the feet of Jesus.

Poor over-worked Jesus! Somehow since the War, he hadn't borne that cross so well. Too heavy, it's too heavy! Lately, Negroes seem to sense that it's not Jesus' cross, anyhow, it's their own. Only old people praise King Jesus any more. On the Norwood plantation, Bert's done told the young people to stop being white folks' niggers. More and more, the Colonel felt it was Bert who brought trouble into the Georgia summer. The revival was a failure.

One day he met the boy coming back from the river where he had been swimming. The Colonel lit into him with all the cuss words at his command. He told him in no uncertain language to get down in the South Field to work. He told him there would be no more school at Atlanta for him; that he would show him that just because Cora happened to be his mother, he was no more than any other nigger on the place. God damn him!

Bert stood silent and red in front of his father, looking as the Colonel must have looked forty years ago—except that he was a shade darker. He did not go down to the South Field to work. And all Cora's pleadings could not make him go. Yet nothing happened. That was the strange thing about it. The Colonel did nothing—to Bert. But he lit into Cora, nagged and scolded her for days, told her she'd better get some sense into her boy's head if she wanted any skin left on his body.

So the summer passed. Sallie, having worked faithfully in the house throughout the hottest months, went away to school again. Bert remained sullenly behind.

The day that ends our story began like this:

The sun rose burning and blazing, flooding the earth with the heat of early autumn, making even the morning oppressive. Folks got out of bed feeling like over-ripe fruit. The air of the morning shimmered with heat and ill-humor. The night before, Colonel Norwood had been drinking. He got up trembling and shaky, yelling for Cora to bring him something clean to put on. He went downstairs cussing.

The Colonel did not want to eat. He drank black coffee, and walked out on the tall-pillared porch to get a breath of air. He was standing there looking through the trees at his cotton, when the Ford swept by in a cloud of dust, past the front of the house and down the highway to town. Bert was driving.

The Colonel cussed out loud, bit his cigar, turned and went into the house, slamming the door, storming to Cora, calling up the stairs where she was working, "What the hell does he think he is, driving off to town in the middle of the morning? Didn't I tell Bert not to touch that Ford, to stay down yonder in the fields and work?"

"Yes, suh, Colonel Tom," Cora said. "You sure did."

"Tell him I want to see him soon as he comes back here. Send him in here. And tell him I'll skin his yellow hide for him." The Colonel spoke of Bert as though he were still a child.

"Yes, suh, Colonel Tom."

VII

The day grew hotter and hotter. Heat waves rose from the fields. Sweat dampened the Colonel's body. Sweat dampened the black bodies of the Negroes in the cotton fields, too, the hard black bodies that had built the Colonel's fortune out of earth and sun and barehanded labor. Yet the Colonel, in spite of the fact that he lived on this labor, sat in his shaded house fanning that morning and wondering what made niggers so contrary—he was thinking of Bert—as the telephone rang. The fat and testy voice of his old friend, Mr. Higgins, trembled at the other end of the wire. He was calling from the Junction.

Accustomed as he was to his friend's voice on the phone, at first the Colonel could not make out what he was saying. When he did understand, his neck bulged and the palms of the hands that held the phone were wet with sweat. Anger and shame made his tall body stoop and bend like an animal about to spring. Mr. Higgins was talking about Bert.

"That yellow nigger . . ." Mr. Higgins said. "One of your yard-niggers sassed . . ." Mr. Higgins said. "I thought I'd better tell you . . ." Mr. Higgins said. "Everybody . . ." Mr. Higgins said.

The whole town was excited about Bert. In the heat of this over-warm autumn day, the hot heads of the white citizens of the town had suddenly become inflamed about Bert. Mr. Higgins, county politician and Postmaster at the Junction, was well qualified to know. His Office had been the center of the news.

It seemed that Bert had insulted the young white woman who sold stamps and made out money-orders at the Post Office. And Mr. Higgins was telling the Colonel about it on the phone, warning him to get rid of Bert, that people around the Junction were getting sick and tired of seeing him.

At the Post Office this is what happened: a simple argument over change. But the young woman who sold the stamps was not used to arguing with Negroes, or being corrected by them when she made a mistake. Bert said, "I gave you a dollar," holding out the incorrect change. "You gave me back only sixty-four cents."

The young woman said, counting the change, "Yes, but you have eight three-cent stamps. Move on now, there're others waiting." Several white people were in line.

Bert said, "Yes, but eight times three is not thirty-six. You owe me twelve cents more."

The girl looked at the change and realized she was wrong. She looked at Bert—light near-white nigger with grey-blue eyes. You gotta be harder on those kind than you have on the black ones. An educated nigger, too! Besides it was hot and she wasn't feeling well. A light near-white nigger with grey eyes! Instead of correcting the change, she screamed, and let her head fall forward in front of the window.

Two or three white men waiting to buy stamps seized Bert and attempted to throw him out of the Post Office. Bert remembered he'd been a football player—and Colonel Norwood's son—so he fought back. One of the white men got a bloody mouth. Women screamed. Bert walked out of the Post Office, got in the Ford and drove away. By that time, the girl who sold stamps had recovered. She was telling everyone how Bert had insulted her.

"Oh, my God! It was terrible," she said.

"That's one nigger don't know his place, Tom," Mr. Higgins roared over the phone. "And it's your fault he don't—sendin' 'em off to school to be educated." The Colonel listened to his friend at the other end of the wire. "Why that yellow buck comes to my store and if he ain't waited on quick as the white folks are, he walks out. He said last week standin' out on my corner, he wasn't *all* nigger no how; said his name was Norwood—not Lewis, like the rest of Cora's family; said your plantation would be his when you passed out—and all that kind o' stuff, boasting to the niggers listening about you being his father." The Colonel almost dropped the phone. "Now, Tom, you know that stuff don't go 'round these parts o' Georgia. Ruinous to other niggers hearing that sort of talk, too. There ain't been no race trouble in our county for three years—since the Deekins lynching—but I'm telling you, Norwood, folks ain't gonna stand for this. I'm speaking on the quiet, but I see ahead. What happened this morning in the Post Office ain't none too good."

"When I get through with him," said the Colonel hoarsely, "you won't need to worry. Goodbye."

The white man came out of the library, yelled for Sam, shouted for Cora, ordered whisky. Drank and screamed.

"God damn that son of yours! I'm gonna kill him," he said to Cora. "Get out of here," he shouted at Sam, who came back with cigars.

Cora wept. The Colonel raved. A car shot down the road. The Colonel rushed out, brandishing a cane to stop it. It was Bert. He paid no attention to the old man standing on the steps of the pillared porch waving his stick. Ashen with fury, the Colonel came back into the house and fumbled with his keys at an old chest. Finally, a drawer opened and he took out a pistol. He went toward the door as Cora began to howl, but on the porch he became suddenly strengthless and limp. Shaking, the old man sank into a chair holding the gun. He would not speak to Cora.

VIII

Late in the afternoon, Colonel Norwood sent Cora for their son. The gun had been put away. At least Cora did not see it.

"I want to talk to that boy," the Colonel said. "Fetch him here." Damned young fool . . . bastard . . . of a nigger. . . .

"What's he gonna do to my boy?" Cora thought. "Son, be careful," as she went across the yard and down toward Willie's cabin to find Bert. "Son, you be careful. I didn't bear you for no white man to kill. Son, you be careful. You ain't white, don't you know that? You be careful. O, Lord God Jesus in heaven! Son, be careful!" Cora was crying when she reached Willie's door, crying all the way back to the Big House with her son.

"To hell with the old man," Bert said. "He ain't no trouble! Old as he is, what can he do to me?"

"Lord have mercy, son, is you crazy? Why don't you be like Willie? He ain't never had no fusses with de Colonel."

"White folks' nigger," Bert said.

"Why don't you talk sense?" Cora begged.

"Why didn't he keep his promise then and let me go back to school in Atlanta, like my sister? You said if I came home this summer he'd lemme go back to the Institute, didn't you? Then why didn't he?"

"Why didn't you act right, son? Oh-o-o!" Cora moaned. "You can't get nothin' from white folks if you don't act right."

"Act like Willie, you mean, and the rest of these cotton pickers? Then I don't want anything."

They had reached the back door now. It was nearly dark in the kitchen where Livonia was making biscuits.

"Don't rile him, Bert, child," Cora said as she took him through the house. "I don't know what he might do to you. He's got a gun."

"Don't worry 'bout me," Bert answered.

The setting sun made long paths of golden light across the parlor floor through the tall windows opening on the West. The air was thick and sultry with autumn heat. The Colonel sat, bent and old, near a table where there were whisky and cigars and a half-open drawer. When Bert entered he suddenly straightened up and the old commanding look came into his eyes. He told Cora to go upstairs to her room.

Of course, he never asked Bert to sit down.

The tall mulatto boy stood before his father, the Colonel. The old white man felt the steel of him standing there, like the steel of himself forty years ago. Steel of the Norwoods darkened now by Africa.[15] The old man got up, straight and tall, too, and suddenly shook his fist in the face of the boy.

"You listen to me," he said, trembling with quiet. "I don't want to have to whip you again like I did when you were a child." He was almost hissing. "The next time I might kill you. I been running this plantation thirty-five years and never had to beat a nigger old as you are. Never had any trouble out of none of Cora's children before either, but you." The old man sat down. "I don't have trouble with my colored folks. They do what I say or what Talbot says, and that's all there is to it. If they turn in crops, they get a living. If they work for wages, they get paid. If they spend their money on licker, or old cars, or fixing up their cabins—they can do what they choose, long as they know their places and it don't hinder their work. To Cora's young ones—you hear me, boy?—I gave all the chances any nigger ever had in these parts. More'n many a white child's had, too. I sent you off to school. I gave your brother, Willie, that house he's living in when he got married, pay him for his work, help him out if he needs it. None of my darkies suffer. You went off to school. Could have kept on, would have sent you back this fall, but I don't intend to pay for no nigger, or white boy either if I had one, that acts the way you been acting." Colonel Norwood got up again, angrily. "And certainly not for no black fool! I'm talking to *you* like this only because you're Cora's child—but you know damn well it's my habit to *tell* people what to do, not discuss it with them. I just want to know what's the matter with you, though—whether you're crazy or not? And if you're not, you'd better change your ways a damn sight or it won't be safe for you here, and you know it—venting your impudence on white women, ruining my niggers, driving like mad through the Junction, carrying on just as you please. I'm warning you, boy, God damn it! . . . Now I want you to answer me, and talk right." The old man sat down in his chair again by the whisky bottle and the partly opened drawer. He took a drink.

"What do you mean, talk right?" Bert said.

"I mean talk like a nigger should to a white man," the Colonel snapped.

"Oh, but I'm not a nigger, Colonel Norwood," Bert said, "I'm your son."

The old man frowned at the boy in front of him. "Cora's son," he said.

"Fatherless?" Bert asked.

"Bastard," the old man said.

Bert's hands closed into fists, so the Colonel opened the drawer where the pistol was. He took it out and laid it on the table.

"You black bastard," he said.

"I've heard that before." Bert just stood there. "You're talking about my mother."

"Well," the Colonel answered, his fingers playing over the surface of the gun, "what can you do about it?"

The boy felt his whole body suddenly tighten and pull. The muscles of his forearms rippled.

"Niggers like you are hung to trees," the old man went on.

"I'm not a nigger," Bert said. "Ain't you my father? And a hell of a father you are, too, holding a gun on me."

"I'll break your black neck for you," the Colonel shouted. "Don't talk to me like that!" He jumped up.

"You'll break my neck?" The boy stood his ground as the father came toward him.

"Get out of here!" The Colonel shook with rage. "Get out! Or I'll do more than that if I ever lay eyes on you again." The old man picked up the pistol from the table, yet the boy did not move. "I'll fill you full of bullets if you come back here. Get off this place! Get to hell out of this county! Now, tonight. Go on!" The Colonel motioned with his pistol toward the door that led to the kitchen and the back of the house.

"Not that way," Bert said. "I'm not your servant. You must think I'm scared. Well, you can't drive me out the back way like a dog. You're not going to run me off, like a field hand you can't use any more. I'll go," the boy said, starting toward the front door, "but not out the back—from my own father's house."

"You nigger bastard!" Norwood screamed, springing between his son and the door, but the boy kept calmly on. The steel of the gun was between them, but that didn't matter. Rather, it seemed to pull them together like a magnet.

"Don't you . . . ," Norwood began, for suddenly Bert's hand grasped the Colonel's arm, "dare put your . . . ," and his old bones began to crack, "black hands on . . ."

"Why don't you shoot?" Bert interrupted him, slowly turning his wrist.

" . . . me!"

"Why don't you shoot, then?"

The old man twisted and bent in fury and pain, but the gun fell to the floor.

"Why don't you shoot?" Bert said again as his hands sought his father's throat. With furious sureness they took the old white neck in their strong young fingers. "Why don't you shoot then, papa?"

Colonel Norwood clawed the air, breathing hoarsely and loud, his tongue growing stiff and dry, his eyes beginning to burn.

"Shoot—why don't you, then? Huh? Why?"

The chemicals of their two lives exploded. Everything was very black around them. The white man's hands stopped clawing the air. His heart stood still. His blood no longer flowed. He wasn't breathing.

"Why don't you shoot?" Bert said, but there was no answer.

When the boy's eyes cleared, he saw his mother standing at the foot of the stairs, so he let the body drop. It fell with a thud, old and white in a path of red from the setting sun.

"Why didn't he shoot, mama? He didn't want me to live. He was white. Why didn't he shoot then?"

"Tom!" Cora cried, falling across his body. "Colonel Tom! Tom! Tom!"

"He's dead," Bert said. "I'm living though."

"Tom!" Cora screamed, pulling at the dead man. "Colonel Tom!"

Bert bent down and picked up the pistol. "This is what my father wanted to use on me," he said. "He's dead. But I can use it on all the white men in Georgia—they'll be coming to get me now. They never wanted me before, but I know they'll want me now." He stuffed the pistol in his shirt. Cora saw what her son had done.

"Run," she said, rising and going to him. "Run, chile! Out the front way quick, so's they won't see you in the kitchen. Make fo' de swamp, honey. Cross de fields fo' de swamp. Go de crick way. In runnin' water, dogs can't smell no tracks. Hurry, son!"

"Yes, mama," Bert said slowly. "But if I see they gonna get me before I reach the swamp, then I'm coming back here. Let them take me out of my father's house—if they can." He patted the gun inside his shirt, and smiled. "They'll never string me up to some roadside tree for the crackers to laugh at. Not me!"

"Hurry, chile," Cora opened the door and the sunset streamed in like a river of blood. "Hurry, chile."

Bert went out across the wide pillared porch and down the road. He saw Talbot and the storekeeper coming, so he turned off through the trees. And then, because he wanted to live, he began to run. The whole sky was a blaze of color as he ran. Then it began to get dark, and the glow went away.

In the house, Cora started to talk to the dead man on the floor, just as though he were not dead. She pushed and pulled at the body, trying

to get him to get up himself. Then she heard the footsteps of Talbot and
the storekeeper on the porch. She rose and stood as if petrified in the
middle of the floor. A knock, and two men were peering through the
screen door into the dusk-dark room. Then Talbot opened the door.

"Hello, Cora," he said. "What's the matter with you, why didn't you
let us in? Where's that damn fool boy o' your'n goin', comin' out the
front way liked he owned the place? What's the matter with you, woman?
Can't you talk? Where's Colonel Norwood?"

"Let's have some light in here," said the storekeeper, turning a button
beside the door.

"Great God!" Talbot cried. "Jim, look at this!" The Colonel's body
lay huddled on the floor, old and purple-white, at Cora's feet.

"Why, he's blue in the face," the storekeeper said bending over the
body. "Oh! Get that nigger we saw walking out the door! That nigger
bastard of Cora's. Get that nigger! . . . Why, the Colonel's dead!"

Talbot rushed toward the door. "That nigger," he cried. "He must be
running toward the swamps now. . . . We'll get him. Telephone town,
Jim, there in the library. Telephone the sheriff. Telephone the Beale
family down by the swamp. Get men, white men, after that nigger."

The storekeeper ran into the library and began to call on the phone.
Talbot looked at Cora standing in the center of the room. "Where's
Norwood's car? In the barn? Talk, you black wench, talk!"

But Cora didn't say a word. She watched the two white men rush out
of the house into the yard. In a few minutes, she heard the roar of a
motor hurtling down the road. It was dark outside. Night had come.

Cora turned toward the body on the floor. "My boy," she said, "he
can't get to de swamp now. They telephoned the white folks down that
way to head him off. He'll come back home." She called aloud, "Colonel
Tom, why don't you get up from there and help me? You know they're
after our boy. You know they got him out there runnin' from de white
folks in de night. Runnin' from de hounds and de guns and de ropes
and all what they uses to kill poor niggers with. . . . Ma boy's out there
runnin'. Why don't you help him?" Cora bent over the body. "Colonel
Tom, you hear me? You said he was ma boy, ma bastard boy. I heard
you. But he's your'n, too—out yonder in de dark runnin'—from your
people. Why don't you get up and stop 'em? You know you could. You's
a power in Polk County. You's a big man, and yet our son's out there
runnin'—runnin' from po' white trash what ain't worth de little finger
o' nobody's got your blood in 'em, Tom." Cora shook the dead body
fiercely. "Get up from there and stop 'em, Colonel Tom." But the white
man did not move.

Gradually Cora stopped shaking him. Then she rose and backed away from this man she had known so long. "You's cruel, Tom," she whispered. "I might a-knowed it—you'd be like that, sendin' ma boy out to die. I might a-knowed it ever since you beat him that time under de feet of de horses. Well, you won't mistreat him no more now. That's finished." She went toward the steps. "I'm gonna make a place for him. Upstairs under ma bed. He's ma chile, and I'll look out for him. And don't you come in ma bedroom while he's up there. Don't you come to my bed either no more a-tall. I calls for you to help me now, Tom, and you just lays there. I calls you to get up now, and you don't move. Whenever you called *me* in de night, I woke up. Whenever you wanted me to love you, I reached out ma arms to you. I bored you five children and now," her voice rose hysterically, "one of 'em's out yonder runnin' from your people. Our youngest boy's out yonder in de dark, runnin'! I 'spects you's out there, too, with de rest of de white folks. Uh-um! Bert's runnin' from *you*, too. You said he warn't your'n—Cora's po' little yellow bastard. But he is your'n, Colonel Tom, and he's runnin' from you. Yes, out yonder in de dark, you, *you* runnin' our chile with a gun in yo' hand, and Talbot followin' behind you with a rope to hang Bert with." She leaned against the wall near the staircase, sobbing violently. Then she went back toward the man on the floor. Her sobs gradually ceased as she looked down at his crumpled body. Then she said slowly, "Listen, I been sleepin' with you too long not to know that this ain't you, Tom, layin' down here with yo' eyes shut on de floor. You can't fool me—you ain't never been so still like this before—you's out yonder runnin' ma boy! Colonel Thomas Norwood runnin' ma boy through de fields in de dark, runnin' ma po' little helpless Bert through de fields in de dark for to lynch him and to kill him. . . . God damn you, Tom Norwood!" Cora cried, "God damn you!"

She went upstairs. For a long time the body lay alone on the floor in the parlor. Later Cora heard Sam and Livonia weeping and shouting in the kitchen, and Negro voices outside in the dark, and feet going down the road. She thought she heard the baying of hounds afar off, too, as she prepared a hiding place for Bert in the attic. Then she came down to her room and put the most beautiful quilts she had on her bed. "Maybe he'll just want to rest here first," she thought. "Maybe he'll be awful tired and just want to rest."

Then she heard a loud knock at the door, and white voices talking, and Sam's frightened answers. The doctor and the undertakers had come to take the body away. In a little while she heard them lifting it up and putting it in the dead wagon. And all the time, they kept talking, talking.

" . . .'ll be havin' his funeral in town . . . ain't nothin' but niggers left out here . . . didn't have no relatives, did he, Sam? . . . Too bad. . . . Nobody to look after his stuff tonight. Every white man's able to walk's out with the posse . . . that young nigger'll swing before midnight . . . what a neck-tie party! . . . Say, Sam!"

"Yes, sah! Yes, sah!"

" . . . that black housekeeper, Cora? . . . murderin' bastard's mother?"

"She's upstairs, I reckon, sah."

" . . . like to see how she looks. Get her down here."

"Yes, sah!" Sam's teeth were chattering.

"And how about a little drink before we start back to town?"

"Yes, sah! Cora's got de keys fo' de licker, sah."

"Well, get her down, double quick, then!"

"Yes, sah!" Cora heard Sam coming up for her.

Downstairs, the voices went on. They were talking about her. " . . . lived together . . . ain't been a white woman here overnight since the wife died when I was a kid . . . bad business, though, livin' with a," in drawling cracker tones, "nigger."

As Cora came down the steps, the undertakers looked at her half-grinning. "So you're the black wench that's got these educated darkie children? Hum-m! Well I guess you'll see one of 'em swinging full o' bullet holes before you get up in the morning. . . . Or maybe they'll burn him. How'd you like a roasted darkie for breakfast, girlie?"

Cora stood quite still on the stairs. "Is that all you wanted to say to me?" she asked.

"Now, don't get smart," the doctor said. "Maybe you think there's nobody to boss you now. We're goin' to have a little drink before we go. Get out a bottle."

"I take ma orders from Colonel Norwood, suh," Cora said.

"Well, you'll take no more orders from him," the undertaker declared. "He's outside in the dead wagon. Get along now and get out a bottle."

"He's out yonder with de mob," Cora said.

"I tell you he's in my wagon, dead as a door nail."

"I tell you he's runnin' with de mob," Cora said.

"I believe this black woman's done gone nuts," the doctor cried. "Sam, you get the licker."

"Yes, sah!" Sam sputtered with fright. "Co-r-r-ra, gimme . . ."

But Cora did not move.

"Ah-a-a-a, Lawd hab mercy!" Sam cried.

"To hell with the licker, Charlie," the undertaker said nervously. "Let's start back to town. We want to get in on some of that excitement, too. They should've found that nigger by now—and I want to see 'em drag him out here."

"All right, Jim," the other agreed. Then, to Cora, "But don't you darkies go to bed until you see the bonfire. You all are gettin' beside yourselves around Polk County. We'll burn a few more of you if you don't watch out."

The men left and the wheels of the wagon turned on the drive. Sam began to cry.

"Hab mercy! Lawd Jesus, hab mercy! Cora, is you a fool? *Is* you? Then why didn't you give de mens de licker, riled as these white folks is? In ma old age, is I gonna be burnt by de crackers? Lawd, is I sinned? Lawd, what has I done?" He looked at Cora. "I sho ain't gonna stay heah tonight. I's gwine."

"Go on," she said. "The Colonel can get his own drinks when he comes back."

"Lawd God Jesus!" Sam, his eyes bucking from their sockets, bolted from the room fast as his old legs could carry him. Cora heard him running blindly through the house, moaning.

She went to the kitchen where pots were still boiling on the stove, but Livonia had fled, the biscuits burnt in the oven. She looked out the back door, but no lights were visible anywhere. The cabins were quiet.

"I reckon they all gone," she said to herself. "Even ma boy, Willie. I reckon he gone, too. You see, Colonel Tom, everybody's scared o' you. They know you done gone with de mob again, like you did that time they hung Luke Jordan and you went to help 'em. Now you's out chasin' ma boy, too. I hears you hollerin'."

And sure enough, all around the Big House in the dark, in a wide far-off circle, men and dog-cries and auto-horns sounded in the night. Nearer they came even as Cora stood at the back door, listening. She closed the door, bolted it, put out the light, and went back to the parlor. "He'll come in by de front," she said. "Back from de swamp way. He wont' let 'em stop him from gettin' home to me agin, just once. Po' little boy, he ain't got no place to go, no how. Po' boy, what growed up with such pride in his heart. Just like you, Colonel Tom. Spittin' image o' you. . . . Proud! . . . And got no place to go."

Nearer and nearer the man-hunt came, the cries and the horns and the dogs. Headlights began to flash in the dark down the road. Off through the trees, Cora heard men screaming. And suddenly feet running, running, running. Nearer, nearer. She knew it was him. She knew they had seen him, too.

Then there were voices shouting very near the house.

"Don't shoot, men. We want to get him alive."

"Close in on him!"

"He must be in them bushes there by the porch."

"Look!"

And suddenly shots rang out. The door opened. Cora saw flashes of fire spitting into the blackness, and Bert's tall body in the doorway. He was shooting at the voices outside in the dark. The door closed.

"Hello, Ma," he said. "One or two of 'em won't follow me no further."

Cora locked the door as bullets splintered through the wood, shattered the window panes. Then a great volley of shots struck the house, blinding head-lights focused on the porch. Shouts and cries of, "Nigger! Nigger! Get the nigger!" filled the night.

"I was waitin' for you, honey," Cora said. "Quick! Your hidin' place's ready for you, upstairs in de attic. I sawed out a place under de floor. Maybe they won't find you, chile. Hurry, 'fore your father comes."

"No time to hide, Ma," Bert panted. "They're at the door now. They'll be coming in the back way, too. They'll be coming in the windows. They'll be coming in everywhere. I got one bullet left, Ma. It's mine."

"Yes, son, it's your'n. Go upstairs in mama's room and lay down on ma bed and rest. I won't let 'em come up till you're gone. God bless you, chile."

Quickly, they embraced. A moment his head rested on her shoulder.

"I'm awful tired running, Ma. I couldn't get to the swamp. Seems like they been chasing me for hours. Crawling through the cotton a long time, I got to rest now."

Cora pushed him toward the stairs. "Go on, son," she said gently.

At the top, Bert turned and looked back at this little brown woman standing there waiting for the mob. Outside the noise was terrific. Men shouted and screamed, massing for action. All at once they seemed to rush in a great wave for the house. They broke the doors and windows in, and poured into the room—a savage crowd of white men, red and wild-eyed, with guns and knives, sticks and ropes, lanterns and flashlights. They paused at the foot of the stairs where Cora stood looking down at them silently.

"Keep still, men," one of the leaders said. "He's armed. . . . Say where's that yellow bastard of yours, Cora—upstairs?"

"Yes," Cora said. "Wait."

"Wait, hell!" the men cried. "Come on, boys, let's go!"

A shot rang out upstairs, then Cora knew it was all right.

"Go on," she said, stepping aside for the mob.

IX

The next morning when people saw a bloody and unrecognizable body hanging in the public square at the Junction, some said with a certain pleasure, "That's what we do to niggers down here," not realizing Bert had been taken dead, and that all the fun for the mob had been sort of stale at the end.

But others, aware of what had happened, thought, "It'd be a hell of a lot better lynching a live nigger. Say, ain't there nobody else mixed up in this here Norwood murder? Where's that boy's brother, Willie? Heh?"

So the evening papers carried this item in the late editions:

DOUBLE LYNCHING IN GEORGIA

A large mob late this afternoon wrecked vengeance on the second of two Negro field hands, the murderers of Colonel Thomas Norwood, wealthy planter found dead at Big House Plantation. Bert Lewis was lynched last night, and his brother, Willie Lewis, today. The sheriff of the county is unable to identify any members of the mob. Colonel Norwood's funeral has not yet been held. The dead man left no heirs.

Laughing to Keep
from Crying

(1952)

To Dorothy

I wish to thank the editors of the following magazines for permission to reprint a number of the stories included in this book which first appeared in their pages: *The African, American Spectator, The Anvil, The Crisis, Esquire, Flight, Negro Story, New Theatre, Scribner's Fiction Parade, Stag,* and *Story Magazine.* The story "Why, You Reckon?" appeared originally in *The New Yorker.*

Contents

When you see me laughing
I'm laughing to keep from crying.
Traditional Blues

Who's Passing for Who?

One of the great difficulties about being a member of a minority race is that so many kindhearted, well-meaning bores gather around to help. Usually, to tell the truth, they have nothing to help with, except their company—which is often appallingly dull.

Some members of the Negro race seem very well able to put up with it, though, in these uplifting years. Such was Caleb Johnson, colored social worker, who was always dragging around with him some nondescript white person or two, inviting them to dinner, showing them Harlem, ending up at the Savoy—much to the displeasure of whatever friends of his might be out that evening for fun, not sociology.

Friends are friends and, unfortunately, overearnest uplifters are uplifters—no matter what color they may be. If it were the white race that was ground down instead of Negroes, Caleb Johnson would be one of the first to offer Nordics the sympathy of his utterly inane society, under the impression that somehow he would be doing them a great deal of good.

You see, Caleb, and his white friends, too, were all bores. Or so we, who lived in Harlem's literary bohemia during the "Negro Renaissance" thought. We literary ones[1] considered ourselves too broad-minded to be bothered with questions of color. We liked people of any race who smoked incessantly, drank liberally, wore complexion and morality as loose garments, and made fun of anyone who didn't do likewise. We snubbed and high-hatted any Negro or white luckless enough not to understand Gertrude Stein, Ulysses, Man Ray, the theremin, Jean Toomer, or George Antheil.[2] By the end of the 1920's Caleb was just catching up to Dos Passos. He thought H. G. Wells good.

We met Caleb one night in Small's. He had three assorted white folks in tow. We would have passed him by with but a nod had he not hailed us enthusiastically, risen, and introduced us with great acclaim to his friends who turned out to be schoolteachers from Iowa, a woman and two men. They appeared amazed and delighted to meet all at once two Negro writers and a black painter in the flesh. They invited us to have a drink with them. Money being scarce with us, we deigned to sit down at their table.

The white lady said, "I've never met a Negro writer before."

The two men added, "Neither have we."

"Why, we know any number of *white* writers," we three dark bohemians declared with bored nonchalance.

"But Negro writers are much more rare," said the lady.

"There are plenty in Harlem," we said.

"But not in Iowa," said one of the men, shaking his mop of red hair.

"There are no good *white* writers in Iowa either, are there?" we asked superciliously.

"Oh, yes, Ruth Suckow came from there."

Whereupon we proceeded to light in upon Ruth Suckow as old hat and to annihilate her in favor of Kay Boyle. The way we flung names around seemed to impress both Caleb and his white guests. This, of course, delighted us, though we were too young and too proud to admit it.

The drinks came and everything was going well, all of us drinking, and we three showing off in a high-brow manner, when suddenly at the table just behind us a man got up and knocked down a woman. He was a brownskin man. The woman was blonde. As she rose he knocked her down again. Then the red-haired man from Iowa got up and knocked the colored man down.

He said, "Keep your hands off that white woman."

The man got up and said, "She's not a white woman. She's my wife."

One of the waiters added, "She's not white, sir, she's colored."

Whereupon the man from Iowa looked puzzled, dropped his fists, and said, "I'm sorry."

The colored man said, "What are you doing up here in Harlem anyway, interfering with my family affairs?"

The white man said, "I thought she was a white woman."

The woman who had been on the floor rose and said, "Well, I'm not a white woman, I'm colored, and you leave my husband alone."

Then they both lit in on the gentleman from Iowa. It took all of us and several waiters, too, to separate them. When it was over the manager requested us to kindly pay our bill and get out. He said we were disturbing the peace. So we all left. We went to a fish restaurant down the street. Caleb was terribly apologetic to his white friends. We artists were both mad and amused.

"Why did you say you were sorry," said the colored painter to the visitor from Iowa, "after you'd hit that man—and then found out it wasn't a white woman you were defending, but merely a light colored woman who looked white?"

"Well," answered the red-haired Iowan, "I didn't mean to be butting in if they were all the same race."

"Don't you think a woman needs defending from a brute, no matter what race she may be?" asked the painter.

"Yes, but I think it's up to you to defend your own women."

"Oh, so you'd divide up a brawl according to races, no matter who was right?"

"Well, I wouldn't say that."

"You mean you wouldn't defend a colored woman whose husband was knocking her down?" asked the poet.

Before the visitor had time to answer, the painter said, "No! You just got mad because you thought a black man was hitting a *white* woman."

"But she *looked* like a white woman," countered the man.

"Maybe she was just passing for colored," I said.

"Like some Negroes pass for white," Caleb interposed.

"Anyhow, I don't like it," said the colored painter, "the way you stopped defending her when you found out she wasn't white."

"No, we don't like it," we all agreed except Caleb.

Caleb said in extenuation, "But Mr. Stubblefield is new to Harlem."

The red-haired white man said, "Yes, it's my first time here."

"Maybe Mr. Stubblefield ought to stay out of Harlem," we observed.

"I agree," Mr. Stubblefield said. "Good night."

He got up then and there and left the café. He stalked as he walked. His red head disappeared into the night.

"Oh, that's too bad," said the white couple who remained. "Stubby's temper just got the best of him. But explain to us, are many colored folks really as fair as that woman?"

"Sure, lots of them have more white blood than colored, and pass for white."

"Do they?" said the lady and gentleman from Iowa.

"You never read Nella Larsen?" we asked.

"She writes novels," Caleb explained. "She's part white herself."

"Read her," we advised. "Also read the *Autobiography of an Ex-Colored Man*." Not that we had read it ourselves—because we paid but little attention to the older colored writers—but we knew it was about passing for white.

We all ordered fish and settled down comfortably to shocking our white friends with tales about how many Negroes there were passing for white all over America. We were determined to *épater le bourgeois* real good via this white couple we had cornered, when the woman leaned over the table in the midst of our dissertations and said, "Listen, gentlemen, you needn't spread the word, but me and my husband aren't white either. We've just been *passing* for white for the last fifteen years."

"What?"

"We're colored, too, just like you," said the husband. "But it's better passing for white because we make more money."

Well, that took the wind out of us. It took the wind out of Caleb, too. He thought all the time he was showing some fine white folks Harlem—and they were as colored as he was!

Caleb almost never cursed. But this time he said, "I'll be damned!"

Then everybody laughed. And laughed! We almost had hysterics. All at once we dropped our professionally self-conscious "Negro" manners, became natural, ate fish, and talked and kidded freely like colored folks do when there are no white folks around. We really had fun then, joking about that red-haired guy who mistook a fair colored woman for white. After the fish we went to two or three more night spots and drank until five o'clock in the morning.

Finally we put the light-colored people in a taxi heading downtown. They turned to shout a last good-by. The cab was just about to move off, when the woman called to the driver to stop.

She leaned out the window and said with a grin, "Listen, boys! I hate to confuse you again. But, to tell the truth, my husband and I aren't really colored at all. We're white. We just thought we'd kid you by passing for colored a little while—just as you said Negroes sometimes pass for white."

She laughed as they sped off toward Central Park, waving, "Good-by!"

We didn't say a thing. We just stood there on the corner in Harlem dumbfounded—not knowing now *which* way we'd been fooled. Were they really white—passing for colored? Or colored—passing for white?

Whatever race they were, they had had too much fun at our expense—even if they did pay for the drinks.

Something in Common

Hong Kong. A hot day. A teeming street. A mélange of races. A pub, over the door the Union Jack.

The two men were not together. They came in from the street, complete strangers, through different doors, but they both reached the bar at about the same time. The big British bartender looked at each of them with a wary, scornful eye. He knew that, more than likely, neither had the price of more than a couple of drinks. They were distinctly down at the heel, had been drinking elsewhere, and were not customers of the bar. He served them with a deliberation that was not even condescending—it was menacing.

"A beer," said the old Negro, rattling a handful of Chinese and English coins at the end of a frayed cuff.

"A scotch," said the old white man, reaching for a pretzel with thin fingers.

"That's the tariff," said the bartender, pointing to a sign.

"Too high for this lousy Hong Kong beer," said the old Negro.

The barman did not deign to answer.

"But, reckon it's as good as some we got back home," the elderly colored man went on as he counted out the money.

"I'll bet you wouldn't mind bein' back there, George," spoke up the old white man from the other end of the bar, "in the good old U.S.A."

"Don't *George* me," said the Negro, " 'cause I don't know you from Adam."

"Well, don't get sore," said the old white man, coming nearer, sliding his glass along the bar. "I'm from down home, too."

"Well, I ain't from no *down home*," answered the Negro wiping beer foam from his mouth. "I'm from the North."

"Where?"

"North of Mississippi," said the black man. "I mean Missouri."

"I'm from Kentucky," vouched the old white fellow swallowing his whisky. "Gimme another one," to the bartender.

"Half a dollar," said the bartender.

"Mex, you mean?"

"Yeah, mex," growled the bartender picking up the glass.

"All right, I'll pay you," said the white man testily. "Gimme another one."

"They're tough in this here bar," said the old Negro sarcastically. "Looks like they don't know a Kentucky colonel when they see one."

"No manners in these damned foreign joints," said the white man seriously. "How long you been in Hong Kong?"

"Too long," said the old Negro.

"Where'd you come from here?"

"Manila," said the Negro.

"What'd you do there?"

"Now what else do you want to know?" asked the Negro.

"I'm askin' you a civil question," said the old white man.

"Don't ask so many then," said the Negro, "and don't start out by callin' me *George*. My name ain't George."

"What is your name, might I ask?" taking another pretzel.

"Samuel Johnson. And your'n?"

"Colonel McBride."

"Of Kentucky?" grinned the Negro impudently toothless.

"Yes, sir, of Kentucky," said the white man seriously.

"Howdy, Colonel," said the Negro. "Have a pretzel."

"Have a drink, boy," said the white man, beckoning the bartender.

"Don't call me *boy*," said the Negro. "I'm as old as you; if not older."

"Don't care," said the white man, "have a drink."

"Gin," said the Negro.

"Make it two," said the white man. "Gin's somethin' we both got in common."

"I love gin," said the Negro.

"Me, too," said the white man.

"Gin's a sweet drink," mused the Negro, "especially when you're around women."

"Gimme one white woman," said the old white man, "and you can take all these Chinee gals over here."

"Gimme one yellow gal," said the old Negro, "and you can take all your white women anywhere."

"Hong Kong's full of yellow gals," said the white man.

"I mean *high-yellow* gals," said the Negro, "like we have in Missouri."

"Or in Kentucky," said the white man, "where half of 'em has white pappys."

"Here! Don't talk 'bout my women," said the old Negro. "I don't allow no white man to talk 'bout my women."

"Who's talkin' about your women? Have a drink, George."

"I told you, don't *George* me. My name is Samuel Johnson. White man, you ain't in Kentucky now. You in the Far East."

"I know it. If I was in Kentucky, I wouldn't be standin' at this bar with you. Have a drink."

"Gin."

"Make it two."

"Who's payin'?" said the bartender.

"Not me," said the Negro. "Not *me*."

"Don't worry," said the old white man grandly.

"Well, I am worryin'," growled the bartender. "Cough up."

"Here," said the white man, pulling out a few shillings. "Here, even if it is my last penny, here!"

The bartender took it without a word. He picked up the glasses and wiped the bar.

"I can't seem to get ahead in this damn town," said the old white man, "and I been here since Coolidge."

"Neither do I," said the Negro, "and I come before the War."

"Where is your home, George?" asked the white man.

"You must think it's Georgia," said the Negro. "Truth is I ain't got no home—no more home than a dog."

"Neither have I," said the white man, "but sometimes I wish I was back in the States."

"Well, I don't," said the Negro. "A black man ain't got a break in the States."

"What?" said the old white man, drawing up proudly.

"States is no good," said the Negro. "No damned good."

"Shut up," yelled the old white man waving a pretzel.

"What do you mean, shut up?" said the Negro.

"I won't listen to nobody runnin' down the United States," said the white man. "You better stop insultin' America, you big black ingrate."

"You better stop insultin' me, you poor-white trash," bristled the aged Negro. Both of them reeled indignantly.

"Why, you black bastard!" quavered the old white man.

"You white cracker!" trembled the elderly Negro.

These final insults caused the two old men to square off like roosters, rocking a little from age and gin, but glaring fiercely at one another, their gnarled fists doubled up, arms at boxing angles.

"Here! Here!" barked the bartender. "Hey! Stop it now!"

"I'll bat you one," said the white man to the Negro.

"I'll fix you so you can't leave, neither can you stay," said the Negro to the white.

"Yuh will, will yuh?" sneered the bartender to both of them. "I'll see about batting—and fixing, too."

He came around the end of the bar in three long strides. He grabbed the two old men unceremoniously by the scruff of their necks, cracked their heads together twice, and threw them both calmly into the street. Then he wiped his hands.

The white and yellow world of Hong Kong moved by, rickshaw runners pushed and panted, motor horns blared, pedestrians crowded the narrow sidewalks. The two old men picked themselves up from the dust and dangers of a careless traffic. They looked at one another, dazed for a moment and considerably shaken.

"Well, I'll be damned!" sputtered the old white man. "Are we gonna stand for this—from a Limey bartender?"

"Hell, no," said the old Negro. "Let's go back in there and clean up that joint."

"He's got no rights to put his Cockney hands on Americans," said the old white man.

"Sure ain't," agreed the old Negro.

Arm in arm, they staggered back into the bar, united to protect their honor against the British.[3]

African Morning

Maurai took off his calico breech-cloth of faded blue flowers. He took two buckets of water and a big bar of soap into the back yard and threw water all over himself until he was clean. Then he wiped his small golden body on an English towel and went back into the house. His mother had told him always to wear English clothes whenever he went out with his father, or was sent on an errand into the offices of the Export Company or onto one of the big steamships that came up the Niger to their little town. So Maurai put on his best white shirt and a pair of little white sailor trousers that his mother had bought him before she died.

She hadn't been dead very long. She was black, pure African, but Maurai was a half-breed, and his father was white. His father worked in the bank. In fact, his father was the president of the bank, the only bank for hundreds of miles on that part of the coast, up the hot Niger delta in a town where there were very few white people. And no other half-breeds.

That was what made it so hard for Maurai. He was the only half-native, half-English child in the village. His black mother's people didn't want him now that she was dead; and his father had no relatives in Africa. They were all in England, far away, and they were white. Sometimes when Maurai went outside of the stockade, the true African children pelted him with stones for being a half-breed and living inside the enclosure with the English.[4] When his mother was alive, she would fight back for Maurai and protect him, but now he had to fight for himself.

In the pale fresh morning, the child crossed the large, square, foreign enclosure of the English section toward that corner where the bank stood, one entrance within the stockade and another on the busy native street. The boy thought curiously how the whites had built a fence around themselves to keep the natives out—as if black people were animals. Only servants and women could come in, as a rule. And already his father had brought another young black woman to live in their house. She was only a child, very young and shy, and not wise like his mother had been.

There were already quite a few people in the bank this morning transacting business, for today was Steamer Day, and Maurai had come to take a letter to the captain for his father. In his father's office there were three or four assistants surrounding the president's desk, and as Maurai opened the door he heard the clink of gold. They were counting money there on the desk, a great pile of golden coins, and when they heard the door close, they turned quickly to see who had entered.

"Wait outside, Maurai," said his father sharply, his hands on the gold, so the little boy went out into the busy main room of the bank again. Evidently they did not want him to see the gold.

Maurai knew that in his village the English did not allow Africans to possess gold—but to the whites it was something very precious. They were always talking about it, always counting it and wrapping it and sending it away by boat, or receiving it from England.

If a black boy stole a coin of gold, they would give him a great many years in prison to think about it. This Maurai knew. And suddenly he thought, looking at his own small hands, "Maybe that's why the black people hate me, because I am the color of gold."

Just then his father came out of his office and handed him the letter. "Here, Maurai, take this note to Captain Higgins of the *Drury* and tell him I shall expect him for tea at four."

"Yes, sir," said Maurai as he went out into the native street and down toward the river where the masts of the big boat towered.

On the dock everyone was busy. There were women selling things to eat and boys waiting for sailors to come ashore. Winches rattled, and the cranes lifted up their loads of palm oil and cocoa beans. Ebony-black men, naked to the waist, the sweat pouring off them, loaded the rope hampers before they swung up and over and down into the dark hole of the big ship. Their sweat fell from shining black bodies onto the bags of cocoa beans and went away to England and came back in gold for the white men to count in banks as though it were the most precious thing in the world.

Maurai went up the steep swinging stairway at the side of the ship, past the sailors leaning over the deck rail, and on up to the bridge and the captain's office. The captain took the letter from the little golden boy without a word.

As Maurai descended from the bridge he could see directly down into the great dark holes where went the palm oil and the cocoa beans, and where more sweating ebony-black men were stowing away the cargo for its trip to England.

One of the white sailors grabbed Maurai on the well deck and asked, "You take me see one fine girl?" because he naturally thought Maurai was one of the many little boys who are regularly sent to the dock on Steamer Days by the prostitutes, knowing only one or two vile phrases in English and the path to the prostitute's door. The sailors fling them a penny, perhaps, if they happen to like the black girls to whom the child leads them.

"I am not a guide boy," said Maurai, as he pulled away from the sailor and went on down the swinging stairs to the dock. There the boys who were runners for the girls in the palm huts laughed and made fun of this little youngster who was neither white nor black. They called him an ugly yellow name. And Maurai turned and struck one of the boys in the face.

But they did not fight fair, these dock boys. A dozen of them began to strike and kick at Maurai, and even the black women squatting on the wharf selling fruits and sweetmeats got up and joined the boys in their attack, while the sailors leaning on the rail of the English steamer had great fun watching the excitement.

The little black boys ran Maurai away from the wharf in a trail of hooting laughter. In the wide grassy street he wiped the blood from his nose and looked down at his white shirt, torn and grimy from the blows of the wharf rats. He thought how, even in his English clothes, a sailor had taken him for a prostitute's boy and had asked him to find "one fine girl" for him.

The little mulatto youngster went slowly up the main street past the bank where his father worked, past the house of the man who sells parrots and monkeys to the sailors, on past the big bayamo tree where the vendors of palm wine have their stands, on to the very edge of town— which is the edge of the jungle, too—and down a narrow path through a sudden tangle of vines and flowers, until he came to a place where the still backwaters of the lagoon formed a pool on whose grassy banks the feet of the obeah dancers dance in nights of moon.

Here Maurai took off his clothes and went into the water, cool to his bruised little body. He swam well, and he was not afraid of snakes or crocodiles. He was not afraid of anything but white people and black people—and gold. Why, he wondered in the water, was his body the color of gold? Why wasn't he black or white—like his mother or like his father, one or the other—but not just (he remembered that ugly word of the wharf rats) a *bastard* of gold?

Filling his lungs with air and holding his breath, down, down, Maurai went, letting his naked body touch the cool muddy bottom of the deep lagoon.

"Suppose I were to stay here forever," he thought, "in the dark, at the bottom of this pool?"

But, against his will, his body shot upward like a cork and his skin caught the sun in the middle of the big pool, and he kept on swimming around and around, loath to go back to the house in the enclosure where his father would soon be having the white captain to tea in the living room, but where he, Maurai, and the little dark girl with whom his father slept, would, of course, eat in the kitchen.

But since he had begun to be awfully hungry and awfully tired, he came out of the water to lie down on the grassy bank and dry in the sun. And probably because he was only twelve years old, Maurai began to cry. He thought about his mother who was dead and his father who would eventually retire and go back to England, leaving him in Africa—where nobody wanted him.

Out of the jungle two bright birds came flying and stopped to sing in a tree above his head. They did not know that a little boy was crying on the ground below them. They paid no attention to the strange sounds that came from that small golden body on the bank of the lagoon. They simply sang a moment, flashed their bright wings, and flew away.

Pushcart Man

The usual Saturday night squalls and brawls were taking place as the Pushcart Man trucked up Eighth Avenue in Harlem. A couple walking straggle-legged got into a fight. A woman came to take her husband home from the corner saloon but he didn't want to go. A man said he had paid for the last round of drinks. The bartender said he hadn't. The squad car came by. A midget stabbed a full-grown man. Saturday night jumped.

"Forgive them, Father, for they know not what they do," said a Sanctified Sister passing through a group of sinners.

"Yes, they do know what they do," said a young punk, "but they don't give a damn!"

"Son, you oughtn't to use such language!"

"If you can't get potatoes, buy tomatoes," yelled the Pushcart Man. "Last call! Pushing this cart on home!"

"Have you got the *Times?*" asked a studious young man at a newsstand where everybody was buying the *Daily News.*

"I got the *News* or *Mirror,*" said the vendor.

"No," said the young man, "I want the *Times.*"

"You can't call my mother names and live with me," said a dark young fellow to a light young girl.

"I did not call your mother a name," said the girl. "I called *you* one."

"You called *me* a son of a—"

"Such language!" said the Sanctified Sister.

"He just ain't no good," explained the girl. "Spent half his money already and ain't brought home a thing to eat for Sunday."

"Help the blind, please," begged a kid cup-shaker pushing a blind man ahead of him.

"That man ain't no more blind than me," declared a fellow in a plaid sport shirt.

"I once knew a blind man who made more money begging than I did working," said a guy leaning on a mailbox.

"You didn't work very hard," said the Sport Shirt. "I never knowed you to keep a job more than two weeks straight. Hey, Mary, where you going?"

"Down to the store to get a pint of ice cream." A passing girl paused. "My mama's prostrate with the heat."

An old gentleman whose eyes followed a fat dame in slacks muttered, "Her backside looks like a keg of ale."

"It's a shame," affirmed a middle-aged shopper on her way in the chicken store, "slacks and no figure."

"If you don't like pomatoes, buy totatoes!" cried the Pushcart Man.

"This bakery sure do make nice cakes," said a little woman to nobody in particular, "but they's so high."

"Don't hit me!" yelled a man facing danger, in the form of two fists.

"Stop backing up!"

"Then stop coming forward—else I'll hurt you." He was cornered. A crowd gathered.

"You children go on home," chided a portly matron to a flock of youngsters. "Fights ain't for children."

"You ain't none of my mama."

"I'm glad I ain't."

"And we don't have to go home."

"You-all ought to be in bed long ago! Here it is midnight!"

"There ain't nobody at my house."

"You'd be home if I was any relation to you," said the portly lady.

"I'm glad you ain't."

"Hit me! Just go on and hit me—and I'll cut you every way there is," said the man.

"I ain't gonna fight you with my bare fists cause you ain't worth it."

"Break it up! Break it up! Break it up!" barked the cop. They broke it up.

"Let's go play in 143rd Street," said a little bowlegged boy. "There's blocks of ice down there we can sit on and cool off."

"If you don't get potatoes, buy tomatoes," cried the Pushcart Man.

A child accidentally dropped a pint of milk on the curb as he passed. The child began to cry.

"When you get older," the Pushcart Man consoled the child, "you'll be glad it wasn't Carstairs you broke. Here's a dime.[5] Buy some more milk. I got tomatoes, potatoes," cried the pushcart vendor. "Come and get 'em—'cause I'm trucking home."

Why, You Reckon?

Well, sir, I ain't never been mixed up in nothin' wrong before nor since and I don't intend to be again, but I was hongry that night. Indeed, I was! Depression times before the war plants opened up.[6]

I was goin' down a Hundred Thirty-third Street in the snow when another colored fellow what looks hongry sidetracks me and says, "Say, buddy, you wanta make a little jack?"

"Sure," I says. "How?"

"Stickin' up a guy," he says. "The first white guy what comes out o' one o' these speak-easies and looks like bucks, we gonna grab him!"

"Oh, no," says I.

"Oh, yes, we will," says this other guy. "Man, ain't you hongry? Didn't I see you down there at the charities today, not gettin' nothin'—like me? You didn't get a thing, did you? Hell, no! Well, you gotta take what you want, that's all, reach out and *take* it," he says. "Even if you are starvin', don't starve like a fool. You must be in love with white folks, or somethin'. Else scared. Do you think they care anything about you?"

"No," I says.

"They sure don't," he says. "These here rich folks comes up to Harlem spendin' forty or fifty bucks in the night clubs and speak-easies and don't care nothin' 'bout you and me out here in the street, do they? Huh? Well, one of 'em's gonna give up some money tonight before he gets home."

"What about the cops?"

"To hell with the cops!" said the other guy. "Now, listen, now. I live right here, sleep on the ash pile back of the furnace down in this basement. Don't nobody never come down there after dark. They let me stay here for keepin' the furnace goin' at night. It's kind of a fast house upstairs, you understand. Now, you grab this here guy we pick out, push him down to the basement door, right here, I'll pull him in, we'll drag him on back yonder to the furnace room and rob him, money, watch, clothes, and all. Then push him out in the rear court. If he hollers— and he sure will holler when that cold air hits him—folks'll just think he's some drunken white man what's fell out with some chocolate baby upstairs and has had to run and leave his clothes behind him. But by that time we'll be long gone. What do you say, boy?"

Well, sir, I'm tellin' you, I was so tired and hongry and cold that night I didn't hardly know what to say, so I said all right, and we decided to do it. Looked like to me 'bout that time a Hundred Thirty-third Street was just workin' with people, taxis cruisin', women hustlin', white folks from downtown lookin' for hot spots.

It were just midnight.

This guy's front basement door was right near the door of the Dixie Bar where that woman sings the kind of blues ofays is crazy about.

Well, sir! Just what we wanted to happen happened right off. A big party of white folks in furs and things come down the street. They musta parked their car on Lenox, 'cause they wasn't in no taxi. They was walkin' in the snow. And just when they got right by us one o' them white women says "Ed-*ward*," she said, "Oh, darlin', don't you know I left my purse and cigarettes and compact in the car. Please go and ask the chauffeur to give 'em to you." And they went on in the Dixie. The boy started toward Lenox again.

Well, sir, Edward never did get back no more that evenin' to the Dixie Bar. No, pal, uh-hum! 'Cause we nabbed him. When he come back down the street in his evenin' clothes and all, with a swell black overcoat on that I wished I had, just a-tippin' so as not to slip up and fall on the snow, I grabbed him. Before he could say Jack Robinson, I pulled him down the steps to the basement door, the other fellow jerked him in, and by the time he knew where he was, we had that white boy back yonder behind the furnace in the coalbin.

"Don't you holler," I said on the way down.

There wasn't much light back there, just the raw gas comin' out of a jet, kind of blue-like, blinkin' in the coal dust. Took a few minutes before we could see what he looked like.

"Ed-*ward*," the other fellow said, "don't you holler in this coal bin."

But Edward didn't holler. He just sat down on the coal. I reckon he was scared weak-like.

"Don't you throw no coal neither," the other fellow said. But Edward didn't look like he was gonna throw coal.

"What do you want?" he asked by and by in a nice white-folks kind of voice. "Am I kidnaped?"

Well, sir, we never thought of kidnapin'. I reckon we both looked puzzled. I could see the other guy thinkin' maybe we *ought* to hold him for ransom. Then he musta decided that that weren't wise, 'cause he says to this white boy, "No, you ain't kidnaped," he says. "We ain't got no time for that. We's hongry right *now*, so, buddy, gimme your money."

The white boy handed out of his coat pocket amongst other things a lady's pretty white beaded bag that he'd been sent after. My partner held it up.

"Doggone," he said, "my gal could go for this. She likes purty things. Stand up and lemme see what else you got."

The white guy got up and the other fellow went through his pockets. He took out a wallet and a gold watch and a cigarette lighter, and he got a swell key ring and some other little things colored folks never use.

"Thank you," said the other guy, when he got through friskin' the white boy, "I guess I'll eat tomorrow! And smoke right now," he said, opening up the white boy's cigarette case. "Have one," and he passed them swell fags around to me and the white boy, too. "What kind is these?" he wanted to know.

"Benson's Hedges," said the white boy, kinder scared-like, 'cause the other fellow was makin' an awful face over the cigarette.

"Well, I don't like 'em," the other fellow said, frownin' up. "Why don't you smoke decent cigarettes? Where do you get off, anyhow?" he said to the white boy standin' there in the coalbin. "Where do you get off comin' up here to Harlem with these kind of cigarettes? Don't you know no colored folks smoke these kind of cigarettes? And what're you doin' bringin' a lot of purty rich women up here wearin' white fur coats? Don't you know it's more'n we colored folks can do to get a black fur coat, let alone a white one? I'm askin' you a question," the other fellow said.

The poor white fellow looked like he was gonna cry. "Don't you know," the colored fellow went on, "that I been walkin' up and down Lenox Avenue for three or four months tryin' to find some way to earn money to get my shoes half-soled? Here, look at 'em." He held up the palms of his feet for the white boy to see. There were sure big holes in his shoes. "Looka here!" he said to that white boy. "Still you got the nerve to come up here to Harlem all dressed up in a tuxedo suit with a stiff shirt on and diamonds shinin' out of the front of it, and a silk muffler on and a big heavy overcoat! Gimme that overcoat," the other fellow said.

He grabbed the white guy and took off his overcoat.

"We can't use that M.C. outfit you got on," he said, talking about the tux. "But we might be able to make earrings for our janes out of them studs. Take 'em off," he said to the white kid.

All this time I was just standin' there, wasn't doin' nothin'. The other fellow had taken all the stuff, so far, and had his arms full.

"Wearin' diamonds up here to Harlem, and me starvin'!" the other fellow said. "Goddamn!"

"I'm sorry," said the white fellow.

"Sorry?" said the other guy. "What's your name?"

"Edward Peedee McGill, III," said the white fellow.

"What third?" said the colored fellow. "Where's the other two?"

"My father and grandfather," said the white boy. "I'm the third."

"I had a father and a grandfather, too," said the other fellow, "but I ain't no third. I'm the first. Ain't never been one like me. I'm a new model." He laughed out loud.

When he laughed, the white boy looked real scared. He looked like he wanted to holler. He sat down in the coal agin. The front of his shirt was all black where he took the diamonds out. The wind came in through a broken pane above the coalbin and the white fellow sat there shiverin'. He was just a kid—eighteen or twenty maybe—runnin' around to night clubs.

"We ain't gonna kill you," the other fellow kept laughin'. "We ain't got the time. But if you sit in that coal long enough, white boy, you'll be black as me. Gimme your shoes. I might maybe can sell 'em."

The white fellow took off his shoes. As he handed them to the colored fellow, he had to laugh, hisself. It looked so crazy handin' somebody else your shoes. We all laughed.

"But I'm laughin' last," said the other fellow. "You two can stay here and laugh if you want to, both of you, but I'm gone. So long!"

And, man, don't you know he went on out from that basement and took all that stuff! Left me standin' just as empty-handed as when I come in there. Yes, sir! He left me with that white boy standin' in the coal. He'd done took the money, the diamonds, and everythin', even the shoes! And me with nothin'! Was I stung? I'm askin' you!

"Ain't you gonna gimme none?" I hollered, runnin' after him down the dark hall. "Where's my part?"

I couldn't even see him in the dark—but I *heard* him.

"Get back there," he yelled at me, "and watch that white boy till I get out o' here. Get back there," he hollered, "or I'll knock your livin' gizzard out! I don't know you."

I got back. And there me and that white boy was standin' in a strange coalbin, him lookin' like a picked chicken—and me *feelin'* like a fool. Well, sir, we both had to laugh again.

"Say," said the white boy, "is he gone?"

"He ain't here," I said.

"Gee, this was exciting," said the white fellow, turning up his tux collar. "This was thrilling!"

"What?" I says.

"This is the first exciting thing that's ever happened to me," said the white guy. "This is the first time in my life I've ever had a good time in Harlem. Everything else has been fake, a show. You know, something you pay for. This was real."

"Say, buddy," I says, "if I had your money, I'd be always having a good time."

"No, you wouldn't," said the white boy.

"Yes, I would, too," I said, but the white boy shook his head. Then he asked me if he could go home, and I said, "Sure! Why not?" So we went up the dark hall. I said, "Wait a minute."

I went up and looked, but there wasn't no cops or nobody much in the streets, so I said, "So long," to that white boy. "I'm glad you had a good time." And left him standin' on the sidewalk in his stocking feet waitin' for a taxi.

I went on up the street hongrier than I am now. And I kept thinkin' about that boy with all his money. I said to myself, "What do you suppose is the matter with rich white folks? Why you reckon they ain't happy?"

Saratoga Rain

The wind blew. Rain swept over the roof. Upstairs the man and woman lay close together. He held her in his arms, drowsily, sleepily, head half buried in the covers, the scent of bodies between them. The rain came down.

She said, "Ben, I love you." To her, thirty years of muddy yesterdays were as nothing.

He said, "I like you, too, babe." And all the dice on all the tables from Reno to Saratoga were forgotten.

It was early morning. The rain came down. They didn't care. They were together in the darkened room, heads half buried in the covers. They had each other. They didn't remember now the many cliffs they'd had to climb nor the lurking tomorrows of marsh and danger.

They would never be angels and have wings—that they knew for sure. But at the moment they had each other.

That moment, that rainy morning, not even that whole day would last very long. Indeed, it might never repeat itself. Things had a way of moving swiftly with each of them, leaving memories, raising scars, and passing on. But they did not choose to remember now the aching loneliness of time, warm in bed as they were, with the rain falling outside.

They did not choose to remember (for her) the stable boy who had been her lover last night, nor the jockey who had been so generous with his money the week before but had fallen yesterday in the steeple chase, lost his mount, and broken his neck.

They did not (for him) choose to remember the swift rattle of crooked dice in the fast fading game at the corner, the recollection of the startled look on that Florida simpleton's face when he saw his month's pay gone.

For neither of them now the memory of muddy water in the gutter of life, because on this early August morning the rain fell straight out of the sky—clean.

The room is pleasantly dark and warm, the house safe and, though neither of them will ever be angels with wings, at the moment they have each other.

"I like you," Ben said.

"I love you," she whispered.

Spanish Blood

In that amazing city of Manhattan where people are forever building things anew, during prohibition times there lived a young Negro called Valerio Gutierrez whose mother was a Harlem laundress, but whose father was a Puerto Rican sailor. Valerio grew up in the streets. He was never much good at school, but he was swell at selling papers, pitching pennies, or shooting pool. In his teens he became one of the smoothest dancers in the Latin-American quarter north of Central Park. Long before the rhumba became popular, he knew how to do it in the real Cuban way that made all the girls afraid to dance with him. Besides, he was very good looking.

At seventeen, an elderly Chilean lady who owned a beauty parlor called La Flor began to buy his neckties. At eighteen, she kept him in pocket money and let him drive her car. At nineteen, younger and prettier women—a certain comely Spanish widow, also one Dr. Barrios' pale wife—began to see that he kept well dressed.

"You'll never amount to nothin'," Hattie, his brown-skinned mother said. "Why don't you get a job and work? It's that foreign blood in you, that's what it is. Just like your father."

"*Qué va?*" Valerio replied, grinning.

"Don't you speak Spanish to me," his mama said. "You know I don't understand it."

"O.K., mama," Valerio said, "*Yo voy a trabajar.*"

"You better *trabajar*," his mama answered. "And I mean work, too! I'm tired o' comin' home every night from that Chinee laundry and findin' you gone to the dogs. I'm gonna move out o' this here Spanish neighborhood anyhow, way up into Harlem where some real *colored* people is, I mean American Negroes. There ain't nobody settin' a decent example for you down here 'mongst all these Cubans and Puerto Ricans and things. I don't care if your father was one of 'em, I never did like 'em real well."

"Aw, ma, why didn't you ever learn Spanish and stop talking like a spook?"

"Don't you spook me, you young hound, you! I won't stand it. Just because you're straight-haired and yellow and got that foreign blood in you, don't you spook me. I'm your mother and I won't stand for it. You hear me?"

"Yes, m'am. But you know what I mean. I mean stop talking like most colored folks—just because you're not white you don't have to get back in a corner and stay there. Can't we live nowhere else but way up in Harlem, for instance? Down here in 106th Street, white and colored families live in the same house—Spanish-speaking families, some white and some black. What do you want to move further up in Harlem for, where everybody's all black? Lots of my friends down here are Spanish and Italian, and we get along swell."

"That's just what I'm talkin' about," said his mother. "That's just why I'm gonna move. I can't keep track of you, runnin' around with a fast foreign crowd, all mixed up with every what-cha-ma-call-it, lettin' all shades o' women give you money. Besides, no matter where you move, or what language you speak, you're still colored less'n your skin is white."

"Well, I won't be," said Valerio, "I'm American, Latin-American."

"Huh!" said his mama. "It's just by luck that you even got good hair."

"What's that got to do with being American?"

"A mighty lot," said his mama, "in America."

They moved. They moved up to 143rd Street, in the very middle of "American" Harlem. There Hattie Gutierrez was happier—for in her youth her name had been Jones, not Gutierrez, just plain colored Jones. She had come from Virginia, not Latin America. She had met the Puerto Rican seaman in Norfolk, had lived with him there and in New York for some ten or twelve years and borne him a son, meanwhile working hard to keep him and their house in style. Then one winter he just disappeared, probably missed his boat in some far-off port town, settled down with another woman, and went on dancing rhumbas and drinking rum without worry.

Valerio, whom Gutierrez left behind, was a handsome child, not quite as light as his father, but with olive-yellow skin and Spanish-black hair, more foreign than Negro. As he grew up, he became steadily taller and better looking. Most of his friends were Spanish-speaking, so he possessed their language as well as English. He was smart and amusing out of school. But he wouldn't work. That was what worried his mother, he just wouldn't work. The long hours and low wages most colored fellows received during depression times never appealed to him. He could live without struggling, so he did.

He liked to dance and play billiards. He hung out near the Cuban theater at 110th Street, around the pool halls and gambling places, in the taxi dance emporiums. He was all for getting the good things out of life. His mother's moving up to black 143rd Street didn't improve conditions any. Indeed, it just started the ball rolling faster, for here Valerio became what is known in Harlem as a big-timer, a young sport, a hep cat. In other words, a man-about-town.

His sleek-haired yellow star rose in a chocolate sky. He was seen at all the formal invitational affairs given by the exclusive clubs of Harlem's younger set, although he belonged to no clubs. He was seen at midnight shows stretching into the dawn. He was even asked to Florita Sutton's famous Thursday midnight-at-homes where visiting dukes, English authors, colored tap dancers, and dinner-coated downtowners vied for elbow room in her small Sugar Hill apartment. Hattie, Valerio's mama, still kept her job ironing in the Chinese laundry—but nobody bothered about his mama.

Valerio was a nice enough boy, though, about sharing his income with her, about pawning a ring or something someone would give him to help her out on the rent or the insurance policies. And maybe, once or twice a week, mama might see her son coming in as she went out in the morning or leaving as she came in at night, for Valerio often slept all day. And she would mutter, "The Lord knows, cause I don't, what will become of you, boy! You're just like your father!"

Then, strangely enough, one day Valerio got a job. A good job, too—at least, it paid him well. A friend of his ran an after-hours night club on upper St. Nicholas Avenue. Gangsters owned the place, but they let a Negro run it. They had a red-hot jazz band, a high-yellow revue, and bootleg liquor. When the Cuban music began to hit Harlem, they hired Valerio to introduce the rhumba. That was something he was really cut out to do, the rhumba. That wasn't work. Not at all, *hombre*! But it was a job, and his mama was glad.

Attired in a yellow silk shirt, white satin trousers, and a bright red sash, Valerio danced nightly to the throbbing drums and seed-filled rattles of the tropics—accompanied by the orchestra's usual instruments of joy. Valerio danced with a little brown Cuban girl in a red dress, Concha, whose hair was a mat of darkness and whose hips were nobody's business.

Their dance became the talk of the town—at least, of that part of the town composed of night-lifers—for Valerio danced the rhumba as his father had taught him to dance it in Norfolk when he was ten years old, innocently—unexpurgated, happy, funny, but beautiful, too—like a gay, sweet longing for something that might be had, some time, maybe, some place or other.

Anyhow, business boomed. Ringside tables filled with people who came expressly to see Valerio dance.

"He's marvelous," gasped ladies who ate at the Ritz any time they wanted to.

"That boy can dance," said portly gentlemen with offices full of lawyers to keep track of their income tax. "He can dance!" And they wished they could, too.

"Hot stuff," said young rum-runners, smoking reefers and drinking gin—for these were prohibition days.

"A natural-born eastman," cried a tan-skin lady with a diamond wristwatch. "He can have anything I got."

That was the trouble! Too many people felt that Valerio could have anything they had, so he lived on the fat of the land without making half an effort. He began to be invited to fashionable cocktail parties downtown. He often went out to dinner in the East 50's with white folks. But his mama still kept her job in the Chinese laundry.

Perhaps it was a good thing she did in view of what finally happened, for to Valerio the world was nothing but a swagger world tingling with lights, music, drinks, money, and people who had everything—or thought they had. Each night, at the club, the orchestra beat out its astounding songs, shook its rattles, fingered its drums. Valerio put on his satin trousers with the fiery red sash to dance with the little Cuban girl who always had a look of pleased surprise on her face, as though amazed to find dancing so good. Somehow she and Valerio made their rhumba, for all their hip-shaking, clean as a summer sun.

Offers began to come in from other night clubs, and from small producers as well. "Wait for something big, kid," said the man who ran the cabaret. "Wait till the Winter Garden calls you."

Valerio waited. Meanwhile, a dark young rounder named Sonny, who wrote number bets for a living, had an idea for making money off of Valerio. They would open an apartment together where people could come after the night clubs closed—come and drink and dance—and love a little if they wanted to. The money would be made from the sale of drinks—charging very high prices to keep the riffraff out. With Valerio as host, a lot of good spenders would surely call. They could get rich.

"O.K. by me," said Valerio.

"I'll run the place," said Sonny, "and all you gotta do is just be there and dance a little, maybe—you know—and make people feel at home."

"O.K.," said Valerio.

"And we'll split the profit two ways—me and you."

"O.K."

So they got a big Seventh Avenue apartment, furnished it with deep, soft sofas and lots of little tables and a huge icebox and opened up. They paid off the police every week. They had good whisky. They sent out cards to a hundred downtown people who didn't care about money. They informed the best patrons of the cabaret where Valerio danced— the white folks who thrilled at becoming real Harlem initiates going home with Valerio.

From the opening night on, Valerio's flat filled with white people from midnight till the sun came up. Mostly a sporty crowd, young blades accompanied by ladies of the chorus, race-track gentlemen, white cabaret entertainers out for amusement after their own places closed, musical comedy stars in search of new dance steps—and perhaps three or four brown-skin ladies-of-the-evening and a couple of chocolate gigolos, to add color.

There was a piano player. Valerio danced. There was impromptu enter- taining by the guests. Often famous radio stars would get up and croon. Expensive night-club names might rise to do a number—or several num- bers if they were tight enough. And sometimes it would be hard to stop them when they really got going.

Occasionally guests would get very drunk and stay all night, sleeping well into the day. Sometimes one might sleep with Valerio.

Shortly all Harlem began to talk about the big red roadster Valerio drove up and down Seventh Avenue. It was all nickel-plated—and a little blonde revue star known on two continents had given it to him, so folks said. Valerio was on his way to becoming a gigolo de luxe.

"That boy sure don't draw no color lines," Harlem commented. "No, sir!

"And why should he?" Harlem then asked itself rhetorically. "Colored folks ain't got no money—and money's what he's after, ain't it?"

But Harlem was wrong. Valerio seldom gave a thought to money— he was having too good a time. That's why it was well his mama kept her job in the Chinese laundry, for one day Sonny received a warning, "Close up that flat of yours, and close it damn quick!"

Gangsters!

"What the hell?" Sonny answered the racketeers. "We're payin' off, ain't we—you and the police, both? So what's wrong?"

"Close up, or we'll break you up," the warning came back. "We don't like the way you're running things, black boy. And tell Valerio to send that white chick's car back to her—and quick!"

"Aw, nuts!" said Sonny. "We're paying the police! You guys lay off."

But Sonny wasn't wise. He knew very well how little the police count when gangsters give orders, yet he kept right on. The profits had gone to his head. He didn't even tell Valerio they had been warned, for Sonny, who was trying to make enough money to start a number bank of his own, was afraid the boy might quit. Sonny should have known better.

One Sunday night about 3:30 A.M., the piano was going like mad. Fourteen couples packed the front room, dancing close and warm. There were at least a dozen folks whose names you'd know if you saw them in any paper, famous from Hollywood to Westport.

They were feeling good.

Sonny was busy at the door, and a brown bar-boy was collecting highball glasses, as Valerio came in from the club where he still worked. He went in the bedroom to change his dancing shoes for it was snowing and his feet were cold.

O, rock me, pretty mama, till the cows come home . . .

sang a sleek-haired Harlemite at the piano.

Rock me, rock me, baby, from night to morn . . .

when just then, a crash like the wreck of the Hesperus resounded through the hall and shook the whole house as five Italian gentlemen in evening clothes who looked exactly like gangsters walked in. They had broken down the door.

Without a word they began to smash up the place with long axes each of them carried. Women began to scream, men to shout, and the piano vibrated, not from jazz-playing fingers, but from axes breaking its hidden heart.

"Lemme out," the piano player yelled. "Lemme out!" But there was panic at the door.

"I can't leave without my wrap," a woman cried. "Where is my wrap? Sonny, my ermine coat!"

"Don't move," one of the gangsters said to Sonny.

A big white fist flattened his brown nose.

"I ought to kill you," said a second gangster. "You was warned. Take this!"

Sonny spit out two teeth.

Crash went the axes on furniture and bar. Splintered glass flew, wood cracked. Guests fled, hatless and coatless. About that time the police arrived.

Strangely enough, the police, instead of helping protect the place from the gangsters, began themselves to break, not only the furniture, but also the *heads* of every Negro in sight. They started with Sonny. They laid the barman and the waiter low. They grabbed Valerio as he emerged from the bedroom. They beat his face to a pulp. They whacked the piano player twice across the buttocks. They had a grand time with their night sticks. Then they arrested all the colored fellows (and no whites) as the gangsters took their axes and left. That was the end of Valerio's apartment.

In jail Valerio learned that the woman who gave him the red roadster was being kept by a gangster who controlled prohibition's whole champagne racket and owned dozens of rum-running boats.

"No wonder!" said Sonny, through his bandages. "He got them guys to break up our place! He probably told the police to beat hell out of us, too!"

"Wonder how he knew she gave me that car?" asked Valerio innocently.

"White folks know everything," said Sonny.

"Aw, stop talking like a spook," said Valerio.

When he got out of jail, Valerio's face had a long night-stick scar across it that would never disappear. He felt weak and sick and hungry. The gangsters had forbidden any of the night clubs to employ him again, so he went back home to mama.

"Umm-huh!" she told him. "Good thing I kept my job in that Chinee laundry. It's a good thing . . . Sit down and eat, son . . . What you gonna do now?"

"Start practicing dancing again. I got an offer to go to Brazil—a big club in Rio."

"Who's gonna pay your fare way down yonder to Brazil?"

"Concha," Valerio answered—the name of his Cuban rhumba partner whose hair was a mat of darkness. "Concha."

"A woman!" cried his mother. "I might a-knowed it! We're weak that way. My God, I don't know, boy! I don't know!"

"You don't know what?" asked Valerio, grinning.

"How women can help it," said his mama. "The Lord knows you're *just* like your father—and I took care o' him for ten years. I reckon it's that Spanish blood."

"*Qué va!*" said Valerio.

Heaven to Hell

There we was dancin' up the steps of glory, my husband, Mackenzie, and me, our earthly troubles over, when who should we meet comin' down but Nancy Smothers!

"That hussy!" I said, "how did she get up here?"

She had her white wings all folded around her, lookin' just like an Easter lily, 'cept that her face was chocolate.

"Nancy Smothers, if you come a-near my husband, I'm gonna crown you!" I said, "I done stood enough from you down on earth, let alone meetin' you in heaven."

All this while, Mackenzie ain't said a word. Shame! He knowed he's done wrong with that woman. Mackenzie lifted up his wings like as if he was gonna fly, but I dared him!

"Don't you lift a feather, you dog, you! Just hold your horses! I'm gonna ask God how come this Harlem hussy got to heaven anyhow."

Mackenzie and I went on up the golden stairs. I could see him strainin' his eyeballs, tryin' to look back without turning his head.

Nancy Smothers switched on down the steps, I reckon.

But I never did find out how she got in heaven—because just then I come out from under the ether.

I looked up and saw a pretty white nurse standin' there by my bed just like a angel. I hollered, "Where is Mackenzie? Was he hurt much, too? You know, he was drivin' when we hit that pole!"

The nurse said, "Don't worry, madam. Your husband's alright. He just got a broken arm when the car turned over. But he'll be in to see you by and by. They're keepin' him in the Men's Ward overnight."

"I'm glad he's safe," I said, "I sure am glad!"

Then the nurse said, "This lady's been here with you a long time, sitting by your bed. An old friend of yours, she says. She brought you some flowers."

So I turned my eyes—and there sat Nancy Smothers, right beside of my bed! Just as long-faced and hypocritical as she could be!

"Nancy," I said, "where am I—in heaven *or in hell*?"

"You's still on earth, Amelia," Nancy said sweetly, "and, honey, I just come from the Men's Ward where I seen Mackenzie. He says to tell you he's doin' well."

Even with three broken ribs I would have tried to kill Nancy—that hussy, bringing me messages from my own Mackenzie—but there was that nice white nurse standing beside me like an angel, and I always did hate to act up in front of white folks.

All I said was, "Nancy, I wish you'd been with us in that wreck! Then I could a-got some pleasure out of it. I'd just love to see you all crippled up."

"Shss-ss-s!" said the nurse. "You're weak! You mustn't talk so loud!"

"You shouldn't excite yourself, dear," said Nancy, rising, "so I'll be going on home. I know you're out of your head."

"I wish you'd go to . . ."

"Shss-sss-s-s!" said the nurse.

Then I realized I was startin' to act up in front of that nice, sweet white nurse, so I tried to smile. "Good-by, Nancy."

She said, "Good-by, Amelia," her eyes gleamin' like a chess-cat's. That snake! Snake!

When the nurse took my temperature again, she said, "That's strange, madam! Your fever's gone away up!"

"Strange, nothin'," I thought to myself.

But then how could that pretty young nurse know I was layin' there worryin' myself to death about whether Nancy Smothers went on home or not—*or if the hussy went back in the Men's Ward to set beside Mackenzie?*

Love can be worse than hell.

Sailor Ashore

"What's your story, Morning Glory?"

"Like your tail, Nightingale."

Azora answered the sailor with as impudent a couplet as she could muster on short notice. This rhymed jive was intended as a compliment, for the sailor was big, brown, and handsome, except that he had sad eyes. Azora was coffee-and-cream colored, leaning slightly to the heavy side.

The sailor took her in with his eyes and decided she would do. Their stools were side by side. The bar was cozy. He was just a little drunk.

"Hold your attitude," he said.

"Solid," affirmed Azora.

"Have a drink?"

"What you think?"

"Well, all reet! That's down my street! Name it!"

"White Horse. Send it trotting!"

"Get a commission?"

"Sure," said Azora. She thought she might as well tell the truth. This bird was probably hep anyhow. But that shouldn't keep him from spending money. Shore leave was short and gay spots scarce after midnight. Colored folks didn't have many after-hour places to go on Central Avenue for, with elections coming, the politicians were cleaning up the city.

"Yes," said Azora, "I get a commission. What's it to you?"

"Set her up," said the sailor to the bartender. "And gimme a gin. What's your name, Miss Fine Brown Frame?"

"Azora."

"Mine's Bill."

"Bill, how are you?"

"Like a ship left to drift. I been looking for you all night. Shall we drink some more here—or go to your house?"

"My house? You act like you know me."

"I feel like I know you. Where's the liquor store?"

"Two doors down, bootleg, extra charge."

"Let's dig it."

Outside the moon was brighter than the street lights, the stars big in the sky. The girl put her arm through Bill's.

"I don't live far," Azora said.

"I'll keep up with you."

"I'm fast as greased lightning and slippery as a pig," jived Azora. "Play my name and you liable to catch a gig."

"Ain't you from Chicago?" asked the sailor.

"Thirty-ninth and State," said Azora.

"I knowed it. All they do in Chicago's play policy. But out here on the Coast the Chinaman's got everything sewed up."

"Tight as Dick's hatband."

"If you beat that Chinese lottery with all them spots to mark—you really beat something," commented the sailor.

The lights in the liquor joint were hard as tin. "What kind of whisky you like, Azora, when you ain't boosting bar sales?"

"Any kind, honey."

They bought a pint and started home to her room. Away from the bright lights of the bar, in the cool night air, the sailor suddenly fell silent. Under the street lights Azora noticed that his face, when he wasn't talking or smiling, was very sad. Well, sometimes she felt sad, too, but she tried not to look it.

She lived in one of those little two-room boxes that sit back in yards in Los Angeles behind two or three more little houses. It was cozy inside. She turned the radio on and got out her tray of glasses. They drank. But the sailor remained quiet. He looked into the brown whisky as if he was looking for something. Maybe he is drunk, Azora thought, or just sleepy. He kept looking down, frowning.

"Why don't you look at me?" Azora asked.

"I don't see no crystal ball in your eyes," the sailor answered.

"Crystal ball?"

"Yah, I'm trying to see my future."

"What old future?"

"My black future."

"What about mine, honey?"

"Yours is sewed up," said the sailor.

"Sewed up?"

"Sure, you ain't gonna be nothing. Neither am I."

"Honey, what makes you talk so serious? We come here to have some fun," said the woman.

"We're colored, ain't we?"

"Sure! Colored as we can be."

"Then we can't get nowhere in this white man's country," said the sailor.

"Yes, we can, too. There ain't no use talking like that, baby. I got a little boy and I'm sure gonna make something out of him."

"I ain't talking about your little boy, Azora. I'm talking about you and me. We ain't gonna be nothing."

"You're something now, honey—a big, strong, fine stud." She leaned toward him. "What does them stripes mean on your arm?"

"Nothing. A colored sailor can have all the stripes he wants on his arm. The white man still cusses him out."

"Who cussed you out, honey? You had trouble on your ship today? Is that why, all a sudden, you so grouchy?"

"Yah, I had trouble. Looks like they think I'm a dog to 'buse around."

"Well, let's not talk about it no more. Leave your troubles aboard."

"Suppose I do leave 'em aboard? I run into 'em all over again ashore," he muttered. "Look how far from the docks *I* have to come to have a little fun. Can't even get a decent drink out at the port. The bars won't serve Negroes."

"Boy, you talk like you just now finding out you're colored. Now, me, I've been colored a long time."

"So've I, but—"

"But what?"

"I don't know. To listen at the radio you would think we never had no Jim Crow and lynchings and prejudice in America at all. Even the Southerners are talking about liberty and freedom. White folks is funny, Azora, especially when they get all noble and speechifying."

"True. But I can deal with 'em, can't you?"

"Naw, they get me in a squirrel cage."

"You take it too serious. I work for white folks every day, cook and scrub. It's hard work, too."

"Then what you doing out ballyhooing all night long?"

"Saturday, ain't it? Besides, suppose I hadn't been out, I wouldn't've run into you."

"You got something there! How old's your kid you mentioned?"

"Eleven. Sixth grade in school. He's a fine boy."

"Un-hum. Wish I had a kid."

"Never been married?"

"No." The sailor shook his head.

"I'm a grass widow. I got nobody either now. You reckon you and me could get along?"

"I been looking for a girl like you. Fix that last drink."

She mixed the whisky and soda.

"I've only got three months more to go in the navy."

"I've been on my job in Beverly Hills for ten years."

"No wonder you got such a sweet little shack. How come you've got no old man?"

"Colored men's all too much like you—got your mind on not being nothing. Always complaining, always discouraged. Always talking about this is a white man's world."

"This *is* a white man's world, ain't it?"

"No, it ain't! I'm in it, too! I'm colored—and I'm gonna make something out of my son."

"You always talking about your son. I'm talking about us now."

"There ain't no just us. There's us—and everybody else. If things is bad, change 'em! You a man, ain't you?"

"I hope so."

"Then talk like a man."

The sad look deepened in the sailor's eyes.

"You a mighty hard chick to get along with," he said.

"What did you ask me tonight when we first met in that bar?"

"I said, 'What's your story, Morning Glory?'" remembered the sailor.

"You've heard my tale, Nightingale," said the girl.

"The whisky is all gone," said the sailor. "I better go—seeing as how I ain't man enough for you."

He looked around for his cap, found it, and opened the door. Azora didn't try to stop him.

"Thanks for the inspiring conversation," he said as he closed the door.

He got a few steps down the path between the houses when he heard her knob turn. A rectangle of light fell into the yard with Azora's shadow silhouetted in the middle.

She called, "Say, listen, sailor! Wait a minute! Com'ere!"

Her voice was harder than before. He turned and saw her standing in the doorway. Slowly he came back to the steps.

"Listen, sailor," said Azora, "ain't neither one of us gonna be nothing! I lied when I told you I had a son. I ain't got nobody. I don't work in Beverly Hills. I work on the streets and in bars. I ain't nothing but a hustler."

"I knowed what you was the minute I saw you," said the sailor.

"Yeah? Well, listen, kid! If I ever *did* have a son—and if I ever do have a job—if I wasn't what I am—I'd make something out of my son, if I had one! I swear to God I would, sailor!"

The man looked at the woman in the doorway a long time.

"I say, I swear to God I would," she repeated as he walked away.

Slice Him Down

In Reno in the 30's, among the colored folks of the town, there were two main social classes—those who came to the city on a freight train and those who did not. The latter, or cushion-riders, were sometimes inclined to turn flat noses high at those who rode the rods by way of entry to the city. Supercilious glances on the part of old settlers and chair-car arrivals tobogganed down broad Negro noses at the black bums who like the white bums, both male and female, streamed through Nevada during the depression years on their way to or from the coast, to remain a while, if the law would let them, in THE BIGGEST LITTLE CITY IN THE WORLD—RENO—according to the official sign in electric lights near the station.

But, of course, the rod-riders got off nowhere near the station. If they were wise, bums from the East got off at Sparks, several miles from the famous mecca of unhappy wives, then they footed it into Reno. (Only passengers with tickets, coaches or Pullmans can afford the luxury of alighting directly at any station, anywhere.)

Terry and Sling came in one day on a fast freight from Salt Lake. Before that they had come from Cheyenne. And before that from Chicago—and then the line went South and got lost somewhere in a tangle of years and cotton fields and God-knows-what fantasies of blackness.

They were Southern shines. Sure, shines—darkies—niggers—Terry and Sling. At least, that's what the railroad bulls called them often enough on the road. And you don't deny anything to a railroad bull, do you? They hit too hard and shoot too fast. And, after all, why argue over a name? It's only when your belly's full and your pride's up that you want people to call you Mr. Terry, Mr. Sling . . . Mr. Man.

"What's your name, boy?" asked a colored voice in the near-darkness.

"What you care? You might be a detective."

Terry grinned from ear to ear at the compliment. He put one hand in a raggedy, pocketless pocket and scratched himself.

"You's a no-name boy like me, heh, fella? Well, maybe you is equally as bad as me, too? Mean and hongry and bad! Listen, let's me and you travel together since we's on the road. What shall I call you?"

"Call me Sling."

Freights were being made up in the Chicago railroad yards at dusk. Rattlers on rollers going somewhere—must be better than here, Lawd, better than here.

"I'm tough, too," said Sling, eying a passing string of boxcars. "I eats pig iron for breakfast."

"Huh! I use cement for syrup on hot cakes made o' steel," said Terry.

"That's why I'm leavin' town," said scarred-up Sling, " 'cause I spit in a bozo's eye yesterday and killed him stone dead! I spit bullets."

Just then they grabbed a Westbound freight on the wing. They lied all the way to Omaha as they squatted in the corner of an open-lathed empty car where plenty of cattle had left plenty of smells on their various trips to the Chicago market.

"Why, man, I done killed me so many mens in my day that I'm scared I'll kill myself some time by accident," said Sling. "When I shaves myself, I tries not to look mean—to keep from pullin' my own razor across my own throat. I'm a bad jigaboo, son."

"Huh! You ain't nowheres near as bad as me," Terry lied, long tall lies, all the way from Omaha to Cheyenne. "Lemme tell you 'bout the last duster that crossed my path. He were an Al Capone—machine gun and all—and I just mowed him down with my little thirty-two on a forty-four frame. Man, I made lace curtains out of his a-nat-toe-mie!"

"Why?"

" 'Cause he were white, and I were mad 'cause he were messin' with my State Street gal."

"Man, you let women mess you up that way?"

"I did that time."

"They ain't worth fightin' about."

"I know it—but I does fight about 'em."

"I does, too, man, but I ain't gonna no mo'. I'm through fightin' 'bout women."

"Me, too."

"Then we's buddies. Womens done messed me up too much."

"And me."

By that time the coal car they were in was running too slow for anybody's good, nearing a town. What town? On the map, Cheyenne.

But no map ever made would have a dot on it for the alley where the garbage can was at the A-1 Café's back door that gave up only a half-dozen rinds of raw squash, a handful of bacon skins, and a few bread crusts to feed two long tall black boys named Terry and Sling.

"Let's get on down the road, boy." As the stars came out.

"Dust my broom, pal."

"Swing your feet, Terry. Let's make this early evenin' rattler."

> *Aw, do it freight train!*
> *Wheelers roll!*
> *Dog-gone my hard,*
> *Unlucky soul!*

Reno! The BIGGEST little CITY in the WORLD blazing its name in lights at night in a big arch of a sign all the way across the street. But they couldn't read the sign too well. Hunger and rain and a bad education all stood between them and the reading of that sign.

Autumn in Reno! Dog-bite my onions! Stacks of shining silver dollars on the tables—even in depression times—wheels spinning in gambling places, folks winning, losing, winning. THE BANK CLUB: big plate glass windows on the main street. Stand right on the sidewalk and look in at the Bank Club. Dice, keno, roulette, piles of silver. Pretty sight.

"There must not be no law in Reno."

"Must ain't," said Sling.

"Must be all the cartwheels in the world in Reno."

"Must is," said Sling.

"Here we stays in Reno."

"Here we stays, Terry," said Sling.

As luck would have it, they got jobs, settled in Reno, got a room, got gambling change, got girls. And there the trouble began—with the girls.

Terry was shining shoes at a stand in front of the station. Sling was elbow-greasing the floor of a Chinese lottery and dice joint, acting as general-janitor, bouncer, and errand boy all in one. Between them, they made ten or twelve dollars a week, not bad in those times. Suits on credit—three dollars down. Two-tone shoes. Near-silk shirts. Key chains—without keys. Who cares about keys? You *wear* the chains. String 'em across your breast! Hang 'em from your pockets. Man, they shine like silver! Shine like gold—them chains! You can't wear keys.

"Boy, you ought to see my gal! Three quarters cat—and didn't come here on no freight train neither," said Terry, putting a stocking cap on his head to make his hair lay down.

"You come on a rattler, so hush," said Sling. "My gal did, too, so don't bring that up!"

"All right, pal! Take it easy! You know I'm a bad man."

"Almost as bad as I is, ain't you?" said Sling, spraying his armpits with rose-colored talcum from a tall ten-cent store box.

"You mean as bad as you would like to be," kidded Terry, at the same time wishing, in his heart of hearts, that he had a big knife scar somewhere on his body like the one Sling had halfway across his neck and down his shoulder blade—a true sign of battle. "You'd like to be tough," kidded Terry.

But Sling let that pass. He was kinda tired and in no mood for joking, nor quarreling, either. A Chinaman sure can work you hard in one day! Poor *hockaway* gets worked hard everywhere by everybody. Almost too tired to wash up and go see my gal. Dog-gone! That's why he used so much talcum powder, he was so tired.

Meanwhile, Terry put on his derby at a cocky angle, got that off his mind, and looked around under the bed for his shoes. As he tied his brown and white oxfords, he kept thinking in his mind how his sweet mama didn't come to Reno on no freight train. No, sir! Not that dame o' mine! Angelina Walls is her name, Mrs. Angelina Walls. Cooks for a white lady from Frisco who come to Reno to get unchained and brought along her maid. And the maid done fell for me! Ha! Ha! Angelina! Fell for a smooth black papa with a deep Chicago line. Old young Terry's done got himself a woman, sure enough.

"Boy, lend me your honey-brown tie, will you?"

"Aw-right," said Sling.

Tonight, Sling's thoughts were on his ladylove, too, tired as he was. Dark and Indian-looking, his particular girl. She didn't work much, neither. Just rested. She made her living—somehow. Wore a rabbit skin coat and a gold wrist-watch . . . Sure, she come to town on a freight train—but she rode in taxis on rainy nights! Had a nice room. Had a good heart. Liked an old long tall boy by the name of Sling, with a razor scar across his shoulder. Hot dog!

Her name was Charlie-Mae. Charlie-Mae what? I dunno! Nobody was ever heard to call her by her last name, if she had one. She might have had one, maybe. Who knows? Probably did. Charlie-Mae—Indian-looking girl in a rabbit skin coat with a gold wrist-watch, Lawd!

"Let's haul it to the club," said Terry, "soon's I go get Angelina."

"I'll pick you up," said Sling, "by and by. You truck on down."

So Terry tapped on down the street in his derby hat and honey-colored tie to get Mrs. Walls.

Shortly thereafter, in a sky-blue suit with wide shoulders, Sling went looking for Charlie-Mae, key chain just a-swinging, shining, and swinging.

Both boys really looked hot in the gorgeous sense—but the sad facts were that it was late November by now and neither one of them had yet worked up to an overcoat to cover their outer finery. So it should be recorded that before donning their stylish suits and ties and hats, they had put on underneath clean shirts, various sweaters, sweatshirts, and other warm but unsightly garments from their meager store in order the better to face the cold Nevada wind.

Saturday night in Reno. Back-alley Reno. Colored Reno by the railroad tracks where you can hear the trains go by. Where do they go, them trains? Where do they come from? What is there where them trains go better than here, Lawd, better than here? Colored folks always live down by the railroad tracks, but is there any train anywhere runnin' where a man ain't black? Far or near, Lawd, is it better than here—Reno on a Saturday night?

"Anyhow, who gives a damn about being black, when he's hard and tough as I is?" said Terry, leaving the house near the park where he had called at the white lady's back door for his girl friend.

"Well, for a woman, it ain't easy being black," said Mrs. Angelina Walls. "I could a-been much better educated, had I been white. Now, down South where I growed up, there wasn't any schools hardly for colored. But as it were, I learned to read and write, and I holds my head high. I ain't common! I come here on a train, myself!"

"You all right with me," Terry said proudly as they walked down the street toward the alley where the colored club was located. "A high-toned woman like you's all right with me."

"Then don't mix me with no dirt," said Mrs. Angelina Walls. "That's one reason I don't like to go to this old club. Any-and-everybody goes there. Womens right off the street. Bums right off the freight."

"They sure do," said Terry, feeling kinda shamed to take her there, educated as she was. "But they ain't no place else for jigs to go in Reno."

"You right, honey," said Mrs. Angelina Walls. "We has to get a glass o' beer somewhere and dance a little bit once in a while."

"We sho' do."

"You can have a right smart good time at that there club," said Sling, as he and his girl came down the steps of the third-rate Japanese rooming house where she lived. "We sho' can," said Charlie-Mae, buttoning her rabbit fur. "Um-m! This air smells good tonight."

"Would smell better if it weren't so cold," said Sling. "I never did like for winter to start coming."

"I do," said Charlie-Mae. "It's better for my business. I don't always have a nice affectionate fella like you to look after me."

"But you got me now," said Sling, "so you don't have to worry."

"When we gonna start living together?"

"Soon's I get my next pay from that Chinaman in the dice house. But I kinda hate to move away from Terry, 'cause me and him's been real good buddies. He's mighty nigh as bad a man as I is, and don't neither one of us take no foolishness. I'm tellin' you, Charlie-Mae," Sling lied, "you ought to seen how we used to do them railroad bulls when we was on the road together. We used to slice 'em right down! I mean, cut 'em to ribbons and leave their carcass in the railroad yard, if they messed with us."

"You did?"

"Sho' did."

"You and Terry?"

"Me and Terry! We used to slice them bulls right down."

"But Terry ain't got no scars."

"He sho ain't," said Sling. "I just now thought o' that. I'm so bad, I done been scarred up two or three times, if not more."

"That's a lovely cut on your right shoulder," said Charlie-Mae. "But, say! Listen, not changing the subject, Terry's sure got a funny taste in women, ain't he? Going around with that old stuck-up yellow hussy they calls Mrs. Angelina Walls. I heard her say she didn't speak to nobody what come here on a freight train, herself."

"She's got a high nose," said Sling. "But Terry, he's all right."

Packed and jammed, the club, on Saturday night. Little colored club in Reno. Six-foot bar and dance floor no bigger than a dime. Old piano with the front wide open, strings showing, and all the hammers of the notes bare, played by a little, fat, coal-black man in shirt sleeves with a glass of gin by his side. A young light-yellow boy beating drums out of this world!

Piano player singing as the dancers dance:

> *I'm goin' down de road and*
> *I won't look back a-tall.*
> *I say, Good-by, mama, it*
> *Ain't no use to call.*

I'm goin' down to Frisco and
I'm goin' by myself.
I'm sorry for you, honey, but
You sho' Lawd will be left.

Sling and Charlie-Mae dancing in a slow embrace. Mrs. Angelina Walls and Terry sitting at the bar drinking.

Angelina really shouldn't have had so many beers, with her education and reserve and all, but when you cook the whole week long for white folks over a hot stove, you need something on a Saturday night.

"A little recreation," she said, "a little recreation!"

"You right," said Terry, downing a straight whisky.

"Gimme another shetland," said Angelina. The barman drew a small glass of beer. "And don't you bother, baby," said Angelina, as Terry reached in his pocket to pay for it. "I make more money'n you do. I'll pay. Hurry up and drink your'n so you can have a glass or two on me."

"O.K.," said Terry, tipsy enough to begin mixing his drinks. "Gimme a shetland, too."

As the music ended, several of the dancers flocked toward the bar, among them Sling and Charlie-Mae, arm in arm.

"Here comes the common herd," said Angelina, but Terry didn't grasp what she said. Charlie-Mae heard, however—and understood, too—as she sat down on a stool and turned her back.

"Gimme two shetlands," Sling called to the barman. "Hy there, buddy," he said to Terry, slapping his pal on the back, "you's huggin' the rail mighty close tonight. Why don't you dance?"

But before Terry could answer, Mrs. Walls explained. "The floor at this club's too full of riffraff for me," she said. "I come here to Reno on a *train,* myself." She was aiming directly at Charlie-Mae sitting beside her.

"That's more'n your boy friend did," said Sling, grinning at Terry.

"Well, if he didn't," said Mrs. Walls in a high half-drunken voice, "he's a real man right on. He earns a decent living shining shoes—not working down in no Chinese rat hole like you, cleaning up after gamblers, and running around with womens what don't know they name."

Sling was shamed into silence—but Charlie-Mae whirled around toward Mrs. Walls and slapped her face. Angelina's beer went all over her dress. Terry pushed Charlie-Mae from her stool. She landed on the floor.

"Don't you touch my woman," Sling yelled at his pal.

"Well, tell her not to touch *my* woman, then," said Terry. "Don't you know who I is? I'm badder'n usual tonight."

"Huh!" said Sling.

"Terry, protect me," Mrs. Walls cried, holding her well-slapped cheek. "A decent girl can't live in this town."

"No, they can't," said Charlie-Mae, rising, "not if they acts like you—and I'm around."

"Don't mess with her," warned Sling, glaring at Terry.

"Man, is you talking to me?" asked Terry of his friend.

"I'm bad," said Sling.

"Is you tryin' to tell *me* who's bad in this town? If there's anybody bad, it's Terry. I'm a terrible terrier this evenin', too!"

"Bark on!" said Sling.

"Listen, honey," pleaded Charlie-Mae loudly in Sling's ear, "do him like you said you did them railroad bulls—slice him down for knocking me off my stool."

Said Terry, "Slice who down?"

"Slice you down," said Sling, "if you fools around with me. You my buddy, and we don't want no trouble, but just leave me and Charlie-Mae alone, that's all, and take your old hinkty heifer out o' here where she belong, 'cause she can't stand no company sides herself. She's a fool!"

"Oh!" screamed Mrs. Walls. "You hear him, Terry? Hit him! Hit him for my sake!"

"If he do, he'll never hit another human," said Sling slowly.

"Boy," said Terry, "I'll pickle you in a minute in your own blood."

"And you'll be sliced baloney," said Sling.

"Not me!" cried Terry drawing a switch-blade and backing toward the wall. His knife was the kind that has a little button in it and double action. When you push the button once, the blade flies out halfway. When you push it twice, it flies out about six inches.

Switch-blades are dangerous weapons, but Sling was prepared. He drew a razor, a good old steel razor, slightly outmoded for shaving, but still useful for defense.

Didn't nobody holler, "Don't let 'em fight!"

On a Saturday night in a little club, down by the railroad track out West, in a town between the mountains, what could be more fun than a good fight with knives and razors? It didn't matter if they were buddies, them boys—didn't nobody holler, "Stop that fight!"

Women stood on stools and tables. The barman got on a beer keg behind the bar. The piano player brought his piano stool nearer the scene of combat.

Folks had to hold Charlie-Mae to keep her from attacking Angelina, for two fights at the same time would have spoilt the fun.

"You women wait," everybody said.

"Boy, I'm tellin' you, I mean business," warned Sling, his eyes red, his teeth shining, and his feelings hurt. "Don't come a-near me!"

"I done heard so much from you about how bad you is," said Terry. "I just want to see. You been my pal, but I believe you's lyin' about your badness."

His long face was a shiny oval under his derby. He was trembling.

"I'll cut you down," said Sling, "like you warn't no friend."

"Cut then—and don't talk," said Terry, " 'cause I'm quicker'n greased lightnin' and I'm liable to get you first."

Suddenly his knife flashed and Sling's left coat sleeve split like a torn ribbon—swiss-ss-sh! But at the same time Sling's razor made a moonlike upward movement and cut straight through the brim of Terry's derby, narrowly missing an eyebrow.

The crowd roared. It was getting good. Didn't nobody say, "Don't let them boys fight."

Sling, with a quick movement of his arm, sent the derby swirling through space and brought his weapon back into play for a slash at Terry's vitals, his flying razor cutting a wide gash straight across his friend's middle, slicing the front of Terry's pants open at the belt and exposing several layers of undergarments. But Terry's switch-blade went deep into Sling's fashionably padded shoulder before either stepped back.

Both began to bleed, but nobody fell. Their new and still unpaid-for suits got cut and stained. Blood dropped down on their two-tone shoes as the fighters stood apart, panting for a few moments.

A loud murmur went up from the crowd, and Mrs. Walls screamed, "My God!" as Sling's razor found the mark it had been looking for— a place where a cut would always show on a man so that people could say that he, Sling, had put it there. He slit the side of Terry's face right down, from temple to chin.

"Sling," Terry cried, "don't do that to me! Man, I'm bad! I'm telling you, I'm bad and I'll hurt you!"

"Lemme see," said Sling, panting against the bar, "I'se heard tell you's bad. Lemme see."

"I'll show you," said Terry, charging so swiftly that before Sling could sidestep, he ran his knife all the way up to the hilt in his companion's side—and left it there.

Sling looked down, saw where the knife had lodged, gasped, trembled, rolled his eyes up, and crumpled backward to the floor.

Terry saw his pal go down, taking the knife with him embedded in his sky-blue coat, his mouth agape, his razor arm limp, his eyes like eggs. And something about the sight of that falling body made his own limbs begin to shake, his knees grow weaker, his bleeding jaw hurt more and more, and his throat fill up with his beating heart. Suddenly, he, too, passed out, sinking prone upon the floor.

"Here! Here! Here!" barked the bartender as he saw them both topple, "you two boys done fought enough now. Cut it out, I say! Cut it out!"

He jumped over the bar and pushed his way through the crowd. As Charlie-Mae shrieked hysterically and strong men turned their heads, the bartender stooped and pulled the knife from Sling's side.

"Funny," he said, frowning sharply, "there ain't no blood on this knife! Some of you-all take care o' Terry yonder while I see after this boy."

The bartender raised Sling up, but his unseeing head fell limply backward. Others crowded near to help and to stare. They took off his sky-blue coat. One arm was bloody. They took off his vest, too, and unbuttoned his lemon-cream shirt. Underneath, he had on a grey sweatshirt. They pulled that off. Under the sweatshirt he wore a ragged purple sweater. They removed that.

"I don't see how any knife ever got to his skin," said one of the helpers, "with all these clothes he's got on."

"I don't believe it did," said the bartender. "His side ain't bleedin'."

And sure enough, when they finally got down to Sling's cocoa-colored skin, he didn't have a scratch on his body—except that old scar across his shoulder. His arm was cut slightly, but his body proper was not harmed in the least.

"Pshaw! That there knife had to go through too many wrappings. He ain't dead," said the bartender disappointedly.

"Boy, you wake up!"

He dropped Sling's head back on the floor with a bang, to turn his attention to Terry. By now, Terry was sitting up, a towel tied around his sliced slit cheek.

"Did I kill him?" Terry moaned. "Is I done kilt my partner?"

"Naw, you ain't killed nobody," the bartender barked. "Both you hucks get up off that floor and let things be as they were before this mess started. Shame on you, lettin' a little blood scare you—till you so weak you have to lay down. Sling, unroll them eyes!"

By this time, Sling's eyes were unrolled, and he felt his half-naked body in amazement at finding it still whole. Only his forearm bled a little where the fleshy part was cut. He sat up to look anxiously across at Terry.

Terry looked back at Sling and then pointed to his wounded jaw.

"Say, boy, is I got me a good scar?"

"Terry," Sling said, his voice shaking, "I thought I'd done killed you."

"I said, boy, is I got me a good scar?"

"Man," Sling said generously, "you got a better scar than I got now— 'cause your'n is gonna be on your face where everybody can see it, and mine's just on my shoulder."

Terry grinned with delight. "All right, then," he said as he rose from the floor.[7] "This fight's been *some* good after all! Get up from there, Sling, and put on your clothes. Let's have a drink."

As Sling gathered up his near-silk shirt and ragged sweater, his well-sliced coat and wrinkled tie, Terry looked around for his "company."

"Where's my lady friend?" he asked.

"Who? Angelina Walls?" some woman answered. "Why, man, she runned out of here no sooner'n she seed you get cut! *She* couldn't be mixed up in no murder trial. She's too respectable."

"A hinkty hussy!" said Sling.

"She is for true," said Terry. "Come on, boy, let's drink."

Sling, his lemon-colored shirt tail out, looked around for his woman. "Charlie-Mae," he said, glaring at his erstwhile sweetie as she emerged all freshly powdered from the Ladies Room, "this boy's my pal, and here you done liked to made me kill him, right this evenin'. You get goin'!"

Charlie-Mae, heeding the look in Sling's eyes, got going. Without a word she donned her rabbit fur and left.

The two big fellows, tattered and torn, key chains dangling and sartorial effects awry, rested their elbows on the bar. They grinned proudly at one another.

"Two shetlands," Sling said to the bartender.

"For two bad men," said Terry, " 'cause we really bad!"

"We slice 'em down," said Sling.

"We really slice 'em down," said Terry.

Tain't So

Miss Lucy Cannon was a right nice old white woman, so Uncle Joe always stated, except that she really did *not* like colored folks, not even after she come out West to California. She could never get over certain little Southern ways she had, and long as she knowed my Uncle Joe, who hauled her ashes for her, she never would call him *Mister*—nor any other colored man *Mister* neither for that matter, not even the minister of the Baptist Church who was a graduate of San Jose State College. Miss Lucy Cannon just wouldn't call colored folks *Mister* nor *Missus*, no matter who they was, neither in Alabama nor in California.

She was always ailing around, too, sick with first one thing and then another. Delicate, and ever so often she would have a fainting spell, like all good Southern white ladies. Looks like the older she got, the more she would be sick and couldn't hardly get around—that is, until she went to a healer and got cured.

And that is one of the funniest stories Uncle Joe ever told me, how old Miss Cannon got cured of her heart and hip in just one cure at the healer's.

Seems like for three years or more she could scarcely walk—even with a cane—had a terrible bad pain in her right leg from her knee up. And on her left side, her heart was always just about to give out. She was in bad shape, that old Southern lady, to be as spry as she was, always giving teas and dinners and working her colored help to death.

Well, Uncle Joe says, one New Year's Day in Pasadena a friend of hers, a Northern lady who was kinda old and retired also and had come out to California to spend her last days, too, and get rid of some parts of her big bank full of money—this old lady told Miss Cannon, "Darling, you just seem to suffer so all the time, and you say you've tried all the doctors, and all kinds of baths and medicines. Why don't you try my way of overcoming? Why don't you try faith?"

"Faith, honey?" says old Miss Lucy Cannon, sipping her jasmine tea.

"Yes, my dear," says the Northern white lady. "Faith! I have one of the best faith-healers in the world."

"Who is he?" asked Miss Lucy Cannon.

"She's a woman, dear," said old Miss Northern white lady. "And she heals by power. She lives in Hollywood."

"Give me her address," said Miss Lucy, "and I'll go to see her. How much do her treatments cost?"

Miss Lucy warn't so rich as some folks thought she was.

"Only Ten Dollars, dearest," said the other lady. "Ten Dollars a treatment. Go, and you'll come away cured."

"I have never believed in such things," said Miss Lucy, "nor disbelieved, either. But I will go and see." And before she could learn any more about the healer, some other friends came in and interrupted the conversation.

A few days later, however, Miss Lucy took herself all the way from Pasadena to Hollywood, put up for the week end with a friend of hers, and thought she would go to see the healer, which she did, come Monday morning early.

Using her customary cane and hobbling on her left leg, feeling a bit bad around the heart, and suffering terribly in her mind, she managed to walk slowly but with dignity a half-dozen blocks through the sunshine to the rather humble street in which was located the office and home of the healer.

In spite of the bright morning air and the good breakfast she had had, Miss Lucy (according to herself) felt pretty bad, racked with pains and crippled to the use of a cane.

When she got to the house she was seeking, a large frame dwelling, newly painted, she saw a sign thereon:

MISS PAULINE JONES

"So that's her name," thought Miss Lucy. "Pauline Jones, Miss Jones."

Ring And Enter said a little card above the bell. So Miss Lucy entered. But the first thing that set her back a bit was that nobody received her, so she just sat down to await Miss Jones, the healer who had, she heard, an enormous following in Hollywood. In fact, that's why she had come early, so she wouldn't have to wait long. Now, it was only nine o'clock. The office was open—but empty. So Miss Lucy simply waited. Ten minutes passed. Fifteen. Twenty. Finally she became all nervous and fluttery. Heart and limb! Pain, pain, pain! Not even a magazine to read.

"Oh, me!" she said impatiently, "What is this? Why, I never!"

There was a sign on the wall that read:

BELIEVE

"I will wait just ten minutes more," said Miss Lucy, glancing at her watch of platinum and pearls.

But before the ten minutes were up, another woman entered the front door and sat down. To Miss Lucy's horror, she was a colored woman! In fact, a big black colored woman!

Said Miss Lucy to herself, "I'll never in the world get used to the North. Now here's a great—my friend says great faith-healer, treating darkies! Why, down in Alabama, a Negro patient wouldn't dare come in here and sit down with white people like this!"

But, womanlike (and having still five minutes to wait), Miss Lucy couldn't keep her mouth shut that long. She just had to talk, albeit to a Negro, so she began on her favorite subject—herself.

"I certainly feel bad this morning," she said to the colored woman, condescending to open the conversation.

"Tain't so," answered the Negro woman placidly—which sort of took Miss Lucy back a bit. She lifted her chin.

"Indeed, it is so," said she indignantly. "My heart is just about to give out. My breath is short."

"Tain't so a-tall," commented the colored woman.

"Why!" gasped Miss Lucy, "such impudence! I tell you *it is so*! I could hardly get down here this morning."

"Tain't so," said the Negro calmly.

"Besides my heart," went on Miss Lucy, "my right hip pains me so I can hardly sit here."

"I say, taint so."

"I tell you it *is* so," screamed Miss Lucy. "Where is the healer? I won't sit here and suffer this—this impudence. I can't! It'll kill me! It's outrageous."

"Tain't so," said the large black woman serenely, whereupon Miss Lucy rose. Her pale face flushed a violent red.

"Where is the healer?" she cried, looking around the room.

"Right here," said the colored woman.

"What?" cried Miss Lucy. "You're the—why—you?"

"I'm Miss Jones."

"Why, I never heard the like," gasped Miss Lucy. "A *colored* woman as famous as you? Why, you must be lying!"

"Tain't so," said the woman calmly.

"Well, I shan't stay another minute," cried Miss Lucy.

"Ten Dollars, then," said the colored woman. "You've had your treatment, anyhow."

"Ten Dollars! That's entirely too much!"

"Tain't so."

Angrily Miss Lucy opened her pocketbook, threw a Ten Dollar bill on the table, took a deep breath, and bounced out. She went three blocks up Sunset Boulevard walking like the wind, conversing with herself.

" 'Tain't so,' " she muttered. " 'Tain't so!' I tell her I'm sick and she says, 'Tain't so!' "

On she went at a rapid gait, stepping like a young girl—so mad she had forgotten all about her infirmities, even her heart—when suddenly she cried, "Lord, have mercy, my cane! For the first time in three years, I'm *without* a cane!"

Then she realized that her breath was giving her no trouble at all. Neither was her leg. Her temper mellowed. The sunshine was sweet and warm. She felt good.

"Colored folks do have some funny kind of supernatural conjuring powers, I reckon," she said smiling to herself. Immediately her face went grim again. "But the impudence of 'em! Soon's they get up North—calling herself *Miss* Pauline Jones. The idea! Putting on airs and charging me Ten Dollars for a handful of *Taint so's*!"

In her mind she clearly heard, "Tain't so!"

One Friday Morning

The thrilling news did not come directly to Nancy Lee, but it came in little indirections that finally added themselves up to one tremendous fact: she had won the prize! But being a calm and quiet young lady, she did not say anything, although the whole high school buzzed with rumors, guesses, reportedly authentic announcements on the part of students who had no right to be making announcements at all—since no student really knew yet who had won this year's art scholarship.

But Nancy Lee's drawing was so good, her lines so sure, her colors so bright and harmonious, that certainly no other student in the senior art class at George Washington High was thought to have very much of a chance. Yet you never could tell. Last year nobody had expected Joe Williams to win the Artist Club scholarship with that funny modernistic water color he had done of the high-level bridge. In fact, it was hard to make out there was a bridge until you had looked at the picture a long time. Still, Joe Williams got the prize, was feted by the community's leading painters, club women, and society folks at a big banquet at the Park-Rose Hotel, and was now an award student at the Art School—the city's only art school.

Nancy Lee Johnson was a colored girl, a few years out of the South. But seldom did her high-school classmates think of her as colored. She was smart, pretty and brown, and fitted in well with the life of the school. She stood high in scholarship, played a swell game of basketball, had taken part in the senior musical in a soft, velvety voice, and had never seemed to intrude or stand out except in pleasant ways, so it was seldom even mentioned—her color.

Nancy Lee sometimes forgot she was colored herself. She liked her classmates and her school. Particularly she liked her art teacher, Miss Dietrich, the tall red-haired woman who taught her law and order in doing things; and the beauty of working step by step until a job is done; a picture finished; a design created; or a block print carved out of nothing but an idea and a smooth square of linoleum, inked, proofs made, and finally put down on paper—clean, sharp, beautiful, individual, unlike any other in the world, thus making the paper have a meaning nobody else could give it except Nancy Lee. That was the wonderful thing about true creation. You made something nobody else on earth could make—but you.

Miss Dietrich was the kind of teacher who brought out the best in her students—but their own best, not anybody else's copied best. For anybody else's best, great though it might be, even Michelangelo's, wasn't enough to please Miss Dietrich dealing with the creative impulses of young men and women living in an American city in the Middle West, and being American.

Nancy Lee was proud of being American, a Negro American with blood out of Africa a long time ago, too many generations back to count. But her parents had taught her the beauties of Africa, its strength, its song, its mighty rivers, its early smelting of iron, its building of the pyramids, and its ancient and important civilizations. And Miss Dietrich had discovered for her the sharp and humorous lines of African sculpture, Benin, Congo, Makonde. Nancy Lee's father was a mail carrier, her mother a social worker in a city settlement house. Both parents had been to Negro colleges in the South. And her mother had gotten a further degree in social work from a Northern university. Her parents were, like most Americans, simple ordinary people who had worked hard and steadily for their education. Now they were trying to make it easier for Nancy Lee to achieve learning than it had been for them. They would be very happy when they heard of the award to their daughter—yet Nancy did not tell them. To surprise them would be better. Besides, there had been a promise.

Casually, one day, Miss Dietrich asked Nancy Lee what color frame she thought would be best on her picture. That had been the first inkling.

"Blue," Nancy Lee said. Although the picture had been entered in the Artist Club contest a month ago, Nancy Lee did not hesitate in her choice of a color for the possible frame since she could still see her picture clearly in her mind's eye—for that picture waiting for the blue frame had come out of her soul, her own life, and had bloomed into miraculous being with Miss Dietrich's help. It was, she knew, the best water color she had painted in her four years as a high-school art student, and she was glad she had made something Miss Dietrich liked well enough to permit her to enter in the contest before she graduated.

It was not a modernistic picture in the sense that you had to look at it a long time to understand what it meant. It was just a simple scene in the city park on a spring day with the trees still leaflessly lacy against the sky, the new grass fresh and green, a flag on a tall pole in the center, children playing, and an old Negro woman sitting on a bench with her head turned. A lot for one picture, to be sure, but it was not there in heavy and final detail like a calendar. Its charm was that everything was light and airy, happy like spring, with a lot of blue sky, paper-white clouds, and air showing through. You could tell that the old Negro woman was looking at the flag, and that the flag was proud in the spring breeze, and that the breeze helped to make the children's dresses billow as they played.

Miss Dietrich had taught Nancy Lee how to paint spring, people, and a breeze on what was only a plain white piece of paper from the supply closet. But Miss Dietrich had not said make it like any other spring-people-breeze ever seen before. She let it remain Nancy Lee's own. That is how the old Negro woman happened to be there looking at the flag—for in her mind the flag, the spring, and the woman formed a kind of triangle holding a dream Nancy Lee wanted to express. White stars on a blue field, spring, children, ever-growing life, and an old woman. Would the judges at the Artist Club like it?

One wet, rainy April afternoon Miss O'Shay, the girls' vice-principal, sent for Nancy Lee to stop by her office as school closed. Pupils without umbrellas or raincoats were clustered in doorways hoping to make it home between showers. Outside the skies were gray. Nancy Lee's thoughts were suddenly gray, too.

She did not think she had done anything wrong, yet that tight little knot came in her throat just the same as she approached Miss O'Shay's door. Perhaps she had banged her locker too often and too hard. Perhaps the note in French she had written to Sallie halfway across the study hall just for fun had never gotten to Sallie but into Miss O'Shay's hands instead. Or maybe she was failing in some subject and wouldn't be allowed to graduate. Chemistry! A pang went through the pit of her stomach.

She knocked on Miss O'Shay's door. That familiarly solid and competent voice said, "Come in."

Miss O'Shay had a way of making you feel welcome, even if you came to be expelled.

"Sit down, Nancy Lee Johnson," said Miss O'Shay. "I have something to tell you." Nancy Lee sat down. "But I must ask you to promise not to tell anyone yet."

"I won't, Miss O'Shay," Nancy Lee said, wondering what on earth the principal had to say to her.

"You are about to graduate," Miss O'Shay said. "And we shall miss you. You have been an excellent student, Nancy, and you will not be without honors on the senior list, as I am sure you know."

At that point there was a light knock on the door. Miss O'Shay called out, "Come in," and Miss Dietrich entered. "May I be a part of this, too?" she asked, tall and smiling.

"Of course," Miss O'Shay said. "I was just telling Nancy Lee what we thought of her. But I hadn't gotten around to giving her the news. Perhaps, Miss Dietrich, you'd like to tell her yourself."

Miss Dietrich was always direct. "Nancy Lee," she said, "your picture has won the Artist Club scholarship."

The slender brown girl's eyes widened, her heart jumped, then her throat tightened again. She tried to smile, but instead tears came to her eyes.

"Dear Nancy Lee," Miss O'Shay said, "we are so happy for you." The elderly white woman took her hand and shook it warmly while Miss Dietrich beamed with pride.

Nancy Lee must have danced all the way home. She never remembered quite how she got there through the rain. She hoped she had been dignified. But certainly she hadn't stopped to tell anybody her secret on the way. Raindrops, smiles, and tears mingled on her brown cheeks. She hoped her mother hadn't yet gotten home and that the house was empty. She wanted to have time to calm down and look natural before she had to see anyone. She didn't want to be bursting with excitement—having a secret to contain.

Miss O'Shay's calling her to the office had been in the nature of a preparation and a warning. The kind, elderly vice-principal said she did not believe in catching young ladies unawares, even with honors, so she wished her to know about the coming award. In making acceptance speeches she wanted her to be calm, prepared, not nervous, overcome, and frightened. So Nancy Lee was asked to think what she would say when the scholarship was conferred upon her a few days hence, both at the Friday morning high-school assembly hour when the announcement would be made, and at the evening banquet of the Artist Club. Nancy Lee promised the vice-principal to think calmly about what she would say.

Miss Dietrich had then asked for some facts about her parents, her background, and her life, since such material would probably be desired for the papers. Nancy Lee had told her how, six years before, they had come up from the Deep South, her father having been successful in achieving a transfer from the one post office to another, a thing he had long sought in order to give Nancy Lee a chance to go to school in the North. Now, they lived in a modest Negro neighborhood, went to see the best plays when they came to town, and had been saving to send

Nancy Lee to art school, in case she were permitted to enter. But the scholarship would help a great deal, for they were not rich people.

"Now Mother can have a new coat next winter," Nancy Lee thought, "because my tuition will all be covered for the first year. And once in art school, there are other scholarships I can win."

Dreams began to dance through her head, plans and ambitions, beauties she would create for herself, her parents, and the Negro people—for Nancy Lee possessed a deep and reverent race pride. She could see the old woman in her picture (really her grandmother in the South) lifting her head to the bright stars on the flag in the distance. A Negro in America! Often hurt, discriminated against, sometimes lynched—but always there were the stars on the blue body of the flag. Was there any other flag in the world that had so many stars? Nancy Lee thought deeply but she could remember none in all the encyclopedias or geographies she had ever looked into.

"Hitch your wagon to a star," Nancy Lee thought, dancing home in the rain. "Who were our flag-makers?"

Friday morning came, the morning when the world would know—her high-school world, the newspaper world, her mother and dad. Dad could not be there at the assembly to hear the announcement, nor see her prize picture displayed on the stage, nor listen to Nancy Lee's little speech of acceptance, but Mother would be able to come, although Mother was much puzzled as to why Nancy Lee was so insistent she be at school on that particular Friday morning.

When something is happening, something new and fine, something that will change your very life, it is hard to go to sleep at night for thinking about it, and hard to keep your heart from pounding, or a strange little knot of joy from gathering in your throat. Nancy Lee had taken her bath, brushed her hair until it glowed, and had gone to bed thinking about the next day, the big day when, before three thousand students, she would be the one student honored, her painting the one painting to be acclaimed as the best of the year from all the art classes of the city. Her short speech of gratitude was ready. She went over it in her mind, not word for word (because she didn't want it to sound as if she had learned it by heart) but she let the thoughts flow simply and sincerely through her consciousness many times.

When the president of the Artist Club presented her with the medal and scroll of the scholarship award, she would say:

"Judges and members of the Artist Club. I want to thank you for this award that means so much to me personally and through me to my people, the colored people of this city who, sometimes, are discouraged and bewildered, thinking that color and poverty are against them. I accept this award with gratitude and pride, not for myself alone, but for my race that believes in American opportunity and American fairness—and the bright stars in our flag. I thank Miss Dietrich and the teachers who made it possible for me to have the knowledge and training that lie behind this honor you have conferred upon my painting. When I came here from the South a few years ago, I was not sure how you would receive me. You received me well. You have given me a chance and helped me along the road I wanted to follow. I suppose the judges know that every week here at assembly the students of this school pledge allegiance to the flag. I shall try to be worthy of that pledge, and of the help and friendship and understanding of my fellow citizens of whatever race or creed, and of our American dream of 'Liberty and justice for all!' "

That would be her response before the students in the morning. How proud and happy the Negro pupils would be, perhaps almost as proud as they were of the one colored star on the football team. Her mother would probably cry with happiness. Thus Nancy Lee went to sleep dreaming of a wonderful tomorrow.

The bright sunlight of an April morning woke her. There was breakfast with her parents—their half-amused and puzzled faces across the table, wondering what could be this secret that made her eyes so bright. The swift walk to school; the clock in the tower almost nine; hundreds of pupils streaming into the long, rambling old building that was the city's largest high school; the sudden quiet of the homeroom after the bell rang; then the teacher opening her record book to call the roll. But just before she began, she looked across the room until her eyes located Nancy Lee.

"Nancy," she said, "Miss O'Shay would like to see you in her office, please."

Nancy Lee rose and went out while the names were being called and the word *present* added its period to each name. Perhaps, Nancy Lee thought, the reporters from the papers had already come. Maybe they wanted to take her picture before assembly, which wasn't until ten o'clock. (Last year they had had the photograph of the winner of the award in the morning papers as soon as the announcement had been made.)

Nancy Lee knocked at Miss O'Shay's door.

"Come in."

The vice-principal stood at her desk. There was no one else in the room. It was very quiet.

"Sit down, Nancy Lee," she said. Miss O'Shay did not smile.

There was a long pause. The seconds went by slowly. "I do not know how to tell you what I have to say," the elderly woman began, her eyes on the papers on her desk. "I am indignant and ashamed for myself and for this city." Then she lifted her eyes and looked at Nancy Lee in the neat blue dress sitting there before her. "You are not to receive the scholarship this morning."

Outside in the hall the electric bells announcing the first period rang, loud and interminably long. Miss O'Shay remained silent. To the brown girl there in the chair, the room grew suddenly smaller, smaller, smaller, and there was no air. She could not speak.

Miss O'Shay said, "When the committee learned that you were colored, they changed their plans."

Still Nancy Lee said nothing, for there was no air to give breath to her lungs.

"Here is the letter from the committee, Nancy Lee." Miss O'Shay picked it up and read the final paragraph to her.

" 'It seems to us wiser to arbitrarily rotate the award among the various high schools of the city from now on. And especially in this case since the student chosen happens to be colored, a circumstance which unfortunately, had we known, might have prevented this embarrassment. But there have never been any Negro students in the local art school, and the presence of one there might create difficulties for all concerned. We have high regard for the quality of Nancy Lee Johnson's talent, but we do not feel it would be fair to honor it with the Artist Club award.' " Miss O'Shay paused. She put the letter down.

"Nancy Lee, I am very sorry to have to give you this message."

"But my speech," Nancy Lee said, "was about . . . ." The words stuck in her throat. " . . . about America. . . ."

Miss O'Shay had risen, she turned her back and stood looking out the window at the spring tulips in the school yard.

"I thought, since the award would be made at assembly right after our oath of allegiance," the words tumbled almost hysterically from Nancy Lee's throat now, "I would put part of the flag salute in my speech. You know, Miss O'Shay, that part about 'liberty and justice for all.' "

"I know," said Miss O'Shay slowly facing the room again. "But America is only what we who believe in it, make it. I am Irish. You may not know, Nancy Lee, but years ago we were called the dirty Irish, and mobs rioted against us in the big cities, and we were invited to go back where we came from. But we didn't go. And we didn't give up, because we believed in the American dream, and in our power to make that dream come true. Difficulties, yes. Mountains to climb, yes. Discouragements to face, yes. Democracy to make, yes. That is it, Nancy Lee! We still have in this world of ours democracy to *make*. You and I, Nancy Lee. But the premise and the base are here, the lines of the Declaration of Independence and the words of Lincoln are here, and the stars in our flag. Those who deny you this scholarship do not know the meaning of those stars, but it's up to us to make them know. As a teacher in the public schools of this city, I myself will go before the school board and ask them to remove from our system the offer of any prizes or awards denied to any student because of race or color."

Suddenly Miss O'Shay stopped speaking. Her clear, clear blue eyes looked into those of the girl before her. The woman's eyes were full of strength and courage. "Lift up your head, Nancy Lee, and smile at me."

Miss O'Shay stood against the open window with the green lawn and the tulips beyond, the sunlight tangled in her gray hair, her voice an electric flow of strength to the hurt spirit of Nancy Lee. The Abolitionists who believed in freedom when there was slavery must have been like that. The first white teachers who went into the Deep South to teach the freed slaves must have been like that. All those who stand against ignorance, narrowness, hate, and mud on stars must be like that.

Nancy Lee lifted her head and smiled. The bell for assembly rang. She went through the long hall filled with students toward the auditorium.

"There will be other awards," Nancy Lee thought. "There're schools in other cities. This won't keep me down. But when I'm a woman, I'll fight to see that these things don't happen to other girls as this has happened to me. And men and women like Miss O'Shay will help me."

She took her seat among the seniors. The doors of the auditorium closed. As the principal came onto the platform, the students rose and turned their eyes to the flag on the stage.

One hand went to the heart, the other outstretched toward the flag. Three thousand voices spoke. Among them was the voice of a dark girl whose cheeks were suddenly wet with tears, " . . . one nation indivisible, with liberty and justice for all."

"That is the land we must make," she thought.

Professor

Promptly at seven a big car drew up in front of the Booker T. Washington Hotel, and a white chauffeur in uniform got out and went toward the door, intending to ask at the desk for a colored professor named T. Walton Brown. But the professor was already sitting in the lobby, a white scarf around his neck and his black overcoat ready to button over his dinner clothes.

As soon as the chauffeur entered, the professor approached. "Mr. Chandler's car?" he asked hesitantly.

"Yes, sir," said the white chauffeur to the neat little Negro. "Are you Dr. Walton Brown?"

"I am," said the professor, smiling and bowing a little.

The chauffeur opened the street door for Dr. Brown, then ran to the car and held the door open there, too. Inside the big car and on the long black running board as well, the lights came on. The professor stepped in among the soft cushions, the deep rug, and the cut glass vases holding flowers. With the greatest of deference the chauffeur quickly tucked a covering of fur about the professor's knees, closed the door, entered his own seat in front beyond the glass partition, and the big car purred away. Within the lobby of the cheap hotel a few ill-clad Negroes watched the whole procedure in amazement.

"A big shot!" somebody said.

At the corner as the car passed, two or three ash-colored children ran across the street in front of the wheel, their skinny legs and poor clothes plain in the glare of the headlights as the chauffeur slowed down to let them pass. Then the car turned and ran the whole length of a Negro street that was lined with pawn shops, beer joints, pig's knuckle stands, cheap movies, hairdressing parlors, and other ramshackle places of business patronized by the poor blacks of the district. Inside the big car the professor, Dr. Walton Brown, regretted that in all the large Midwestern cities where he had lectured on his present tour in behalf of his college, the main Negro streets presented the same sleazy and disagreeable appearance: pig's knuckle joints, pawn shops, beer parlors—and houses of vice, no doubt—save that these latter, at least, did not hang out their signs.

The professor looked away from the unpleasant sight of this typical Negro street, poor and unkempt. He looked ahead through the glass at the dignified white neck of the uniformed chauffeur in front of him. The professor in his dinner clothes, his brown face even browner above the white silk scarf at his neck, felt warm and comfortable under the fur rug. But he felt, too, a little unsafe at being driven through the streets of this city on the edge of the South in an expensive car, by a white chauffeur.

"But, then," he thought, "this is the wealthy Mr. Ralph P. Chandler's car, and surely no harm can come to me here. The Chandlers are a power in the Middle West, and in the South as well. Theirs is one of the great fortunes of America. In philanthropy, nobody exceeds them in well-planned generosity on a large and highly publicized scale. They are a power in Negro education, too.[8] That is why I am visiting them tonight at their invitation."

Just now the Chandlers were interested in the little Negro college at which the professor taught. They wanted to make it one of the major Negro colleges of America. And in particular the Chandlers were interested in his Department of Sociology. They were thinking of endowing a chair of research there and employing a man of ability for it. A Ph.D. and a scholar. A man of some prestige, like the professor. For his *The Sociology of Prejudice* (that restrained and conservative study of Dr. T. Walton Brown's) had recently come to the attention of the Chandler Committee. And a representative of their philanthropies, visiting the campus, had conversed with the professor at some length about his book and his views. This representative of the Committee found Dr. Brown highly gratifying, because in almost every case the professor's views agreed with the white man's own.

"A fine, sane, dependable young Negro," was the description that came to the Chandler Committee from their traveling representative.

So now the power himself, Mr. Ralph P. Chandler, and Mrs. Chandler, learning that he was lecturing at one of the colored churches of the town, had invited him to dinner at their mansion in this city on the edge of the South. Their car had come to call for him at the colored Booker T. Washington Hotel—where the hot water was always cold, the dresser drawers stuck, and the professor shivered as he got into his dinner clothes; and the bellboys, anxious for a tip, had asked him twice that evening if he needed a half pint or a woman.

But now he was in this big warm car and they were moving swiftly down a fine boulevard, the black slums far behind them. The professor was glad. He had been very much distressed at having the white chauffeur call for him at this cheap hotel in what really amounted to the red-light district of the town. But, then, none of the white hotels in this American city would house Negroes, no matter how cultured they might be. Marian Anderson herself had been unable to find decent accommodations there, so the colored papers said, on the day of her concert.

Sighing, the professor looked out of the car at the wide lawns and fine homes that lined the beautiful well-lighted boulevard where white people lived. After a time the car turned into a fashionable suburban road and he saw no more houses, but only ivy-hung walls, neat shrubs, and boxwoods that indicated not merely homes beyond but vast estates. Shortly the car whirled into a paved driveway, past a small lodge, through a park full of fountains and trees, and up to a private house as large as a hotel. From a tall portico a great hanging lantern cast a soft glow on the black and chrome body of the big car. The white chauffeur jumped out and deferentially opened the door for the colored professor. An English butler welcomed him at the entrance and took his coat, hat, and scarf. Then he led the professor into a large drawing room where two men and a woman were standing chatting near the fireplace.

The professor hesitated, not knowing who was who; but Mr. and Mrs. Chandler came forward, introduced themselves, shook hands, and in turn presented their other guest of the evening, Dr. Bulwick of the local Municipal College—a college that Dr. Brown recalled did *not* admit Negroes.

"I am happy to know you," said Dr. Bulwick. "I am also a sociologist."

"I have heard of you," said Dr. Brown graciously.

The butler came with sherry in a silver pitcher. They sat down, and the whites began to talk politely, to ask Dr. Brown about his lecture tour, if his audiences were good, if they were mostly Negro or mixed, and if there was much interest in his college, much money being given.

Then Dr. Bulwick began to ask about his book, *The Sociology of Prejudice,* where he got his material, under whom he had studied, and if he thought the Negro Problem would ever be solved.

Dr. Brown said genially, "We are making progress," which was what he always said, though he often felt he was lying.

"Yes," said Dr. Bulwick, "that is very true. Why, at our city college here we've been conducting some fine interracial experiments. I have had several colored ministers and high-school teachers visit my classes. We found them most intelligent people."

In spite of himself Dr. Brown had to say, "But you have no colored students at your college, have you?"

"No," said Dr. Bulwick, "and that is too bad! But that is one of our difficulties here. There is no Municipal College for Negroes—although nearly forty per cent of our population is colored. Some of us have thought it might be wise to establish a separate junior college for our Negroes, but the politicians opposed it on the score of no funds. And we cannot take them as students on our campus. That, at present, is impossible. It's too bad."

"But do you not think, Dr. Brown," interposed Mrs. Chandler, who wore diamonds on her wrists and smiled every time she spoke, "do you not think *your* people are happier in schools of their own—that it is really better for both groups not to mix them?"

In spite of himself Dr. Brown replied, "That depends, Mrs. Chandler. I could not have gotten my degree in any schools of our own."

"True, true," said Mr. Chandler. "Advanced studies, of course, cannot be gotten. But when your colleges are developed—as we hope they will be, and our Committee plans to aid in their development—when their departments are headed by men like yourself, for instance, then you can no longer say, 'That depends.'"

"You are right," Dr. Brown agreed diplomatically, coming to himself and thinking of his mission in that house. "You are right," Dr. Brown said, thinking too of that endowed chair of sociology and himself in the chair, the six thousand dollars[9] a year that he would probably be paid, the surveys he might make and the books he could publish. "You are right," said Dr. Brown diplomatically to Ralph P. Chandler. But in the back of his head was that ghetto street full of sleazy misery he had just driven through, and the segregated hotel where the hot water was always cold, and the colored churches where he lectured, and the Jim Crow schools where Negroes always had less equipment and far less money than white institutions; and that separate justice of the South where his people sat on trial but the whites were judge and jury forever; and all the segregated Jim Crow things that America gave Negroes and that were never equal to the things she gave the whites. But Dr. Brown said, "You are right, Mr. Chandler," for, after all, Mr. Chandler had the money!

So he began to talk earnestly to the Chandlers there in the warm drawing room about the need for bigger and better black colleges, for more and more surveys of *Negro* life, and a well-developed department of sociology at his own little institution.

"Dinner is served," said the butler.

They rose and went into a dining room where there were flowers on the table and candles, white linen and silver, and where Dr. Brown was seated at the right of the hostess and the talk was light over the soup, but serious and sociological again by the time the meat was served.

"The American Negro must not be taken in by communism," Dr. Bulwick was saying with great positiveness as the butler passed the peas.

"He won't," agreed Dr. Brown. "I assure you, our leadership stands squarely against it." He looked at the Chandlers and bowed. "All the best people stand against it."

"America has done too much for the Negro," said Mr. Chandler, "for him to seek to destroy it."

Dr. Brown bobbed and bowed.

"In your *Sociology of Prejudice*," said Dr. Bulwick, "I highly approve of the closing note, your magnificent appeal to the old standards of Christian morality and the simple concepts of justice by which America functions."

"Yes," said Dr. Brown, nodding his dark head and thinking suddenly how on six thousand dollars a year he might take his family to South America in the summer where for three months they wouldn't feel like Negroes. "Yes, Dr. Bulwick," he nodded, "I firmly believe as you do that if the best elements of both races came together in Christian fellowship, we would solve this problem of ours."

"How beautiful," said Mrs. Chandler.

"And practical, too," said her husband. "But now to come back to your college—university, I believe you call it—to bring that institution up to really first-class standards you would need . . . ?"

"We would need . . ." said Dr. Brown, speaking as a mouthpiece of the administration, and speaking, too, as mouthpiece for the Negro students of his section of the South, and speaking for himself as a once ragged youth who had attended the college when its rating was lower than that of a Northern high school so that he had to study two years in Boston before he could enter a white college, when he had worked nights as redcap in the station and then as a waiter for seven years until he got his Ph.D., and then couldn't get a job in the North but had to go back down South to the work where he was now—but which might develop into a glorious opportunity at six thousand dollars a year to make surveys and put down figures that other scholars might study to get their Ph.D.'s, and that would bring him in enough to just once take his family on a vacation to South America where they wouldn't feel that they were Negroes. "We would need, Mr. Chandler, . . ."

And the things Dr. Brown's little college needed were small enough in the eyes of the Chandlers. The sane and conservative way in which

Dr. Brown presented his case delighted the philanthropic heart of the Chandlers. And Mr. Chandler and Dr. Bulwick both felt that instead of building a junior college for Negroes in their own town they could rightfully advise local colored students to go down South to that fine little campus where they had a professor of their own race like Dr. Brown.

Over the coffee, in the drawing room, they talked about the coming theatrical season. And Mrs. Chandler spoke of how she loved Negro singers, and smiled and smiled.

In due time the professor rose to go. The car was called and he shook hands with Dr. Bulwick and the Chandlers. The white people were delighted with Dr. Brown. He could see it in their faces, just as in the past he could always tell as a waiter when he had pleased a table full of whites by tender steaks and good service.

"Tell the president of your college he shall hear from us shortly," said the Chandlers. "We'll probably send a man down again soon to talk to him about his expansion program." And they bowed farewell.

As the car sped him back toward town, Dr. Brown sat under its soft fur rug among the deep cushions and thought how with six thousand dollars a year earned by dancing properly to the tune of Jim Crow education, he could carry his whole family to South America for a summer where they wouldn't need to feel like Negroes.

Name in the Papers

I always did wonder what I'd do if some husband or other came home some time and caught me with his wife. Now it's happened. I'm reading about it in the papers.

Her name was Deedee, but that was the only thing French about her. Otherwise she was pure Harlem.

I met her at a party and the drinks were mixed. How should I know she was married? She came in alone, so I took her under my wing. There were too many other wolves around to leave her unprotected.

I said, "Have one."

She said, "Sure."

The next time they turned on the radio we got together and danced the rest of the evening. She was 100%! I liked her style, so I said, "Baby, who's the big boss?"

She said, "He works nights."

I said, "That's the old gag, honey. So do I."

She said, "Aw, now, you quit!"

I said, "I'm not made that way."

By that time she was tickled all over. Me, too.

I said, "Have one more."

She said, "Sure."

I mixed it myself. Then some guy sat down at the piano and started playing that old song about the Lazy River and the old mill stream.

I said, "I can't stand it no more. Let's go."

Of all the homes to stay away from, I'm tellin' you now, avoid those where the husband works nights. I could tell she was really married the minute I got in her door. The house had a no-place-like-home look.

I said, "Honey, are you *sure* he works all night?"

She said, "Of course, he does. I wouldn't lie to you."

But somehow, neither one of us realized night was nearly up then! We'd left that party pretty late. (And I had really *mixed* those drinks!) Besides, you know how long it stays dark on winter mornings!

It was dark that day, I tell you! Because the next thing I knew, her husband was home. He came right home at daybreak like a good husband. The afternoon papers said he arrived at seven A.M., but it seemed like the middle of the night to me. Nevertheless, he arrived. When I saw him, I said, "Hy, Buddy!"

He said, "Hy, hell!" And pulled out a pistol.

Now, that was the moment I had always wondered about. Just what would I do? Fight, run, or holler? But the truth is, I didn't do anything—because the next thing I knew I was in the hospital, shot everywhere but in my big toe. He fired on me point-blank—and barefooted. I was nothing but a target.

"Nurse, is there anything about me in the *Daily News?* Is my name in the papers?"

Powder-White Faces

It was good to feel the sea spray on his face again, to look up at the stars rocking in the sky, to breathe the great, clean rush of wind from the open ocean as the deck swayed beneath his feet.

The little old freighter had slipped down the East River past the lights of New York like a glittering wall to starboard. Charlie Lee, messboy, lit a cigarette, inhaled once, and threw it into the water.

"We're off, heh, mate?" said a white seaman leaning on the rail beside the Oriental.

"Yep," Charlie Lee said. "Long gone this time."

The Statue of Liberty holding its light moved back into the darkness. Staten Island sliding by, Brooklyn on the other side starry with lights, moved back into darkness.

"Goodnight," said the seaman, "I'm turnin' in."

" 'Night," said Charlie Lee. He lit another cigarette, and listened to the heavy beat of the engines settle into an even rhythm of full steam ahead, a beat that would not be silent for several weeks to come. In a certain steady way the waves hit the boatside, the masts rocked against the sky, the weight of the rail pressed on Charlie's chest and then fell away. All this sea movement would go on for many days. Charlie was glad his next port would be Cape Town, thousands of miles from Manhattan—for that morning Charlie had killed a woman.

As Charlie Lee stood by the ship's side looking out into the watery darkness of the Atlantic, he tried to think why he had done it. But he could not think why, he could only *feel* why. He could feel again, standing by the rail, all the hatred and anger of a lifetime that had suddenly that morning collected in his heart and gathered in his fingers at the sight of a white face and a red mouth on the pillow beneath him.

Charlie Lee had killed a *white* woman just twelve hours ago.

Charlie Lee. That wasn't his real name. Charlie had almost forgotten his real name. But Charlie Lee was a good name, he thought. It didn't sound oriental like the names of most of the people on the little American possession in the Pacific from which he had come. It was better than a name like Ali Woo or Kakawali or Chung Sing.

But the name didn't really matter. What mattered was that Charlie's face was brown, his eyes slanted, and his hair heavy and black like a Chinese. Because of his color and perhaps his eyes, American ships wouldn't hire him for any work but a steward's or a kitchen boy's. American or English officers on his own island wouldn't give him a clerk's job if they could find a white person to fill it. And no white woman would marry him unless she were down and out.

But a white man, very long ago, had taken his youngest sister for a mistress, and she had borne him four children.

That was before Charlie grew up, changed his name, and went away to sea as a cabin boy on a tramp steamer bound for Frisco. For nearly ten years Charlie had never been back home. Sailing all the world. The Pacific, the Atlantic, the Mediterranean. Many cities, many people. White, brown, and yellow people. Stopping a while to work ashore in California vineyards; one winter as a Santa Barbara houseboy; another winter in a New York elevator on Riverside Drive, up and down, up and down. And between times, the sea, the great, clean, old sea rocking beneath his feet—like tonight.

Now, Charlie Lee stood at the tramp's rail with the wind blowing in his face wondering why he had killed that white woman this morning. He had never killed anybody in his life before. And this woman had really done nothing to him. Not *this* woman. Then why did he kill *her*? But when he tried to figure it out, he kept remembering other white women (not the one he had killed, but *other* women), port-town women, taxi-dance-hall women, women with powder-white faces who took all they could get from him and then let him go, called him names, kicked him out, or had him beaten up.

It began with the girls in Mollie's Tropical Beer Garden where he had worked at home out in the Pacific before he grew up and changed his name. There he ran errands for the white hostesses and the American marines. There, he often heard the girls declare they couldn't have anything to do with a native because if they did Uncle Sam's boys wouldn't have anything to do with them. So the policy of Mollie's Beer Garden was WHITE ONLY insofar as her customers went. (There was a sign over the bar to that effect.) And although the waiters were native brown boys, the bartender—the only one who got a salary—was Irish. The brown boys worked for tips alone.

When Charlie went away to sea, the next foreign women he knew were White Russians under the carnival lights of Shanghai, rapacious females, hungry and diseased, who haunted the bars, dives, and dance halls, sleeping with anyone who could pay them, and picking pockets in the bargain. They cleaned Charlie out of all his money while his ship was in dock. And the doctors put him in the Marine Hospital when he reached San Francisco ill.

When he got better, he found a job in the grape orchards on the coast and experienced all the prejudices of white California toward the brown people from across the Pacific. Even if you were from an *American* island, it didn't seem to make any difference.

After two years in California Charlie went to sea again as a cabin boy on a freighter. San Diego, Colon, Havana, the Gulf ports. Then he got in jail, for the first time, at New Orleans.

All the messboys went out together their first night in port, to a wineshop on St. Louis Street. Along the street the shutters kept clicking and white women kept looking out at the little Orientals in their broad-shouldered suits and highly polished shoes. Sometimes the women whispered, "Come in, baby." But the boys kept on to a place where they were sure they were welcome, for in this wineshop there were women, too. Rather faded women, it's true, a little old or a little ugly or a little droopy—but the best the Italian proprietor could get for a bar that catered to yellow-brown boys from the ships, for seldom did white sailors come there, and almost never men of the city.

But tonight, by chance, a group of white men did come—not sailors, but young Southern rowdies about town looking for fun. They were already half drunk, and they weren't used to seeing (as sailors would have been) brown men and white women mixing. They felt hurt about it as they stood drinking at the bar. They felt insulted. They got mad. They wanted to protect white womanhood.

"Let's clean out the spicks," one of them whispered.

A big guy turned on Charlie.

"Take your eyes off that white woman, coon," he said, hitting him across the mouth, wham! without warning.

Charlie staggered to his feet. His friends drew knives. The girls screamed and gathered behind the white men. Fists flew. A fight was on.

The next thing Charlie knew, he regained consciousness in a cell. Alone, his face battered, his clothes torn, his money and watch gone, he felt sick and his head whirled. There were iron bars all around him like a cage. His body hurt. And his soul hurt, too.

The last thing he remembered before the big white fellow knocked him out was that the girl whom he had just treated to a drink suddenly spat in his face. Charlie never forgot that. The judge gave him ten days in jail for disturbing the peace, and he missed his boat. For nearly a month he went hungry in New Orleans, but finally he managed to ship out on a coastwise steamer to New York. The salt of the sea healed the purple bruises on his face.

In Manhattan he got a job as elevator boy in a busy house on the Drive. Nights he spent in the taxi-dance halls above Columbus Circle frequented by sleek-haired little brown fellows, Filipinos, Hawaiians, and Chinese, dancing and dancing to rhumbas that were like the palm trees swaying in his native islands.

There were lots of white girls, powdered pink and blonde, who worked in these dance halls and lived on the boys who went to dance there. Once Charlie was in love with one of these hostesses. He kept bringing her all his money every week, until she said one night, "Darling, you don't make enough for me. Why don't you gamble or something and get some real dough?"

So Charlie began to lose all his wages trying to win more for her. Every week he lost. He worried about her, kept stopping the elevator at the wrong floors with her on his mind, and finally got fired from his job. Of course she left him.

When he found work again it was as houseboy for a rich young man named Richards who had an apartment on lower Fifth Avenue.

He had plenty to do, but he was well paid. He liked the boss, and the boss liked him. But Charlie didn't like Mr. Richards' mistress. He found her too much like the girls in the taxi-dance halls, or in St. Louis Street in New Orleans, hard, rapacious, and crude. But sometimes, for days, he wouldn't see Mr. Richards—only this woman. And, as time went on, she became more and more familiar with Charlie, said things to him that she shouldn't say to a servant, kidded him, walked around before him in pink silk things that were only shadows, smiling. Charlie hated her. Even when she put all her jewels on—blonde as a beauty shop and sprinkled with perfume—she still made him think of Shanghai[10] and the hungry little Russian girls of Avenue Joffre who had stolen his money and left him ill years ago, and the white woman who spat in his face in New Orleans, and the dance-hall girl who left him when he went broke and had no job.

"Why can't Mr. Richards see what she's like?" Charlie wondered. "Me see."

Yet she was always nice to Charlie. Bold and invitingly nice. Even when she asked him to go out and buy dope for her and he refused, she didn't really mind. She only purred, "Don't tell Richie, will you?" as she went to the phone to order the white powder from a druggist she knew.

Now, Charlie recalled as he stood by the ship's rail, she and Mr. Richards kept talking about the dog races last night at the table during dinner. Later they went out and returned long after midnight. Charlie didn't hear them come in, but early in the morning the telephone rang. Long distance, Chicago calling. He woke Mr. Richards, who got all excited as he listened to the voice at the other end of the line. He kept talking about a merger, merger, merger. Finally he said, "I'll be there today." Then he called Charlie to pack his bag. "Flying to Chicago right away," he said. "Call a cab."

He kissed his blonde woman lying drowsy on the silken bed and, without eating, rushed out at dawn. Charlie didn't see him any more. In a few minutes the tragedy happened.

The blonde woman said, "Come here, Charlie." When Charlie came near the bed, she took him by his silky hair and pulled him down close to her breast.

"You're a cute China boy!" she said. "Kiss me."

But Charlie drew away. A sudden combination of anger and loathing came into his eyes. Fear and hatred. Distrust, suspicion, contempt for her lack of loyalty. What do you want with me? What's your game? What are you trying to gyp me out of? What do you want to do? I'm not your color! I know you too well—you and all your kind! You never played square by me, just like you don't play square by Mr. Richards. You white women, you cheats!

"Charlie," she said.

His brown hands gently sought her face, her chin. And suddenly closed on her throat. She did not even scream. Her mouth opened, but was silent. No breath, no sound. And Charlie didn't know why he did it.

Charlie suddenly remembered three Americans who killed a brown man in Honolulu over a white woman. He remembered the iron bars around him in New Orleans. And the powder-white faces of the Russian girls in Shanghai. And the hostesses in Mollie's Beer Garden, FOR WHITE ONLY. All the hidden resentment of years seemed to collect in his heart and gather in his fingers as the red mouth slowly opened on the pillow beneath him.

He did not want her. He only wanted to kill her—this woman who became suddenly *all* white women to him.

As he locked the apartment and went out into the early morning air he smelled the sea again—the sea into which you can pour all the filth of the world, but the water never gets dirty.

Rouge High

Two streetwalkers came in and began to powder their faces. The waiter slid a couple of glasses of water along the counter and was about to take their order when a tall young fellow entered and knocked one of the girls plumb off the stool with a blow in the face.

"Here, honey! Take it! Here it is!" she began to yell.

Before she got up off the floor, she took a wrinkled bill from somewhere down in her bosom and gave it to him.

"Tryin' to hold out on me," said the fellow as he turned on his heel and left.

The girl got back up on the stool and went on powdering her face. She didn't shed a single tear.

"Ham and eggs, scrambled," said her companion.

"Nothin' but coffee for me," said the one who had been hit. "Them shots the doc gave me this mornin' made me sick. I can't eat a thing."

"Shots are hell," said the other one. "But, say, girlie, listen. What made Bunny think you was holdin' out on him?"

"He didn't think it, he knew it! He's pretty smart at figgerin' out what a John'll pay—that's why he's always on the corner lookin' 'em over when they come along. Bunny's an old hand at gettin' his."

"Then why didn't you give it to him then?"

"Aw, he ain't so wise as he thinks he is," said the girl as the waiter put her cup of coffee down in front of her. "Listen, I stole that last customer's pocketbook, too. And, believe me, I ain't splittin' these extra bucks with nobody!"

From somewhere under her clothes she pulled out a man's brown wallet, took out the money, and tossed the pocketbook across the counter to the waiter.

"Hey, kid," she said, "put that way down in the garbage can, underneath the coffee grounds. Get me?"

"I got you," the waiter said.

"What you gonna do, buy a new dress?" asked the other girl enviously.

"Naw, I got to pay the doctor for them shots."

She drank her coffee. When they went out, she gave the waiter a good tip.

"Honey," said the other girl as she opened the door, "your eye's gettin' black where Bunny hit you. Put a little more powder on it—or else rouge high."

On the Way Home

Carl was not what you would call a drinking man. Not that he had any moral scruples about drinking, for he prided himself on being broad-minded. But he had always been told that his father (whom he couldn't remember) was a drunkard. So in the back of his head, he didn't really feel it right to get drunk. Except for perhaps a glass of wine on holidays, or a bottle of beer if he was out with a party and didn't want to be conspicuous, he was a teetotaler.

Carl had promised his mother not to drink *at all*. He was an only child, fond of his mother. But she had raised him with almost too much kindness. To adjust himself to people who were less kind had been hard. But since there were no good jobs in Sommerville, he came away to Chicago to work. Every month, for a Sunday, he went back home, taking the four o'clock bus Saturday afternoon, which put him off in front of his boyhood door in time for supper—with country butter, fresh milk, and home-made bread.

After supper he would go uptown with his mother in the cool of evening, if it was summer, to do her Saturday-night shopping. Or if it was winter, they might go over to a neighbor's house and pop corn or drink cider. Or friends might come to their home and sit around the parlor talking and playing old records on an old victrola—Sousa's marches, Nora Bayes, Bert Williams, Caruso—records that most other people had long ago thrown away or forgotten.[11] It was fun, old-fashioned, and very different from the rum parties most of his office friends indulged in in Chicago.

Carl had definitely promised his mother and himself not to drink. But this particular afternoon, he stood in front of a long counter in a liquor store on Clark Street and heard himself say, strangely enough, "A bottle of wine."

"What kind of wine?" the clerk asked brusquely.

"That kind," Carl answered, pointing to a row of tall yellow bottles on the middle shelf. It just happened that his finger stopped at the yellow bottles. He did not know the names or brands of wines.

"That's sweet wine," the clerk said.

"That's all right," Carl affirmed, for he wanted to get the wine quickly and go.

The clerk wrapped the bottle, made change, and turned to another customer. Carl took the bottle and went out. He walked slowly, yet he could hardly wait to get to his room. He had never been so anxious to drink before. He might have stopped at a bar, since he passed many, but he was not used to drinking at bars. So he went to his room.

It was quiet in the big, dark, old rooming house. There was no one in the hall as he went up the wide, creaking staircase. All the roomers were at work. It was Tuesday. He would have been at work, too, had he not received at the office about noon a wire that his mother was suddenly very ill, and he had better come home. He knew there was no bus until four o'clock. It was one now. He would get ready to go soon. But he needed a drink. Did not men sometimes drink to steady their nerves? In novels they took a swig of brandy—but brandy made Carl sick. Wine would be better—milder.

In his room he tore open the package and uncorked the bottle even before he hung his hat in the closet. He took his toothbrush out of a glass on his dresser and poured the glass a third full of the amber-yellow wine. He tried to keep himself from wondering if his mother was going to die.

"Please, no!" he prayed. He drank the wine.

He sat down on the bed to get his breath back. That climb up the steps had never taken his breath before, but now his heart was beating fast, and sweat had come out on his brow, so he took off his coat, tie, shirt, and got ready to wash his face.

He had better pack his bag first. Then, he suddenly thought, he had no present for his mother—but he caught himself in the middle of the thought. This was not Saturday, not one of his monthly Saturdays when he went home. This was Tuesday and there was this telegram from the Rossiters in his pocket that had suddenly broken the whole rhythm of his life:

YOUR MOTHER GRAVELY ILL STOP COME HOME AT ONCE.

John and Nellie Rossiter had been neighbors since childhood. They would not frighten him needlessly. His mother must be very ill indeed, so he need not think of taking her a present. He went to the closet door to pull out the suitcase, but his hands did not move. The wine, amber-yellow in its tall bottle, stood on the dresser beside him. Warm, sweet, forbidden.

There was no one in the room. Nobody in the whole house perhaps except the landlady. Nobody really in all Chicago to talk to in his trouble. With a mother to take care of on a small salary, room rent, a class at business college, books to buy, there's not much time left to make friends or take girls out. In a big city it's hard for a strange young man to know people.

Carl poured the glass full of wine again—drank it. Then he opened the top drawer, took out his toilet articles and put them on the bed. From the second drawer he took a couple of shirts. Maybe three would be better, or four. This was not a week end. Perhaps he had better take some extra clothing—in case his mother was ill long, and he had to stay a week or more. Perhaps he'd better take his dark suit in case she . . .

It hit him in the stomach like a fist. A pang of fear spread over his whole body. He sat down trembling on the bed.

"Buck up, old man!" The sound of his own voice comforted him. He smiled weakly at his face in the mirror.

"Be a man!"

He filled the glass full this time and drank it without stopping. He had never drunk so much wine before and this was warm, sweet, and palatable. He stood, threw his shoulders back, and felt suddenly tall as though his head were touching the ceiling. Then, for no reason at all, he looked at himself in the mirror and began to sing. He made up a song out of nowhere that repeated itself over and over:

> *In the spring the roses*
> *In the spring begin to sing*
> *Roses in the spring*
> *Begin to sing . . .*

He took off his clothes, put on his bathrobe, carefully drained the bottle, then went down the hall to the bathroom, still singing. He ran a tub full of water, climbed in, and sat down. The water in the tub was warm like the wine. He felt good remembering a dark grassy slope in a corner of his mother's yard where he played with a little girl when he was very young at home. His mother came out, separated them, and sent the little girl away because she wasn't of a decent family. But now his mother would never dismiss another little girl be—

Carl sat up quickly in the tub, splashed water over his back and over his head. Drunk? What's the matter? What's the matter with you? Thinking of your mother that way and maybe she's dy— Say! Listen, don't you know you have to catch a four o'clock bus? And here he was getting drunk before he even started on the way home. He trembled. His heart beat fast, so fast that he lay down in the tub to catch his breath, all but his head covered with the warm water.

To lie quiet that way was fine. Still and quiet. Tuesday. Everybody working at the office. And here he was, Carl Anderson, lying quiet in a deep tub of warm water. Maybe someday in a few years with a little money saved up, and no expenses at home, and a car to take girls out in the spring,

> *When the roses sing*
> *In the spring . . .*

He had a good voice and the song that he had made up himself about roses sounded good with wine on his breath as he sang, so he stood up in the tub, grabbed a towel, and began to sing quite lustily. Suddenly there was a knock at the door.

"What's going on in there?"

It was the landlady's voice in the hall outside. She must have heard him singing downstairs.

"Nothing, Mrs. Dyer! Nothing! I just feel like singing."

"Mr. Anderson? Is that you? What're you doing in the house this time of day?"

"I'm on the way home to see my mother. She . . ."

"You sound happier than a lark about it. I couldn't imagine . . ."

He heard the landlady's feet shuffling off down the stairs, back to her ironing.

"She's . . ." His head began to go round and round. "My mother's . . ." His eyes suddenly burned. To step out of the tub, he held tightly to the sides. Drunk, that's what he was! Drunk!

He lurched down the hall, fell across the bed in his room, and buried his head in the pillows. He stretched his arms above his head to the rods of the bedstand. He felt ashamed. With his head in the pillows all was dark. His mother dying? No! No! But he was drunk.

In the dark he seemed to feel his mother's hand on his head when he was a little boy, and her voice saying, "Be sweet, Carl. Be a good boy. Keep clean. Mother loves you. She'll look out for you. Be sweet—and remember what you're taught at home."

Then the roses in the song he had made up and the wine he had drunk began to go around and around in his head and he felt as if he had betrayed his mother and home singing about roses and spring and dreaming of cars and pretty girls with that yellow telegram in his coat pocket on the back of the chair beside the bed that suddenly seemed to go around and around.

But when he closed his eyes, it stopped. He held his breath. He buried his head deeper in the pillows. He lay very still. It was dark and warm. And quiet, and darker than ever. A long time passed, a very long time, dark, and quiet, and peaceful, and still.

"Mr. Anderson! Hey, Mr. Anderson!"

In the darkness far off, somebody called, then nearer—but still very far away—then knocking on a distant door.

"Mr. Anderson!"

The voice was quite near now, sharper. The door opened, light streamed in. A hand shook his shoulder. He opened his eyes. Mrs. Dyer stood there, looking down at him in indignant amazement.

"Mr. Anderson, are you drunk?"

"No, Mrs. Dyer," he said in a daze, blinking at the landlady standing above him. The electric light bulb she had switched on hurt his eyes.

"Mr. Anderson, they's a long-distance call for you on the phone down in the hall. Get up. Tie up that bathrobe. Hurry on down there and get it, will you? I've been yelling for you for five minutes."

"What time is it?" Carl sat bolt upright. The landlady stopped in the door.

"It's after dinnertime," she said. "Must be six-thirty, seven o'clock."

"Seven o'clock?" Carl gasped. "I've missed my bus!"

"What bus?"

"The four o'clock bus."

"I guess you have," said the landlady. "Alcohol and timetables don't mix, young man. That must be your mother on the phone now." Disgusted, she went downstairs, leaving his door open.

The phone! Carl felt sick and unsteady on his legs. He pulled his bathrobe together and stumbled down the stairs. The phone! A kind of weakness rushed through his veins. The telephone! He had promised his mother not to drink. She said his father . . . He couldn't remember his father. He died long ago. Now his mother was . . . Anyhow, he should have been home by seven o'clock, at her bedside, holding her hand. He could have been home an hour ago. Now, maybe she . . .

He picked up the receiver. His voice was hoarse, frightened. "Hello. Yes, this is Carl . . . Yes, Mrs. Rossiter . . ."

"Carl, honey, we kept looking for you on that six o'clock bus. My husband went out on the road a piece to meet you in his car. We thought it might be quicker. Carl, honey . . ."

"Yes, Mrs. Rossiter . . ."

"Your mother . . ."

"Yes, Mrs. Rossiter . . ."

"Your mother just passed away. I thought maybe you ought to know in case you hadn't already started. I thought maybe . . ."

For a moment he couldn't hear what she said. Then he knew that she was asking him a question—that she was repeating it.

"I could have Jerry drive to Chicago and get you tonight. Would you like to have me do that, since there's no bus now until morning?"

"I wish you would, Mrs. Rossiter. But then, no—listen! Never mind! There's two or three things I ought to do before I come home. I ought to go to the bank. I must. But I'll catch that first bus home in the morning. First thing in the morning, Mrs. Rossiter, I'll be home."

"We're your neighbors and your friends. You know *this* is your home, too, so come right here."

"Yes, Mrs. Rossiter, I know. I will. I'll be home."

He ran back upstairs and jumped into his clothes, feeling that he had to get out. Had to get out! His body burned. His throat was dry. He picked up the wine bottle and looked at the label. Good wine! Warm and easy to the throat! Hurry before perhaps the landlady came. Hurry! She wouldn't understand this haste.

Did she die alone?

Quickly he put on his coat and plunged down the steps. Outside it was dark. The street lights seemed dimmer than usual.

Did she die alone?

At the corner, there was a bar, palely lighted. He had never stopped there before, but this time he went in. He could drink all he wanted to now.

Alone, at home, alone! Did she die alone?

The bar was big and dismal, like a barn. A juke box played a raucous hit song. A woman stood near the machine singing to herself.

Carl went up to the bar.

"What'll it be?" The bartender passed his towel over the counter in front of him.

"A drink," Carl said.

"Whisky?"

"Yes."

"Can you make it two?" asked the woman in a warm low voice.

"Sure," Carl said. "Make it two."

"What's the matter? You're shivering!" she exclaimed.

"Cold," Carl said.

"You've been drinking?" the woman said. "But it don't smell like whisky."

"Wasn't," Carl said. "Was wine."

"Oh! I guess you can mix up your drinks, heh? O.K. Try it. But if that wine along with this whisky knocks you out," she purred, "I'll have to take you home to my house, little boy."

"Home?" Carl asked.

"Yes," the woman said, "home with me. You and me—home."

She put her arm around his shoulders.

"Home?" Carl said.

"Home, sure, baby! Home to my house."

"Home?" Carl was about to repeat when suddenly a volley of uncontrolled sobs shook his body, choking the word, "Home." He leaned forward with his head in his arms and wept like a kid.

"Home. . . . . home . . . home . . ."

The bartender and the woman looked at him in amazement. The juke box stopped.

The woman said gently, "You're drunk, fellow. Come on, buck up! I'll take you home. It don't have to be to my house either—if you don't want to go. Where do you live? I'll see that you get home."

Mysterious Madame Shanghai

We other roomers occasionally met her in the entrance hall, coming in or going out. She was a tall old woman. Her olive skin was leathery and seared, heavily lined, with the lines of her face and neck well-filled with a covering of rice powder. She spoke pleasantly enough in a deep, almost masculine voice, a simple, "Good day." That was all. But she never tried to make friends with any of the other roomers in the house. She was Mrs. Dyer's woman of mystery. Because she occasionally went down the second-floor hall to the bathroom in an amazing Chinese kimono of blue silk heavily brocaded with golden dragons, somebody had nicknamed her Madame Shanghai. The name stuck.

Mrs. Dyer, the landlady, certainly did not like her, and would wonder about her in a series of constantly varying and uncomplimentary suppositions—for nobody in the house really *knew* anything about Madame Shanghai. She looked like a gypsy, a fair East Indian, or a mulatto. But since she was no trouble and paid her rent on time, Mrs. Dyer had no good cause to ask her to move. Indeed, Mrs. Dyer did not honestly want her to move until she had wormed out of her who she was, had been, and why. Simply to know that her current name was Ethel Cunningham and that she worked now in the stock room of a downtown department store was really to know nothing at all—since it was written all over the woman that she had had a past.

Mrs. Dyer had great curiosity about her roomers' pasts. If they didn't have one, or failed to reveal it, our landlady usually made one up for them out of her own imagination, nourished by the novels she had read and the movies she had seen. The past which Mrs. Dyer created for Ethel Cunningham hardly became a lady.

"No woman could be so quiet today," Mrs. Dyer said to me one evening, "except that her morals've been loose in the past!"

I laughed, because I really didn't care about Madame Shanghai's morals, past or present. She was old enough to be my mother. So was Mrs. Dyer.

"Furthermore, no old woman would wear so much powder if she hadn't been used to wearing more when she was young!"

"Mrs. Dyer, could I have one of those big bath towels this week?"

"And forty years ago no nice girl covered up her complexion with rouge . . . A big bath towel, you say? Them big towels is for my front rooms, young man. You don't occupy no walnut suite. How would them little towels of yours look hanging on a towel rack in them big rooms?"

"But I'm a big man, Mrs. Dyer, and I need a big towel to wipe myself on."

"Well, here—since it's to be drying yourself. Fact is, you are a pretty big fellow. But mind, you don't go putting your pal in the back room up to wanting a big towel, too. I haven't got but a dozen and they're for the front rooms, like I'm telling you."

"Yes, Mrs. Dyer. Thank you."

She waddled off down the hall. I gave her the polite raspberries—after I shut the door. Then I got out my clothes and started for the bathroom, but somebody was in there, so I came back, laid out a clean shirt on the bed and wiped off my tan shoes. When I finally got washed and dressed it was almost eight o'clock, a blue summer dusk, cool and pleasant. To take the girl to a show, or for a walk in the park? The park would be better, I thought, as I started down the dimly lighted steps in Mrs. Dyer's hall. At the curve of the stairs I almost ran over Ethel Cunningham. She was coming up very slowly, breathing heavily.

"Why, Madame Shang—Miss Cunningham," I stammered. She frightened me. "Are you sick?"

"I'm not sick—but—but—could you come upstairs with me, please a minute, Mr. Shields?"

"Let me help you."

I took her arm to the top of the steps and walked with her down the hall to her room. She fumbled nervously for her key, then opened the door. I had never been in her room before. It was a small room, not of the type to which Mrs. Dyer gave big towels. On the dresser were a number of photographs of a man—all the same man. In most of the pictures he wore a riding habit and carried a whip. He had a mustache. The pictures were faded, as though taken many years ago.

"That's him," Madame Shanghai gasped. "And he's waiting downstairs to kill me!"

"What?" I cried astonished, envisioning a man rushing into the room that very moment with drawn pistol.

"On the sidewalk," she said. "He hasn't seen me yet. But I saw him just as I started out."

I felt relieved that he had not seen her, but puzzled. Was she crazy?

"Go downstairs and tell him I love him," Madame Shanghai said, her

eyes wide and anxious, her voice full of pleading. "Go tell him that God
has punished me enough all these years."

"But what is it all about? I don't know what you mean. Who is he,
Miss Cunningham?"

"My husband."

"Your husband?"

"Come back from the grave! I thought he was dead. I haven't seen
him for twenty years—and then—now—oh, my God!" She sat on the
bed and covered her face with her hands. "He was covered with blood."

"What?"

"I had tried to kill him. I let Tamaris tear the skin from his body and
didn't even stop her."

"Tamaris?"

"The biggest cat in the world!"

"Cat?" I wanted to laugh because I thought she was talking about
another woman.

"A tiger, Mr. Shields. I told Tamaris myself to claw him to death."

"But where did you get a tiger?"

She sat up and looked at me in surprise.

"Why, we were the greatest wild animal act in the business—before
you were born, I guess. They billed us as the Daring Darnells. We played
every circus and hippodrome in the world. But I was in love with him—
too much in love—and jealous. He was in love with me, too—but cruel.
Oh, so cruel! He thought *I* was an animal that needed to be tamed. So
we fought all the time—with our fists, with whips, with our fingernails,
with ropes. That was because we loved each other, I know now. I still
love him. I want you to go downstairs and tell him I didn't mean to kill
him. I'd go, but I'm afraid he'll shoot me before I get a chance to speak.
Shoot me, or knife me, or slap my head off, I don't know which. He's a
jealous man about women, Mr. Shields."

Again I wanted to laugh. Madame Shanghai was so wrinkled, ugly,
and old, what man would want to knock her head off now?

"You tried to kill him once?"

"I thought I *had* killed him. I certainly wanted to. I sic'ed the wildest
of the cats on him one night in the center of the big top before five
thousand people. I thought he was dead when they dragged him out in
front of a crowd sick with horror."

"Why did you try to kill him?"

"Over a ring, a ring my mother gave me, an old old ring with a
hundred years of circus life behind it in Bohemia. That night, just as

we went into the cage, Marie, the French bareback rider passed on her white horse leaving the arena, blowing kisses in answer to the applause—and there on her finger was my ring! I turned green with rage, jealousy, anger, hate. I knew my husband must have taken it from our trunk and given it to her to wear. She was beautiful and blonde—and he had a weakness for blonde women. I was dark as a gypsy. After I saw that ring on her finger, I said to him while we got the lions snarling into place on their stools, 'So you've stolen my ring and given it to that French hussy?'

" 'Shut up and take care of these cats,' was his answer. 'We're giving a performance.'

" 'I'll not shut up,' I said, 'you double-crossing no-good . . .'

"Just then the tigers leaped into the cage.

" 'My fist'll make you shut up as soon as I get out of this cage,' he said.

" 'You'll never get out,' I answered. 'Tamaris!'

"Tamaris was the largest and most beautiful of tigers, a tiger I had raised from a cub who obeyed me like a dog. I pointed my whip at the man in the ring whom I loved and hated more than anybody else in the world—my husband—whom I permitted to beat me, curse me, but whom I could not let give *my ring* to Marie.

" 'Tamaris!' I said, giving her the signal to spring.

"All the blood left my husband's face. Like lightning the sleek young animal crouched, then swept through the air. He screamed. Her great paws ripped into his flesh from the skull down. She bore him to the ground, mangled him with her tiger's teeth. The crowd gasped, sat tense, held its breath, then let loose a mighty groan of fright and horror as people saw the blood.

"From outside, the guards shot Tamaris. They opened the doors of the cage and took Jim out, a mass of bloody pulp. The show went on. They rushed him to the hospital. I walked back to the dressing tent. A dozen circus women crowded around to comfort me. But I wanted one thing only—that was my ring.

"The women were all astonished that I didn't cry. 'I can't cry,' I said. I was too humiliated, hurt, and angry. Just then Marie, that French woman, came in. I grabbed her hand, she thought for comfort, but really to see if my ring was there.

"Suddenly my heart stopped. It was *not* my ring, after all, on her finger! Merely one that looked like it! I could see it plainly now. The stone wasn't even the same kind of stone in her ring. It was paste.

"My blood turned to water. I stumbled across the tent to my trunk. I almost broke the lock. I could hardly wait to get it open. There, inside, safe as always, was my ring—the old gypsy ring of my mother's.

"Then I began to sob. I had deceived myself about my husband. I began to shriek. I howled like a mad woman. I tore my hair and rolled on the ground. Life can never hold another hour as bitter as that hour was for me.

"It was six weeks before Jim regained consciousness. The show went on across the country, but I remained behind by his side. When he opened his eyes at last and recognized me the first words he said were, 'Get away! Ethel, get away! Before I kill you.'

"The doctors would not allow me in the room with him after that. The sight of me sent him into a fury that endangered his life. The sound of my name caused him to burn with fever. I was forbidden to come into the hospital. So I went back to the circus. Always a great drawing card, as an animal tamer I was famous. I continued to make a great deal of money. I spent it all on my husband trying to bring him back to life and health—though he cursed me with every breath he drew into his slowly healing body. I knew that now for me from his scarred lips came nothing but hate. Still I sent him all the delicacies I could find that I thought he might like. I sent him champagne. I sent him money. I paid the hospital bills promptly. All he ever sent back was a curse or a threat, if he could persuade the doctors or nurses to write the profane words for him.

"Finally, without my knowledge, he was released from the hospital. I had wanted to see him to tell him I loved him, to beg his forgiveness on my knees, to devote the rest of my life to making him happy. I had hoped he would let me. Instead there came a wire from the head doctor at the hospital saying, 'Beware! He threatens to kill you.'

"And in a letter from his nurse that followed, I was told that he had spoken often of his intention to buy a gun, to trail the circus, to sit there in the audience some day and shoot me down as I stood in the center cage among my beautiful animals.

"Don't think, Mr. Shields, that I minded dying. It wasn't that. I simply did not want to die without a chance to speak to him, without a word of sorrow and love and apology for his ears. I wanted a chance to fall on my knees in front of him and say, 'Jim, forgive me.' Even though his gun was ready to blow my brains out.

"But to be shot without knowing when or where, without seeing Jim's face that I loved—even though mangled by tiger's claws and distorted with hate for me—to die without touching his hand even though it held my death! No! I couldn't bear that! Daily I went through hell after that letter came. Every time I entered the ring I expected a bullet to whistle out of the crowd. I lost control of my beasts. I went to pieces. I spent all my time in the cage peering into the crowd trying to see if he was there—my husband. Before my act I haunted the front of the big tent from noon on, looking to see if he entered the grounds. The managers thought I was going crazy. Though they liked freaks in the circus, they didn't like fools, so I gave up. I had to quit.

"I hid in a little town whose name I've forgotten now and let the circus go on without me. I let them have my animals. I changed my name. I worked as a cook, a maid, traveling everywhere looking for him, but I couldn't find him. Finally, I thought perhaps he had died. Then I came here to Chicago. Now, thank God, he's found me. But, oh, please, Mr. Shields, help me! Prepare him! Go downstairs and tell him not to kill me until I have a chance to say, 'Forgive me! Just forgive me. Jim, forgive me!' "

"I'll go," I said, still doubting, "and tell him—if he's still there."

"He'll never leave," the woman declared.

I went down the steps and out of Mrs. Dyer's rooming house, half smiling for I expected to see nobody on the sidewalk. I thought it was all just some crazy dream in Madame Shanghai's rice-powdered old head—but I was mistaken. Sure enough, in the half dark of the street lights just outside a man limped back and forth, a man bent sidewise as though by some old wound, an elderly man whose leather-colored face was crisscrossed by scars. His mouth was twisted. Now I was afraid, too.

"Pardon me," I said timidly, "but I've been told you are looking for a woman who lives in this house?"

"I am," he said, "since you seem to know. I'm looking for my wife."

"To—to—kill her?" I asked.

He said nothing.

"She wants to speak to you before you do," I said.

"Then tell her to come to me," he answered.

"You'll give her a chance?"

"Tell her to come and see."

I went back into the house and told her what he had said.

"I'll go," she answered. I was trembling, but she was not.

Madame Shanghai went bravely down the steps walking like a woman used to going into a cage with wild animals. I followed her to the door, cold sweat on my forehead. Already, as if in anticipation of drama, three or four people had gathered on the sidewalk. Mrs. Dyer had raised her window.

The man in the street waited quite still for his wife to come toward him beneath the street light. She went, holding out her arms in a gesture of the greatest love I have ever seen. But then she swayed, put her hands to her mouth, called weakly, "Jim!" and fell in a faint at his feet.

The man with the crooked body hesitated, then bent down swiftly and lifted her in his arms. He came up the steps into the house.

"Where is her room?" he asked.

I pointed upward. He went ahead and I followed, trailed now by a half-dozen roomers. He burst in through the half-open door and laid her on the bed. As he bent over a pistol fell from his pocket. But he did not pick it up.

"You are not going to kill her?" I said.

"No," he answered tensely, "I'm just going to slap the life back into her . . . then I'm going to kiss her."

He began to slap her face soundly on one cheek, then the other, and a dusty haze of rice powder floated upward.

Madame Shanghai opened her eyes. "Jim!" she cried, "you love me— or you wouldn't be slapping me like this. You love me! You love me!"

They kissed, crushed in each other's arms. We closed their door, but it was hard to get our landlady out of the hall.

Never Room with a Couple

Even if they don't pay very much, you can have lots of fun working in a summer camp and you meet plenty of funny people. Last summer at a big camp in upstate New York I was head chief dishwasher and bottle-wiper, with plenty else to do besides. For one thing, I had to help the cook get all the vegetables ready. I peeled so many potatoes that if you'd put all them spuds eye to eye they'd reach from Waycross to Jalapy and back. But who's gonna worry 'bout that? Summer's gone now.

One afternoon me and the second cook was sitting out in the shade behind the cook shack peeling spuds, when up from the lake comes a Jewish couple quarreling to beat the band. They was in bathing suits, a man and his wife, and they was both kinda fat and old. When they quarreled their stomachs wobbled up and down. I wanted to laugh, but I didn't.

"You see that?" said the second cook. "I bet she's been flirtin' under-water with some other man."

"Might be the other way round," I said. "Maybe it was him and another woman."

"Which ever way it was," said the cook, "some woman is to blame."

"What makes you figger that?" I asked.

"It's always a woman is to blame," said the cook as he grabbed a potato I had just peeled, and looked at me. "Pick out them eyes good, boy," he said, although I knew perfectly well how to peel potatoes and *was* picking out the eyes good. But then I was only eighteen and Allie was an old guy about forty, always giving me advice. He sort of took it upon himself to look out for me, so he was always telling me stories with morals, like I was a kid.

"I never will forget that last family quarrel I was mixed up in," Allie went on as we peeled and cut. "Who was to blame? A woman! Son, they's terrible! That hussy like to ruint me!"

"Who?" I said. "Where? When?"

"Never room with a couple," Allie counseled gravely. He paused to let this warning sink in. "Son, as long as you away from your mother's home, no matter where you may be, never room with a married couple. It's dangerous!" He looked me solemnly in the eye over our bucket of potatoes. "You are young and you don't know! But, boy, I'm tellin' you, if you rent a room when you go back to Harlem, rent from a widow or an orphan, a West Indian or a Geechee, but never room with a couple! A man and his wife, plus a roomer—son, that's poison!"

"Why?" I said to keep the tale going and get the potatoes peeled so I could take a swim before supper.

"Why?" Allie answered, looking at me as if I was a child. "I'm gonna tell you why. Look at me, here peeling potatoes! Well, I used to be a first-class captain-waiter who could carry more orders on one tray than any waiter in New York—and look at me now! All from roomin' with a couple."

"What!" I said in astonishment.

"Sure, just look at me!" Allie said. "Their name was Wilkins. A nice young couple, Joe and his wife, Fannie. I used to run on the road with Joe before I quit the dining cars. So when he told me one day, 'Me and my wife's got a nice little apartment in 143rd. Why don't you come on up and room with us, fellow? Quiet and homelike—and only three bucks a week,' I said, 'I believe I will.' Which I did, cause I knowed they needed the rent. So long about this time last year I moved in and paid my rent. They gimme the rear back room. They had a nice apartment on the third floor, with my window looking across the alley at more third floors. Nighttime, all them radios goin', it was swell! Harlem just full o' music—not like up here in these woods where all you can hear is yourself snorin'."

"Then what happened?" I said.

"Funny thing, son," Allie went on. "Before I went there to room, Joe's wife ain't never appealed to me a-tall. I like 'em three-quarters pink, and she were just a ordinary light brown-skin. But seemed like to me Fannie blossomed out and got prettier after I moved in. Or maybe seein' her every day at close range got me used to overlookin' her fizziogomy. Anyhow, one Sunday morning when Joe's train was out and I was goin' to the bath to shave, I met her trippin' down the hall on her way to church. I said, 'Baby, I could go for you!' When Fannie flashed them pearly teeth o' her'n in my face, I said, 'When do Joe come home?'

"She said, 'Not till twelve o'clock tonight.'

"I said, 'That'll do!' And, son, don't you know that woman got crazy about me?"

"Naturally," I answered, sarcastic-like, because in every tale he told, the women were always crazy about him.

Allie went on, "Fannie wanted to give me a diamond ring, but I wouldn't take it. I said, 'No, honey, your husband's just a working man.'

"She said, 'That don't make no difference, Allie. I'd take Joe's money and buy *you* a diamond—just to see you smile.'

"But I said, 'No, baby, I really don't need nary diamond. Just let me wear somethin' o' your'n. Any old thing—to think of you by!'

"She said, 'What?'

"I said, 'How about that little old horseshoe ring you got on your finger there?'

"She said, 'Aw, no, sugar! That belongs to Joe. He lets me wear it, but it ain't no good.'

"So I said, 'You thinks more of Joe than you does of me?'

" 'No, I don't, honey!' she said real quick. 'You can have it, if you want it. Here!' And she gimme Joe's ring. 'But don't wear it around the house,' she said.

" 'Do you think I'm a fool?' I told her.

"I really didn't want the ring nohow, but I knowed it was Joe's—and I just wanted to see would she give it to me. Well, sir, to make a long story short, it wasn't no time till Joe found out that that ring was gone. Then it was that I should've moved, but I didn't have the sense—not thinkin' he'd suspicion *me*. We was always such good friends on the road.

"But one night I come home from the hotel where I was workin' and I'd no more than put my key in the latch when I heard 'em quarrelin'. I tipped down the hall real easy past their bedroom door, but when I went to unlock my own door, since I had done left my window open in the morning, the wind blew the door back with a bang. I heard Joe open his door and say, 'There's that so-and-so now!' So I knew they was quarrelin' 'bout me!

" 'Baby,' Fannie said to Joe, 'come in here and shut the door. Can't you see I ain't got no clothes on?'

" 'Shut up!' said Joe, and he called her out of her name.

" 'Don't call me that,' said Fannie, 'cause I'm a pure woman.'

" 'You don't say!' said Joe.

" '*Say,* nothin', Joe Wilkins,' she hollered, 'you know I am,' said Fannie.

" 'Yes, until that roomer come here,' yelled Joe. 'Right up till last August when Allie King showed up?'

" 'Till now, as far as Allie is concerned,' yelled Fannie.

" 'Then where is my horseshoe ring?'

" 'In the drawer,' she lied.

" 'Lemme see!'

"I could hear Fannie lookin' through the drawers for that ring she knew wasn't there—cause I had it in my pocket. Then she begins to cry—and I was sweatin' blood! I ain't even turned on the light yet in my room. Just holdin' my hat in my hand *sweatin' blood*—cause there wasn't but one way to get out of my room without passin' their door, and that was to jump. The third floor is pretty high—but Joe's a fightin' man.

" 'Fannie,' he said, 'who's got my ring?'

" 'What do you mean, who?' cried Fannie.

" 'You know what *who* means,' said Joe.

" 'Somebody must-a stole it,' said Fannie.

" 'Who'd steal a no-good horseshoe ring?' said Joe. 'You give it to Allie King.'

" 'Ow-o-o-o-o-o!' cried Fannie. I knowed he'd raised his hand to hit her—so I put on my hat to go.

" 'And you ain't the only one I'm gonna hit,' yelled Joe. 'I'm goin' in there and beat that no-good son-of-a-so-and-so to death right now.' He started down the hall for me.

" 'Aw-ooo-oo-o!' Fannie yelled as I heard Joe chargin' towards my door—but before he could put his hand on the knob, I was gone!"

"Gone where?" I asked, dropping a potato.

"Gone out," said Allie. "I stepped right through that third-floor window down into the yard."

"Three stories down?"

"I didn't miss it," said Allie. "I like to took that window with me, too—I was in such a hurry. Don't think I lingered in the back yard neither. No, sir! I crawled right on up to Lenox and grabbed me a taxi."

"Crawled?" I said.

"Sure, *crawled!* I'd done broke both my ankles! That's why I'm peelin' spuds out here in this lonesome camp today. I can't wait table no mo' with these crippled-up feet—and all from roomin' with a couple!"

Allie looked at me with a warning eye over our bucket of potatoes.

"*Never* room with a couple, son," he said solemnly, "less'n they are over eighty."

Little Old Spy

A number of years ago, toward the end of one of Cuba's reactionary regimes, on the evening of my second day in Havana, I realized I was being followed. I had walked too far for the same little old man, trailing a respectable distance behind me, to be there accidentally. I noticed him first standing quite close to me when I stopped to buy a paper at the big newsstand across from the Alhambra.[12] He seemed to be trying to see what I was buying.

Then I forgot about him. I walked down the Prado in the warm dusk looking at the American tourists on parade, watching the fine cars that passed, and seeing the lights catch fire from the sunset. When I got to the bandstand by the fort at the waterfront, I stopped, leaned against the wall, and put my foot out for a ragged little urchin to shine. I was lighting a cigarette when the little old man of the newsstand strolled by in front of me. He stopped a few paces beyond, and called a boy to shine his shoes. Even then I thought nothing of his being there. But I did notice his strange get-up, the tight suit, the cream-colored spats, and the floppy Panama with its bright band that a youth, but not an old man, could have worn. He was a queer little withered Cuban, certainly sixty years old, but dressed like a fop of twenty.

A mile away on the Malecon—for I had continued to walk along the sea wall—I looked at my watch and saw the hour approaching seven, when I was to meet some friends at the Florida Café. I turned to retrace my steps. In turning, whom should I face on the sidewalk but the little old man! Then I became suspicious. He said nothing, and strolled on as though he had not seen me. But when I looked back after walking perhaps a quarter mile toward the center, there he was, a respectable distance behind.

Later that evening at the restaurant, midway through the salad, I noticed him alone at a far table sipping coffee and looking sort of out of place in the fashionable dining room.

"Say, who is that fellow?" I asked my friend, the newspaper editor, as we sat with his cousin, the poet, and a little dancer named Mata. Carlos, the editor, looked across the restaurant toward the table I indicated.

"Don't everybody look," I said as Mata and Jorge began bending their necks, too. "It might embarrass him."

But when Carlos turned his head toward us again and answered in a whispering voice, "A spy," none of us could keep our eyes from glancing quickly across the café.

"What?" I said.

"Yes," Carlos affirmed, "a government spy."

"But why should he be following me?" I asked.

"He has been following you?"

"All afternoon."

"Maybe he thinks you're Communist," Carlos said. "That's what they are afraid of here."

"But they've got a lot more to be afraid of than that," Jorge added.

"I guess they have," I answered, for everybody knew Cuba was on the verge of a revolution. All the schools were closed, and the public buildings guarded. The "they" we so discreetly referred to meant the government and the tyrant at its head. But nobody mentioned the tyrant's name in public; and nobody talked very loud, if they talked at all.

For months there had been political murders in the streets of the capital, riots in the provinces, and American gunboats in the harbors. Mobs were becoming bolder and bolder, crying in public places, "Down with the Yankees! Down with the government that supports them!" But the tourists seemed blissfully unaware of all this. They still flocked to the Casino, wore their fine clothes through quaint streets of misery, danced nightly rhumbas at the big hotels, and took tours into the countryside, exclaiming before the miserable huts of the sugar-cane cutters, "How picturesque! How cute!"

"Yes," went on Carlos (this time in English), pouring a beer. "He ees spy. I know heem. On newspaper you know everybody. But he ees no dangerous."

"Not dangerous?" I said.

"Not, joust a poor little *viejo*, once pimp, now spy."

"Oh," I said.

"But tomorrow the government will know with whom you dined," said Mata, "and that maybe will be dangerous."

"Why?" I asked.

"To dine with anyone in Havana is dangerous," Jorge laughed, "unless it is with the big boss himself. Everybody else, except the police, are against the government. And that paper of my cousin's," indicating Carlos, "*Caramba!* It has been suppressed ten times."

"But I thought it was your best paper."

"It is—but they think they are our *best* government."

Just then the waiter came bringing more beer. We switched our conversation into Spanish again and the domestic troubles of the Pickford-Fairbanks ménage—then of great interest to the readers of Carlos' paper.

"But what shall I do about the spy?" I asked, when the waiter had gone. "I never imagined such open spying."

"They are that way down here," Carlos said. "Not very subtle."

"Make friends with him," suggested Jorge, eating a *flan*. "That would be amusing."

"Buy heem a few drinks," said Carlos, "I know his kind. All they looking for, after all, ees easiest way to get few drinks. The government ees full of drunkards."

Meanwhile the little spy kept mournfully sipping his coffee across the room. Evidently his allowance for spying called for nothing better than coffee when his job took him into an expensive restaurant. I pitied him sitting there looking at all the good food going by and getting nothing.

"Say," I said to Carlos and Jorge, "won't it be dangerous for you and Mata, sitting here with me—if I'm suspected of being a dangerous man."

"To sit with anybody is dangerous in Havana," Jorge replied. "But they can't lock up everyone. Or kill all of us. After all, it is not writers like my cousin and me that they are really afraid of. Or visiting dancers like Mata. No, it is the workers. You see, they can stop refineries from running. They can keep ships from being loaded, and sugar cane from being cut. They can hit in the pocketbook—and that's all our damned government's here for—to protect foreign dividends."

"Sure, I know that," I said. "But why's that man watching me?"

"Because strangers who don't at once make for the Casino to start gambling are watched. *Poor* strangers may be sympathetic with our revolution. They may be bearers of messages from our group in exile. That's why they watch you."

"But if you want heem to forget all about it, buy heem few drinks," shrugged Carlos. "We kill all their best spies. We don't bother with little old bums like heem. Bullets too valuable."

The little man across the way took out a pack of cheap cigarettes and began to smoke. Carlos, Mata, Jorge, and I sat talking until almost midnight. Well-dressed Americans and portly Cubans passed and repassed between the tables. A famous Spanish actress came in with her man on her arm. There was music somewhere at the back of the café, and talk, laughter, and clatter of dishes everywhere. We stopped thinking about the spy and began to speak of Mayakovsky—for Jorge, who was putting his verse into Spanish, declared him the greatest poet of the twentieth century, but Carlos disagreed in favor of Lorca, so a discussion sprang up.[13]

When I left my friends, the little brown man was right at my heels. He trailed behind me until I finally got into a taxi. As the car drew off, I knew he was taking down the license number. Later the police would find out from the chauffeur where I had been driven.

I was not a little flattered to be so assiduously spied upon. At home in Harlem I was nobody, just a Negro writer. Down here in Havana I was suddenly of governmental importance. And I knew pretty well why. The government of Cuba had grown suddenly terribly afraid of its Negro population, its black shine boys and cane field hands, its colored soldiers and sailors who make up most of the armed forces, its taxi drivers and street vendors. At last, after all the other elements of the island's population had openly revolted against the tyrant in power, the Negroes had begun to rise with the students and others to drive the dictator from Cuba.

For a strange New York Negro to come to Havana might mean— *quién sabe?*—that he had come to help stir them up—for the Negroes of Harlem were reputed in Cuba to be none too docile, and none too dumb. Had not Marcus Garvey come out of Harlem to arouse the whole black world to a consciousness of its potential strength?

"They," the Cuban dictatorship, were afraid of Negroes from Harlem. The American steamship lines at that time would not sell colored persons tickets to Cuba. The immigration at the port of Havana tried to keep them out, if they got that far. But here was I—and I was being shadowed.

The next day I went downstairs to breakfast in the café-bar of my hotel. The iron shutters were up and the whole front of the building open to the street, dust, and sunshine.

Across the way in a Spanish wineshop, I saw the little old man of the day before waiting patiently.

"Today," I thought to myself, "we will make friends. There ought to be an amusing story in you, old top, if I can get it out."

But after breakfast, for the fun of it, I gave him a merry chase first. By streetcar, by taxi, on foot, down narrow old streets and up broad new ones, all over the central part of Havana, he trotted after me. I had a number of errands to do and I did them in as zigzag a manner as possible. Once I lost him. But just as I was beginning to regret it (for the game was not unamusing), I looked around and there, not ten feet away from me in El Centro, was the little old man, puffing and blowing to be sure, but nevertheless there. I laughed. But the sweating little spy did not seem to find the situation entertaining. One of his spats had become unbuttoned from running, and his watch chain was hanging.

That afternoon I had tea with Señora Barrios, the Chilean novelist, my spy waiting patiently the while outside the hedge of her Vedado villa. No taxi being in sight when I emerged, I walked along toward the center of the city, giving the old man some exercise.

On a quiet corner near the statue of Gomez, I sighted a little bar and went across for a drink before dinner. My withered dandy stood forlornly without.

"It'll be fun to tire him," I thought. "I'll sit here drinking nice cool beers until he can stand it no longer and will have to come in, too. Then I'll invite him to have a drink and see what happens."

It worked. The little old man could not forever stand on that corner and watch me drinking comfortably within. I knew his throat was dry. At last he entered, wiping his brow, and called for an anisette at the small bar.

"Have a Bacardi with me," I invited. "I don't like to drink alone."

The little old man started, stared, seemed hesitant as to whether he should answer at all or not, and finally slid into the chair across from my own. The waiter brought us two drinks and put them on the marble-topped table.

"Hot," I said pleasantly.

"*Si, señorito,* like steam," the little old man answered.

"You've been walking quite a lot, too," I laughed.

"Too much for my age," the old man said. "You Americanos are *muy activo.* That's no good in this climate."

"Have another drink," I said.

The old man accepted with alacrity. Just as Carlos said, he loved his Bacardi. He smiled and nodded as I called the waiter.

"Say," I said, "you have a hell of a job."

"I know it," he said, "but, señorito, I took it to keep out of jail."

"How come," I asked, "jail?"

"A woman," he said, "they had me for cutting a woman. I caught her giving her money to some other man after all I did for her, so I nearly killed her."

"Aren't you pretty old for that girl-racket, señor?"

"Not too old to knife one if she crosses me. They had me in jail locked up. But I said to them, I'm no good here, not to you nor me either. I know languages, I know people, I'm smart—so the Porra turned me out to help them scent revolutionists. Now they've switched me to the foreign squad. I get two dollars a day for just running around behind you. 'They' don't like strange foreigners."

We were speaking in Spanish, but when I switched to English he understood me equally well.

He spoke the English of the wharf rats and the bad Spanish of one who wants to speak Castilian. He was provincial and grandiloquent. But when he began to speak of women, as he did shortly, he was poetical too.

For years he had been a procurer on the waterfront, I learned as we drank. Even to his own wife, when he had one, he would bring lovers from among the sailors. The crumpled bills in his hand, the round silver dollars, meant more to him than any woman could ever mean, I gathered from his talk.

That afternoon he was quite out of breath from trailing me. He needed to rest, drink, sit, and talk to somebody. I was interested, so I began to ask him questions as I kept his glass filled.

"Those women," I said, "that you exploited, didn't they care?"

"Couldn't care," he said. "Most of 'em are poor, some of 'em are black, all of 'em loved me. They couldn't afford to care. Without me they might have died, anyhow. I looked out for them. Man, when I was young, the money they brought me! Whew-oo-o!"

As he told his story, I discovered that the little brown man was the very essence of those people who want a good time in life—and don't care how they get it. He had no morals. He had no qualms about using for gain the women who loved him or sought his protection. But, as he grew older, naturally they sought the favors of younger men; new kings arose in the brothels. Then he took to intimidations, to knives and beatings to hold his power. When he could no longer pay off the police, they put him in jail, so he became a spy.

"Drink," I said.

"*Sí, señor.*"

As he put his glass down, he twirled his little wax mustache and looked at me across the marble table in the darkening café. Outside the street lights had come on and the tropical evening deepened into night.

"Come, let us go to San Isidro Street, señorito," said the little man. "Along about now the girls are coming out."

"What's there," I asked, "in San Isidro Street?"

"Just women," said the little man, "of the waterfront."

"Pretty?" I asked.

"Yes," said the little man, "very pretty."

"So!" I said. "Have a drink."

This time I asked the waiter to bring a whole bottle of rum and leave it on our table. As the little man partook, he became more and more grandiloquent on the subject of women.

"The women of Cuba," he said, "are like the pomegranates of Santa Clara. Their souls are jeweled, *joven,* their blood is red, their lips are sweet. And sweetest of all are the mulattoes of Camagüey, *Americanito.* They are the sweetest of all."

"Why the mulattoes?" I said.

"Because," said the old man, "they are a mixture of two worlds, two extremes, two bloods. You see, señorito, the passion of the blacks and the passion of the whites combine in the smoldering heat that is *la mulata.* The rose of Venus blooms in her body. She's pain and she's pleasure. You see, señorito, I know. In the pure Negro, soul and body are separate. In the white they work badly together. But in the mulatto they strangle each other—and their strangulation produces that sweet juice that is a yellow woman's love."

With this amazing observation the little brown man, once a merchant in bodies, lifted his glass of rum and drank. He swayed a little in his chair as he put the glass down. He looked at me with funny far-off eyes. "I wish I were young again," he said. "Come, let's go down to San Isidro Street, sonny."

"Alright, wait a minute."

I got up and left the table. The little brown man's head was in his arms when I looked back. His eyes were closed. I slipped the barman a bill and went out, leaving more than half a bottle of Bacardi on the table.

That night I delivered all the messages that the exiles in the Latin-American quarter of Harlem had sent by me to their revolutionary co-workers in Havana.

On the boat to New York two days later, off the coast of Georgia, the wireless brought the news that the Cuban government was falling, and that a "pack of Negresses from the waterfront had torn the clothes off the backs of a party of cabinet wives as they came to visit their husbands in jail."

I wonder, I thought to myself, what the women of San Isidro Street would have done to that withered little old man had I gone there with him that night and whispered to them that he was a spy? They probably would have torn him to pieces and given his gold watch chain to some younger man. On the end of the chain I felt sure he had no watch.

Tragedy at the Baths

"That it should happen in my Baths!" was all she could say. "That it should happen in my Baths!" And try as they would, nobody could console her. Señora Rueda was quite hysterical. Being a big strong woman, her screams alarmed the neighborhood.

She and her now-deceased husband had owned the Baths for years—the Esmeralda Baths—among the cleanest and most respectable in Mexico City, family baths where only decent people came for their weekly tub or shower or *baño de vapor*.[14] Indeed, her establishment, with its tiled courtyard and splashing fountain, was a monument to the neighborhood, a middle-class section of flats and shops near the Loreto. Now this had happened!

Why! Señora Rueda had known the young man for years—that is, he had been a customer of the Esmeralda Baths since his youth, coming there for his weekly shower and swim in the little tiled tank. Sometimes, when he was flush, he took a private tub, and a good steaming out—which cost a *peso*. Juan Maldonado was the young man's name. He was a tall nice-looking boy.

That Sunday morning when he presented himself at the wicket and asked for a private tub for two—himself and his wife—Señora Rueda was not especially surprised. Even by reading the papers, one can't keep up with all the marriages that take place—and young men will eventually get married.

As she handed Juan his change she looked up to see beside him a vibrant black-haired girl with the soft Indian-brown complexion of a Mexican *mestiza*.[15] Señora Rueda smiled. A nice couple, she thought as the attendant showed them to their room and their tub. Two beautiful youths, she thought, and sighed.

Some bathhouses, she knew, did not allow the sexes to mingle within their walls, but Señora Rueda did not mind when they were legally married. Being respectable neighborhood baths, nothing but decent people were her patrons, anyway. She had no reason to suspect young Maldonado.

But an hour later there was another tale to tell! Not even smelling salts then could calm poor Señora Rueda. Oh, why did it have to happen in her Baths? *Por dios,* why?

This is the story as it came to me. It may not be wholly true for, in the patios and courtyards of Loreto, romantic and colorful additions have probably been added by those who know Juan and his family. The Mexicans love sad, romantic tales with many embroidered touches of sentimental heartbreak and ironic frustration. But, although versions of what led up to that strange Sunday morning in the Esmeralda Baths may vary in the telling, what actually happened therein—everybody knows. And it was awful!

In the first place, they were not married, Juan and that woman!

He met her in a very strange way, anyhow. The mounted police were charging a demonstration against the government. The Zocalo was filled with people trampling the grass and the flowers.[16] Juan crossed the square on the way to the shop where he worked, giving the demonstrators a wide berth—as his particular politics were not involved that day. But just as he got midway across the Zocalo, the police began to charge on horses and the crowd began to run, so Juan was forced to run, too.

Everyone was trying to reach the shelter of the *portales*[17] opposite the Palace, or the gates of the Cathedral, or the safety of a side street. Juan was heading toward Avenida Madero, the clatter of the horses' hoofs behind him when, just in front of him, a woman stumbled and fell.

Juan stopped running and picked her up, lifted her in his arms and went on. Once out of the square, in the quiet of a side street, he put her down on her feet and offered her his handkerchief to wipe the dust and tears from her face. Then he saw that she was young and very beautiful with the soft Indian-brown complexion of a Mexican mestiza.

"Ay, Señor," she said to the tall young man in front of her, "how can I ever thank you?"

But just at that moment a man approached, hatless and wild-eyed. He, too, had been caught in the spinning crowd, had seen his wife fall, but could not get to her—and then she had disappeared! For a while, the husband was frantic, but finally he caught sight of her around the corner faced by a tall young man who was offering her his handkerchief and gazing deep into her lovely eyes.

"You don't need to thank me," the young man was saying, "just let me look at you," as the girl caught sight of her approaching husband.

"Sunday at the Maximo," she whispered. "I want to thank you alone."

"At your service," said the young man, as the panting husband arrived.

Now, the husband was also a fairly young man, but neither as tall nor as handsome as Maldonado. He was much too short and frail to be married to so charming a woman. He kept an *escritorio,* a writing room, in the Portal of Santo Domingo on the little square, where letters were written for peasants who had no education, and where people could get legal documents copied on the typewriter, or have their names penned with decorative flourishes on a hundred calling cards.

The husband, too, there in the side street that day, thanked young Maldonado for having rescued his wife from the feet of the crowd and the hoofs of the police horses. Then they all shook hands and went their way, the tall young man going south, the pretty girl and her prosaic husband north.

But the following Sunday Maldonado waited at the entrance of the Cinema Maximo, where a Bogart film was being shown, and about five o'clock, sure enough, she appeared, alone. She was even prettier than the day he had picked her up in the Zocalo, and very shy, as if ashamed of what she was doing.

They took seats way up in the balcony, where lovers sit and hold hands in the dark. And soon they were holding hands, too.

"There was something about the strength of your arms the other day," she said, "even before I looked into your eyes, that made me want to stay with you forever."

"Stop!" yelled a cop, firing across the screen.

"And there was something in the feel of your body lying in my arms that made me never want to put you down," said Juan.

"My name is Consuelo Aguilar," the girl said softly. "You have met my husband."

"Tell me about him," said Juan.

"He is crazy about me," Consuelo answered, "and terribly jealous! He wants to be a writer, but all he writes is letters for peasants."

"And if he knew you were here—?"

"But he won't know. He stays home on Sundays and writes poems! When I tell him they're no good, he says I don't love him and threatens to commit suicide. He is very emotional, my little husband."

"And where does he think you are now?"

"At my aunt's."

It was really love, and at first sight, so they say in the patios of Loreto. But they also say that Juan was a little dumb, and a little inexperienced in the ways of women.

They kept on meeting in *cines*[18] and dance halls, and things began to be more and more dangerous for both of them, for husbands very often kill lovers in Mexico—and go free. It is the thing to do! But what this husband did was even worse! At least, Señora Rueda thought so.

But what his wife did was terrible, too. In Catholic lands where divorces are practically impossible, and where women are never supposed to leave their husbands, anyhow—this wife planned to run away with Maldonado! But, being young and foolish (or so they say in Loreto), for some strange reason or other, on the Sunday of their elopement, they planned to take a bath first. And that is how the couple happened to be in Señora Rueda's quiet Esmeralda Baths.

There the husband came and caught them! Or, rather, he deliberately followed them there. The miracle was that he did not kill them both! Instead, he bought a season's ticket for a whole year of baths (probably not realizing what he was doing) then went into the corridor outside the room where Juan and Consuelo were bathing—and shot *himself!*

Then it was that the uproar began, and such an uproar! People commenced to emerge from their tubs, clad and unclad, to run and scream. Doors began to open, and steam escaped into the courtyard. In the excitement, someone turned off the water main and the fountain stopped running. Naturally, Consuelo and Maldonado came out to see what was going on—and stumbled over the bleeding body of Señor Aguilar at their feet.

"Oh, my God!" Consuelo cried. "He said he would kill himself if I ran away with you."

"How did he ever know you were coming away with *me?*" asked the young man in astonishment.

"I told him," said Consuelo. Her eyes were hard. "I wanted to see if he really would commit suicide. He threatened to so often. But now, darling," she turned softly toward Juan, "with him gone, we can be married."

"But suppose he had killed *us!*" said Maldonado, trembling in the doorway with only a towel about his body.

"That little coward," sneered Consuelo, "wasn't man enough!"

"But he did kill himself," said Maldonado slowly, turning back into the room away from the body on the floor and the crowd that had gathered.

"Kiss me," purred Consuelo, lifting her pretty face toward Juan's, as she closed their door.

"Get away from me!" cried Juan, suddenly sickened with horror. Flinging open the door, he gave her a terrific push into the hall.

Consuelo fell prone over the body of her husband and, beginning to realize that she was, after all, a widow, and that there were six good typewriters to be inherited from the escritorio, she commenced to sob in approved fashion on the floor, embracing the corpse of her late spouse, hysterically—as a good wife should.

When the police got through asking questions of them both, and of Señora Rueda, Juan went home alone and left Consuelo still crying at the Baths. It took him a long time to get over the fact that she had told her husband—and the sound of that single pistol shot echoed in his head for months.

But the saddest thing of all, so they say in Loreto, was that when the details of their tragic triangle appeared in the papers, Juan's employer read them with such scandalized interest that he promptly dismissed him from his work. Consuelo lost only a husband she didn't want. But young Maldonado lost his *job*.

As for Señora Rueda, she swore never to rent another tub to a couple.

Trouble with the Angels

At every performance lots of white people wept. And almost every Sunday while they were on tour some white minister invited the Negro actor who played God to address his congregation and thus help improve race relations—because almost everywhere they needed improving. Although the play had been the hit of the decade in New York, its Negro actors and singers were paid much less than white actors and singers would have been paid for performing it. And, although the white producer and his backers made more than half a million dollars, the colored troupers on tour lived in cheap hotels and often slept in beds that were full of bugs. Only the actor who played God would sometimes, by the hardest, achieve accommodations in a white hotel, or be put up by some nice white family, or be invited to the home of the best Negroes in town. Thus God probably thought that everything was lovely in the world. As an actor he really got very good write-ups in the papers.

Then they were booked to play Washington, and that's where the trouble began. Washington, the capital of the United States is, as every Negro knows, a town where no black man was allowed inside a downtown theater, not even in the gallery until very recently. The legitimate playhouses had no accommodations for colored people. Incredible as it may seem, until Ingrid Bergman made her stand, Washington was worse than the Deep South in that respect.[19]

But God wasn't at all worried about playing Washington. He thought surely his coming would improve race relations. He thought it would be fine for the good white people of the Capital to see him—a colored God—even if Negroes couldn't. Not even those Negroes who worked for the government. Not even the black Congressman.

But several weeks before the Washington appearance of the famous "Negro" play about charming darkies who drank eggnog at a fish fry in heaven, storm clouds began to rise. It seemed that the Negroes of Washington strangely enough had decided that they, too, wanted to see this play. But when they approached the theater management on the question, they got a cold shoulder. The management said they didn't have any seats to sell Negroes. They couldn't even allot a corner in the upper gallery—there was such a heavy ticket demand from white folks.

Now this made the Negroes of Washington mad, especially those who worked for the government and constituted the best society. The teachers at Howard got mad, too, and the ministers of the colored churches who wanted to see what a black heaven looked like on the stage.

But nothing doing! The theater management was adamant. They really couldn't sell seats to Negroes. Although they had no scruples about making a large profit on the week's work of Negro actors, they couldn't permit Negroes to occupy seats in the theater.

So the Washington Negroes wrote directly to God, this colored God who had been such a hit on Broadway. They thought surely he would help them. Several organizations, including the Negro Ministerial Alliance, got in touch with him when he was playing Philadelphia. What a shame, they said by letter, that the white folks will not allow us to come to see you perform in Washington. We are getting up a protest. We want you to help us. Will you?

Now God knew that for many years white folks had not allowed Negroes in Washington to see any shows—not even in the churches, let alone in theaters! So how come they suddenly thought they ought to be allowed to see God in a white playhouse?

Besides, God was getting paid pretty well, and was pretty well known. So he answered their letters and said that although his ink was made of tears, and his heart bled, he couldn't afford to get into trouble with Equity. Also, it wasn't his place to go around the country spreading dissension and hate, but rather love and beauty. And it would surely do the white folks of the District of Columbia a lot of good to see Him, and it would soften their hearts to hear the beautiful Negro spirituals and witness the lovely black angels in his play.

The black drama lovers of Washington couldn't get any real satisfaction out of God by mail—their colored God. So when the company played Baltimore, a delegation of the Washington Negroes went over to the neighboring city to interview him. In Baltimore, Negroes, at least, were allowed to sit in the galleries of the theaters.

After the play, God received the delegation in his dressing room and wept about his inability to do anything concerning the situation. He had, of course, spoken to his management about it and they thought it might be possible to arrange a special Sunday night performance for Negroes. God said it hurt him to his soul to think how his people were mistreated, but the play must go on.

The delegation left in a huff—but not before they had spread their indignation to other members of the cast of the show. Then among the angels there arose a great discussion as to what they might do about the Washington situation. Although God was the star, the angels, too, were a part of the play.

Now, among the angels there was a young Negro named Johnny Logan who never really liked being an angel, but who, because of his baritone voice and Negro features, had gotten the job during the first rehearsals in New York. Now, since the play had been running three years, he was an old hand at being an angel.

Logan was from the South—but he hadn't stayed there long after he grew up. The white folks wouldn't let him. He was the kind of young Negro most Southern white people hate. He believed in fighting prejudice, in bucking against the traces of discrimination and Jim Crow, and in trying to knock down any white man who insulted him. So he was only about eighteen when the whites ran him out of Augusta, Georgia.

He came to New York, married a waitress, got a job as a redcap, and would have settled down forever in a little flat in Harlem, had not some of his friends discovered that he could sing. They persuaded him to join a Red Cap Quartette. Out of that had come this work as a black angel in what turned out to be a Broadway success in the midst of the depression.

Just before the show went on the road, his wife had their first kid, so he needed to hold his job as a singing angel, even if it meant going on tour. But the more he thought about their forthcoming appearance in a Washington theater that wasn't even Jim Crow—but barred Negroes altogether—the madder Logan got. Finally he got so mad that he caused the rest of the cast to organize a strike!

At that distance from Washington, black angels—from tenors to basses, sopranos to blues singers—were up in arms. Everybody in the cast, except God, agreed to strike.

"The idea of a town where colored folks can't even sit in the gallery to see an all-colored show. I ain't gonna work there myself."

"We'll show them white folks we've got spunk for once. We'll pull off the biggest actors' strike you ever seen."

"We sure will."

That was in Philadelphia. In Baltimore their ardor had cooled down a bit and it was all Logan could do to hold his temper as he felt his fellow angels weakening.

"Man, I got a wife to take care of. I can't lose no week's work!"

"I got a wife, too," said Logan, "and a kid besides, but I'm game."

"You ain't a trouper," said another, as he sat in the dressing room putting on his make-up.

"Naw, if you was you'd be used to playing all-white houses. In the old days . . ." said the man who played Methuselah, powdering his gray wig.

"I know all about the old days," said Logan, "when black minstrels blacked up even blacker and made fun of themselves for the benefit of white folks. But who wants to go back to the old days?"

"Anyhow, let's let well enough alone," said Methuselah.

"You guys have got no guts—that's all I can say," said Logan.

"You's just one of them radicals, son, that's what you are," put in the old tenor who played Saul. "We know when we want to strike or don't."

"Listen, then," said Logan to the angels who were putting on their wings by now, as it was near curtain time, "if we can't make it a real strike, then let's make it a general walk-out on the opening night. Strike for one performance anyhow. At least show folks that we won't take it lying down. Show those Washington Negroes we back them up—theoretically, anyhow."

"One day ain't so bad," said a skinny black angel. "I'm with you on a one-day strike."

"Me, too," several others agreed as they crowded into the corridor at curtain time. The actor who played God was standing in the wings in his frock coat.

"Shss-ss!" he said.

Monday in Washington. The opening of that famous white play about black life in a scenic heaven. Original New York cast. Songs as only Negroes can sing them. Uncle Tom come back as God.

Negro Washington wanted to picket the theater, but the police had an injunction against them. Cops were posted for blocks around the playhouse to prevent a riot. Nobody could see God. He was safely housed in the quiet home of a conservative Negro professor, guarded by two detectives. The papers said black radicals had threatened to kidnap him. To kidnap God!

Logan spent the whole day rallying the flagging spirits of his fellow actors, talking to them in their hotel rooms. They were solid for the one-day strike when he was around, and weak when he wasn't. No telling what Washington cops might do to them if they struck. They locked Negroes up for less than that in Washington. Besides, they might get canned, they might lose their pay, they might never get no more jobs on the stage. It was all right to talk about being a man and standing up for your race, and all that—but hell, even an actor has to eat. Besides, God was right. It was a great play, a famous play! They ought to hold up its reputation. It did white folks good to see Negroes in such a play. Logan must be crazy!

"Listen here, you might as well get wise. Ain't nobody gonna strike tonight," one of the men told him about six o'clock in the lobby of the colored Whitelaw Hotel. "You'd just as well give up. You're right. We ain't got no guts."

"I won't give up," said Logan.

When the actors reached the theater, they found it surrounded by cops and the stage was full of detectives. In the lobby there was a long line of people—white, of course—waiting to buy standing room. God arrived with motorcycle cops in front of his car. He had come a little early to address the cast. With him was the white stage manager and a representative of the New York producing office.

They called everybody together on the stage. The Lord wept as he spoke of all his race had borne to get where Negroes are today. Of how they had struggled. Of how they sang. Of how they must keep on struggling and singing—until white folks see the light. A strike would do no good. A strike would only hurt their cause. With sorrow in his heart—but more noble because of it—he would go on with the play. He was sure his actors—his angels—his children—would continue, too.

The white men accompanying God were very solemn, as though hurt to their souls to think what their Negro employees were suffering, but far more hurt to think that Negroes had wanted to jeopardize a week's box-office receipts by a strike! That would really harm everybody!

Behind God and the white managers stood two big detectives.

Needless to say, the Negroes finally went downstairs to put on their wings and make-up. All but Logan. He went downstairs to drag the cast out by force, to make men of darkies, to carry through the strike. But he couldn't. Not alone. Nobody really wanted to strike. Nobody wanted to sacrifice anything for race pride, decency, or elementary human rights. The actors only wanted to keep on appearing in a naïve dialect play about a quaint, funny heaven full of niggers at which white people laughed and wept.

The management sent two detectives downstairs to get Logan. They were taking no chances. Just as the curtain rose they carted him off to jail—for disturbing the peace. The colored angels were all massed in the wings for the opening spiritual when the police took the black boy out, a line of tears running down his cheeks.

Most of the actors *wanted* to think Logan was crying because he was being arrested—but in their souls they knew that was not why he wept.

On the Road

He was not interested in the snow. When he got off the freight, one early evening during the depression, Sargeant never even noticed the snow. But he must have felt it seeping down his neck, cold, wet, sopping in his shoes. But if you had asked him, he wouldn't have known it was snowing. Sargeant didn't see the snow, not even under the bright lights of the main street, falling white and flaky against the night. He was too hungry, too sleepy, too tired.

The Reverend Mr. Dorset, however, saw the snow when he switched on his porch light, opened the front door of his parsonage, and found standing there before him a big black man with snow on his face, a human piece of night with snow on his face—obviously unemployed.

Said the Reverend Mr. Dorset before Sargeant even realized he'd opened his mouth: "I'm sorry. No! Go right on down this street four blocks and turn to your left, walk up seven and you'll see the Relief Shelter. I'm sorry. No!" He shut the door.

Sargeant wanted to tell the holy man that he had already been to the Relief Shelter, been to hundreds of relief shelters during the depression years, the beds were always gone and supper was over, the place was full, and they drew the color line anyhow. But the minister said, "No," and shut the door. Evidently he didn't want to hear about it. And he *had* a door to shut.

The big black man turned away. And even yet he didn't see the snow, walking right into it. Maybe he sensed it, cold, wet, sticking to his jaws, wet on his black hands, sopping in his shoes. He stopped and stood on the sidewalk hunched over—hungry, sleepy, cold—looking up and down. Then he looked right where he was—in front of a church. Of course! A church! Sure, right next to a parsonage, certainly a church.

It had *two* doors.

Broad white steps in the night all snowy white. Two high arched doors with slender stone pillars on either side. And way up, a round lacy window with a stone crucifix in the middle and Christ on the crucifix in stone. All this was pale in the street lights, solid and stony pale in the snow.

Sargeant blinked. When he looked up the snow fell into his eyes. For the first time that night he *saw* the snow. He shook his head. He shook the snow from his coat sleeves, felt hungry, felt lost, felt not lost, felt cold. He walked up the steps of the church. He knocked at the door. No answer. He tried the handle. Locked. He put his shoulder against the door and his long black body slanted like a ramrod. He pushed. With loud rhythmic grunts, like the grunts in a chain-gang song, he pushed against the door.

"I'm tired . . . Huh! . . . Hongry . . . Uh! . . . I'm sleepy . . . Huh! I'm cold . . . I got to sleep somewheres," Sargeant said. "This here is a church, ain't it? Well, uh!"

He pushed against the door.

Suddenly, with an undue cracking and screaking, the door began to give way to the tall black Negro who pushed ferociously against the door.

By now two or three white people had stopped in the street, and Sargeant was vaguely aware of some of them yelling at him concerning the door. Three or four more came running, yelling at him.

"Hey!" they said. "Hey!"

"Un-huh," answered the big tall Negro, "I know it's a white folks' church, but I got to sleep somewhere." He gave another lunge at the door. "Huh!"

And the door broke open.

But just when the door gave way, two white cops arrived in a car, ran up the steps with their clubs and grabbed Sargeant. But Sargeant for once had no intention of being pulled or pushed away from the door.

Sargeant grabbed, but not for anything so weak as a broken door. He grabbed for one of the tall stone pillars beside the door, grabbed at it and caught it. And held it. The cops pulled and Sargeant pulled. Most of the people in the street got behind the cops and helped them pull.

"A big black unemployed Negro holding onto our church!" thought the people. "The idea!"

The cops began to beat Sargeant over the head, and nobody protested. But he held on.

And then the church fell down.

Gradually, the big stone front of the church fell down, the walls and the rafters, the crucifix and the Christ. Then the whole thing fell down, covering the cops and the people with bricks and stones and debris. The whole church fell down in the snow.

Sargeant got out from under the church and went walking on up the street with the stone pillar on his shoulder. He was under the impression that he had buried the parsonage and the Reverend Mr. Dorset who said,

"No!" So he laughed, and threw the pillar six blocks up the street and went on.

Sargeant thought he was alone, but listening to the crunch, crunch, crunch on the snow of his own footsteps, he heard other footsteps, too, doubling his own. He looked around and there was Christ walking along beside him, the same Christ that had been on the cross on the church—still stone with a rough stone surface, walking along beside him just like he was broken off the cross when the church fell down.

"Well, I'll be dogged," said Sargeant. "This here's the first time I ever seed you off the cross."

"Yes," said Christ, crunching his feet in the snow. "You had to pull the church down to get me off the cross."

"You glad?" said Sargeant.

"I sure am," said Christ.

They both laughed.

"I'm a hell of a fellow, ain't I?" said Sargeant. "Done pulled the church down!"

"You did a good job," said Christ. "They have kept me nailed on a cross for nearly two thousand years."

"Whee-ee-e!" said Sargeant. "I know you are glad to get off."

"I sure am," said Christ.

They walked on in the snow. Sargeant looked at the man of stone.

"And you been up there two thousand years?"

"I sure have," Christ said.

"Well, if I had a little cash," said Sargeant, "I'd show you around a bit."

"I been around," said Christ.

"Yeah, but that was a long time ago."

"All the same," said Christ, "I've been around."

They walked on in the snow until they came to the railroad yards. Sargeant was tired, sweating and tired.

"Where you goin'?" Sargeant said, stopping by the tracks. He looked at Christ. Sargeant said, "I'm just a bum on the road. How about you? Where you goin'?"

"God knows," Christ said, "but I'm leavin' here."

They saw the red and green lights of the railroad yard half veiled by the snow that fell out of the night. Away down the track they saw a fire in a hobo jungle.

"I can go there and sleep," Sargeant said.

"You can?"

"Sure," said Sargeant. "That place ain't got no doors."

Outside the town, along the tracks, there were barren trees and bushes below the embankment, snow-gray in the dark. And down among the trees and bushes there were makeshift houses made out of boxes and tin and old pieces of wood and canvas. You couldn't see them in the dark, but you knew they were there if you'd ever been on the road, if you had ever lived with the homeless and hungry in a depression.

"I'm side-tracking," Sargeant said. "I'm tired."

"I'm gonna make it on to Kansas City," said Christ.

"O.K.," Sargeant said. "So long!"

He went down into the hobo jungle and found himself a place to sleep. He never did see Christ no more. About six A.M. a freight came by. Sargeant scrambled out of the jungle with a dozen or so more hoboes and ran along the track, grabbing at the freight. It was dawn, early dawn, cold and gray.

"Wonder where Christ is by now?" Sargeant thought. "He must-a gone on way on down the road. He didn't sleep in this jungle."

Sargeant grabbed the train and started to pull himself up into a moving coal car, over the edge of a wheeling coal car. But strangely enough, the car was full of cops. The nearest cop rapped Sargeant soundly across the knuckles with his night stick. Wham! Rapped his big black hands for clinging to the top of the car. Wham! But Sargeant did not turn loose. He clung on and tried to pull himself into the car. He hollered at the top of his voice, "Damn it, lemme in this car!"

"Shut up," barked the cop. "You crazy coon!" He rapped Sargeant across the knuckles and punched him in the stomach. "You ain't out in no jungle now. This ain't no train. You in jail."

Wham! across his bare black fingers clinging to the bars of his cell. Wham! between the steel bars low down against his shins.

Suddenly Sargeant realized that he really was in jail. He wasn't on no train. The blood of the night before had dried on his face, his head hurt terribly, and a cop outside in the corridor was hitting him across the knuckles for holding onto the door, yelling and shaking the cell door.

"They must-a took me to jail for breaking down the door last night," Sargeant thought, "that church door."

Sargeant went over and sat on a wooden bench against the cold stone wall. He was emptier than ever. His clothes were wet, clammy cold wet, and shoes sloppy with snow water. It was just about dawn. There he was, locked up behind a cell door, nursing his bruised fingers.

The bruised fingers were his, but not the *door.*

Not the *club,* but the fingers.

"You wait," mumbled Sargeant, black against the jail wall. "I'm gonna break down this door, too."

"Shut up—or I'll paste you one," said the cop.

"I'm gonna break down this door," yelled Sargeant as he stood up in his cell.

Then he must have been talking to himself because he said, "I wonder where Christ's gone? I wonder if he's gone to Kansas City?"

Big Meeting

The early stars had begun to twinkle in the August night as Bud and I neared the woods. A great many Negroes, old and young, were plodding down the dirt road on foot on their way to the Big Meeting. Long before we came near the lantern-lighted tent we could hear early arrivals singing, clapping their hands lustily and throwing out each word distinct like a drumbeat. Songs like "When the Saints Go Marching Home" and "That Old-Time Religion" filled the air.

In the road that ran past the woods, a number of automobiles and buggies belonging to white people had stopped near the tent so that their occupants might listen to the singing. The whites stared curiously through the hickory trees at the rocking figures in the tent. The canvas, except behind the pulpit, was rolled up on account of the heat, and the meeting could easily be seen from the road, so there beneath a tree Bud and I stopped, too. In our teens, we were young and wild and didn't believe much in revivals, so we stayed outside in the road where we could smoke and laugh like the white folks. But both Bud's mother and mine were under the tent singing, actively a part of the services. Had they known we were near, they would certainly have come out and dragged us in.

From frequent attendance since childhood at these Big Meetings held each summer in the South, we knew the services were divided into three parts. The testimonials and the song-service came first. This began as soon as two or three people were gathered together, continuing until the minister himself arrived. Then the sermon followed, with its accompanying songs and shouts from the audience. Then the climax came with the calling of the lost souls to the mourners' bench, and the prayers for sinners and backsliders. This was where Bud and I would leave. We were having too good a time being sinners, and we didn't want to be saved—not yet, anyway.

When we arrived, old Aunt Ibey Davis was just starting a familiar song:

> *Where shall I be when that first trumpet sound?*
> *Lawdy, where shall I be when it sound so loud?*

The rapidly increasing number of worshipers took up the tune in full volume sending a great flood of melody billowing beneath the canvas roof. With heads back, feet and hands patting time, they repeated the chorus again and again. And each party of new arrivals swung into rhythm as they walked up the aisle by the light of the dim oil lanterns hanging from the tent poles.

Standing there at the edge of the road beneath a big tree, Bud and I watched the people as they came—keeping our eyes open for the girls. Scores of Negroes from the town and nearby villages and farms came drawn by the music and the preaching. Some were old and gray-headed; some in the prime of life; some mere boys and girls; and many little barefooted children. It was the twelfth night of the Big Meeting. They came from miles around to bathe their souls in a sea of song, to shout and cry and moan before the flow of Reverend Braswell's eloquence, and to pray for all the sinners in the county who had not yet seen the light. Although it was a colored folks' meeting, whites liked to come and sit outside in the road in their cars and listen. Sometimes there would be as many as ten or twelve parties of whites parked there in the dark, smoking and listening, and enjoying themselves, like Bud and I, in a not very serious way.

Even while old Aunt Ibey Davis was singing, a big red Buick drove up and parked right behind Bud and me beneath the tree. It was full of white people, and we recognized the driver as Mr. Parkes, the man who owned the drugstore in town where colored people couldn't buy a glass of soda at the fountain.

> *It will sound so loud it will wake up the dead!*
> *Lawdy, where shall I be when it sound?*

"You'll hear some good singing out here," Mr. Parkes said to a woman in the car with him.

"I always did love to hear darkies singing," she answered from the back seat.

Bud nudged me in the ribs at the word *darkie*.

"I hear 'em," I said, sitting down on one of the gnarled roots of the tree and pulling out a cigarette.

The song ended as an old black woman inside the tent got up to speak. "I rise to testify dis evenin' fo' Jesus!" she said. "Ma Saviour an' ma Redeemer an' de chamber wherein I resuscitates ma soul. Pray fo' me, brothers and sisters. Let yo' mercies bless me in all I do an' yo' prayers go with me on each travelin' voyage through dis land."

"Amen! Hallelujah!" cried my mother.

Just in front of us, near the side of the tent, a woman's clear soprano voice began to sing:

> *I am a po' pilgrim of sorrow*
> *Out in this wide world alone . . .*

Soon others joined with her and the whole tent was singing:

> *Sometimes I am tossed and driven,*
> *Sometimes I don't know where to go . . .*

"Real pretty, ain't it?" said the white woman in the car behind us.

> *But I've heard of a city called heaven*
> *And I've started to make it my home.*

When the woman finished her song she rose and told how her husband left her with six children, her mother died in a poorhouse, and the world had always been against her—but still she was going on!

"My, she's had a hard time," giggled the woman in the car.

"Sure has," laughed Mr. Parkes, "to hear her tell it."

And the way they talked made gooseflesh come out on my skin.

"Trials and tribulations surround me—but I'm goin' on," the woman in the tent cried. Shouts and exclamations of approval broke out all over the congregation.

"Praise God!"

"Bless His Holy Name!"

"That's right, sister!"

"Devils beset me—but I'm goin' on!" said the woman. "I ain't got no friends—but I'm goin' on!"

"Jesus yo' friend, sister! Jesus yo' friend!" came the answer.

"God bless Jesus! I'm goin' on!"

"Dat's right!" cried Sister Mabry, Bud's mother, bouncing in her seat and flinging her arms outward. "Take all this world, but gimme Jesus!"

"Look at mama," Bud said half amused, sitting there beside me smoking. "She's getting happy."

"Whoo-ooo-o-o! Great Gawd-a-Mighty!" yelled old man Walls near the pulpit. "I can't hold it dis evenin'! Dis mawnin', dis evenin', dis mawnin', Lawd!"

"Pray for me—cause I'm goin' on!" said the woman. In the midst of the demonstration she had created she sat down exhausted, her armpits wet with sweat and her face covered with tears.

"Did you hear her, Jehover?" someone asked.

"Yes! He heard her! Halleloo!" came the answer.

"Dis mawnin', dis evenin', dis mawnin', Lawd!"

Brother Nace Eubanks began to line a song:

> *Must Jesus bear his cross alone*
> *An' all de world go free?*

Slowly they sang it line by line. Then the old man rose and told of a vision that had come to him long ago on that day when he had been changed from a sinner to a just man.

"I was layin' in ma bed," he said, "at de midnight hour twenty-two years past at 714 Pine Street in dis here city when a snow-white sheep come in ma room an' stood behind de wash bowl. Dis here sheep, hit spoke to me wid tongues o' fiah an' hit said, 'Nace, git up! Git up, an' come wid me!' Yes, suh! He had a light round 'bout his head like a moon, an' wings like a dove, an' he walked on hoofs o' gold an' dis sheep hit said, 'I once were lost, but now I'm saved, an' you kin be like me!' Yes, suh! An' ever since dat night, brothers an' sisters, I's been a chile o' de Lamb! Pray fo' me!"

"Help him, Jesus!" Sister Mabry shouted.

"Amen!" chanted Deacon Laws. "Amen! Amen!"

> *Glory! Hallelujah!*
> *Let de halleluian roll!*
> *I'll sing ma Saviour's praises far an' wide!*

It was my mother's favorite song, and she sang it like a paean of triumph, rising from her seat.

"Look at ma," I said to Bud, knowing that she was about to start her nightly shouting.

"Yah," Bud said. "I hope she don't see me while she's standing up there, or she'll come out here and make us go up to the mourners' bench."

"We'll leave before that," I said.

> *I've opened up to heaven*

All de windows of ma soul,
An' I'm livin' on de halleluian side!

Rocking proudly to and fro as the second chorus boomed and swelled beneath the canvas, mama began to clap her hands, her lips silent now in this sea of song she had started, her head thrown back in joy—for my mother was a great shouter. Stepping gracefully to the beat of the music, she moved out toward the center aisle into a cleared space. Then she began to spring on her toes with little short rhythmical hops. All the way up the long aisle to the pulpit gently she leaped to the clap-clap of hands, the pat of feet, and the steady booming song of her fellow worshipers. Then mama began to revolve in a dignified circle, slowly, as a great happiness swept her gleaming black features, and her lips curved into a smile.

I've opened up to heaven
All de windows of my soul ...

Mama was dancing before the Lord with her eyes closed, her mouth smiling, and her head held high.

I'm livin' on de halleluian side!

As she danced she threw her hands upward away from her breasts as though casting off all the cares of the world.

Just then the white woman in Mr. Parkes' car behind us laughed, "My Lord, John, it's better than a show!"

Something about the way she laughed made my blood boil. That was *my mother* dancing and shouting. Maybe it was better than a show, but nobody had any business laughing at her, least of all white people.

I looked at Bud, but he didn't say anything. Maybe he was thinking how often we, too, made fun of the shouters, laughing at our parents as though they were crazy—but deep down inside us we understood why they came to Big Meeting. Working all day all their lives for white folks, they *had* to believe there was a "Halleluian Side."

I looked at mama standing there singing, and I thought about how many years she had prayed and shouted and praised the Lord at church meetings and revivals, then came home for a few hours' sleep before getting up at dawn to go cook and scrub and clean for others. And I didn't want any white folks, especially whites who wouldn't let a Negro drink a glass of soda in their drugstore or give one a job, sitting in a car laughing at mama.

"Gimme a cigarette, Bud. If these dopes behind us say any more, I'm gonna get up and tell 'em something they won't like."

"To hell with 'em," Bud answered.

I leaned back against the gnarled roots of the tree by the road and inhaled deeply. The white people were silent again in their car, listening to the singing. In the dark I couldn't see their faces to tell if they were still amused or not. But that was mostly what they wanted out of Negroes—work and fun—without paying for it, I thought, work and fun.

To a great hand-clapping, body-rocking, foot-patting rhythm, mama was repeating the chorus over and over. Sisters leaped and shouted and perspiring brothers walked the aisles bowing left and right, beating time, shaking hands, laughing aloud for joy, and singing steadily when, at the back of the tent, the Reverend Duke Braswell arrived.

A tall, powerful, jet-black man, he moved with long steps through the center of the tent, his iron-gray hair uncovered, his green-black coat jim-swinging to his knees, his fierce eyes looking straight toward the altar. Under his arm he carried a Bible.

Once on the platform, he stood silently wiping his brow with a large white handkerchief while the singing swirled around him. Then he sang, too, his voice roaring like a cyclone, his white teeth shining. Finally he held up his palms for silence and the song gradually lowered to a hum, hum, hum, hands and feet patting, bodies still moving. At last, above the broken cries of the shouters and the undertones of song, the minister was able to make himself heard.

"Brother Garner, offer up a prayer."

Reverend Braswell sank on his knees and every back bowed. Brother Garner, with his head in his hands, lifted his voice against a background of moans:

"Oh, Lawd, we comes befo' you dis evenin' wid fear an' tremblin'—unworthy as we is to enter yo' house an' speak yo' name. We comes befo' you, Lawd, cause we knows you is mighty an' powerful in all de lands, an' great above de stars, an' bright above de moon. Oh, Lawd, you is bigger den de world. You holds de sun in yo' right hand an' de mornin' star in yo' left, an' we po' sinners ain't nothin', not even so much as a grain o' sand beneath yo' feet. Yet we calls on you dis evenin' to hear us, Lawd, to send down yo' sweet Son Jesus to walk wid us in our sorrows to comfort us on our weary road cause sometimes we don't know which-a-way to turn! We pray you dis evenin', Lawd, to look down at our wanderin' chilluns what's gone from home. Look down in St. Louis, Lawd, an' look in Memphis, an' look down in Chicago if they's usin' Thy name in vain dis evenin', if they's gamblin' tonight, Lawd, if they's doin' any ways wrong—reach down an' pull 'em up, Lawd, an' say, 'Come wid me, cause I am de Vine an' de Husbandman an' de gate dat leads to Glory!' "

Remembering sons in faraway cities, "Help him, Jesus!" mothers cried.

"Whilst you's lookin' down on us dis evenin', keep a mighty eye on de sick an' de 'flicked. Ease Sister Hightower, Lawd, layin' in her bed at de pint o' death. An' bless Bro' Carpenter what's come out to meetin' here dis evenin' in spite o' his broken arm from fallin' off de roof. An' Lawd, aid de pastor dis evenin' to fill dis tent wid yo' Spirit, an' to make de sinners tremble an' backsliders shout, an' dem dat is widout de church to come to de moaners' bench an' find rest in Jesus! We ask Thee all dese favors dis evenin'. Also to guide us an' bless us wid Thy bread an' give us Thy wine to drink fo' Christ de Holy Saviour's sake, our Shelter an' our Rock. Amen!"

There's not a friend like de lowly Jesus . . .

Some sister began, high and clear after the passion of the prayer,

No, not one! . . . No, not one!

Then the preacher took his text from the open Bible. "Ye now therefore have sorrow: but I will see you again, and your hearts shall rejoice, and your joy no man taketh from you."

He slammed shut the Holy Book and walked to the edge of the platform. "That's what Jesus said befo' he went to the cross, children—'I will see you again, and yo' hearts shall rejoice!' "

"Yes, sir!" said the brothers and sisters. " 'Deed he did!"

Then the minister began to tell the familiar story of the death of Christ. Standing in the dim light of the smoking oil lanterns, he sketched the life of the man who had had power over multitudes.

"Power," the minister said. "Power! Without money and without titles, without position, he had power! And that power went out to the poor and afflicted. For Jesus said, 'The first shall be last, and the last shall be first.' "

"He sho did!" cried Bud's mother.

"Hallelujah!" mama agreed loudly. "Glory be to God!"

"Then the big people of the land heard about Jesus," the preacher went on, "the chief priests and the scribes, the politicians, the bootleggers, and the bankers—and they begun to conspire against Jesus because *He had power!* This Jesus with His twelve disciples preachin' in Galilee. Then came that eve of the Passover, when he set down with His friends to eat and drink of the vine and the settin' sun fell behind the hills of Jerusalem. And Jesus knew that ere the cock crew Judas would betray Him, and Peter would say, 'I know Him not,' and all alone by Hisself He would go to His death. Yes, sir, He knew! So He got up from the table and went into the garden to pray. In this hour of trouble, Jesus went to pray!"

Away at the back of the tent some old sister began to sing:

Oh, watch with me one hour
While I go yonder and pray . . .

And the crowd took up the song, swelled it, made its melody fill the hot tent while the minister stopped talking to wipe his face with his white handkerchief.

Then to the humming undertone of the song, he continued, "They called it Gethsemane—that garden where Jesus fell down on His face in the grass and cried to the Father, 'Let this bitter hour pass from me! Oh, God, let this hour pass.' Because He was still a young man who did not want to die, He rose up and went back into the house—but His friends was all asleep. While Jesus prayed, His friends done gone to sleep! But, 'Sleep on,' he said, 'for the hour is at hand.' Jesus said, 'Sleep on.'"

"Sleep on, sleep on," chanted the crowd, repeating the words of the minister.

"He was not angry with them. But as Jesus looked out of the house, He saw that garden alive with men carryin' lanterns and swords and staves, and the mob was everywhere. So He went to the door. Then Judas come out from among the crowd, the traitor Judas, and kissed Him on the cheek—Oh, bitter friendship! And the soldiers with handcuffs fell upon the Lord and took Him prisoner.

"The disciples was awake by now, Oh, yes! But they fled away because they was afraid. And the mob carried Jesus off.

"Peter followed Him from afar, followed Jesus in chains till they come to the palace of the high priest. There Peter went in, timid and afraid, to see the trial. He set in the back of the hall. Peter listened to the lies they told about Christ—and didn't dispute 'em. He watched the high priest spit in Christ's face—and made no move. He saw 'em smite Him with the palms of they hands—and Peter uttered not a word for his poor mistreated Jesus."

"Not a word! . . . Not a word! . . . Not a word!"

"And when the servants of the high priest asked Peter, 'Does you know this man?' he said, 'I do not!'

"And when they asked him a second time, he said, 'No!'

"And yet a third time, 'Do you know Jesus?'

"And Peter answered with an oath, 'I told you, No!'

"Then the cock crew."

"De cock crew!" cried Aunt Ibey Davis. "De cock crew! Oh, ma Lawd! De cock crew!"

"The next day the chief priests taken counsel against Jesus to put Him to death. They brought Him before Pilate, and Pilate said, 'What evil hath he done?'

"But the people cried, 'Crucify Him!' because they didn't care. So Pilate called for water and washed his hands.

"The soldiers made sport of Jesus where He stood in the Council Hall. They stripped Him naked, and put a crown of thorns on His head, a red robe about His body, and a reed from the river in His hands.

"They said, 'Ha! Ha! So you're the King! Ha! Ha!' And they bowed down in mockery before Him, makin' fun of Jesus.

"Some of the guards threw wine in His face. Some of the guards was drunk and called Him out o' His name—and nobody said, 'Stop! That's Jesus!' "

The Reverend Duke Braswell's face darkened with horror as he pictured the death of Christ. "Oh, yes! Peter denied Him because he was afraid. Judas betrayed Him for thirty pieces of silver. Pilate said, 'I wash my hands—take him and kill Him.'

"And His friends fled away! . . . Have mercy on Jesus! . . . His friends done fled away!"

"His friends!"

"His friends done fled away!"

The preacher chanted, half moaning his sentences, not speaking them. His breath came in quick, short gasps with an indrawn, "Umn!" between each rapid phrase. Perspiration poured down his face as he strode across the platform wrapped in this drama that he saw in the very air before his eyes. Peering over the heads of his audience out into the darkness, he began the ascent to Golgotha, describing the taunting crowd at Christ's heels and the heavy cross on His shoulders.

"Then a black man named Simon, blacker than me, come and took the cross and bore it for Him. Umn!

"Then Jesus were standin' alone on a high hill, in the broilin' sun, while they put the crosses in the ground. No water to cool His throat! No tree to shade His achin' head! Nobody to say a friendly word to Jesus! Umn!

"Alone, in that crowd on the hill of Golgotha, with two thieves bound and dyin', and the murmur of the mob all around. Umn!

"But Jesus never said a word! Umn!

"They laid they hands on Him, and they tore the clothes from His body—and then, and then," loud as a thunderclap, the minister's voice broke through the little tent, "they raised Him to the cross!"

A great wail went up from the crowd. Bud and I sat entranced in spite of ourselves, forgetting to smoke. Aunt Ibey Davis wept. Sister Mabry moaned. In their car behind us the white people were silent as the minister went on:

> *They brought four long iron nails*
> *And put one in the palm of His left hand.*
> *The hammer said . . . Bam!*
> *They put one in the palm of His right hand.*
> *The hammer said . . . Bam!*
> *They put one through His left foot . . . Bam!*
> *And one through His right foot . . . Bam!*

"Don't drive it!" a woman screamed. "Don't drive them nails! For Christ's sake! Oh! Don't drive 'em!"

> *And they left my Jesus on the cross.*
> *Nails in His hands! Nails in His feet!*
> *Sword in His side! Thorns circlin' His head!*
> *Mob cussin' and hootin' my Jesus. Umn!*
> *The spit of the mob in His face! Umn!*
> *His body hangin' on the cross! Umn!*
> *Gimme piece of His garment for a souvenir! Umn!*
> *Castin' lots for His garments! Umn!*
> *Blood from His wounded side! Umn!*
> *Streamin' down His naked legs! Umn!*
> *Droppin' in the dust—umn—*
> *That's what they did to my Jesus!*
> *They stoned Him first, they stoned Him!*

Called Him everything but a child of God.
Then they lynched Him on the cross.

In song I heard my mother's voice cry:

Were you there when they crucified my Lord?
Were you there when they nailed Him to the tree?

The Reverend Duke Braswell stretched wide his arms against the white canvas of the tent. In the yellow light his body made a cross-like shadow on the canvas.

Oh, it makes me to tremble, tremble!
Were you there when they crucified my Lord?

"Let's go," said the white woman in the car behind us. "This is too much for me!" They started the motor and drove noisily away in a swirl of dust.

"Don't go," I cried from where I was sitting at the root of the tree. "Don't go," I shouted, jumping up. "They're about to call for sinners to come to the mourners' bench. Don't go!" But their car was already out of earshot.

I didn't realize I was crying until I tasted my tears in my mouth.

Something in Common
and Other Stories

(1963)

The following stories are from *The Ways of White Folks,* reprinted with the permission of the publisher, Alfred A. Knopf, Inc.: "Little Dog," "A Good Job Gone," "Father and Son."

The following stories are from *Laughing to Keep from Crying,* published by Henry Holt and Company: "Who's Passing for Who?," "African Morning," "Pushcart Man," "Why, You Reckon?," "Saratoga Rain," "Spanish Blood," "Heaven to Hell," "Sailor Ashore," "Slice Him Down," "Tain't So," "Professor," "Powder-White Faces," "Rouge High," "On the Way Home," "Mysterious Madame Shanghai," "Never Room with a Couple," "Tragedy at the Baths," "Trouble with the Angels," "On the Road," "Big Meeting," "Something in Common."

The following stories are from *The Langston Hughes Reader,* published by George Braziller, Inc.: "Thank You, M'am," "Patron of the Arts."

Other stories originally appeared in magazines as follows: "Gumption" in *The New Yorker* under the title "Oyster's Son"; "The Gun" in the *Brooklyn Daily Eagle* under the title "Flora Belle"; "Sorrow for a Midget" in *The Literary Review* of Fairleigh Dickinson University; "Fine Accommodations" in *Negro Story* under the title "The Negro in the Drawingroom"; "Breakfast in Virginia" in *Common Ground* under the title "I Thank You for This."

To Gwendolyn

My thanks to *The New Yorker, Esquire, The American Spectator, Story Magazine, Common Ground, The American Mercury, The Crisis, The Literary Review, Negro Story, Stag, The African, Scribner's Fiction Parade,* and *The Brooklyn Daily Eagle* in whose pages some of these stories first appeared.

Contents

Thank You, M'am

She was a large woman with a large purse that had everything in it but a hammer and nails. It had a long strap, and she carried it slung across her shoulder. It was about eleven o'clock at night, dark, and she was walking alone, when a boy ran up behind her and tried to snatch her purse. The strap broke with the sudden single tug the boy gave it from behind. But the boy's weight and the weight of the purse combined caused him to lose his balance. Instead of taking off full blast as he had hoped, the boy fell on his back on the sidewalk and his legs flew up. The large woman simply turned around and kicked him right square in his blue-jeaned sitter. Then she reached down, picked the boy up by his shirt front, and shook him until his teeth rattled.

After that the woman said, "Pick up my pocketbook, boy, and give it here."

She still held him tightly. But she bent down enough to permit him to stoop and pick up her purse. Then she said, "Now ain't you ashamed of yourself?"

Firmly gripped by his shirt front, the boy said, "Yes'm."

The woman said, "What did you want to do it for?"

The boy said, "I didn't aim to."

She said, "You a lie!"

By that time two or three people passed, stopped, turned to look, and some stood watching.

"If I turn you loose, will you run?" asked the woman.

"Yes'm," said the boy.

"Then I won't turn you loose," said the woman. She did not release him.

"Lady, I'm sorry," whispered the boy.

"Um-hum! Your face is dirty. I got a great mind to wash your face for you. Ain't you got nobody home to tell you to wash your face?"

"No'm," said the boy.

"Then it will get washed this evening," said the large woman, starting up the street, dragging the frightened boy behind her.

He looked as if he were fourteen or fifteen, frail and willow-wild, in tennis shoes and blue jeans.

The woman said, "You ought to be my son. I would teach you right from wrong. Least I can do right now is to wash your face. Are you hungry?"

"No'm," said the being-dragged boy. "I just want you to turn me loose."

"Was I bothering *you* when I turned that corner?" asked the woman.

"No'm."

"But you put yourself in contact with *me*," said the woman. "If you think that that contact is not going to last awhile, you got another thought coming. When I get through with you, sir, you are going to remember Mrs. Luella Bates Washington Jones."

Sweat popped out on the boy's face and he began to struggle. Mrs. Jones stopped, jerked him around in front of her, put a half nelson about his neck, and continued to drag him up the street. When she got to her door, she dragged the boy inside, down a hall, and into a large kitchenette-furnished room at the rear of the house. She switched on the light and left the door open. The boy could hear other roomers laughing and talking in the large house. Some of their doors were open, too, so he knew he and the woman were not alone. The woman still had him by the neck in the middle of her room.

She said, "What is your name?"

"Roger," answered the boy.

"Then, Roger, you go to that sink and wash your face," said the woman, whereupon she turned him loose—at last. Roger looked at the door—looked at the woman—looked at the door—*and went to the sink.*

"Let the water run until it gets warm," she said. "Here's a clean towel."

"You gonna take me to jail?" asked the boy, bending over the sink.

"Not with that face, I would not take you nowhere," said the woman. "Here I am trying to get home to cook me a bite to eat, and you snatch my pocketbook! Maybe you ain't been to your supper either, late as it be. Have you?"

"There's nobody home at my house," said the boy.

"Then we'll eat," said the woman. "I believe you're hungry—or been hungry—to try to snatch my pocketbook!"

"I want a pair of blue suede shoes," said the boy.

"Well, you didn't have to snatch *my* pocketbook to get some suede shoes," said Mrs. Luella Bates Washington Jones. "You could of asked me."

"M'am?"

The water dripping from his face, the boy looked at her. There was a long pause. A very long pause. After he had dried his face and not knowing what else to do, dried it again, the boy turned around, wondering what next. The door was open. He could make a dash for it down the hall. He could run, run, run, *run!*

The woman was sitting on the day bed. After a while she said, "I were young once and I wanted things I could not get."

There was another long pause. The boy's mouth opened. Then he frowned, not knowing he frowned.

The woman said, "Um-hum! You thought I was going to say *but*, didn't you? You thought I was going to say, *but I didn't snatch people's pocketbooks*. Well, I wasn't going to say that." Pause. Silence. "I have done things, too, which I would not tell you, son—neither tell God, if He didn't already know. Everybody's got something in common. So you set down while I fix us something to eat. You might run that comb through your hair so you will look presentable."

In another corner of the room behind a screen was a gas plate and an icebox. Mrs. Jones got up and went behind the screen. The woman did not watch the boy to see if he was going to run now, nor did she watch her purse, which she left behind her on the day bed. But the boy took care to sit on the far side of the room, away from the purse, where he thought she could easily see him out of the corner of her eye if she wanted to. He did not trust the woman *not* to trust him. And he did not want to be mistrusted now.

"Do you need somebody to go to the store," asked the boy, "maybe to get some milk or something?"

"Don't believe I do," said the woman, "unless you just want sweet milk yourself. I was going to make cocoa out of this canned milk I got here."

"That will be fine," said the boy.

She heated some lima beans and ham she had in the icebox, made the cocoa, and set the table. The woman did not ask the boy anything about where he lived, or his folks, or anything else that would embarrass him. Instead, as they ate, she told him about her job in a hotel beauty shop that stayed open late, what the work was like, and how all kinds of women came in and out, blondes, redheads, and Spanish. Then she cut him a half of her ten-cent cake.

"Eat some more, son," she said.

When they were finished eating, she got up and said, "Now here, take this ten dollars and buy yourself some blue suede shoes. And next time, do not make the mistake of latching onto *my* pocketbook *nor nobody else's*—because shoes got by devilish ways will burn your feet. I got to get my rest now. But from here on in, son, I hope you will behave yourself."

She led him down the hall to the front door and opened it. "Good night! Behave yourself, boy!" she said, looking out into the street as he went down the steps.

The boy wanted to say something other than, "Thank you, m'am," to Mrs. Luella Bates Washington Jones, but although his lips moved, he couldn't even say that as he turned at the foot of the barren stoop and looked up at the large woman in the door. Then she shut the door.

Little Dog

Reprinted from *The Ways of White Folks*. See p. 104.

Rock, Church

Elder William Jones was one of them rock-church preachers who know how to make the spirit rise and the soul get right. Sometimes in the pulpit he used to start talking real slow, and you'd think his sermon warn't gonna be nothing; but by the time he got through, the walls of the temple would be almost rent, the doors busted open, and the benches turned over from pure shouting on the part of the brothers and sisters.

He were a great preacher, was Reverend William Jones. But he warn't satisfied—he wanted to be greater than he was. He wanted to be another Billy Graham or Elmer Gantry or a resurrected Daddy Grace.[1] And that's what brought about his downfall—ambition!

Now, Reverend Jones had been for nearly a year the pastor of one of them little colored churches in the back alleys of St. Louis that are open every night in the week for preaching, singing, and praying, where sisters come to shake tambourines, shout, swing gospel songs, and get happy while the Reverend presents the Word.

Elder Jones always opened his part of the services with "In His Hand," his theme song, and he always closed his services with the same. Now, the rhythm of "In His Hand" was such that once it got to swinging, you couldn't help but move your arms or feet or both, and since the Reverend always took up collection at the beginning and ending of his sermons, the dancing movement of the crowd at such times was always toward the collection table—which was exactly where the Elder wanted it to be.

"In His hand!
In His hand!
I'm safe and sound
I'll be bound—
Settin' in Jesus' hand!"

"Come one! Come all! Come, my Lambs," Elder Jones would shout, "and put it down for Jesus!"

Poor old washer-ladies, big fat cooks, long lean truck drivers and heavy-set roustabouts would come up and lay their money down, two times every evening for Elder Jones.

That minister was getting rich right there in that St. Louis alley.

> *"In His hand!*
> *In His hand!*
> *I'll have you know*
> *I'm white as snow—*
> *Settin' in Jesus' hand!"*

With the piano just a-going, tambourines a-flying, and people shouting right on up to the altar.

"Rock, church, rock!" Elder Jones would cry at such intensely lucrative moments.

But he were too ambitious. He wouldn't let well enough alone. He wanted to be a big shot and panic Harlem, gas Detroit, sew up Chicago, then move on to Hollywood. He warn't satisfied with just St. Louis.

So he got to thinking, "Now, what can I do to get everybody excited, to get everybody talking about my church, to get the streets outside crowded and my name known all over, even unto the far reaches of the nation? Now, what can I do?"

Billy Sunday had a sawdust trail, so he had heard. Reverend Becton had two valets in the pulpit with him as he cast off garment after garment in the heat of preaching, and used up dozens of white handkerchiefs every evening wiping his brow while calling on the Lord to come. Meanwhile, the Angel of Angelus Temple had just kept on getting married and divorced and making the front pages of everybody's newspapers.[2]

"I got to be news, too, in my day and time," mused Elder Jones. "This town's too small for me! I want the world to hear my name!"

Now, as I've said before, Elder Jones was a good preacher—and a good-looking preacher, too. He could cry real loud and moan real deep, and he could move the sisters as no other black preacher on this side of town had ever moved them before. Besides, in his youth, as a sinner, he had done a little light hustling around Memphis and Vicksburg—so he knew just how to appeal to the feminine nature.

Since his recent sojourn in St. Louis, Elder Jones had been looking for a special female Lamb to shelter in his private fold. Out of all the sisters in his church, he had finally chosen Sister Maggie Bradford. Not that Sister Maggie was pretty. No, far from it. But Sister Maggie was well fed, brownskin, good natured, fat, and *prosperous*. She owned four two-family houses that she rented out, upstairs and down, so she made a good living. Besides, she had sweet and loving ways as well as the interest of her pastor at heart.

Elder Jones confided his personal ambitions to said Sister Bradford one morning when he woke up to find her by his side.

"I want to branch out, Maggie," he said. "I want to be a really big man! Now, what can I do to get the 'tention of the world on me? I mean, in a religious way?"

They thought and they thought. Since it was a Fourth of July morning, and Sister Maggie didn't have to go collect rents, they just lay there and thought.

Finally, Sister Maggie said, "Bill Jones, you know something I ain't never forgot that I seed as a child? There was a preacher down in Mississippi named old man Eubanks who one time got himself dead and buried and then rose from the dead. Now I ain't never forgot that. Neither has nobody else in that part of the Delta. That's something mem'rable. Why don't you do something like that?"

"How did he do it, Sister Maggie?"

"He ain't never told nobody how he do it, Brother Bill. He say it were the Grace of God, that's all."

"It might a-been," said Elder Jones. "It might a-been."

He lay there and thought awhile longer. By and by he said, "But honey, I'm gonna do something better'n that. I'm gonna be nailed on a cross."

"Do, Jesus!" said Sister Maggie Bradford. "Jones, you's a mess!"

Now, the Elder, in order to pull off his intended miracle, had, of necessity, to take somebody else into his confidence, so he picked out Brother Hicks, his chief deacon, one of the main pillars of the church long before Jones came as pastor.

It was too bad, though, that Jones never knew that Brother Hicks (more familiarly known as Bulldog) used to be in love with Sister Bradford. Sister Bradford neglected to tell the new reverend about any of her former sweethearts. So how was Elder Jones to know that some of them still coveted her, and were envious of him in their hearts?

"Hicks," whispered Elder Jones in telling his chief deacon of his plan to die on the cross and then come back to life, "that miracle will make me the greatest minister in the world. No doubt about it! When I get to be world renowned, Bulldog, and go traveling about the firmament, I'll take you with me as my chief deacon. You shall be my right hand, and Sister Maggie Bradford shall be my left. Amen!"

"I hear you," said Brother Hicks. "I hope it comes true."

But if Elder Jones had looked closely, he would have seen an evil light in his deacon's eyes.

"It will come true," said Elder Jones, "if you keep your mouth shut and follow out my instructions—exactly as I lay 'em down to you. I trust you, so listen! You know and I know that I ain't gonna *really* die. Neither is I *really* gonna be nailed. That's why I wants you to help me. I wants you to have me a great big cross made, higher than the altar—so high I has to have a stepladder to get up to it to be nailed thereon, and you to nail me. The higher the better, so's they won't see the straps—cause I'm gonna be tied on by straps, you hear. The light'll be rose-colored so they can't see the straps. Now, here you come and do the nailin' nobody else but you. Put them nails *between* my fingers and toes, not through 'em—*between*—and don't nail too deep. Leave the heads kinder stickin' out. You get the jibe?"

"I get the jibe," said Brother Bulldog Hicks.

"Then you and me'll stay right on there in the church all night and all day till the next night when the people come back to see me rise. Ever so often, you can let me down to rest a little bit. But as long as I'm on the cross, I play off like I'm dead, particularly when reporters come around. On Monday night, hallelujah! I will rise, and take up collection!"

"Amen!" said Brother Hicks.

Well, you couldn't get a-near the church on the night that Reverend Jones had had it announced by press, by radio, and by word of mouth that he would be crucified *dead,* stay dead, and rise. Negroes came from all over St. Louis, East St. Louis, and mighty nigh everywhere else to be present at the witnessing of the miracle. Lots of 'em didn't believe in Reverend Jones, but lots of 'em *did.* Sometimes false prophets can bamboozle you so you can't tell yonder from whither—and that's the way Jones had the crowd.

The church was packed and jammed. Not a seat to be found, and tears were flowing (from sorrowing sisters' eyes) long before the Elder even approached the cross which, made out of new lumber right straight from the sawmill, loomed up behind the pulpit. In the rose-colored lights, with big paper lilies that Sister Bradford had made decorating its head and foot, the cross looked mighty pretty.

Elder Jones preached a mighty sermon that night, and hot as it was, there was plenty of leaping and jumping and shouting in that crowded church. It looked like the walls would fall. Then when he got through preaching, Elder Jones made a solemn announcement. As he termed it, for a night and a day, his last pronouncement.

"Church! Tonight, as I have told the world, I'm gonna die. I'm gonna be nailed to this cross and let the breath pass from me. But tomorrow, Monday night, August the twenty-first, at twelve P.M., I am coming back to life. Amen! After twenty-four hours on the cross, hallelujah! And all the city of St. Louis can be saved—if they will just come out to see me. Now, before I mounts the steps to the cross, let us sing for the last time 'In His Hand'—cause I tell you, that's where I am! As we sing, let everybody come forward to the collection table and help this church before I go. Give largely!"

The piano tinkled, the tambourines rang, hands clapped. Elder Jones and his children sang:

> *"In His hand!*
> *In His hand!*
> *You'll never stray*
> *Down the Devil's way—*
> *Settin' in Jesus' hand!*
>
> *Oh, in His hand!*
> *In His hand!*
> *Though I may die*
> *I'll mount on high—*
> *Settin' in Jesus' hand!"*

"Let us pray." And while every back was bowed in prayer, the Elder went up the stepladder to the cross. Brother Hicks followed with the hammer and nails. Sister Bradford wailed at the top of her voice. Woe filled the Amen Corner. Emotion rocked the church.

Folks outside was saying all up and down the street, "Lawd, I wish we could have got in. Listen yonder at that noise! I wonder what *is* going on!"

Elder Jones was about to make himself famous—that's what was going on. And all would have went well had it not been for Brother Hicks—a two-faced rascal. Somehow that night the Devil got into Bulldog Hicks and took full possession.

The truth of the matter is that Hicks got to thinking about Sister Maggie Bradford, and how Reverend Jones had worked up to be her No. I Man. That made him mad. The old green snake of jealousy began to coil around his heart, right there in the meeting, right there on the steps of the cross. Lord, have mercy! At the very high point of the ceremonies!

Hicks had the hammer in one hand and his other hand was full of nails as he mounted the ladder behind his pastor. He was going up to nail Elder Jones on that sawmill cross.

"While I'm nailin', I might as well nail him right," Hicks thought. "A low-down klinker—comin' here out of Mississippi to take my woman away from me! He'll never know the pleasure of my help in none o' his schemes to out-Divine Father![3] No, sir!"

Elder Jones had himself all fixed up with a system of straps round his waist, round his shoulder blades, and round his wrists and ankles, hidden under his long black coat. These straps fastened in hooks on the back of the cross, out of sight of the audience, so he could just hang up there all sad and sorrowful-looking, and make out like he was being nailed. Brother Bulldog Hicks was to plant the nails *between* his fingers and toes. Hallelujah! Rock, church, rock!

Excitement was intense.

All went well until the nailing began. Elder Jones removed his shoes and socks and, in his bare black feet, bade farewell to his weeping congregation. As he leaned back against the cross and allowed Brother Hicks to compose him there, the crowd began to moan. But it was when Hicks placed the first nail between Elder Jones's toes that they became hysterical. Sister Bradford outyelled them all.

Hicks placed that first nail between the big toe and the next toe of the left foot and began to hammer. The foot was well strapped down, so the Elder couldn't move it. The closer the head of the nail got to his toes, the harder Hicks struck it. Finally the hammer collided with Elder Jones's foot, *bam* against his big toe.

"Aw-oh!" he moaned under his breath. "Go easy, man!"

"Have mercy," shouted the brothers and sisters of the church. "Have mercy on our Elder!"

Once more the hammer struck his toe. But the all-too-human sound of his surprised and agonized "Ouch!" was lost in the tumult of the shouting church.

"Bulldog, I say, go easy," hissed the Elder. "This *ain't* real."

Brother Hicks desisted, a grim smile on his face. Then he turned his attention to the right foot. There he placed another nail between the toes, and began to hammer. Again, as the nail went into the wood, he showed no signs of stopping when the hammer reached the foot. He just kept on landing cruel metallic blows on the Elder's bare toenails until the preacher howled with pain, no longer able to keep back a sudden hair-raising cry. The sweat popped out on his forehead and dripped down on his shirt.

At first the Elder thought, naturally, that it was just a slip of the hammer on the deacon's part. Then he thought the man must have gone crazy—like the rest of the audience. Then it hurt him so bad, he didn't know what he thought—so he just hollered, "Aw-ooo-oo-o!"

It was a good thing the church was full of noise, or they would have heard a strange dialogue.

"My God, Hicks, what are you doing?" the Elder cried, staring wildly at his deacon on the ladder.

"I'm nailin' you to the cross, Jones! And man, I'm *really* nailin'."

"Aw-oow-ow! Don't you know you're hurting me? I told you *not* to nail so hard!"

But the deacon was unruffled.

"Who'd you say's gonna be your right hand when you get down from here and start your travelings?" Hicks asked.

"You, brother," the sweating Elder cried.

"And who'd you say was gonna be your left hand?"

"Sister Maggie Bradford," moaned Elder Jones from the cross.

"Naw she ain't," said Brother Hicks, whereupon he struck the Reverend's toe a really righteous blow.

"Lord, help me!" cried the tortured minister. The weeping congregation echoed his cry. It was certainly real. The Elder *was* being crucified!

Brother Bulldog Hicks took two more steps up the ladder, preparing to nail the hands. With his evil face right in front of Elder Jones, he hissed: "I'll teach you nappy-headed jack-leg ministers to come to St. Louis and think you-all can walk away with any woman you's a mind to. I'm gonna teach you to leave my women alone. Here—here's a nail!"

Brother Hicks placed a great big spike right in the palm of Elder Jones's left hand. He was just about to drive it in when the frightened Reverend let out a scream that could be heard two blocks away. At the same time he began to struggle to get down. Jones tried to bust the straps, but they was too strong for him.

If he could just get one foot loose to kick Brother Bulldog Hicks!

Hicks lifted the hammer to let go when the Reverend's second yell, this time, was loud enough to be heard in East St. Louis. It burst like a bomb above the shouts of the crowd—and it had its effect. Suddenly the congregation was quiet. Everybody knew that was no way for a dying man to yell.

Sister Bradford realized that something had gone wrong, so she began to chant the song her beloved pastor had told her to chant at the propitious moment after the nailing was done. Now, even though the nailing was not done, Sister Bradford thought she had better sing:

> *"Elder Jones will rise again,*
> *Elder Jones will rise again,*
> *Rise again, rise again!*
> *Elder Jones will rise again,*
> *Yes, my Lawd!"*

But nobody took up the refrain to help her carry it on. Everybody was too interested in what was happening in front of them; so Sister Bradford's voice just died out.

Meanwhile Brother Hicks lifted the hammer again, but Elder Jones spat right in his face. He not only spat, but suddenly called his deacon a name unworthy of man or beast. Then he let out another frightful yell and, in mortal anguish, called, "Sister Maggie Bradford, lemme down from here! I say, come and get . . . me . . . down . . . *from here!*"

Those in the church that had not already stopped moaning and shouting did so at once. You could have heard a pin drop. Folks were petrified.

Brother Hicks stood on the ladder, glaring with satisfaction at Reverend Jones, his hammer still raised. Under his breath the panting Elder dared him to nail another nail, and threatened to kill him stone-dead with a forty-four if he did.

"Just lemme get loost from here, and I'll fight you like a natural man," he gasped, twisting and turning like a tree in a storm.

"Come down, then," yelled Hicks, right out loud from the ladder. "Come on down! As sure as water runs, Jones, I'll show you up for what you is—a woman-chasing no-good low-down faker! I'll beat you to a batter with my bare hands!"

"Lawd, have mercy!" cried the church.

Jones almost broke a blood vessel trying to get loose from his cross. "Sister Maggie, come and lemme down," he pleaded, sweat streaming from his face.

But Sister Bradford was covered with confusion. In fact, she was petrified. What could have gone wrong for the Elder to call on her like this in public in the very midst of the thing that was to bring him famous-glory and make them all rich, preaching throughout the land with her at his side? Sister Bradford's head was in a whirl, her heart was in her mouth.

"Elder Jones, you means you really wants to get down?" she asked weakly from her seat in the Amen Corner.

"Yes," cried the Elder, "can't you hear? I done called on you twenty times to let me down!"

At this point Brother Hicks gave the foot nails one more good hammering. The words that came from the cross were not to be found in the Bible.

In a twinkling, Sister Bradford was at Jones's side. Realizing at last that the Devil must've done got into Hicks (like it used to sometimes in the days when she knowed him), she went to the aid of her battered Elder, grabbed the foot of the ladder, and sent Hicks sprawling across the pulpit.

"You'll never crucify my Elder," she cried, "not for real." Energetically she began to cut the straps away that bound the Reverend. Soon poor Jones slid to the floor, his feet too sore from the hammer's blows to even stand on them without help.

"Just lemme get at Hicks," was all the Reverend Jones could gasp. "He knowed I didn't want them nails that close." In the dead silence that took possession of the church, everybody heard him moan, "Lawd, lemme get at Hicks," as he hobbled away on the protecting arm of Sister Maggie.

"Stand back, Bulldog," Sister Maggie said to the deacon, "and let your pastor pass. Soon as he's able, he'll flatten you out like a shadow—but now, I'm in charge. Stand back, I say, and let him pass!"

Hicks stood back. The crowd murmured. The minister made his exit. Thus ended the ambitious career of Elder William Jones. He never did pastor in St. Louis any more. Neither did he fight Hicks. He just snuck away for parts unknown.

Little Old Spy

Reprinted from *Laughing to Keep from Crying*. See p. 254.

A Good Job Gone

Reprinted from *The Ways of White Folks*. See p. 49.

Who's Passing for Who?

Reprinted from *Laughing to Keep from Crying*. See p. 163.

African Morning

Reprinted from *Laughing to Keep from Crying*. See p. 171.

Pushcart Man

Reprinted from *Laughing to Keep from Crying*. See p. 175.

Why, You Reckon?

Reprinted from *Laughing to Keep from Crying*. See p. 177.

Saratoga Rain

Reprinted from *Laughing to Keep from Crying*. See p. 182.

Spanish Blood

Reprinted from *Laughing to Keep from Crying*. See p. 183.

Gumption

You young folks don't remember the depression, but I do. No jobs for nobody. That winter there wasn't a soul working in our house but my wife, and she was evil as she could be! She was doing a few washings now and then for the white folks—before hand laundry went out of style—so we kinder made out. But she didn't like to see me sitting around, even if I couldn't find a job. There wasn't no work to be got in our town, nor any other place, for that matter. We had a couple of roomers, a man and his girl friend, but they were out of a job also. And, like me and my wife, they hadn't been in town long enough to get any consideration, since the relief folks were hard on strangers. All of us was just managing to get by on beans and mush all winter.

One cold February morning we was sitting around the stove in the kitchen trying to keep warm, the roomers and me, my wife was ironing, when who should pass by outside in the alley but old man Oyster and his son.

"There goes Oyster and that boy of his," I said, "ragged as a jaybird, both of 'em."

"They ain't even on relief work, is they?" Jack, the roomer, asked.

"They did have a few hours' work a month," I answered. "They messed up, though."

"Messed up, you call it, heh?" my wife put in, in her nervous way. "Well, they got gumption, anyhow. They told them white folks up yonder in the office just what they thought of 'em. That's what they did."

"And look at 'em now," I said, "going through the alley looking for something to eat."

"Well, they got gumption," my wife yelled, "and that's something!"

"You can't eat gumption," Jack remarked, which made my wife mad.

"You can't eat sitting-around-on-your-rumpus, neither," she broke out, slamming her iron down on the white man's shirt and looking real hard at our roomer—a look that said, You oughtn't to talk, cause you ain't paid your rent for a month.

I sure was glad I hadn't said nothing, boy.

"What's it all about?" Jack's girl asked. "What's old man Oyster done to get in bad with them relief folks, Miss Clara?"

She had heard about it before from me, but she just wanted to get my wife to running her mouth—and keep her mind off the fact that they hadn't paid their rent that month.

"You ain't heard?" my wife said, choosing a new hot iron. "It's a story worth telling, to my mind, cause they got *gumption*—them Oysters." She looked hard at Jack and me. "Now, old man Oyster—this story goes way back, child—he ain't never amounted to much, just poor and honest. But he always did want to make something out of that boy o' his'n, Charlie—little and runty as he was. He worked hard to do it, too. He portered, bellhopped, did road work, did anything he could get to do. Kept that boy in school after his wife died, washed his ears, kept him clean, tried to make a gentleman out of him—and that boy did pretty well. Grew up and took a commercial bookkeeping-typewriter course in the school, and come out Grade A. *Grade A,* I'm telling you. Graduated and got a job with the white folks. Yes, sir! First time I ever heard tell of a colored boy typewriting or keeping books or anything like that in this white man's town. But Mr. Bartelson what owned the coalyard and fuel office where young Oyster worked, he was from Maine and didn't have no prejudice to speak of, so he give this colored boy a chance in his place. And was them white truck drivers jealous—seeing a Negro working in the office and they out driving trucks! But old man Oyster's boy was *prepared.* I'm telling you, *prepared!* He had a good education and could do the work, black as he was. And he was lucky to find somebody to give him a break, because you know and I know you don't see no colored men working in white folks' offices nowhere hardly.

"Well, sir, old man Oyster was proud as he could be of his boy. We was all proud. The church was proud. The white business school what graduated him was proud. Everything went fine for two or three years. Oyster and Charlie even started to buy a little house, cause the old man was working on the road digging for forty cents a hour. Then the depression came. They stopped building roads, and folks stopped buying fuel to keep warm by. Poor old man Bartelson what owned the coalyard finally had to close up, bankrupted and broke—which left young Oyster without a job, like the rest of us. Old man Oyster was jobless, too, cause the less roads they built and sewers they laid, the less work they gave to colored folks, and give it to the white instead. You know how it is—first to be fired and last to be hired."

Clara was just a-ironing and a-talking. "Then along come this Government relief and WPA and everybody thought times was surely gonna get better. Well, they ain't got no better, leastwise not for colored. Everybody in this town's on relief now but me and you-all—what ain't been here long enough to be on it. I've still got a few washings to do and a little house cleaning now and then, thank God! But look at Sylvester," pointing at me. "They done cut every porter off at the bus station but one. And Syl is jobless as a greyhound.

"Anyhow, to go ahead with Oyster, it were a crying shame to see this poor old man and that fine young colored boy out o' work—and they both ambitious, and steady, and good race men. Well, when relief opened up and they started giving out so many hours of work a month, they put old man Oyster back on the road. Now, his boy, Charlie, ain't never done no kind of work like road work, being a office man. But he thought he'd have to do it, too, and Charlie wasn't objecting, mind you—when the Government opened up a office for what they calls white-collar workers. All the white folks what's been doing office work in good times, insurance people and store clerks and such, they went there to get the kind o' work they was used to doing. Oyster's son went, too. But don't you know they discriminated against him! Yes, sir—the Government discriminating him because he were black! They said. 'You're not no office worker,' in spite of all the proofs Charlie had that he were in Mr. Bartelson's office for three years—the letter Bartelson gave him and all. But they sent old man Oyster's boy right on out yonder to work on the road with his father.

"Well, that made the old man mad. He said, 'What am I working all these years for you, educating you to come out here and dig on the road with me, and you with a education?'

"The old man stopped his work then and there that morning, laid off, and went right on up to that government office to see the white man about it. And that's where the trouble commenced!"

Clara was just a-talking and a-ironing. "The Government white man said, 'You ought to be glad for your boy to get any kind o' work, these days and times. You can't be picking and choosing now.'

"But old man Oyster stood there and argued with the man for his son's rights. That's why I say he's got *gumption*. He said, 'I ain't asking to be picking and choosing, and I ain't asked nothing for *myself*. I'm speaking about that boy o' mine. Charlie's got a education. True, he's colored, but he's worked for three years in a office for one of the finest white men that ever lived and breathed, Mr. Bartelson. Charlie's got experience. My boy's a typewriter and a bookkeeper. What for you send him out to work on a road with me? Ain't this the place what's giving all the white folks jobs doing what they *used* to doing and know how to do? My boy ain't know nothing about no pick and shovel. Why don't you treat Charlie Oyster like you do the rest of the people and give him some o' his kind o' work?'

" 'We have no office jobs here for Negroes,' said the man, right flat out like that. 'That's why I sent your son over to where they give out road work. I classify all Negroes as laborers on our relief rolls.'

"Well, that made old man Oyster mad as hell. He said, 'Drat it, I'm a citizen! Is that what WPA is for—to bring more discrimination than what is? I want to know why my boy can't be a typewriter like the rest of 'em what's got training, even if it is on relief. If he could work in a white man's office, ain't he good enough to get work from you—and you the gobernment?'

"Well, this made the white man mad, and he yelled, 'You must be one o' them Communists, ain't you?' And he pressed some kind o' buzzer and sent out for a cop.

"Now, old man Oyster ain't never had no trouble of any kind in this town before, but when them cops started to put their hands on him and throw him out o' that office, he raised sand. He was right, too! But them cops didn't see it that way, and one of 'em brought his stock down on that old man's head and knocked him out.

"When Oyster come to, he was in jail.

"Then old man Oyster's son showed he was a man! Charlie heard about the trouble when he come home from off the road that evening, and he went to the jail to see his papa, boiling mad. When he heard how it was, that white man calling the cops in to beat up his father, he said, 'Pa, I'll be in jail here with you tomorrow.' And sure enough, he was. He went up to that there white-collar relief office the next morning and beat that white man so bad, he ain't got over it yet.

" 'The idea,' young Oyster said, 'of you having my father knocked down and dragged out because he came here to talk to you like a citizen about our rights! Who are you anyway, any more'n me? Try to throw me out o' yere and I'll beat you to a pulp first!'

"Well, that man reached for the buzzer again to call some more cops. When he reached, young Oyster had him! It would a-done me good to see the way that black boy give that white man a fit—cause he turned him every way but loose. When the cops come, they put Charlie in jail all right —but that white man was beat by then! The idea of relief coming here adding prejudice to what we already got, and times as hard as they is."

Clara planked down her iron on the stove. "Anyhow, they didn't keep them Oysters in jail very long, neither father or son. Old Judge Murray give 'em a month apiece, suspended sentence, and let 'em out. But when they got out o' jail, don't you know them relief people wouldn't give Oyster and his boy no more work a-tall! No, sir! They told 'em they wasn't feeding no black reds. Now old man Oyster nor Charlie neither ain't never heard o' Communists—but that's what they called 'em, just cause they went up there and fought for what they ought to have. They didn't win—they're out there in the alleys now hauling trash. But they got gumption!"

"You can't live on gumption," I said, trying to be practical.

"No, but you can choke on shame!" my wife yelled, looking hard at Jack and me. "I ain't never seen you-all fighting for nothing yet. Lord knows you both bad enough off to go out and raise hell somewhere and get something!" She put the iron down with a bang. "If I had a young boy, I'd want him to be like Oyster's son, and not take after none of you—sitting around behind the stove talking 'bout you 'can't live on gumption.' *You* can't live on it cause you ain't got none, that's why! Get up from behind that stove, get out o' here, both of you, and bring me something back I can use—bread, money, or a job, I don't care which. Get up and go on! Scat!"

She waved her iron in the air and looked like she meant to bring it down on my head instead of on a shirt. So Jack and me had to leave that nice warm house and go out in the cold and scuffle. There was no peace at home that morning, I mean. I had to try and work up a little gumption.

Heaven to Hell

Reprinted from *Laughing to Keep from Crying*. See p. 191.

Sailor Ashore

Reprinted from *Laughing to Keep from Crying*. See p. 193.

Slice Him Down

Reprinted from *Laughing to Keep from Crying*. See p. 198.

His Last Affair

Every five or six years, Henry Q. Marston came to New York. He loved New York for the very good reason that he didn't know anybody there. In his home town in Indiana Mr. Marston knew everybody, from the Mayor who asked him to serve on civic committees to the junk man who expected a ham at Christmas—for Marston was a wealthy man, a prominent citizen, and a good Christian.

In Terre Haute his virtues were fully recognized. As a result, his time was not his own. All the charities, from the Red Cross to the foreign missions, all the lodges, clubs, and various organizations connected with the church, were constantly calling on him. Besides, the demands of his business were many and time-taking. He was a man of affairs.

Mr. Marston was in real estate, feed, grain, apples, and a number of other commercial activities connected with the soil of Indiana. He was a trustee of two or three banks. His offices took up a whole floor in a downtown building, with branches in Indianapolis and Gary. But Mr. Marston preferred to live in the small city of Terre Haute, where he had lived all his life, in spite of ambitious wives and daughters who always seemed to want to live elsewhere, even in Chicago.

At fifty, fat, bluff, and bold, he had been married three times, but had buried two wives. One wife, however, was still very much alive, former president of the Federated Women's Clubs of the state and a great worker in temperance and the church. She was a large lady who wore glasses and presided over their stately home with a firm and proper grace, caring for her own children and stepchildren alike in a most capable manner.

Mr. Marston couldn't complain about his home life, for it was exemplary, a model for all homes, and a pattern of Christian virtue. But every two or three years Mr. Marston just had to get away! This spring his wife had gone to California to attend an important congress of clubwomen meeting in Pasadena. She was gone three weeks. No sooner had she departed than Mr. Marston went to New York. It had been a long time since the smell of Broadway struck his small-town nostrils.

Mr. Marston needed Broadway like a colt needs a pasture. He found it madder and gayer than ever, and there were still plenty of hot spots for suckers. When Mr. Marston was spending money in a town where he didn't know anybody, he didn't give a damn about being a sucker. At home such sportiveness would have been un-Christian, but in New York nobody cared, nobody was even unduly impressed, and there were no prosaic hangovers in the way of requests for periodical donations, committees demanding services, or missionaries asking him to pay and pray for the heathen. Broadway didn't go in for salvation of any sort. Self-sufficient, that street.

In New York Mr. Marston wined, dined, danced, and gambled until two of his three weeks were nearly up. He went to the Latin Quarter and the Peppermint Lounge. He had a few dates with ladies, but never at his own hotel, and never telling any of them his real name. Oh, he had a fine time being incognito in a town where he didn't know anybody.

Imagine his surprise when, early one morning, right on the corner of Forty-seventh and Broadway, where the lights are brighter than the noonday sun, somebody called his name. Somebody called his *right* name, "Hello, Henry Marston," in a sweetly feminine voice.

Mr. Marston wondered, "Now, who can that be?" He started to walk on, but curiosity got the best of him, so he turned to see. There on the corner stood a smartly dressed young woman, or rather a *young-looking* woman, tall and cool, saying, "Hello, Henry."

"Why—er—good evening," Mr. Marston replied, thinking perhaps it was one of his renters from Indiana, or an unknown lady of his church who would, of course, know him—a trustee. But this woman, although having a faint Midwestern aura about her, was distinctly New Yorkish. Mr. Marston was puzzled.

"How are you, Henry?" she said familiarly, offering a gloved hand. "It's been years since I've seen you."

That was a relief—years. But there was such a thrill to her hand that Mr. Marston said as he held it, "I'm mighty glad to see you *now*," wondering all the time who in the world she could be.

"Years and years," she said. "Don't you remember, Henry?"

An old schoolmate perhaps? Or some friend's daughter? Her age was indefinite. But Mr. Marston finally had to ask her when and where.

"Don't you really remember?" she said, smelling very sweet as her blue eyes looked into his.

He was ashamed, but he didn't. Maybe he could recollect if given time, he said. Evidently she felt he should have time, because she suggested stepping into Lindy's for coffee and a little chat. Because she was so charming, Mr. Marston agreed to go that far, at least, on the road to recollection.

"I seem to know you," he said, feeling in her nearness something pleasurably familiar.

"Quite well," the lady answered. "Don't you recall?"

"Here, in New York?" Mr. Marston asked, thinking perhaps of the days when he used to come to Manhattan under his own name, before he was so prominent or so wealthy.

"Oh, no," she said, "back home in Indiana."

"Indiana?"

"Yes, Indiana."

"Who are you?" asked Mr. Marston, unable to stand it any longer.

"Callie," the woman said simply.

"Callie!" gasped Mr. Marston. "Callie?" he cried staring at her.

"Calista now," she said, "Calista Lowery."

"Callie Lowery!"

"After all these years"—smiling. "Do you, perhaps, still love me?"

The trouble with that question was that Mr. Marston even now could not be sure whether he did or didn't. He could only sit and stare at her and notice the growing familiarity of her face and features, delicately powdered and even more beautiful; womanly, not girlish, but strange and vital as ever; and her hair twice as golden as it used to be. Callie!

The waiter came. They ordered dinner—for neither had eaten.

"We were waiting for each other," said Calista, smiling.

Henry was not hungry, confusion and surprise having taken his appetite away, although he ate, forcing the food down. He was too perturbed by—Calista. He remembered too well the last time he had seen her. Suddenly he recalled her mother's face, and his mother's face; the tears and cuss words of that awful day; and the fact that his father had had a pretty hard time getting him out of that scrape—his first "affair."

Back home in Indiana years ago in high school, he met Callie. She was from the wrong side of town, and wanted to be an actress. An incredible calling in those days, indecent and not befitting a lady—but glamorous to a young girl, and to a boy in high school who hadn't met many actresses. Every time a road show or a stock company came to town, Henry would be in the gallery of the Opera House; and Callie would be there, too, sometimes alone, sometimes with her mother. She was "sweet sixteen" then, poor but ambitious, and had never been kissed.

One night, when he had met her at the show alone, young Marston took her home—to the wrong side of town. He kissed her. He was never so thrilled before—or since. The memory of that thrill came back to him now as he looked at her across the table in Lindy's.

All that winter long ago, years ago now, before radio or the inroads of television, they met at the movies or in the gallery of the Opera House in their general admission seats, looking at *Under Two Flags* or *East Lynne*, *Uncle Tom's Cabin* or *Buster Brown*. Once they saw *Camille*, and Callie said, her eyes like stars, "Henry, one of my dreams is to go to Paris."

Henry agreed that he would like to go, also. Then, after the show, he walked her home through the snow to her side of town; and walked alone all the way back to his parents' house in a section where "decent" people lived.

One night in the spring Henry and Callie stopped in the park on their way home. They stopped several times thereafter. The next thing he knew, Callie was announcing dramatically, in the tragic manner of the leading lady in a stock company, "Henry, darling, I am with child!"

That bowled young Marston over—just about to graduate from high school as president of his class. That bowled over his father, too, when he heard of it. And it put his poor mother in bed for two weeks.

"That Lowery girl, my God! Why, she rouges and powders and wants to be an actress! I expect she smokes cigarettes. And nobody knows a thing about her family."

Well, they got Henry out of it by the hardest. There were tears, scenes—and money paid to her gypsy-looking mama. Then Callie and her mother went away to Chicago. He never heard of them again. That was long, long ago, really long ago.

The scent of the old Opera House and Callie's hair came back to him as he sat there at the table in Lindy's and looked at her again. He wondered if her hair—now blonde—still smelled as sweet, if her lips tasted the same. She had retained her looks remarkably well, indeed she had improved, was slim and smart in the best New York manner (although she must be well over forty). In spite of himself, Henry compared her to the three big wholesome small-town women he had married and spent his life with. "Did you ever get to be an actress?" he asked.

"Have you never heard of Calista Lowery?" she demanded mockingly.

"I've heard of Callie," he said wryly. They both laughed.

"I am an actress, but not a very famous one," she said. "At least, not a leading lady. I've played a lot of bit parts in stock, and once or twice on Broadway, but nothing big. You were the biggest thing in my life, Henry."

"I wish I had been," Mr. Marston said.

"I wish you had remained so," she answered. "Do you remember the Opera House?"

"I should say I do," Mr. Marston said, "and the park." Then he leaned across the table. "Did we, Callie . . . did we—er . . . ever have a child?"

"Don't you remember?" Callie said. "Your father wouldn't let us."

Broadway, lane of lights, strange romances, and the beginning and end of funny fragile things. Hard surfaces, delicate hearts. Birdland. Jazz bands that sob their mad caprices. Fancies and dreams.

"Callie," Mr. Marston said, "let's walk in a park again."

During the week that remained to him in Manhattan, Mr. Marston discovered that Calista's—Callie's complexion was made by a popular beauty shop; that her hair smelled like a French hairdresser's pomade; her lips were strawberry rouge; but her softness and her sweetness were still the same—the same as years ago, back home in Indiana.

Mr. Marston had never spent such a joyous seven days in New York, never spent such a seven days in his life, as the days of that week that was the last in Manhattan. Youth and romance came back all over again with Calista. They even went to see a play and sat in the gallery of the theatre just as in the past. Although the play wasn't anything like the old melodramas they had once loved, they were so absorbed in each other that they didn't notice its theme.

Then Mr. Marston had to go back home. His time was up.

In the meanwhile, he decided this would be just an interlude for them, or rather a postlude—for of course Mr. Marston couldn't keep this up now that he was married, had five children, was a pillar in the church and a leading citizen of the West. No, this would have to end when he got on the train.

Callie—Calista—agreed. But when she parted from the fat gray-haired Henry, she acted like her heart was broken. She let two tears stream down her well-enameled face. Mr. Marston could hardly stand to tear himself away. It was almost as bad as that first parting, years and years ago. But once on the train, as the miles retreated beneath the wheels while the Pullmans went forward toward Indiana, Henry gradually began to forget Callie—Calista Lowery—and to think of his wife. They would probably have chicken for dinner next Sunday. All the children would probably be there. And everybody would be delighted to see him home once more, safe and sound.

It was too bad poor Callie had not become an actress of fame. But at least she had become the shining Calista Lowery of New York, well dressed and beautiful, even at her age, and that was something toward an ambition generated in the gallery of the old Indiana Opera House. Beautiful—and dumb as ever, too, poor child. Suppose he had married her in his youth, in spite of his parents? Tut! Tut! She could never have managed his affairs as well as the three large ladies who had been his wives. Probably he would not have prospered at all, Mr. Marston thought. There was something *too* alluring about Calista. There always had been. She took a man's mind off his work.

He arrived in Terre Haute in the morning, just in time to welcome Mrs. Marston, who came in on the afternoon train from Chicago. Henry's life settled down once more to the calm and comfortable routine that is the lot of a middle-aged man of business in a small city.

Then one afternoon about a fortnight later at his office, just when Mr. Marston was beginning to think about a game of golf, the telephone rang.

His secretary said, "Long distance calling you, Mr. Marston. A personal call from New York. Would you care to take it?"

He picked up the receiver and put it to his ear.

"Henry Quentin Marston speaking."

"Hello." A sweetly feminine voice came over the wire. "This is Callie, Henry darling. I am again with child."

"Good God!" Mr. Marston cried. "My God! What—what do you want?" the middle-aged man at the desk in Indiana asked, visions of his wife, his children, his home, his church, dancing before him.

"Darling," said Calista, "money."

"Money?" The sweat popped out on his forehead. "How—how—how much money?"

"The last time it was *so* little," Callie said. "Do you remember? Just enough to take mother and me to Chicago. This time I think I should really like to go to Paris. I have never been abroad—and Paris is one of my dreams. Our child could be born there, Henry."

"Would two thousand do?" asked Mr. Marston naïvely, having no one to guide him.

"Multiplied by ten," said Calista, "it *might* do."

"Oh-rr-r-r!" groaned Mr. Marston. "Callie! *Calista!* Callie!"

"I have no mother to protect me any more," the voice at the other end of the wire said sadly. "I have only some old lawyers now, Henry."

"Don't," said Henry trembling, "just a minute, wait."

"I'll try to wait a minute," said Calista.

"I—er—you—you shall have it, Callie," he panted, "I'll mail a draft to you this week."

"Better to my lawyers," the charming voice said, "just to make it legal." She gave him their address.

"All right," said Mr. Marston hoarsely, writing the number down. "O.K. All right."

"Perhaps you'll come to Europe," purred the lovely voice at his ear.

"Perhaps," panted Mr. Marston, "but I'm a very busy man."

"Then good-by, Henry," said the woman on the phone, considerately. "I'm so sorry, darling, to bother you with this."

When Mr. Marston could move from his chair, weak as he was, he wiped the sweat from his neck, rang for a glass of water, and prepared to arrange for the transfer of twenty thousand dollars to one Calista Lowery of New York.

A week later at the first-class canopy-covered entrance to a transatlantic jet, her hair newly waved, her face freshly fixed, an orchid at her neckline, and a smile of triumph on her lips, Callie emplaned for Paris—the city of her dreams.

" '*I am with child*'—that is the best line I ever delivered," she said to herself. "I made it up myself—*both times*! I'm almost as good a playwright as I am an actress. But Henry's *such* a dumb leading man! And he never did even suspicion that I'm colored."

Tain't So

Reprinted from *Laughing to Keep from Crying*. See p. 209.

Father and Son

Reprinted from *Laughing to Keep from Crying*. See p. 128.

Professor

Reprinted from *Laughing to Keep from Crying*. See p. 221.

Sorrow for a Midget

No grown man works in a hospital if he can help it—the pay is too low. But I was broke, jobs hard to find, and the employment office sent me there that winter.

Right in the middle of Harlem.

Work wasn't hard, just cleaning up the wards, serving meals off a rolling table, bulling around, pushing a mop. I didn't mind. I got plenty to eat.

It was a little special kind of hospital; there was three private rooms on my floor, and in one of them was a female midget. Miss Midget—a little lady who looked like a dried-up child to me. But they told me (so I wouldn't get scared of her) that she was a midget. She had a pocketbook bigger than she was. It laid on a chair beside her bed. Generous, too—nice, that little midget lady. She gave me a tip the first day I was there.

But she was dying.

The nurses told me Countess Midget was booked to die. And I had never seen nobody die. Anyhow, I hung around her. It was profitable.

"Take care of me good," she said. "I pay as I go, I always did know how to get service." She opened her big fat pocketbook, as big as she was, and showed me a thick wad of bills. "This gets it anytime, anywhere," she said.

It got it with me, all right. I stuck by. Tips count up. That's how I know so much about what happened in them few days she was in that hospital room, game as she could be, but booked to die.

"Not even penicillin can save her," the day nurse said, "not her." That was when penicillin was new.

Of course, the undertakers that year was all complaining about penicillin. They used to come to the hospital looking for corpses.

"Business is bad," one undertaker told me. "People don't die like they used to since this penicillin come in. Un-huh! Springtime, in the old days, you could always count on plenty of folks dying of pneumonia and such, going outdoors catching cold before it was warm enough, and all. Funerals every other day then. Not no more. The doctors stick 'em with penicillin now—and they get well. Damn if they don't! Business is bad for morticians."

But that midget did not have pneumonia, neither a cold. She had went without an operation she needed too long. Now operations could do her no good. And what they put in the needle for her arm was not penicillin. It was something that did her no good either, just eased down the pain. It were kept locked up so young orderlies like me would not steal it and sell it to junkies. The nurses would not even tell me where it was locked up at.

You know, I did not look too straight when I come in that hospital. Short-handed—not having much help—they would hire almost anybody for an orderly in a hospital in Harlem, even me. So I got the job.

Right off, after that first day, I loved that midget. I said, "Little Bits, you're a game kiddie. I admire your spunk."

Midget said, "I dig this hospital jive. Them nurses ain't understandable. Nice, but don't understand. You're the only one in here, boy, I would ask to do me a favor. Find my son."

"You look like a baby to me, Countess. Where and when on earth did you get a son?" I asked.

"Don't worry about that," said Countess Midget. "I got him—and he's mine. I want him *right now*. He do not know I am in here sick—if he did, he would come—even were he ashamed of the way he looked. You find my son." She gave me twenty bucks for subway fare and taxi to go looking.

I went and searched and found her son. Just like she had said he might be, he were ashamed to come to the hospital. He was not doing so well. Fact is, her son was ragged as a buzzard feeding on a Lenox Avenue carcass. But when I told him his mama was sick in the Maggie Butler Pavilion of the Sadie Henderson Hospital, he come. He got right up out of bed and left his old lady and come.

"My mama has not called for me for a long, long time," he said. "If she calls me now, like this boy says," he told his girl, "wild horses could not hold me. Baby, I am going to see my mama," he said.

"I did not even know you had a mama," whined the sleepy old broad in the bed, looking as if she did not much care.

"Lots of things you do not know about this Joe," said the cat to the broad. He got up and dressed and went with me, quick.

"That little bitty woman," I asked him in the street, "she is your mama?"

"Damn right she's my mama," said the guy, who was near six feet, big, heavy-set, black, and ragged. No warm coat on. I thought I was beat, but he was the most. I could tell he had *been* gone to the dogs, long gone. Still, he was a young man. From him I took a lesson.

"I will never get this far down," to myself I said. "No, *not never!*"

"Is she very low sick?" he asked about his mama. "Real sick?"

"Man, I don't know," I said. "She is sunk way down in bed. And the sign on the door says NO VISITORS."

"Then how am I gonna get in?"

"Relatives is not visitors," I said. "Besides, I know the nurses. Right now is not even visiting hours. Too early. But come with me. You'll get in."

I felt sorry for a guy with a mama who was a midget who was dying. A midget laying dying! Had she been my mama, I guess I would have wanted to be there, though, in spite of the fact she was a midget. I couldn't help wondering how could she be so small and have this great big son? Who were his papa? And how could his papa have had her?

Well, anyhow, I took him in to see the little Countess in that big high hospital bed, so dark and small, in that white, white room in that white bed.

They had just given his mama a needle, so she were not right bright. But when she saw her son, her little old wrinkled face lighted up. Her little old tiny matchstick arms went almost around his neck. And she hollered, "My baby!" real loud. "My precious baby son!"

"Mama," he almost cried, "I have not been a good son to you."

"You have been my *only* son," she said.

The nurse hipped me, "Let's get out of here and leave 'em alone." So we went. And we left them alone for a long time, until he left.

That afternoon that midget died. Her son couldn't hardly have more than gotten home when I had to go after him again. I asked him on the way back to the hospital was he honest-to-God sure enough her son.

He shook his head. "No."

That is when I felt most sorry for that midget, when I heard him say No. He explained to me that he was just a took-in son, one she had sort of adopted when he was near-about a baby—because he had no father and no mother and she had no son. But she wanted people to *think* she had a son.

She was just his midget mama, that's all. He never had no real mama that he knew. But this little tiny midget raised him as best she could. Being mostly off in sideshows and carnivals the biggest part of the time, she boarded him out somewhere in school in the country. When he got teen-age and came back to Harlem, he went right straight to the dogs. But she loved him and he loved her.

When he found out, about 5:30 P.M., that she had died, that big old ragged no-good make-believe son of hers cried like a child.

Powder-White Faces

Reprinted from *Laughing to Keep from Crying*. See p. 229.

Rouge High

Reprinted from *Laughing to Keep from Crying*. See p. 234.

The Gun

Picture yourself a lone bird in a cage with monkeys, or the sole cat in a kennel full of dogs. Even if the dogs became accustomed to you, they wouldn't make the best of playmates; nor could you, being a cat, mate with them, being dogs. Although, in the little town of Tall Rock, Montana, the barriers were less natural than artificial (entirely man-made barriers, in fact), nevertheless, to be the only Negro child in this small white city made you a stranger in a strange world; an outcast in the house where you lived; a part of it all by necessity, and yet no part at all.

Flora Belle Yates, as a child, used to shield herself from the frequent hurts and insults of white children with tears, blows, and sometimes curses. Even with only one Negro family, the Yateses, in Tall Rock, race relations were not too good. Her father and mother had come up from Texas years ago. Flora Belle had heard them tell about the night they left Texarkana, looking back to see their hut in flames and a mob shouting in the darkness. The mob wanted to lynch Flora Belle's father. It seemed that, in an argument about wages, he had beaten up a white man. Through some miracle, her mother said, they had gotten away in the face of the mob, escaping in a rickety Ford, crossing the state line and driving for three days, somehow making it to the Northwest. Her father had an idea of getting to Canada, fleeing like the slaves in slave days clean out of the United States, but gas and money ran out. He and his wife stopped to work along the way, and finally ended up by staying in Tall Rock. Flora's father had gotten a job there, tending to the horses and equipment of a big contractor. Her mother worked in the contractor's house as cook, maid, and washwoman. Shortly after their arrival, Flora Belle was born in a large room over the contractor's stable.

She was never a pretty baby, Flora Belle, for her parents were not beautiful people. Poor food and hard work had lined their faces and bent their bodies even before she was born. The fear and strain of their hegira, with the mother pregnant, did not help to produce a sweet and lovely child. Flora Belle's face, as she grew up, had a lugubrious expression about it that would make you laugh if you didn't know her—but would make you sorry for her if you did know her.

Then, too, from helping her mother with the white folks' washing and her father to tend the horses, Flora Belle grew up strong and heavy, with rough hands and a hard chest like a boy's. She had hard ways, as well. A more attractive colored girl might have appealed to the young white men of the town for illegitimate advances, but nobody so much as winked at Flora Belle. She graduated from high school without ever having had a beau of any kind. The only colored boys she had ever seen were the ones who came through Tall Rock once with a circus.

Just before her graduation, her mother laid down and died—quite simply—"worked to death," as she put it. Tired! A white preacher came to the house and preached her funeral with a few white neighbors present. After that Flora Belle lived with her aging father and cooked his meals for him—the two of them alone, dark souls in a white world. She did the contractor's family washing, as the new Irish maid refused to cook, clean—and then wash, too. Flora Belle made a few dollars a week washing and ironing.

One day, the second summer after she came out of high school, her father said, "I'm gonna leave here, Flora Belle." So they went to Butte. That was shortly after World War I ended, in the days of Prohibition. Things were kind of dead in Butte, and most of the Negroes there were having a hard time, or going into bootlegging. Flora Belle and her father lived in the house with a family who sold liquor. It was a loud and noisy house, with people coming and going way up in the night. There was gambling in the kitchen.

There were very few Negroes in Butte, and Flora Belle made friends with none of them. Their ways were exceedingly strange to her, since she had never known colored people before. And she to them was just a funny-looking stuck-up ugly old girl. They took her shyness to mean conceit, and her high-school English to mean superiority. Nobody paid any attention to Flora.

Her father soon took up with a stray woman around town. He began to drink a lot, too. Months went by and he found no steady work, but Flora Belle did occasional house cleaning. They still had a little money that they had saved, so one day Flora Belle said, "Pa, let's buy a ticket and leave this town. It's no good."

And the old man said, "I don't care if I do."

Flora Belle had set her mind on one of the big cities of the coast where there would be lots of nice colored people she could make friends with. So they went to Seattle, her and Pa. They got there one winter morning in the rain. They asked a porter in the station where colored people could stop, and he sent them to a street near the depot where Negroes, Filipinos, Japanese, and Chinese lived in boxlike buildings. The street had a busy downtown atmosphere. Flora Belle liked it very much, the moving people, the noise, the shops, the many races.

"I'm glad to get to a real city at last," she said.

"This rain is chillin' me to the bone," her father answered, walking along with their suitcases. "I wish I had a drink." He left Flora Belle as soon as their rooms were rented and went looking for a half-pint.

In Seattle it rained and rained. In the gray streets strange people of many shades and colors passed, all of them going places, having things to do. In the colored rooming house, as time went by, Flora Belle met a few of the roomers, but they all were busy, and they did not ask her to join them in their activities. Her father stayed out a good deal, looking for a job, he said—but when he came back, you could smell alcohol on his breath. Flora Belle looked for a job, also, but without success.

She was glad when Sunday came. At least she could go to church, to a colored church—for back in Tall Rock there had been no Negro church, and the white temples were not friendly to a black face.

"I'm A.M.E., myself," the landlady said. "The Baptists do too much shoutin' for me. You go to my church."

So Flora Belle went to the African Methodist Episcopal Church— alone, because the landlady was too busy to take her. That first day at services quite a few members shook hands with her. This made Flora Belle very happy. She went back that evening and joined the church. She felt warm and glad at just meeting people. She was invited to attend prayer meeting and to become a member of the Young Women's Club, dues ten cents a week. She in turn asked some of the sisters, with fumbling incoherence, if they knew where she could get a job. The churchwomen took her phone number and promised to call her if they heard of anything. Flora Belle walked home through the rain that night feeling as if she had at last come to a welcome place.

Sure enough, during the week, a woman did call up to let her know about a job. "It's a kinder hard place," the woman said over the phone, "but I reckon you can stand it awhile. She wants a maid to sleep in, and they don't pay much. But since you ain't workin', it might beat a blank."

Flora Belle got the job. She was given the servant's room. It was damp and cold; the work was hard, and the lady exacting; the meager pay came once a month, but Flora Belle was thankful to have work.

"Now," she thought to herself, "I can get some nice clothes and meet nice people, 'cause I'm way behind, growing up in a town where there wasn't none of my color to be friends with. I want to meet some boys and girls and have a good time."

But she had only one night off a week, Sunday evening to go to church. Then Flora Belle would fix herself up as nice as she knew how and bow and bow in her friendliest fashion, fighting against shyness and strangeness, but never making much of an impression on folks. At church everybody was nice enough, to be sure, but nobody took up more time with her than brotherly love required. None of the young men noticed her at all, what with dozens of pretty girls around, talkative and gay—for Flora Belle stood like she was tongue-tied when she was introduced to anybody. Just stood staring, trying to smile. She didn't know the easy slang of the young people, nor was she good at a smart comeback if someone made a bright remark. She was just a big, homely silent woman whose desire for friends never got past that lugubrious look in her wistful eyes and that silence that frightened folks away.

A crippled man after Sunday services tried to make up to her once or twice. He talked and talked, but Flora Belle could manage to say nothing more than "Yes, sir," or, "No, sir," to everything he said, like a dumb young girl—although she was now twenty-five, and too unattractive to play coy.

Even the sporting men—to whom women give money—used to laugh about Flora Belle. "Man, I wouldn't be seen on the streets with that truck horse," was their comment in the pool halls.

So a year went by and Flora Belle had no more friends than she had had back in Butte or Tall Rock. "I think I'll go away from here," she said to herself. "Try another town. I reckon all cities ain't like Seattle, where folks is so cold and it rains all the time."

So she went away. She left Pa living in sin with some old Indian woman and shining shoes in a white barber shop for a living. He had begun to look mighty bowed and wrinkled, and he drank increasingly.

Flora Belle went to San Francisco. She had a hard time finding work, a hard time meeting people, a hard time trying to get a boy friend. But in California she didn't take up so much time with the church. She met, instead, some lively railroad porters and maids who gave parties and lived a sort of fast life. Flora Belle managed to get in good with the porters' crowd, mostly by handing out money freely to pay for food and drinks when parties were being arranged.

She was usually an odd number, though, having no man. Nevertheless, she would come by herself to the parties and try her best to be a good sport, to drink and be vulgar. But even when she was drunk, she was still silent and couldn't think of anything much to say. She fell in love with a stevedore and used to give him her pay regularly and buy him fine shirts, but he never gave her any matrimonial encouragement, although he would take whatever she offered him. Then she found out that he was married already and had four children. He told her he didn't want her, anyway.

"I'm gonna leave this town," Flora Belle said to herself, "if the bus station still sells tickets."

So the years went on. The cities on the coast, the fog cities of fruit trees and vineyards, passed in procession—full of hard work and loneliness. Cook in a roadhouse, maid for a madam, ironer in a laundry, servant for rich Mexicans—Monterrey—Berkeley—San Diego—Marysville—San Jose. At last she came to Fresno. She was well past thirty. She felt tired. She wanted sometimes to die. She had worked so long for white folks, she had cooked so many dinners, made so many beds.

Working for a Fresno ranch owner, looking after his kids, trying to clean his house and keep things as his wife desired, passing lonely nights in her room over the garage, she felt awful tired, awful tired.

"I wish I could die," she said to herself. By now she often talked out loud. "I wish I could die."

And one day, she asked, "Why not?"

The idea struck her all of a sudden, "Why not?"

So on her Thursday afternoon off from work, she bought a pistol. She bought a box of bullets. She took them home—and somehow she felt better just carrying the heavy package under one arm along the street.

That night in her room over the garage she unwrapped the gun and looked at it a long time. It was black, cold, steel-like, heavy and hard, dependable and certain. She felt sure it could take her far away—whenever she wanted to go. She felt sure it would not disappoint her—if she chose to leave Fresno. She was sure that with the gun, she would never again come to an empty town.

She put in all the bullets it would hold, six, and pressed its muzzle to her head. "Maybe the heart would be better," she thought, putting its cold nose against her breast. Thus she amused herself in her room until late in the night. Then she put the pistol down, undressed, and went to bed. Somehow she felt better, as though she could go off anytime now to some sweet good place, as though she were no longer a prisoner in the world, or in herself.

She slept with the pistol under her pillow.

The following morning she locked it in her trunk and went down to work. That day her big ugly body moved about the house with a new lightness. And she was very kind to the white lady's children. She kept thinking that in the tray of her trunk there was something that meant her good, and would be kind to her. So the days passed.

Every night in her little room, over the garage, after she had combed her hair for bed, she would open the trunk and take the pistol from its resting place. Sometimes she would hold it in her lap. Other nights she would press the steel-black weapon to her heart and put her finger on the trigger, standing still quite a long time. She never pulled the trigger, but she knew that she could pull it whenever she wished.

Sometimes, in bed in the dark, she would press the gun between her breasts and talk to it like a lover. She would tell it all the things that had gone on in her mind in the past. She would tell it all that she had wanted to do, and how, now, she didn't want to do anything, only hold this gun, and be sure—*sure* that she could go away if she wanted to go—anytime. She was sure!

Each night the gun was there—like she imagined a lover might be. Each night it came to bed with her, to lie under the pillow near her head or to rest in her hand. Sometimes she would touch that long black pistol in the dark and murmur in her sleep, "I love . . . you."

Of course, she told nobody. But everybody knew that something had happened to Flora Belle Yates. She knew what. Her life became surer and happier because of this friend in the night. She began to attend church regularly on Sunday, to sing, shout, and take a more active part in the week-night meetings. She began to play with her employer's children, and to laugh with his wife over the little happenings in the house. The white lady began to say to her neighbors, "I've got the best maid in the world. She was awfully grouchy when she first came, but now that she's gotten to like the place, she's simply wonderful!"

As the months went by, Flora Belle began to take on weight, to look plump and jolly, and to resemble one of those lovable big dark-skinned mammies in the picture books. It was the gun. As some people find assurance in the Bible or in alcohol, Flora Belle found assurance in the sure cold steel of the gun.

She is still living alone over the white folks' garage in Fresno—but now she can go away anytime she wants to.

Fine Accommodations

In two seconds they'd be pulling out of Atlanta, going North. The long platform was busy with people, redcaps, baggage trucks, travelers, and relatives waving farewell. The New York Limited had a heavy load. Peter Johnson, porter, stood beside the Pullman steps. He looked down toward the engine and saw the last mail bags being thrown into a coach ahead. " 'Bout to be hitting it," he thought, when a hurrying redcap, bending under the weight of three big brown bags that seemed, from the way he was panting, to be loaded with iron, cried, "Here we are, buddy!"

Behind the redcap came a large elderly well-dressed Negro, followed by a young colored man with a portable typewriter and two brief cases. Porter Peter Johnson smiled as he took one of the heavy bags from the redcap, reaching at the same time for the two brief cases which the young man carried.

"Never mind," said the young fellow, "these are very valuable. Here, you take the typewriter."

"Drawing room A," said the redcap.

"Rich colored folks," thought Peter Johnson, and a thrill of pride ran through him that two members of his own race were riding the crack New York Limited—in an expensive drawing room at that!

Peter Johnson knew that in the South the railroad people sometimes gave Negroes the drawing room for the price of an ordinary berth, just to have them out of sight, but that would never happen on a crowded extra-fare train where space was booked a week ahead. No, these Negroes had obviously paid good money for a de-luxe trip north in such fine accommodations.

"They ain't sporting people," Peter Johnson said to himself, noting the quiet attire and beribboned spectacles of the elderly man, and the nervous college-boy face of the younger passenger. "He must be some big shot, the old fellow, professor, or a bishop, or a race leader. I'll find out directly."

But before Peter Johnson could ask the sweating redcap who the man was, he had pocketed his tip and gone. The train was pulling out. The porter hurried down the corridor to close the car doors.

By and by, as the train hit the suburbs and gathered speed, and the porter had changed into his white jacket, he came back to drawing room A and knocked on the door.

"Come," said a heavy voice inside.

The porter entered and smiled, bowed, and began to put the huge bags up out of the way. The elderly brownskin man was sitting by the window, his hands full of papers covered with notes and figures. The young man was not in the room.

"Going all the way?" asked the porter as he busied himself with the bags.

"Washington," said the elderly man, "to the White House."

"Oh," said the porter, with admiration. "It's a honor to be carrying you on this train." He must be a *big* Negro, Peter Johnson thought. I'm glad we've got race men like him.

"I am called to see the President," went on the elderly man pompously, "concerning Negro labor."

"They're gonna raise wages, ain't they?" asked the porter.

"In some instances, yes," replied the man, studying his papers.

"I thought for everybody," said the porter.

"We are hoping to adjust that," answered the man. The race leader said no more. He seemed intensely occupied with his papers, so the porter went out.

That night when Peter Johnson came to make up the berths, the elderly Negro was in the club car. The young man closed his portable typewriter to exchange a few friendly words with the porter.

"I used to work on the road, too," he said, "dining car, on the Central."

"Where did you run?" the porter asked.

"New York to Buffalo mostly," the young man said.

"Nice run," said the porter. "What's your business now, might I ask? You look like a educated fellow."

"I graduated from Columbia," said the young man, sorting out the carbons of something he had been copying. "Now I'm assistant secretary to Dr. Jenkins here, president of Attucks Institute, perhaps the most important Negro school in the South."

"I'd like to send my son there when he's big enough," said the porter. "I got a boy twelve years old."

"Where do you live?" the young man asked.

"Harlem," the porter replied.

"Well, I'd send him to a Northern school then," advised the secretary. "I work down South, but I don't like it. It's still full of prejudice."

"Something in that," said the porter, making down the berths. "But Dr. Jenkins is a great leader, ain't he? I want my boy to know some of the big men of his own color."

"I guess you're right," said the young man a little uncertainly, "but . . ."

"Anybody the President calls to Washington must be a fine man," declared the porter simply.

"Not always," the young man said with a sudden bitter intenseness—then he looked as though he wished he hadn't said it. "I guess I'd better shut up."

"Listen, I don't talk," said the porter.

"It's your saying you'd like to send your son to that school that gets me," said the young man slowly. "Don't send him there!"

"What's the matter?" asked the porter. "You don't like the school or your boss, or what?"

"It's not that," said the young man. "Personally, he's fine to work for, but I—" he hesitated again, and then blurted out, "I don't like what he's doing."

"I thought he was a fine man," said the porter.

"My father was a better man," said the young fellow, "and he was a porter."

"Your father was a porter, too, you say? Where'd he run?"

"On the Pennsy to Pittsburgh the last two years before he died. Jim Palmer was his name."

"Jim Palmer?" said the porter. "Why, I knew him! Big tall fellow? Why, me and him used to run together on Number Nine years ago. We used to pal around together."

"Well, you know what he was like then," said the young man. "He was a real man, wasn't he?"

"He sure was," cried the porter. "Why, he helped to form our union."

"Yes," said the young fellow. "He wanted colored people to stand up and be somebody, didn't he? To fight for their rights! To organize. If you knew my father, you know that. He worked like hell to put me and my brothers through school. And he wouldn't like what I'm doing now, not by a damn sight."

"What do you mean, son, he wouldn't like it?" asked the porter. "I can call you *son* if you're Jim Palmer's boy."

"And I can talk to you like a father," said the young man. "I got to talk to somebody. I'm going to give this job up—even if it does pay a good salary, even if it is a 'position.' Dr. Jenkins is a big man, I know,

and a famous Negro—but the way he keeps *big* is by *not playing square.*
Don't send your boy to his school."

"What do you mean?" asked the porter.

"Well, take this labor relations thing," said the young man. "He's *not*
going to Washington to help Negroes get higher wages, nor the same
wages the whites get, nor what the code promises them down South.
Do you know why he's going to Washington?"

"No," said the porter.

"To get the authorities to except from the code those industries in
the South where Negroes are employed, to get them to allow white
factory owners to pay Negroes less than they pay white workers—to
permit them to do that *with Government sanction!*" He rose and stood
looking at the porter. "Why? Because the white trustees of that Southern
school of his are men who employ Negroes, who make their money off of
Negroes, and who don't want to pay us a living wage. You see, that's the
way he keeps on being a *big* man—bowing to Southern white customs.
That's how much Dr. Jenkins cares about his race! His people! He never
opened his mouth about the boy who was beaten to death by the police
near his campus last month. I'm fed up. It makes me feel guilty just
typing out these polite surveys and reports, toned down, conciliatory,
understated, for him to take to Washington. They look scholarly as hell,
but are intended to help keep poor black people just where we've been
all the time—poor and black! You understand me! I don't want to be
secretary to that kind of man. I can't be!"

"I thought he was a *real* leader," said the porter sadly.

Just then the door opened and Dr. Jenkins entered, the butt of a nearly
smoked-out cigar in his mouth.

"Did you finish copying the survey?" he asked his secretary.

"Yes," said the young man, "but I didn't agree with it."

"It's not necessary that you agree," snapped Dr. Jenkins as the porter
went out. The rest of his words were lost as the door closed and the train
roared through the night.

For a moment the porter stood thinking in the corridor. "The last Negro passenger I had in that drawing room was a pimp from Birmingham.
Now I got a professor. I guess both of them have to have ways of paying
for such fine accommodations."

No Place to Make Love

We had no place to make love. We could kiss in doorways, or hold hands in the movies, or somebody might lend us a car. But most of the time we had no place at all to make love. I tell you all that, Mister, so you'll understand how come we're here, me and Mary, and not looking for charity, either.

Poor and young. But old enough to work, old enough for our parents to make us bring home the bacon every week. But never old enough for anybody to worry about our love life, Mister. Kids in our kind of families have to worry about that themselves. The old folks are all loved out, so they don't care how we get along—just so we don't get hitched too soon and take their pay checks away.

Me and Mary wasn't hardly making enough to get married. I had my mother to take care of and two kid sisters. Pa died on us last year. Both of us had to quit school in our teens. Mary had a big family, too, house full of sisters and brothers. Being the oldest, she had to bring home every cent she made in the hosiery mill. Even white like me and Mary, it's no fun growing up down South in a poor family, I tell you, Mister.

Though poor, our parents were awful religious. They liked revivals, liked to put money in the church and help support the Bible school. If me and Mary went to the movies on Sunday, they'd kick because we didn't go to church, too. Her parents didn't like me worth a damn, nohow. They knew I wanted to marry her—and they thought they'd lose a paying boarder if Mary left.

Me, I wanted to take her away. Sure! Come up North somewhere. But there was Ma on my hands, sufferin' and complainin' all the time. Mister, you know, sometimes I think kids ought to be born without parents.

The old folks knew we didn't have no place even to make love. They didn't care. A small town ain't like a big one where you can find a place. When you're too poor to own even an old Ford, what can you do—with your house full of family all the time?

Well, last summer we went out in the woods. And we found a hill. And we pretended we was in the Garden of Eden—only we could always hear the cars and busses passing in the road below.

Then one night coming home about dusk-dark, with the sun gone down and the first stars coming out, Mary said, "Honey, I guess I ought to tell you. I drunk that stuff again twice last week, but it didn't do no good—and it's almost two months now."

I said, "Listen! I don't care if it don't work. Let's get married. I like kids, don't you?"

So I found out how much a license costs—and the next Sunday when we went out on our hill, we was man and wife. I took her home to sleep on the davenport in the parlor with me—and Ma raised hell. Said we'd starve to death getting married, young as we was—and she'd be glad of it. Said what right did we have getting married anyhow, and she not knowing about it? What business did we have birthing a child with no money? My mother got sick and went to bed. All our folks like to died. Yet and still, Mary's parents told everybody they was glad to have her out of the house, glad to get rid of her, pregnant as she was. But they did everything they could to break us up. For the first time in history her mother got friendly with my mother, and they would spend hours talking about how foolish we was, and how ungrateful for all their raising.

My mother was as nasty to Mary as she could be. So was my sisters. Before we'd get home from work, they'd have their dinner all fixed and et. Mary would have to go cook another dinner for ourselves—and me buying all the food for them, too. Relatives sure can be mean when they want to!

Ma kept saying she was going to tell the authorities how we'd put our ages up to get married without telling our parents, and she'd have the whole thing annulled. But then there was our baby on the road. She knew when it came, I'd have to take care of the kid anyhow—so she didn't do nothing but talk.

"Hardly dry behind the ears yet, and a baby coming," she'd say.

I'd grin, but it made me mad. She didn't mean it in fun. Old folks are fierce. Between the lot of 'em, they made us so tired, Mary and me, that we just got on the evening train one night and come to New York. We both want our kid to be born in a friendly place, that's why, away from relatives.

Of course, I didn't know it was so hard to get a job in New York, or so cold up here. You see, Mister, I ain't never been away from home before. With the kid coming and all, I *got* to have something to do, recession or not. Mary ain't able to work, and they won't even let me shovel snow for the city. You got to be a registered voter, the man says.

You're the second welfare investigator what's been here. The first one, the white man, said he couldn't do a thing. We don't come under his jurisdiction. Maybe you can tell us what jurisdiction we do come under? What about young folks like us who want a decent place for our kid to be born in? I'm getting desperate, Mister! Mary is, too. We got rent to pay. We don't want our kid to be born out in the cold, maybe growing up like we did—without even a place to make love. I don't want relief, Mister, but I do want a job. I know you understand. You niggers have a hard time, too, don't you?

On the Way Home

Reprinted from *Laughing to Keep from Crying*. See p. 236.

Mysterious Madame Shanghai

Reprinted from *Laughing to Keep from Crying*. See p. 243.

Patron of the Arts

Although it was only four o'clock of an autumn afternoon, the lights were on in the corners of Darby's little fifth-floor studio apartment, those soft rose-colored lights that make even an ugly woman look charming—particularly if she is as smartly groomed as many New York women of color are. Through the windows with their *tête de negre* drapes, one saw a wind-blown, autumn-leafed view of aristocratic Sugar Hill, and southward, the less well-kept regions of Harlem, through which, in spite of poverty, fame had stalked to carry off a Josephine Baker or an Eartha Kitt.

Darby looked out, puffing impatiently on a cigarette and waiting for the lady to arrive. She was thirty-five and, according to the poets, there is no woman so charming as the woman of thirty-five. Darby had read this somewhere. He was twenty-one, fresh out of college. Today he had everything in readiness—the little anchovies, the ice in the bowl, the Bacardi, and the limes. He knew what she liked, this green-eyed brownskin Mrs. Oldham who had been one of his first friends in New York. Back home in Oklahoma over his drawing board in art class in high school, Darby had dreamed of women like Cornelia Oldham. There were none in the Southwest that a Negro boy might meet.

Now that he knew her—and had known her—there was a little creole girl at the Art Students League downtown he liked much better—a struggling young artist like himself in a strange city. He wished he could marry her.

Standing in reverie, Darby heard the elevator door close. He straightened his tie—despite the fact that he might shortly take it off. You see, he was only twenty-one, and he wanted to look his best at first.

The bell rang. He went to his door, and there was Cornelia. Taller than Darby, sleek in black and white, green-eyed and wise and old. Oh, so charming—a brownskin woman with sea-green eyes! He took her in his arms, but the very first words she said caused him to jump halfway across the room.

"Darling," she whispered, panting, looking at him with her great green eyes like a cat's, "I have told . . . my husband . . . all."

Something stopped beating in Darby's breast. It was his heart. "What?" he cried.

"Yes, dear, I have told him I love you!"

Darby stood behind the sofa. He stared at her with wide young eyes. He knew she had a husband, to be sure, a large dark man, a solid figure in the Negro community. But that personage had always seemed quite remote, far away at home in St. Albans, or working at his Seventh Avenue office. This was Darby's first experience with a married woman. And he never dreamed that they told their husbands all.

"What—what," stuttered the young man as soon as he could talk, "what—did—your husband say?"

"He rose," Cornelia panted, "and stalked out of the room."

Her green eyes in her *café-au-lait* face were full of tragedy. At once Darby had visions of an irate spouse still stalking—right on up to his apartment with a pistol in his hand.

"Lord!" Darby cried. "Cornelia, why did you do that?"

"I love you," she said, "that's why."

"But—but maybe he'll come here and shoot up the place!"

"Let him," she cried. "First we'll mix a cocktail." She took off her wraps and sat down. The youth stood behind the sofa, shaking his head.

"I—I will not fix a cocktail," he said. She leaned her head back for a kiss. "Suppose he were tailing you! Why, he'd find us in a—a compromising position!" Darby retreated toward the wall.

"Darling!" Cornelia cried, rising to come swiftly toward him, her green eyes gleaming, her dark hair done by Rose Meta. "Don't worry . . ."

Just then there was a ring at the door. Darby stood as if petrified while Cornelia returned to the sofa. Finally he managed to move his legs, close his mouth, and turn the doorknob.

The janitor stood in the hall.

"I'll take them socks, Mr. Middlefield, you said you wanted my wife to mend."

"Could you come back later, *please?*" said Darby.

"Yes, suh," said the man.

"Let's get out of here," Darby said as he closed the door. "Your husband might come at any moment, Cornelia."

"He's still in his office, darling."

"I don't care," said Darby, "let's go."

Thinking how his mother back home in Tulsa would feel if she read in the papers that he was killed over a *married* woman, Darby opened the closet and took out his coat.

"If you leave me," Cornelia said, "I will shoot myself."

"There's nothing here for you to shoot yourself with," said Darby, putting on his coat.

"Then I'll grind up glass and eat it."

"Don't be a fool!" cried Darby.

"I am," said Cornelia, "about you!"

"I want *you* to go home," Darby begged desperately.

"I won't," answered Cornelia.

"Then I'm going out to a phone and call your husband and explain everything to him. After all, you're just my patron, Mrs. Oldham. You paid me well to paint your portrait."

"Is that all I am to you?" cried Cornelia. She poured herself a huge drink, not bothering to mix it.

"That's all I'll ever admit," said the young man. "I'm going to explain fully to your husband *now*—our relationship. After that, please take your portrait home. It's finished." He pointed toward the easel where rested the oil painting he had made of her.

"You coward!" said Mrs. Oldham. "Afraid of my husband! Why, you and I could go to Paris and be free."

"I don't want to go to Paris," said Darby, "I'm going to a phone."

He left Cornelia in front of the cocktail shaker as he rushed out. From the pay station in the drugstore at the corner, Darby finally got Dr. Oldham on the phone.

"I am Darby Middlefield," said the young man nervously.

"Who?" asked Dr. Oldham.

"Middlefield, the artist."

"The artist?"

"I'm calling you about your wife."

"My wife? Why about *my* wife?"

"Because I want to make it plain to you, Dr. Oldham, we are nothing to each other."

"What? But why?"

Darby repeated what he had just said.

"My dear boy," said Dr. Oldham, "my wife and I have lived apart for years. Our divorce is pending."

"But—but—"

"Whoever you are," said Dr. Oldham, "from the sound of your voice, you must be very young. You need not worry about me."

"But I thought she had told you all?" said Darby plaintively.

"She probably did," explained Dr. Oldham. "But I am so bored at Cornelia's frequent affairs with young men immature enough to be her sons that I usually walk out of the room when she begins her confidences. I've heard them for years, so I am no longer amused, damn it!"

"You mean you don't care?"

"I certainly don't," said Dr. Oldham. "Cornelia's a woman of forty-seven who can take care of herself."

"Forty-seven?" said Darby. "She told me she was thirty-five!"

"I can smell your youth!" said Dr. Oldham. He hung up the phone.

"Thirty-five! *Forty-seven!*" Darby murmured to himself as he left the booth. "Thirty-five! That lying chick!"

When he got back to his apartment Cornelia had gone. Without partaking of any ground glass, she had drunk *half* of his bottle of Bacardi instead.

Resting on the tray beside the bottle was a little note:

Dearest Darby:

Please keep the picture you painted of me to take with you when you go back to Oklahoma. Perhaps, when you are older, you might like to remember how your patron looked.

Love,
CORNELIA

Early Autumn

When Bill was very young, they had been in love. Many nights they had spent walking, talking together. Then something not very important had come between them, and they didn't speak. Impulsively, she had married a man she thought she loved. Bill went away, bitter about women.

Yesterday, walking across Washington Square, she saw him for the first time in years.

"Bill Walker," she said.

He stopped. At first he did not recognize her, to him she looked so old.

"Mary! Where did you come from?"

Unconsciously, she lifted her face as though wanting a kiss, but he held out his hand. She took it.

"I live in New York now," she said.

"Oh"—smiling politely. Then a little frown came quickly between his eyes.

"Always wondered what happened to you, Bill."

"I'm a lawyer. Nice firm, way downtown."

"Married yet?"

"Sure. Two kids."

"Oh," she said.

A great many people went past them through the park. People they didn't know. It was late afternoon. Nearly sunset. Cold.

"And your husband," he asked her.

"We have three children. I work in the bursar's office at Columbia."

"You're looking very . . ." (he wanted to say *old*) " . . . well," he said.

She understood. Under the trees in Washington Square, she found herself desperately reaching back into the past. She had been older than he then in Ohio. Now she was not young at all. Bill was still young.

"We live on Central Park West," she said. "Come and see us sometime."

"Sure," he replied. "You and your husband must have dinner with my family some night. Any night. Lucille and I'd love to have you."

The leaves fell slowly from the trees in the Square. Fell without wind. Autumn dusk. She felt a little sick.

"We'd love it," she answered.

"You ought to see my kids." He grinned.

Suddenly the lights came on up the whole length of Fifth Avenue, chains of misty brilliance in the blue air.

"There's my bus," she said.

He held out his hand, "Good-by."

"When . . ." she wanted to say, but the bus was ready to pull off. The lights on the avenue blurred, twinkled, blurred. And she was afraid to open her mouth as she entered the bus. Afraid it would be impossible to utter a word.

Suddenly she shrieked very loudly, "Good-by!" But the bus door had closed.

The bus started. People came between them outside, people crossing the street, people they didn't know. Space and people. She lost sight of Bill. Then she remembered she had forgotten to give him her address— or to ask him for his—or tell him that her youngest boy was named Bill, too.

Never Room with a Couple

Reprinted from *Laughing to Keep from Crying*. See p. 250.

Tragedy at the Baths

Reprinted from *Laughing to Keep from Crying*. See p. 262.

Trouble with the Angels

Reprinted from *Laughing to Keep from Crying*. See p. 267.

On the Road

Reprinted from *Laughing to Keep from Crying*. See p. 272.

Big Meeting

Reprinted from *Laughing to Keep from Crying*. See p. 277.

Breakfast in Virginia

Two colored boys during the war. For the first time in his life one of them, on furlough from a Southern training camp, was coming North. His best buddy was a New York lad, also on furlough, who had invited him to visit Harlem. Being colored, they had to travel in the Jim Crow car until the Florida Express reached Washington.

The train was crowded and people were standing in WHITE day coaches and in the COLORED coach—the single Jim Crow car. Corporal Ellis and Corporal Williams had, after much insistence, shared for a part of the night the seats of other kindly passengers in the coach marked COLORED. They took turns sleeping for a few hours. The rest of the time they sat on the arm of a seat or stood smoking in the vestibule. By morning they were very tired. And they were hungry.

No vendors came into the Jim Crow coach with food, so Corporal Ellis suggested to his friend that they go into the diner and have breakfast. Corporal Ellis was born in New York and grew up there. He had been a star track man with his college team, and had often eaten in diners on trips with his teammates. Corporal Williams had never eaten in a diner before, but he followed his friend. It was midmorning. The rush period was over, although the dining car was still fairly full. But, fortunately, just at the door as they entered there were three seats at a table for four persons. The sole occupant of the table was a tall, distinguished gray-haired man. A white man.

As the two brownskin soldiers stood at the door waiting for the steward to seat them, the white man looked up and said, "Won't you sit here and be my guests this morning? I have a son fighting in North Africa. Come, sit down."

"Thank you, sir," said Corporal Ellis. "This is kind of you. I am Corporal Ellis. This is Corporal Williams."

The elderly man rose, gave his name, shook hands with the two colored soldiers, and the three of them sat down at the table. The young men faced their host. Corporal Williams was silent, but Corporal Ellis carried on the conversation as they waited for the steward to bring the menus.

"How long have you been in the service, Corporal?" the white man was saying as the steward approached.

Corporal Ellis could not answer this question because the steward cut in brusquely, "You boys can't sit here."

"These men are my guests for breakfast, steward," said the white man.

"I am sorry, sir," said the white steward. "But Negroes cannot be served now. If there's time, we may have a fourth sitting before luncheon for them, if they want to come back."

"But these men are soldiers," said the white man.

"I am sorry, sir. We will take *your* order, but I cannot serve them in the state of Virginia."

The two Negro soldiers were silent. The white man rose. He looked at the steward a minute, then said, "I am embarrassed, steward, both for you and for my guests." To the soldiers he said, "If you gentlemen will come with me to my drawing room, we will have breakfast there. Steward, I would like a waiter immediately, Room E, the third car back."

The tall, distinguished man turned and led the way out of the diner. The two soldiers followed him. They passed through the club car, through the open Pullmans, and into a coach made up entirely of compartments. The white man led them along the blue-gray corridor, stopped at the last door, and opened it.

"Come in," he said. He waited for the soldiers to enter.

It was a roomy compartment with a large window and two long comfortable seats facing each other. The man indicated a place for the soldiers, who sat down together. He pressed a button.

"I will have the porter bring a table," he said. Then he went on with the conversation just as if nothing had happened. He told them of recent letters from his son overseas, and of his pride in all the men in the military services who were giving up the pleasures of civilian life to help bring an end to Hitlerism. Shortly the porter arrived with the table. Soon a waiter spread a cloth and took their order. In a little while the food was there.

All this time Corporal Williams from the South had said nothing. He sat, shy and bewildered, as the Virginia landscape passed outside the train window. Then he drank his orange juice with loud gulps. But when the eggs were brought, suddenly he spoke, "This here time, sir, is the first time I ever been invited to eat with a white man. I'm from Georgia."

"I hope it won't be the last time," the white man replied. "Breaking bread together is the oldest symbol of human friendship." He passed the silver tray. "Would you care for rolls or muffins, Corporal? I am sorry there is no butter this morning. I guess we're on rations."

"I can eat without butter," said the corporal.

For the first time his eyes met those of his host. He smiled. Through the window of the speeding train, as it neared Washington, clear in the morning sunlight yet far off in the distance, they could see the dome of the Capitol. But the soldier from the Deep South was not looking out of the window. He was looking across the table at his fellow American.

"I thank you for this breakfast," said Corporal Williams.

Blessed Assurance

Unfortunately (and to John's distrust of God) it seemed his son was turning out to be a queer. He was a brilliant queer, on the Honor Roll in high school, and likely to be graduated in the spring at the head of the class. But the boy was colored. Since colored parents always like to put their best foot forward, John was more disturbed about his son's transition than if they had been white. Negroes have enough crosses to bear.

Delmar was his only son, Arletta, the younger child, being a girl. Perhaps John should not have permitted his son to be named Delmar— Delly for short—but the mother had insisted on it. Delmar was *her* father's name.

"And he is *my* son as well as yours," his wife informed John.

Did the queer strain come from *her* side? Maternal grandpa had seemed normal enough. He was known to have had several affairs with women outside his home—mostly sisters of Tried Stone Church of which he was a pillar.

God forbid! John, Delly's father thought, could he himself have had any deviate ancestors? None who had acted even remotely effeminate could John recall as being a part of his family. Anyhow, why didn't he name the boy at birth *John, Jr.,* after himself? But his wife said, "Don't saddle him with Junior." Yet she had saddled him with Delmar.

If only Delly were not such a sweet boy—no juvenile delinquency, no stealing cars, no smoking reefers ever. He did the chores without complaint. He washed dishes too easily, with no argument, when he might have left them to Arletta. He seldom, even when at the teasing stage, pulled his sister's hair. They played together, Delly with dolls almost as long as Arletta did. Yet he was good at marbles, once fair at baseball, and a real whizz at tennis. He could have made the track team had he not preferred the French Club, the Dramatic Club, and Glee Club. Football, his father's game in high school, Delly didn't like. He couldn't keep his eye on the ball in scrimmage. At seventeen he had to have glasses. The style of rather exaggerated rims he chose made him look like a girl rather than a boy.

"At least he didn't get rhinestone rims," thought John half-thought didn't think felt faint and aloud said nothing. That spring he asked, "Delmar, do you have to wear *white* Bermuda shorts to school? Most of the other boys wear levis or just plain pants, don't they? And why wash them out yourself every night, all that ironing? I want you to be clean, son, but not *that* clean."

Another time, "Delmar, those school togs of yours don't have to match so perfectly, do they? Colors *blended*, as you say, and all like that. This school you're going to's no fashion school—at least, it wasn't when I went there. The boys'll think you're sissy."

Once again desperately, "If you're going to smoke, Delmar, hold your cigarette between your *first* two fingers, not between your thumb and finger—like a woman."

Then his son cried.

John remembered how it was before the boy's mother packed up and left their house to live with another man who made more money than any Negro in their church. He kept an apartment in South Philly and another in Harlem. Owned a Cadillac. Racket connections—politely called *politics*. A shame for his children, for the church, and for him, John! His wife gone with an uncouth rascal!

But although Arletta loathed him, Delly liked his not-yet-legal step-father. Delly's mother and her burly lover had at least had the decency to leave Germantown and change their religious affiliations. They no longer attended John's family church where Delmar sang in the Junior Choir.

Delly had a sweet high tenor with overtones of Sam Cooke. The women at Tried Stone loved him. Although Tried Stone was a Baptist church, it tended toward the sedate—Northern Baptist in tone, not down-home. Yet it did have a Gospel Choir, scarlet robed, since a certain untutored segment of the membership demanded lively music. It had a Senior Choir, too, black robed, that specialized in anthems, sang *Jesu, Joy of Man's Desiring*, the Bach cantatas, and once a year presented *The Messiah*. The white robed Junior Choir, however, even went so far as to want to render a jazz recessional—Delly's idea—which was vetoed. This while he was trying to grow a beard like the beatniks he had seen when the Junior Choir sang in New York and the Minister of Music had taken Delly on a trip to the Village.

"God, don't let him put an earring in his ear like some," John prayed. He wondered vaguely with a sick feeling in his stomach should he think it through then then think it through right then through should he try then and think it through should without blacking through think blacking out then and there think it through?

John didn't. But one night he remembered his son had once told his mother that after he graduated from high school he would like to study at the Sorbonne. The Sorbonne in Paris! John had studied at Morgan in Baltimore. In possession of a diploma from that *fine* (in his mind) Negro institute he took pride. Normally John would have wanted his boy to go there, yet the day after the Spring Concert he asked Delmar, "Son, do you still want to study in France? If you do, maybe—er—I guess I could next fall—Sorbonne. Say, how much is a ticket to Paris?"

In October it would be John's turn to host his fraternity brothers at his house. Maybe by then Delmar would—is the Sorbonne like Morgan? Does it have dormitories, a campus? In Paris he had heard they didn't care about such things. Care about such what things didn't care about what? At least no color lines.

Well, anyhow, what happened at the concert a good six months before October came was, well—think it through clearly now, get it right. Especially for that Spring Concert, Tried Stone's Minister of Music, Dr. Manley Jaxon, had written an original anthem, words and score his own, based on the story of Ruth:

> *"Entreat me not to leave thee,*
> *Neither to go far from thee.*
> *Whither thou goeth, I will go.*
> *Always will I be near thee. . . ."*

The work was dedicated to Delmar who received the first handwritten manuscript copy as a tribute from Dr. Jaxon. In spite of its dedication, one might have thought that in performance the solo lead—Ruth's part—would be assigned to a woman. Perversely enough, the composer allotted it to Delmar. Dr. Jaxon's explanation was, "No one else can do it justice." The Minister of Music declared, "The girls in the ensemble really have *no* projection."

So without respect for gender, on the Sunday afternoon of the program, Delmar sang the female lead. Dr. Jaxon, saffron robed, was at the organ. Until Delmar's father attended the concert that day, he had no inkling as to the casting of the anthem. But, when his son's solo began, all John could say was, "I'll be damned!"

John had hardly gotten the words out of his mouth when words became of no further value. The "Papa, what's happening?" of his daughter in the pew beside him made hot saliva rise in his throat—for what suddenly had happened was that as the organ wept and Delmar's voice soared above the Choir with all the sweetness of Sam Cooke's *tessitura*,[4] backwards off the organ stool in a dead faint fell Dr. Manley Jaxon. Not only did Dr. Jaxon fall from the stool, but he rolled limply down the steps from the organ loft like a bag of meal and tumbled prone onto the rostrum, robes and all.

Amens and *Hallelujahs* drowned in the throats of various elderly sisters who were on the verge of shouting. Swooning teenage maidens suddenly sat up in their pews to see the excitement. Springing from his chair on the rostrum, the pastor's mind deserted the pending collection to try to think what to say under the unusual circumstances.

"One down, one to go," was all that came to mind. After a series of pastorates in numerous sophisticated cities where Negroes did everything whites do, the Reverend Dr. Greene had seen other choir directors take the count in various ways with equal drama, though perhaps less physical immediacy.

When the organ went silent, the choir died, too—but Delmar never stopped singing. Over the limp figure of Dr. Jaxon lying on the rostrum, the "Entreat me not to leave thee" of his solo flooded the church as if it were on hi-fi.

The members of the congregation sat riveted in their pews as the deacons rushed to the rostrum to lift the Minister of Music to his feet. Several large ladies of the Altar Guild fanned him vigorously while others sprinkled him with water. But it was not until the church's nurse-in-uniform applied smelling salts to Dr. Jaxon's dark nostrils, did he lift his head. Finally, two ushers led him off to an anteroom while Delmar's voice soared to a high C such as Tried Stone Baptist Church had never heard.

"Bless God! Amen!" cried Reverend Greene. "Dr. Jaxon has only fainted, friends. We will continue our services by taking up collection directly after the anthem."

"Daddy, why did Dr. Jaxon have to faint just when brother started singing?" whispered John's daughter.

"I don't know," John said.

"Some of the girls say that when Delmar sings, they want to scream, they're so overcome," whispered Arletta. "But Dr. Jaxon didn't scream. He just fainted."

"Shut up," John said, staring straight ahead at the choir loft. "Oh,

God! Delmar, *shut up*!" John's hands gripped the back of the seat in front of him. "Shut up, son! *Shut up*," he cried. "Shut up!"

Silence. . . .

"We will now lift the offering," announced the minister. "Ushers, get the baskets." Reverend Greene stepped forward. "Deacons, raise a hymn. Bear us up, sisters, bear us up!"

His voice boomed:

> *"Blessed assurance!"*

He clapped his hands once.

> *"Jesus is mine!"*

"Yes! Yes! Yes!" he cried.

> *"Oh, what a fortress*
> *Of glory divine!"*

The congregation swung gently into song:

> *"Heir of salvation,*
> *Purchase of God!"*

"Hallelujah! Amen! Halle! Halle!"

> *"Born of the Spirit"*

"God damn it!" John cried. "God *damn* it!"

> *"Washed in His blood. . . ."*

Something in Common

Reprinted from *Laughing to Keep from Crying*. See p. 167.

Uncollected Stories

Mary Winosky

Many of the metropolitan daily papers, crowded with news of the war, the Russian situation, and heated editorials against bolshevism, gave two lines of their precious space to a small article sent out by the Associated Press of New York. It read like this:

New York, May 5. —Mary Winosky, who scrubbed floors and picked rags, died and left $8,000.

Many parents read the little item and pointed it out to their children as an excellent example of thrift and industry. Patriotic Americans spoke about it as showing what an opportunity the United States gives to foreigners. A scrubwoman earning eight thousand dollars. In other countries that would be impossible. But few people read between the printed lines the dull tragedy of Mary Winosky's life. A drab-colored life of floors to scrub and rags to pick, having at its end eight thousand dollars as a result of the drudgery.

When Mary and her father and a younger sister came from the Old Country in the steerage of a big liner, their hearts beat high with expectation and their eyes were full of hope. In this great new world, America, they found city streets ugly and crowded. They found filthy tenements, squalid, stifling, and the skies blurred with a gray smoke, so different from the blue heavens they had known. And where were the flowers in summer, the trees and the wide green fields? Here they found only brick and stone and hard, hot surfaces. And there were no birds to sing. Only above the street noises the heavy rumble of the elevated all day long and in the night its intermittent roar breaking the city silence.

Within a year or so the Winosky family became a part of the big town's composite life. The younger sister learned English rapidly and soon procured a position as bundle wrapper in a downtown store. Old man Winosky, whose hands had grown callous from much plowing and reaping, now became a pushcart peddler and a buyer of old junk such as scrap iron, bottles, and rags. Later when he had gotten enough money, he quit the peddling business and opened a junk shop of his own, where he bought scrap iron and old rags from other men. Mary Winosky, however, did not fit into the new life very well. She never learned to speak the new language readily. She was solidly built and her features were heavy and dull. She was not slim and pretty and deft of movement like her younger sister, so it was hard for Mary to find a job. For a while she worked in a steam laundry but they fired her. Then she washed dishes in a large hotel, but the china was too delicate for Mary's clumsy hands and so they gave her her money before the week was up.

Then one day Fortune smiled a wry smile at Mary and offered her a job. A woman who lived in the same building told Mary to come with her and she could get work. "I scrub," said the woman. "Easy work. Jest scrubbing from ten in the night till two in the morning. Good pay." And so Mary Winosky became a scrubwoman.

For more than a year she scrubbed the floors of a big office building on lower Broadway. Miles and miles of marble halls were cleaned by the dull swish-swash of Mary's scrub brush. From ten at night until two in the morning she washed away the dirt and the grime of the day's footsteps, then she rode home before dawn with the other scrubwomen, jabbering about their husbands or their beaus, leaving the car in ones or twos, arriving home in the heavy grayness of early morning.

Spring came, and with it balmy nights full of stars and a love moon. A vague longing took possession of Mary Winosky. She sat on the park benches at night, before going to work, and watched the spooning couples sitting close together in the soft darkness. She put on her best white dress on Sundays and went out walking, her simple face shining and her hands red from recent contact with lye and scrub water. Mary Winosky wanted to be loved.

Then one night she met Andrew Czarnac. He was a ditchdigger and he belonged to the union. He had a curled mustache and flashing black eyes and he wore a red bandanna handkerchief inside his collar on hot days. He began to like Mary and Mary liked him. Late in June old man Winosky died, leaving the junk shop and a little sum of money. Mary divided the money with her younger sister, who was already married, and took charge of the junk shop herself. Two months after her father's death she married Andrew Czarnac. They celebrated their honeymoon by a whole day at Coney Island. Mary was very happy. Life to her became a joyous thing. She had someone to love. She gave all her money to Andrew, so he quit digging in the ditch. Mary still scrubbed floors at night and tended the junk shop in the day, weighing the scrap iron and sorting out the rags. Andrew wore his best suit all the time and worked very seldom. Mary supported him.

Soon, however, Czarnac began to grow tired of married life. He was restless. One day he went away without saying good-bye and he did not come back. Mary waited for him that evening in the door of the shop but he never came. She did not go to work that night but she stood and cried softly to herself. The next day she waited and the next night and for a whole week after that, then she went back to the office building, scrubbing the dirt from the floors at night.

Spring came again and found her still waiting for Andrew Czarnac, but he never returned. Many springtimes came with the golden moons and lovers spooning on the park benches, but each year found Mary Czarnac a little older, a little more stoop-shouldered, loneliness resting a little heavier on her simple heart.

Then the war came to America. She made money in the junk business and added to her already snug bank account. Mary lived frugally, but she was not interested in the money that she made. She was not much interested in anything. She just sat sorting the rags into piles all day and waiting for him.

Of course Mary read the war news, for her people were fighting in Europe, too. One day she sat on a box reading an afternoon paper in the little junk shop, among the rags and bottles and rusty iron scattered about on the floor. Under the Honor Roll List she saw six names, and one of them was Andrew Czarnac—killed in action! He had gone to war and given up his life. He had been killed. He would never come back. All of this came to her in an instant. She gave a little moan and sank down among the rags. A heaviness pressed upon her heart. Andrew, her husband, was dead. She uttered a soft low cry and lay quite still . . .

The neighbors found her afterwards stiff and cold on the floor of the shop. In the bedroom under the mattress they found some money and in the bureau drawer her bankbook. The next day the papers carried this item:

Mary Winosky, who scrubbed floors and picked rags, died and left $8,000.

Many parents read it to their children as an excellent example of thrift and economy.

Those Who Have No Turkey

A stretch of farmland, gray in the dawning, a flash of blue lake water, long lines of freight cars, the sound of many whistles and the shrill shriek of the brakes, with the sleepy voice of the porter calling "Cleveland," told the girl that she had arrived at the end of her journey. One big puff, a final jolt, and the long limited came to a stop. Clasping her old traveling bag in one hand, a bundle under her arm and a shawl over her shoulder, fifteen-year-old Diane Jordan stepped to the platform, for the first time in her life in a large city.

It was early Thanksgiving morning, sometimes called the Day of Big Dinners, that Diane got her first view of Cleveland. Of course, her two cousins with Aunt Ruth were at the station to meet her. After many kisses and exclamations of welcome they guided the rather dazed little country girl out to their big limousine and whirled away uptown. Diane looked out of the auto window and enjoyed the ride, while Aunt Ruth asked about her only sister, Diane's mother, and her activities in the country, for Mrs. Crane had not been to visit her relative for some years.

The Jordan family and the Crane family were in no wise alike, as the two sisters had married into vastly different positions in life. One went to a farm down in the southern part of Ohio with her husband and tilled the soil for a living. Their crops were usually good and they did well, but their mode of living remained that of simple, generous-hearted countryfolk. The other girl married Samuel Crane, a wealthy banker. The whisper of gossips said that she loved his money and not the man, but be that as it may, she gained an enviable social position; she lived in one of the finest houses on upper Euclid Avenue and sent her daughter to an exclusive private school. Mr. Crane died four years after their marriage. Mrs. Crane, busy with her social duties, seldom saw her country sister, but since her two children had spent a summer on the farm, she had always intended to have her niece, Diane, visit in the city. So that accounts for the presence of countrified, tomboyish, unsophisticated Diane Jordan seated in a richly lined limousine between the stylishly clad daughters of Mrs. Samuel P. Crane.

Soon the big auto rolled up a cement driveway and stopped under the porte cochere of the largest house Diane had ever seen. She marveled at its size, but the inside was still more wonderful. It is useless to attempt to describe Diane's feelings upon entering this mansion, so different from her rural home, as no one but a Dickens could do it.

However, after an hour or so of this indoor splendor and her doll-like cousins, Diane, a hardy child of the out-of-doors, grew a bit tired and decided to inspect the yard since Aunt Ruth would not let her help get dinner. Once in a while the scent of turkey floated in from the kitchen. In the country she always helped her mother cook, but here they seemed to hire folks to do the work. Well, city people were queer. Even their yards were not the same. Why, in the country, one had a whole farm to play in, but here the houses took up all the room, so finding the space between the house and the fence too small, Diane's adventurous feet led her to examine the neighborhood.

She had walked a block or two, stopping now and then to stare at some strange new object, when she reached a corner where two car lines crossed and many autos were passing in all directions. The scene was interesting, so she leaned against a lamppost and watched the city people go by until her attention was attracted to a small red-haired boy yelling at the top of his voice, "Extra papers, just out!" He reminded Diane of little brother at home. Her gaze must have attracted his attention for he demanded, "Paper, lady?" Perhaps he called her lady because her dresses were unusually long for a girl of fifteen, but on the farm clothes are not of the latest fashion.

"What kind o' paper you got?" asked the girl.

"*Press* or *News*," replied the little urchin.

Diane pondered. "Well, give me the best one," she said, " 'cause Pa told me to bring him a city paper."

"I've only got two left and if you take 'em both you'll be sure and get the best one," urged the little newsie, anxious to sell out.

"All right, I'll take them," she agreed. "You're in a hurry to get home and eat some turkey, aren't you?"

"Turkey! What do yuh mean?" asked the boy to whom the word was but a name. "We ain't got no turkey."

This answer was surprising to Diane. The girl could not imagine anyone not having turkey for Thanksgiving. All the people in the country had one. Truly, city ways were strange! Why, she had never known anybody to be without a turkey on Thanksgiving Day except once when her Uncle Si said that he was "just durned tired of having what other folks had," so his wife cooked two ducks and a chicken instead of the usual fowl. Perhaps this boy's mother intended to have duck.

"Well, you're going to have duck for dinner, then?" Diane said.

"Naw, we ain't got no duck," he replied.

"Poor little boy," she thought. "Why then, it must be chicken, isn't it?" her voice suggested.

"Naw, we ain't got no chicken, either."

"Well, what in the world have you got?" she demanded of this peculiar boy who had neither turkey, duck, nor chicken for dinner on Thanksgiving.

"We ain't got nothin' yet," he said, and looking up into Diane's sympathetic face, he added, "and we won't have much if dere's not enough pennies in my pocket to get somethin'. My mother's sick."

"Oh-o—," said Diane, looking down at the ragged little boy. It took her a long time to comprehend. She had never heard of anybody having nothing for dinner except the poor war-stricken Belgians, and that was because the Germans had eaten up everything. "Oh," she repeated. "Are you going to buy something?"

"Sure I am," he replied proudly. "Want to help me count my change?"

He had a dollar fifty-four cents.

"Gee, I kin get a dandy dinner with this," he said. "Ma's able to cook now."

However, Diane was not very sure about how much a dollar fifty-four cents would buy, especially for a Thanksgiving meal. Suddenly a big thought came to her. She would ask the little boy and his mother to her aunt's house for dinner. Surely Aunt Ruth would not mind. In the country they always had lots of extra company at the Thanksgiving table.

The newsie was rather puzzled at the strange girl's generosity. Nothing like this had ever happened to him before and he had sold papers in the streets since the age of three. Finally Diane forced him to accept her invitation, the lure of unknown turkey being too much for the little fellow. He promised to come at three.

"Where do you live?" he asked skeptically.

"Down there," Diane pointed to the large house not far away. "I mean I don't live there but I am staying there now and you and your mother can come down today for dinner."

"But I got two sisters," said the boy.

"Oh, bring them along." What were two sisters added to a dinner party? Why, her mother's table at home could feed twenty at once, if necessary.

"And I got a little brother, too," he continued.

"Well," murmured Diane, "bring him with you. I like babies." However, she hoped that he had no more relatives. "Now, tell me your name," she demanded, "so I can tell Aunt Ruth who's coming."

"Tubby Sweeny," he replied, "and we'll sure be there. S' long." Off he ran down the street to deliver the invitation.

Diane went back to the great house without a doubt in the world but that her aunt would be "tickled to death" to have extra company for dinner. Mrs. Crane had been worried about her niece for the last twenty minutes and when she learned of the invitation, that august lady was too shocked for words. At first she hotly refused to admit the coming guests to her home. However, after many hugs and kisses and tearful entreaties from her two daughters, who thought it would be great fun to have such queer company, and from Diane, who declared she would not eat unless the newsboy and his family could eat, too, the elderly lady finally consented. She gave one of the maids instructions to have every one of the guests, when they came, wash their face and hands thoroughly before entering the drawing room. Diane was satisfied, although she thought the washing unnecessary. They never sterilized visitors at her house.

About three o'clock the family came. They were of foreign extraction and none of them, except Tubby, spoke English well. There was the weak little mother, who did not understand the invitation at all but came only because her son insisted; the small twin sisters; and the cute, but none too fat, baby with big black eyes and tiny, mischievous hands that kept Mrs. Crane's nerves on edge. They always wanted to touch something and babies quite often break things!

During dinner the quiet little mother did not talk much, but the young Sweenys—they ate and jabbered to their hearts' content. They expressed a marvelous joy and delight over the turkey, as they had never even tasted that fowl before. And as for the plum pudding and large, round pies, no words in the world could express their feelings! But when they had finished, their stomachs were as tight as kettledrums from very fullness, and the baby resembled a pert little cherub like those painted around Madonna's pictures. Indeed, the tired-looking woman who held the babe would have made a wonderful model if some artist wished to paint "A Madonna of the Poor."

After the ice cream had been eaten and each one of the children had a handful of nuts, the little mother said that they must go, much to Mrs. Crane's relief. The woman thanked them very sincerely for the grand dinner and each one of the little Sweenys kissed Diane and would have kissed the others too, but the Cranes refused to go through the ordeal as they said kissing breeds germs. After the door had closed upon the departing Sweeny party, Mrs. Crane declared: "Those people were the strangest dinner guests I have ever entertained!" And when Diane got back to the farm, she told her mother all about it and ended her story with "Well, Ma, I never knew before that there are people in the world who have no turkey on Thanksgiving."

Seventy-Five Dollars

Primrose Street was a most dejected looking thoroughfare. It was one of the poorest and ugliest streets in the poor district and contained not a single beautiful thing. From its beginning at Detroit Avenue to its end at the edge of a big ravine where the neighborhood threw empty tin cans and other refuse, Primrose Street was simply a jumble of dilapidated frame houses monotonously alike, all the same dull color. A few of them had tumbledown fences in front and one or two had porches, but most of the houses were both fenceless and porchless. Landlords spent little money on their property in that vicinity. Since every house contained from one to a dozen children, the main thoroughfare was always rubbish-strewn, as it was their only playground, but to the residents of Primrose Street, filth and squalor mattered little. The gaunt gray wolf of hunger was their most formidable enemy.

The last house on the street, a narrow two-story frame on which the paint had long since faded, had a more dejected air than all the rest of the houses. It was situated on the edge of the ravine and its windows gave an extensive view of the tin cans and rubbish in the hollow. Today, however, the worn shades were drawn and a wreath with a wisp of black crepe hung on the door. Death had visited Primrose Street.

In the afternoon the neighbors came to the house and the priest delivered the last rites over the dead.

"Poor woman," said Mrs. Mahoney as they watched the little funeral procession going toward Detroit Avenue. "Poor woman, and what will the six children be a-doin' without neither mother nor father?"

"It's hard," said Mrs. Cohn. "Awful hard."

"Yes, it is hard," repeated Mrs. Mahoney.

"It's hard the way she's worked and struggled to take care of them children after her husband died. All day in the factory and then she'd come home and wash and iron and cook for 'em. Only three's big enough to take care of themselves. She tried so hard to keep the little ones in the grades and to help Joe finish high school. The other two big ones quit school, but Joe always did have a hankerin' after education and his mother wanted to give it to him. That poor woman just worked herself to death. It was too much for her."

"Yes," said Mrs. Cohn. "She got so thin."

"And to think she had to die and leave the children! Poor dears! I'd take one myself if I didn't have seven of me own and Mr. Mahoney with none too much work to do. I guess the burden'll fall on Martha now. She's been a-workin' at Weinbolt's store for over a year, and maybe if Joe and the biggest boy helps, she can manage to take care of the little tots. Maybe somehow they can get along."

"Maybe they can, somehow," said Mrs. Cohn.

That evening the parentless children sat around the white oilcloth-covered table in the small combination kitchen-dining room and talked of the "somehow" they were to get along. There were six of them: three small ones—a frail little girl just old enough to go to school; one still younger, who might be sent to a kindergarten; and a boy large enough to sell papers on the street. The others were Martha, the oldest, who worked at Weinbolt's; Joe, who had somehow managed to reach his third year in high school; and Eddie, otherwise "Tough," who had quit school in the seventh grade to take a job in a bowling alley. Upon these three older ones depended the fate of the little family. They talked of the future. The scent of their dead mother's funeral flowers still gave the house a death smell.

"Joe," Martha said, "I guess you'll have to quit school and get a job. There ain't no other way. My ten dollars a week won't go very far, so you and Eddie'll have to help a lot. Mother worked so hard for us and now we must take care of the little ones." Martha's face reflected the grayness of Primrose Street. Her eyes were a dull, drab color, empty of dreams.

"Sure, we'll help you," Joe said. "I won't go back to school." But a lump came in his throat. School meant so much to Joe. "We'll go to work, won't we, Tough?"

"Aw, don't worry, Martha." Tough's voice had a growl in it. "I'll get a regular job and give my money to you. I'll stop hanging around with the gang so much." His cigarette-stained fingers beat a tattoo on the table. His hands were never still. Tough's eyes had a wild look. "We'll get along, Mart," he added.

"I hope we will," Martha said. "Mother wanted me to take care of the children if she died and now I'm going to try. I'll try hard for her sake. I know you boys will help, but it won't be easy and I'll be so lonesome without my m-mother." Martha bowed her head on the table and wept. Her sobs were the dry, nervous sobs of one who has cried too much.

Tough, although the biggest bully on his street, could not stand the sight of tears, so he went out to smoke a cigarette and tell the gang of his resolution to take a "regular" job. Joe put his arm about his sister and tried to soothe her, but he wanted to cry himself. During the time between his mother's death and the funeral, he had shown no signs of grief. He had comforted Martha and played with the little tots and now he felt a lump rising in his own throat. Joe, although a big boy, would miss his mother and he wanted to keep on going to school, but now he could not for Martha must have help to support his little brother and sisters, so he would have to go to work. Joe loved school but he tried to think of other things. It took all his sixteen-year-old courage to keep the tears out of his eyes.

From the time of the mother's death in April to the opening of school in September, the fortunes of the little family were better than they had expected. Martha received a raise at Weinbolt's and Tough, true to his word, finally procured a regular job as delivery boy and performer of any other odd duties that might fall to his lot in old man Steiner's bargain store at the corner of Primrose Street and Detroit Avenue. Although he played pool with the gang every night, smoked excessively, and quite often took Judy Mahoney, the red-haired little Irish girl next door, to the cheap vaudeville shows on the avenue, Tough never forgot to give Martha a goodly portion of his wages every week. He and the gang sometimes derived income from sources unknown. It worried Martha. Some of Tough's friends had been caught in the act of pickpocketing, burglary, and other shady pursuits. The morals of the Primrose Street boys were none too good, but happily Joe was of a different sort. However, Martha worried about Joe. His old happy smile was gone and he seldom laughed.

When Joe left school he took a job in a factory across the ravine and did a man's work. Every payday he gave his money to Martha, but by September the boy had grown tired of the noise of machinery and the dull monotony of his work. He longed to return to school. He wanted to go to the football games and he missed his old companions. Joe was very lonesome. The boys in Primrose Street were so rowdy and uncouth. He did not care much for Tough's chums, and his fellow workers at the factory were mostly foreigners; thus he had no friends, no pals. The autumn nights were long and lonely. High school had been the one happy thing in Joe's life. He would have made the basketball team the coming season and in a little while he would have been a senior. He was the sort of boy who does big things. Joe had been a leader in his class.

Generous-hearted Martha noticed her brother's discontent and it troubled her. She knew how much school meant to Joe, so she tried to think of a way to help him. Perhaps if she skimped and saved a little more she could manage to put away enough of his wages to let him return at the beginning of the February term, so one night after Tough had gone out to play pool and the little ones were asleep, the sister and brother talked it over. If they could save seventy-five dollars before the opening of the midwinter semester, they decided it would be possible for Joe to return to school.

"That would be enough to last you until summer," Martha said, as her weary hands darned stockings for the youngest boy. "You could work on Saturdays and when the basketball season's over you could take an after-school job. Mother wanted you to finish high school and since I've taken her place in our little family I do, too." The warm light of love filled Martha's drab eyes. "I can do overtime work at the store, Joe. I'll help you."

Joe was overjoyed at any prospect of returning to school. "Gee, you're bully, Mart!" He smiled his big happy smile and gave his sister a joyous hug. That night he dreamed of getting a zero in every class and chasing a basketball over the gym floor. Joe laughed aloud in his sleep.

That week and all the following weeks he worked harder at the factory. His envelope contained a little more on paydays. Martha stayed overtime at Weinbolt's. She skimped at home. Together they watched the little school fund grow. Joe's hopes were happy.

The gray days of autumn changed to grayer days of winter. Dry brown leaves on the scraggy trees of Primrose Street fell to the ground. Cold winds swept them away. Snow came and covered the dejected looking houses of the poor with its whiteness. Imitation holly and cheap tinsel ornaments hanging in the store windows on Detroit Avenue told of an approaching Yuletide, while the younger children in Primrose Street began to speak of Santa Claus, although they knew he never had very much to bring them. Christmas, the season of great joy for some and of a great deal of work for others, made its approach. Martha stood on her tired feet all day at Weinbolt's, and old man Steiner had so many deliveries that even Tough was quite weary at night and, instead of going out, remained at home and went to bed. Joe worked on at the factory. Fatigue mattered little to him. His soul was full of joy for in February he would go back to school.

Early in December Joe went to see the athletic coach and was assured that if he returned the next term he would be given a chance to play basketball on the team, so he worked harder and saved more. A few weeks before Christmas, with the aid of Martha, Joe had saved his school money, seventy-five dollars. He kept it in a little iron bank in his bedroom upstairs. February seemed so far off that he could hardly wait. He longed to be among his companions again and to enjoy the happy carefree school days once more. He dreamed of school at night. Joe's eyes were bright and his smile merrier than for many months. The future seemed so full of promise.

Then something happened that put an end to all of Joe's hopes and dreams. The week before Christmas Tough stole three twenties and three fives from old man Steiner's cash drawer and some cheap jewelry out of a case. That evening just before closing the store his employer discovered the loss. They searched Tough and found the jewelry in his overcoat pocket. They did not find the money. Old man Steiner's little eyes gleamed.

"I want my money back," he said.

Tough was sullenly silent.

Mama Steiner wished to call the police "right away yet," but her husband desired his money more than he wished Tough's arrest. Putting the boy in jail would not get his seventy-five dollars back.

"What you do with that money?" he demanded. "Gimme it back and I let you go. I fire you and not call cops."

"Aw, I spent the money," Tough growled.

"What!" The old man made a gesture of despair. "You spend seventy-five dollars already so soon? Maybe your sister can pay it back to me, huh? I need it. I must have my money so I go home with you now and see."

Tough refused to go. He did not want to see Martha, but when his employer threatened to get the police, he went. Tough had rather face his sister than to face arrest, and, maybe, somehow Martha might be able to pay back the money that he had stolen.

The two little girls were "playing house" in one corner of the warm kitchen. Martha was retrimming her last winter's hat and Joe was drawing a diagram of a play in basketball for his little brother, who had just begun to be interested in the game, when they heard a nervous rap on the front door. It opened to admit Mr. Steiner, sullenly followed by Tough. Martha, rather surprised, led the way to the kitchen. The little old man's leather-like skin was flushed. His eyes gleamed excitedly. He wasted no time on preliminaries but began without answering Martha's good evening.

"Your brother steal from me." The little old merchant's voice was shrill with excitement. "Your brother take out of my cash drawer seventy-five dollars and two rings out of my case. I get rings back. I no get seventy-five dollars. He say he spent it already, so I come see you. Maybe you pay me back. If I no get my money I call cops and have your brother 'rested." The old man's thin voice rose to a wail. "I can no lose that many dollars!"

Martha sat dumbfounded. The little children listened with open mouths to the tale of their brother's theft. Finally Joe's voice broke the tension.

"Tough, did you do that?" he demanded.

Tough growled an answer.

"Sure he did it," Steiner broke in. "What you think, I lie to you? He take my money and I want it back or I call cops."

"I have no money now, Mr. Steiner," Martha said. "But I will give it back to you. Every Saturday I'll bring you part of my wages."

The old man would not agree to that. "I give no credit at my store, so for why should I credit you?" Seeing that there seemed no way of getting his money, he snapped, "I let your brother go to jail."

"Oh, please don't, Mr. Steiner," Martha pleaded. She bowed her head on the table and wept. Her tears made a tiny pool on the smooth white oilcloth.

Tough's surliness vanished when he saw his sister cry. "Aw, Mart, don't take on so," he said. "There's other guys on this street that's stole and got by with it. I thought I could, too. I needed clothes and I wanted to get somethin' for the kids for Christmas. I couldn't stand the looks of that there money so I took it." There were shadows in Tough's eyes. The growl in his voice deepened. "I'm sorry, sis," he said.

"You no need be sorry," interrupted old man Steiner. "That don't get my money back. I let cops take you." Then Martha said, "Well, Joe, I guess you'll have to give back to Mr. Steiner his seventy-five dollars. There ain't no other way. You'll have to take your school money, for I ain't got none and we mustn't let Eddie go to jail." Martha sobbed again. "Oh, what would Mother think if she were alive!"

Tough turned to Joe. The sullen, worried look in his eyes changed to one of appeal. His cigarette-stained fingers moved nervously.

"Don't cry, Martha," Joe said. "I'll pay it." This meant he couldn't go back to school, but Tough was his brother and he had to help him. Joe went upstairs and opened the little bank. When he returned he put the seventy-five dollars in old man Steiner's hands and with it went all his hopes of school.

That night after the others had gone to bed, Joe sat in his tiny room for a long time in the dark beside the window. He thought of school. He couldn't go back and he had worked so hard to save his money. His mother wanted him to finish his education and now his mother was dead. His brother had become a thief, a common thief. And he couldn't go back to school, because they were too poor. The lump in Joe's throat grew larger and larger. He tried to think of other things but it wouldn't go. For the first time since he was a little boy Joe cried. Two big teardrops trickled down to the tip of his freckled nose and fell upon the windowsill. Outside, the moonlight veiled the poor houses of Primrose Street in misty radiance. Stars sparkled and glimmered in the far reaches of the night.

Bodies in the Moonlight

Sailors call it the Fever Coast—that two or three thousand miles of West Africa from Senegal to Luanda.

For four weeks now our ship had been anchored "in the stream" loading cocoa beans. There had been some mix-up in the schedule and the old man had no orders to move on. Six of our men had been sent ashore with tropic fever to the European hospital. The potatoes were running out and the captain no longer issued money to his mixed crew. The sun blazed by day and the moon shone at night and more men fell ill with the fever. Or developed venereal diseases. And there our steamer lay tossing wearily in the blue water, a half mile off the coast beyond the beating surf.

At eighteen when one is a rover, the world is wonderful—I was a mess-boy on my first trip to sea. I had thrown all my schoolbooks overboard and for several months I had not written to my parents. People I had known as a boy had not been kind to me, I thought, but now I was free. The sea had taken me like a mother and a freight ship named the *West Illana* had become my home.

The sun was setting, and the sea and sky were all stained with blood. With a wet cloth full of soap powder, I scoured the sink in my mess pantry, where I had just finished washing the dinner dishes. Then I went into the saloon and closed the portholes. The water was purple now and the sky blue-violet. The first stars popped out. The chief mate came down looking for his cap. It was on the deck under the table and he stooped to pick it up.

"Christ, mess, I'm tired o' this damn place," he said. Then, "Did ya leave any ginger cakes out for lunch tonight?"

"No," I replied. "The steward didn't gimme any."

"Lousy runt! Food must be gettin' low." I heard the chief mate going up the iron stairs to his room. I threw my white coat in a drawer of the buffet, carefully concealed a flat can of salmon in my shirt, and went on deck. It was dark.

"Goin' ashore?" the young Swede on watch at the gangplank called out.

"Sure," I replied.

"Well, I ain't. Them women over there's got me burnt up. You and Porto Rico better watch out!"

"You the one that oughta been careful," I laughed back. "Jesus, you're dumb! Porto Rico and I are in love."

"Yea, and with the same girl," said the Swede. "*You* had better watch out now."

I went on down the deck past the lighted ports of the engineers' rooms and around to the door of the officers' mess.

"Ain't you through yet?" I said.

"Hell, no! The damn bo'sun was late comin' to eat again but the way I told him about it, he won't be late no more." Porto Rico was washing knives and forks in a very dirty bucket of water. "*Cabrón!*" he said. "Just when I wanted to go ashore!" As though he didn't go ashore every night.

"I'm goin' on back aft. Hurry up and we'll catch the next boat when it comes out. I s'pose you gonna see her, too . . . What you gonna take her tonight?"

"*Hombre!*" Then in a whisper, "Couldn't save a damn thing but a hunk o' bread today. Looks like to me in two weeks won't be nothin' to eat on this tank. Ain't much here now—but I got a bar o' soap to give that mutty boatman if he takes us ashore. I'm gonna . . ."

The conversation died as the steward came down the corridor. He stepped into the galley where the Jamaican cooks were peeling potatoes. I went on back aft. Five bells.

For a cake of soap as payment we were paddled ashore. An African in a loincloth at either end, Porto Rico and I in the middle, we sat in a narrow little canoe so deep in water that one momentarily expected it to fill with the sea and sink. Under the stars. The ocean deep and evil. The lights of the *West Illana* at our stern. The palm-fringed line of shore and the boom of surf ahead. Off on the edge of the water the moon rose round, golden, and lazy. The sky seemed heavy with its weight of stars and the sea deep and weary, lipping the sides of the little boat.

"*Estoy cansado,*" said Porto Rico.

"I wish I was back in New York. I swear I do," I said. "Damn Nunuma."

But the excitement of landing in the surf loosened us from our momentary melancholy and we stood on the sand not far from the line of palm trees. The canoe and its two silent natives put to sea again. "Gimme a cigarette." Feet crossing the hard sand. "Gimme a cigarette." We were going to see Nunuma.

Nunuma—because I remember her I write this story. Because of her and the scar across my throat. At eighteen, women are strange bodies, strange, taunting, desirable bodies. Flesh and spirit. And the song is in the flesh even more than in the spirit.

We saw Nunuma the first day my "buddy" and I went ashore at Lonbar. A slender dark young girl, ripe breasts bare, a single strip of cloth about her body, squatted on her heels behind a pile of yams in the public square. There were many old women and young girls in the marketplace, but none other like Nunuma, delicate and lovely as a jungle flower, beautiful as a poem.

"Oh, you sweetie," said Porto Rico. "Some broad," said Mike from Newark. And the sailors bought all her yams.

That night when we came ashore again, a little barefoot boy, professional guide, showed Porto Rico and me to Nunuma's house—the usual native hut with its thatched roof and low eaves. She stood in the doorway, bright cloth about her body, face dusk-bronze in the moonlight. O, lovely flower growing too near the sea! Sailors must have passed her way before that night, but Nunuma had received none of them. "Me no like white sailor man," she explained later in her West African English. "He rough and mean."

The little boy guide padded off down the grassy road, coin in hand. "Hello, kid." In a few minutes another girl appeared from somewhere, joined us, and we sat down together in front of the hut. We four. The other girl never told her name. She was solid and well-built, but not beautiful like Nunuma. There wasn't much to say. Hands touch. Lips touch. The moon burned. By and by we went into the hut . . . In the morning Porto Rico and I gave each of the girls two shillings when we left.

Wide and white and cool the dawn as the slender native canoe paddled us back to the ship an hour before breakfast. Wide and cool and green the morning sea as the white sun shot up. The *West Illana* lay solemnly at anchor. We paid the boatman and were about to climb the gangway stairs when a black girl ran down. "Get the hell off here!" It was the third mate's voice. "I should think the men would see enough o' you women on shore without bringing you on the damn ship. Don't lemme catch you here again," and he swore roundly several great seamen's oaths. The woman was very much frightened. She chattered to the boatmen as they paddled away and her hands trembled. She was fat. Her face was not beautiful like Nunuma's.

That day the sun boiled. The winches rattled with their loads of cocoa beans lifted from native boats. The Kru-boys chipped the deck. And two sailors fell ill with the fever. That night Porto Rico and I went to see Nunuma—and the other girl. Neither one of us cared about the name of the other girl. She was just a body—a used thing of the port towns.

Days, nights. Nights, days. The vast impersonal African sky, now full of stars, now white with sun. The *West Illana* quiet and sober. Cocoa beans all loaded. Six men with fever ashore in the hospital. No orders. The captain impatient. Mahogany logs to load in Grand-Bassam. Christ, when are we moving on? The chief cook sick with a disease of the whorehouses. Steward worried about the food running low. "Nobody but a fool goes to sea anyhow," says the bo'sun.

Porto Rico and I were ashore every night. Almost every afternoon between meals—ashore . . . Nunuma. Nunuma . . . Oh, mother of God! . . . Sometimes I see her alone. Sometimes she and Porto Rico, I and the other girl are together. Sometimes she and Porto Rico alone are with each other . . . Nunuma! Nunuma! . . . I have given her the red slippers I bought in Dakar. Porto Rico has given her the Spanish shawl he picked up at Cádiz coming down. And now that we have no money we smuggle her stolen food from the ship's pantries. And Porto Rico gave her a string of beads.

He is my friend but I wish he wouldn't put his hands on Nunuma. Nunuma is beautiful and Porto Rico is not a man to know beauty. Besides he is jealous. One morning in the galley he asked me why I didn't fool with the other girl sometimes and leave him Nunuma alone. "You don't own the woman, do you?" I demanded. His large hands slowly clenched to fists and a sneer crossed his face. "Fight!" yelled the second cook. "Hell," I said, "we ain't gonna fight about a port-town girl." "No," he replied, and smiled.

"You bloody young niggers," said the old Jamaican baker.

Nunuma was beautiful. Nunuma's face was like a flower in the moonlight and her body soft and slender. At eighteen one has not known many soft bodies of women. One has not often kissed lips like the petals of pansies—unless one has been a sailor like Porto Rico. Porto Rico, hard, and rough, and strong, with a knowledge of women in half the port towns of the world. Porto Rico, who did not know that Nunuma's face was like a flower in the moonlight. Who did not care that her body was soft and tender. I wanted Porto Rico to keep his hands off Nunuma's body. He shouldn't touch her. He who had known so many dirty women . . . Yet Porto Rico was my friend . . . But Nunuma was beautiful. At eighteen one can go mad over the beauty of a woman. And forget a friend . . . I believe I loved Nunuma.

Feet crossing the dry sand. We were going to see her. "Gimme a cigarette," I repeated. Feet crossing the dry sand carrying one to the line of palm trees, carrying one to the grassy roads running between the thatched huts. Native fires gleaming, sailors in white pants drinking palm wine and feeling the breasts of girls, laughing. Africans with bare black feet, single cloths about their bodies, walking under the moon. The ship's carpenter drunk beneath a mango tree.

"Say, mess, did you hear the news?" calls the young wireless-man and the super-cargo who are passing in the road. We stop. "No," says Porto Rico. "What is it?"

"Haul anchor tomorrow for Grand-Bassam. Old Man's glad as hell," says the wireless.

"Lord knows I am," adds the super-cargo. "Die before I'd make another trip down this coast."

Sailing in the morning . . . Nunuma. Nunuma . . . Grand-Bassam, Accra, Freetown, Cape Verde Islands, New York . . . Nunuma! Nunuma! . . . Sailing in the morning.

She is standing in her doorway, the Spanish shawl wrapped about her body instead of the customary bright cloth. Her lips are red and her face like a flower, dusk-dark in the moonlight. " 'Lo kid," she smiles.

"You're vamping the boys tonight."

"Look just like Broadway."

"Me no like white sailor man."

Bantering talk.

Grotesque gifts to offer an African flower-girl—Porto Rico undoes his half loaf of bread and extends it awkwardly. I take a flat can of salmon from inside my shirt. We offer them both. She laughs and takes them inside the hut. Silence. When she comes out we sit down on the ground. And she is in the middle between we two men. The other girl is not there. Nunuma's body is slender and brown. She sings a tribal song about the moon. She points to the moon. Hands touch. Lips touch. A dusk-dark girl in the golden night, my buddy and I.

"We're sailing in the morning," I said.

"Yep, we haul anchor," added Porto Rico. "We leave."

"Mornin' go? In mornin' ship he go?" Nunuma's eyes grew wide in the moonlight. "Then you love me tonight," she said. "You love me tonight." And her lips were like flower petals. But she clasped her hands and the dark face looked into the moonlight. Her warm brown body sat between us. Her twin breasts pointed into the moonlight. Her slender feet in red slippers. Her eyes looking at the moon.

"You go back to the ship," said Porto Rico to me, "and get your sleep."

"No," I said.

"Go back to the ship, kid." He and I both rose. One can be a fool over a woman at eighteen.

"I won't go back! You can't make me!" My hand sought the clasp-knife in my pocket.

"*Hijo de la* . . ." he began an oath in Spanish and his lips trembled.

Like a dart of moonlight, Nunuma ran, without a scream, into her hut.

"Keep your hands off her," I shouted. "Keep your damn dirty hands off her!"

Before my fingers could leave my pocket, something silver flashed in the pale light. A flood of oaths in English and Spanish drenched my ears. And a warm red fluid ran from my throat, stained and spread on the whiteness of my shirt, dripped on my suddenly weak and useless hands.

"Keep your hands . . . off . . . her," I stammered. "Keep your hands off . . . Nunuma." And I fell face forward in the grass and dug my fingers in the earth and cried, "Keep your damn dirty hands off her," until the world lurched and grew dark. And all the stars fell down.

At sea in a bunk with a bandage about my neck. Porto Rico saying, "Jesus, kid, you know I didn't mean to do it. I was crazy, that's all." White caps of waves through the portholes. White blazing sun in the sky. Those things are almost forgotten now—but the scar, and the memory of Nunuma, make me write this story.

The Childhood of Jimmy

Six Pictures in the Head of a Negro Boy

The Town

I lived with my aunt in a small town. There were lots of colored people there. It was a nice town with trees in it and at the end of our street a river and a little house where a colored man sold whisky and sometimes beer . . . My aunt liked our town. She said she always lived there. My uncle liked our town, too . . . He washed his overalls in the backyard on Sundays . . . There were two churches in our town.

The School

There were colored children in the town school. All the little colored children were in one room and the teacher was colored, too. I don't think she liked the school . . . When I was in the third grade I went into another room with the white children and the teacher was white, too. I don't think she liked the school either. She said we were all bad children . . . Sometimes they slapped me in the school.

The Difference

You're a nigger. You ain't as good as I am 'cause you're a nigger . . . Paul said that to me but he didn't mean to hurt me when he said it. He was my friend. We played games together all the time and we went to the woods on Saturdays to look for mayapples and birds . . . He said you ain't as good as I am. You're a nigger, but he didn't mean to hurt me . . . I asked my aunt what I should say when Paul said you're a nigger. I liked Paul so I asked my aunt what I should say.

The Soul

God! I ain't afraid of God! Earl said, and God didn't strike him dead . . . Come all ye who love the Lord and lay your burdens down. They sang slow in church Sunday morning. It was Revival Day and Earl went up and sat on the mourners' bench . . . And I went up, too, ashamed . . . Come all ye who love the Lord . . . and my aunt was kneeling down beside me praying . . . and the old folks in the amen corner were praying . . . And the preacher said, Do you love God? And I said yes. And the preacher said, Do you accept Him? And I said yes. And I was converted . . . And my aunt got up and the old folks screamed hallelujah and sang glory to the name of the Lord . . . And I went home and cried in bed because I was ashamed . . . I didn't love God . . . And I was ashamed to lie about I didn't love God.

The Body

My aunt said be careful about girls . . . Clarence, next door, was the father of a baby . . . Clarence was sixteen years old . . . Clarence was arrested and had to marry the mother of his baby . . . My aunt said be careful about girls . . . I went to her house at four o'clock in the afternoon. She said I should come . . . My aunt said be careful about girls . . . I didn't know much about girls . . . Her mother worked all day in Mrs. Ronnermann's kitchen. Her mother didn't get home until after supper . . . My aunt said be careful about girls . . . She said I should come. Her mother didn't get home until after supper . . . Be careful about girls.

Death

My grandmother died on Thursday . . . Grandmother . . . I didn't want her to die on Thursday . . . Every Thursday I sold papers and I missed selling papers because she died on Thursday . . . Somebody woke me up at three o'clock in the morning because my grandmother was dead. I went outdoors looking for my grandmother . . . She wasn't there. The moon was there, cold and ugly, but no ghost of my grandmother . . . They wrapped her up in sheets and sent her away to the undertaker's. I didn't sell any papers on Thursday . . . I missed my grandmother . . . We moved away to another town. I went to another school. I didn't sell any more papers on Thursdays. I went to work in a big hotel . . . I missed my grandmother.

The Young Glory of Him

She had written in her diary in a thin schoolgirl's hand: "Oh, the young glory of him! His name is Eric Gynt and he is the handsomest sailor on the ship. I met him yesterday. It was my first time out on deck because I had been seasick for four days since leaving New York. I was sitting in my deck chair reading Browning when all my college class-notes on 'The Ring and the Book' blew away. He was going to the bridge, but he ran and caught some of my papers for me. The others went into the sea. I didn't mind the loss of half my notes, though—because I met him. I must have been greatly confused, for all I could stammer was, 'Thank you very much.' And he went on up to the bridge. But this morning I met him again and he said, 'Good morning,' and I said, 'Good morning,' too."

We had been at sea ten days when I read this in her diary. Of course, I had no business reading her diary at all, but then I was cabin boy on the *West Illana*, New York to West Africa, and it was my duty to clean the passengers' rooms. But as the *West Illana* was essentially a freight ship, there were only four passengers aboard—a trader, the girl who kept the diary, and her parents—two well-meaning middle-aged New England missionaries. One morning the girl left her diary open on the little desk near her bunk and I read it. There wasn't much, because it began with her getting on the ship. And the book was new.

All the boys in the fo'c'sle, though, were already "wise" to her liking Eric. They had for three days now been teasing him about it. But I thought she was, like him, just passing the time away—until I read her diary. There in all seriousness she had written: "I want him to love me. I have been so lonesome all my life." And further down for July 2: "Suppose he really would love me. I always dreamed of being loved by a sailor. And he is truly wonderful! His hair is all golden and curly and he says he never loved any girl before. I told him I had never loved any boy either. And I told him about how I had been in a girls' school (church school, too), where I never saw any men . . . I do love him! I do! I do!"

It was my duty to serve the meals to the officers and passengers—nine in all. That evening at dinner the girl wore a stiff white dress and a knitted scarf about her shoulders. Her name was Daisy Jones. With her thin body, sandy hair, dry little freckled face, and the spectacles she wore for reading, she looked thirty although she was only eighteen. At the fifth evening meal served at sea, I heard the two missionaries tell the captain all about their daughter. As I poured water and passed dishes between heads, I listened. For ten years the elderly couple had been stationed in Africa and only once in all this time had they returned to America to see Daisy. Her high-school and college years had been spent in a very Christian Methodist Seminary for girls. Now that she was graduated, they had returned for the graduation exercises and to take their daughter back with them. They didn't know her very well, they said. She had always been away from them, but they hoped to make a missionary of her, too. She seemed willing and meek. They smiled at the daughter across the table and she smiled back—a wan, strange little smile. The captain said, "Well, you're doing a good work." The trader agreed. Then the missionaries and the trader began a conversation concerning the necessity for more Christian Protestant missions along the Congo in order to combat the spread of Catholicism. I passed the bread pudding. The *West Illana,* the ship in which we all lived, pushed slowly and solemnly through the night. Six bells.

Back aft in the sailors' quarters. Twelve days from New York. Double bunks on four sides. A box. Two chairs. Sailors, wipers, oilers, messboys amid a confusion of laughter, oaths, and bits of song. The men are "kidding" Eric about Daisy.

"Ain't satisfied with the girls in port. Must be gettin' good an' holy now—makin' love to missionaries' daughters."

"Oh, you sweet-looking blond boy!"

"Some lady-killer. Even passengers fallin' fer 'im."

"Why don't you take on the old lady, too? She's better lookin' than the daughter. Daisy looks like she's been through the war—all washed out and everything."

"Man, I had a girl in Havre ten times as good looking as she is." And the conversation began to turn, as usual, to the girls of the ports, the merits and defects of those of Havre as compared with those of Barcelona, and to intimate details of nights of love.

"Sure, I've had plenty o' women. And I got something to show for mine," said Eric, the Dane.

"I guess you have," jibed Porto Rico.

"Oh, not what you mean," said the young sailor. And he pulled out his seabag from under a bunk. "I got a box of souvenirs, and letters, and pictures from damn near every girl I ever knew anywhere."

He took up a long cardboard box and opened it. "See this little jeweled dagger. I took it away from a girl in San Isidro Street in Havana."

Roars of laughter. Score of vulgar jibes.

"And see this red silk stocking. A burlesque dame in New York found it missing when I left one morning."

Ha! Ha! Ha! Ha! Some lover the boy was!

"My first girl in Copenhagen gave me this bit of hair. I was sixteen then. Just started to sea." And he held up a bunch of flaxen curls tied with a blue ribbon. He had rings, too, and a piece of filmy silk lingerie; and a pack of letters scrawled in badly spelled language; and pictures taken in Yokohama and Seattle and Naples.

He put the box away and began to talk about Daisy. "She's a good kid, but dumb. Gave me a little black Bible the other day and I'm keeping it over my heart." He showed the men the small leather-bound book in the left-hand pocket of his shirt. "She wanted me to kiss her last night, and Christ! you know I wasn't going to refuse." And he acted in pantomime how he had taken her in his arms and crushed her against the bulkhead. "And then she ran away across the deck like she was afraid." It was a joke among the crew for the next two weeks to ask the Dane, "Is she still running away?"

Port of Horta in the Azores—toy city on the edge of the sea, lonely. Not much cargo to unload. We stay a half day and sail at midnight. Porto Rico and I, as well as most of the crew, have been ashore buying wine at the wineshops, ambling up and down the cobblestone streets among oxcarts and peasants, and going after sundown to promenade on the seawall with the girls of the town who like to walk with young sailors. Now it is growing late. Porto Rico and I return to the ship at ten o'clock. For a quarter each a Portuguese boatman rows us out to the *West Illana* anchored in the harbor. Through a confusion of little boats and barges receiving cargo from the steamer, we reach the ladder and climb aboard.

I went straight to the saloon to close the portholes and lower the lights for the night. There at the entrance to the corridor stood our youngest passenger, Daisy Jones. I knew she was waiting for Eric. "Good evening," I said and passed on.

Five minutes afterwards I came on deck and stood near the galley door watching the cranes unloading from the midship hatch, swinging over and out, lowering bags of wheat into the little boats below. I had never seen a boat unload at night before. Daisy Jones stood in the corridor of the saloon looking not at the cargo rising out of the hatch and falling toward the sea, but at the gangway up which Eric must come. He came with some fellow seamen, six or eight, laughing and swearing. He had lost his cap and his blond hair was tousled. His blue eyes sparkled and his boy's face flushed with the joy of wine. He saw Daisy. "I'm gonna have some fun," he said. And he went across the deck under the swinging bags of wheat, held out his hand, and spoke to her. Half fascinated by the careless beauty of his face and the blue gaiety of his eyes, yet half afraid, she drew back in the shadow of the dark hall, stood for a moment while he whispered something in her ear, then turned and ran into her room. The sailors standing with me near the galley laughed. Then we all went back aft to our quarters. At one o'clock we sailed.

The next morning at sea when I went in to clean her room I read this in her diary: "Last night he looked like a blond Greek god returning from a festival. Oh, the young glory of him! . . . And he asked me if I would go ashore with him sometime, too. In Dakar he said . . . I would like to see an African town at night and I believe he would take care of me. But I don't dare go. I'm afraid."

I laughed because I knew she would go. Her mother and father retired early always. And Eric said no woman refused to do what he asked. Well, it was none of my business. I closed her diary, shut the desk, and began to sweep the rug on the deck.

Dakar in Senegal, one of the most fascinating ports in all Africa, and one of the few with dock and harbor facilities. The *West Illana* pushes in to a pier and we look down on a jetty crowded with sweltering humanity. Natives in long Mohammedan robes; French colonial officials; black traders from the desert bartering feathers, statuettes of brass and ivory, dates and strange fruits; women and children; missionaries waiting for papers or news; and those little boy guides one sees in so many sea-towns sent to pick up sailors to bring to the houses of prostitution. Port of Dakar on a day when the sun blazes.

Port of Dakar when the sun has fallen into the sea and darkness comes. The tiny garden café in M. Brousard's Grand Hotel de Nice et Lyon. Native music, a fountain, black waiters, smoke, wine, and the stars. A crowd of boisterous seamen about the tables, a dozen little dark girls and a few French women. The fat proprietor rubs his hands, well pleased at the business the bar is doing. One of the French girls begins singing

"Madelon," but Mike from Newark drowns her out with "Why Should I Cry over You." The bo'sun has gone to sleep sprawled across a table. Jerry is doing a sailor's hornpipe on the edge of the fountain. A drunken babble of laughter and voices fills the little garden. Through a haze of wine in the brain and smoke in the air, I see Chips coming toward our table.

"Just walked up the street," he said. "And guess who I saw—Eric and the dumb-looking missionary girl by themselves. They was comin' out o' that hotel down the way yonder and she was cryin'. And they was headin' back toward the ship."

"I'll bet he had her where she couldn't run this time," said Porto Rico.

"That boy ain't so pure and innocent," croaked an old oiler. "She'll learn to fool with sailors."

"She'll pray tonight all right."

"She was cryin'," Chips went on. "And him just laughin' at her like he didn't give a damn."

Splash! The sailor who had been dancing the hornpipe fell backwards in the fountain! "Bravo!" yelled the French girls. "Hee! Hee! Hee!" cried the little African ladies. "Hooray!" shouted the drunken seamen. And the noise of falling glasses, laughter, applause, women's voices, ironic music rose to the stars. "Let's get another bottle of cognac," said Porto Rico.

The sun is blazing the next day when we leave Dakar. My head aches and I am in no mood for extra work, yet Daisy Jones stays in bed all morning and I must carry a luncheon of soup and toast to her room on a tray.

"She is ill," her mother said. "I tell her about staying up so late of nights reading those books."

I would have laughed but my head throbbed and burned. I went back to the bunk and slept all the afternoon.

That evening at dinner Daisy Jones did not appear. "She has been crying," her mother said. "It must be her nerves."

"Young folks are hard to understand," added the father.

When I knocked on her door to ask if she wished anything, she said, "No, I'm going to get up and sit on deck for a while." So I went away. After I had cleared the table and cleaned the pantry, I went back to her room, got fresh linen from the steward, and made up her bed while she sat on deck between her parents. Then I went into the galley and talked to the cooks for a while as they peeled potatoes for breakfast. A warm breeze came in the door. The stars seemed near enough to touch.

When I returned to lower the lights in the saloon I could see that the missionaries were getting ready for bed. The girl still sat on the deck, but she was alone now.

It must have been near midnight that it happened. I was lying in my berth reading, Porto Rico snoring in the bunk above, when I heard the bells clang in the engine room and felt the ship slow down. Then I heard the shrill blasts of the whistle and jumped up, slid into my pants, and ran out on deck. "Man overboard!" Mates running and shouting. Commands being issued. I saw the sailors lowering a lifeboat. Then I knew what happened: Daisy Jones had jumped into the sea.

I ran up the iron stairs to the midship deck, past the galley door, past the covered hatch, through the saloon corridor and into her room. I knew she wasn't there. The lights were burning and the berth just as I had made it up after dinner. But on the white spread near the pillow lay a note in a sealed envelope addressed to "Father and Mother." On the desk her diary was open. But all she had written that day had been obliterated with heavy pen and ink lines, except for a few words at the bottom of the page: "I thought he loved me, but I know he doesn't. I can't bear it." Tears had fallen, too, on that page.

Slowly I closed the diary, slipped it under my shirt, and went out on deck. When no one was looking I let it fall over the rail into the sea. With all the confusion outside, the two old missionaries had not awakened. Then I remembered how they had slept at Horta and Dakar in spite of the noise of unloading cargo. Ten years of Africa, I thought, makes one want to sleep. But soon the captain came to wake them. The lifeboat still moved about on the quiet moon-washed face of the sea, but there was not a trace of her body. A great sky full of stars looked down quietly and gave no comment.

Next morning, of course, Eric felt badly enough. Some of the men were angry with him for having anything to do with the girl at all. Nobody, though, seemed to feel that he in any way had caused her death. Chips said, "Women just can't help it. They go wild over the kid, clean crazy. See what a fool this skirt was." And the captain called him to his room and talked with him after breakfast.

But in a few days the youngster was all right again, laughing, singing, joking, and swearing as usual. And the night we docked at Freetown I saw him take the little black Bible that had once belonged to Daisy Jones and put it in his box along with a garter from Horta, a red silk stocking from New York, a jeweled dagger from Havana, and a bunch of flaxen curls that a girl in Copenhagen gave him.

The Little Virgin

The *West Illana* dipped slowly through the green water seven days out from the port of New York. But in a week at sea even a crew made up of Greeks, West Indian Negroes, Irish, Portuguese, and Americans can become pretty well acquainted. When the weather is warm and sailors lounge on the afterdeck of evenings telling stories, men learn to know one another. The sea breeds a strange comradeship, a strict fraternity, and many a time I have seen the most heterogeneous crew imaginable stick together like brothers in a sailors' fight in a foreign port. Nor is there ever any separation in that vast verbal warfare all seamen wage against all chief stewards over the always bad food. The sea is like a wide-armed mother and the humble toilers of the sea, blood brothers.

But sometimes there comes one to whom the ways of the water folk are strange . . . The sailors called him the Little Virgin because they discovered that he had never known a woman and because of his polite manners. He was a blond boy, sixteen or so, probably a runaway from some neat middle-class home in an inland village. He came looking for adventure at sea. He admitted he had not worked on ship before but he proved an apt apprentice, and soon learned to chip decks and scrub bulkheads with the rest of the ordinaries. But he didn't learn their way of talking so easily and he was very shy. He didn't grab for the potato pan at meals and try to snatch the largest potato. Indeed, if he got no potatoes at all he said nothing.

> *Oh, give us some time to*
> *Blow the man down!*

On the hatch in front of the afterdeck house in the early evening, dinner over, the talk had been of sailing ships and the old days of the sea. Paddy, in a deep Irish brogue, was telling his wild experiences on whalers. Over against the rail the Swede sang, to himself, a chantey which some of the steamship men had never even heard:

> *What do you think*
> *We had for breakfast?*

> *Wey, hey!*
> *Blow the man down!*

The warm wind came from the south and the faint throb of the engines and the chug, chug of the propeller accompanied his song:

> *A monkey's heart*
> *And a donkey's liver.*
> *Give us some time to*
> *Blow the man down!*

"Yez," said Paddy, "when the old *John Emory* went to Rio, them was the days."

> *Oh, they sailed us down*
> *The Congo River*
> *Wey, hey!*
> *Blow the man down!*

One of the A.B.'s on watch passed with lighted lantern, went up the iron stairs, and hung it over the stern of the ship. It was getting dark. The blue depths of the sky began to be dotted with stars and the little waves below lapped languidly, one on the other.

> *And O! I'll sail*
> *The seas forever.*
> *Give us some time to*
> *Blow the man down!*

"Say, was everybody in your town as dumb as you?" Eric demanded suddenly of the Little Virgin.

"Heck, no!" the kid answered. "My father—"

"Why don't you say, 'Hell, no,' you pink angel?" Jerry drawled.

"Hell—no," said the boy slowly, for he hadn't yet learned to swear with the facility of the sea.

"Women won't think you're a sailor 'less you learn to cuss better 'an that there 'Gol darn' and 'By heck' you got—like some country hayseed 'stead of a seaman."

"Yes, sir," said the boy.

"*Hombre!* Who ever says he was a seaman," laughed Porto Rico.

"And we're gonna show you some women in Horta next week. I been there before, Virgin, and I know 'em. They're wild and they'll lead you to slaughter. Show us how you make love, kid."

And then the torture of the self-conscious and embarrassed boy began —he who was the daily butt of sailors' jibes and vulgar jokes. The men liked him and the cleanness of him, but the fun of seeing him red and confused was too great to resist. So everything the youngster did or said by day became a subject for ribald wit and ridicule at night on the after-hatch. And the lad, who was unable to banter jokes and obscenities, looked lost and alone and very miserable. Everyone seemed his enemy, no one his friend. Words can be terribly cruel when a person does not know how to construct a defense or laugh at a joke.

"I don't know how to make love," the boy said.

"Oh, you Little Virgin! Mama's nice baby!" Chips sang in falsetto. "Pretty Percy!"

"What kind a sailor is this?"

> *Now he was all*
> *Most twenty-three.*
> *But still sat on*
> *His mother's knee.*
> *He'd never . . .*

"Say, kid, tell us . . ." began one of the Greek firemen.

"Don't tell that Greek nothin', Virgin." It was Mike from Newark speaking. "Get up an' sock him in the eye!"

The absurdity of this command brought a gale of laughter from the men on the hatch. Chips rolled over and over. But for some reason or other it angered the fireman.

"What a hell you tell da kid to hit me for? You would ain't do it yourself," the Greek yelled.

"Stand up an' see if I won't," countered Mike. There hadn't been a fight on board for three days now and the ship plowed slowly and calmly through the water under the starry darkness. Things were dull and quiet like the slow move of the steamer. "I'm tired o' you guys ridin' the Virgin anyhow. You must think he likes it. He's a good kid and he don't bother none o' you."

"He's no you brother," said the Greek. And he made a sudden plunge at Mike from Newark, but in an instant the fireman was going backward toward the bulkhead sent there by a blow from the Nev Jersey man's fist. Then, before the Greek could recover his balance, the bo'sun sprang between them.

"Stop this fight," he commanded. "You dumb fools!" And two or three sailors grabbed each of the combatants by the arms.

"Damn!" said Eric. "The bo'sun's always stoppin' fights."

"That's dirty," I agreed, because I wanted to see the fight go on, too.

But Mike and the Greek were held apart until, each struggling nobly to get at the other, their vocabulary of insults in both the language of the Hellespont and Newark were exhausted. Then Mike, with a final oath regarding the parentage of all Greeks, turned to the frightened Little Virgin and said, "Come on, kid, let's go inside. I'll teach you to play pinochle." And the two of them left the deck.

"Sure, that's the best you can do is play pinochle," somebody jeered, while the fireman began to talk rapidly to a fellow countryman. An hour later when I passed the mess-room door on my way to bed I saw the Little Virgin and Mike from Newark leaning on the wooden table deep in conversation. And the young boy looked happy for the first time since leaving New York. He had seemingly found a friend.

So the days passed filled with sunshine and the slow roll of the little waves. And the nights passed warm and starry as the old freighter steamed unhurriedly through the black waters toward Africa. And the dawns came pink and gold, strangely cool and calm with a magic vastness about them lying softly on the wide circle of the waters. Then the sun would shoot up, disturbing the colorful quiet. And some mornings there would be flying fish lying on the deck which the third mate, coming down from the bridge, would pick up and take to the galley to have cooked for his breakfast. At eight bells the watch changed and the Little Virgin, along with the rest of the ordinaries, would come out for work.

The Virgin and Mike from Newark were boon companions now. They worked together during the day and played cards or talked at night. From Mike the kid learned how to tie sailor's knots, how to do the least work with the greatest appearance of effort, and how to lower a lifeboat during fire drill. He began to learn, too, the vocabulary of the sea, to pick up a varied string of true seamen's oaths, and to acquire an amusing collection of filthy stories. Everything that Mike did, the Little Virgin tried to do, too. Before the village boy this young sailor from Newark seemed a model of all the manly virtues. And Mike had lived a life which the Virgin envied and wished to emulate. He, like the Virgin, had left home without telling anybody and in his three years away from the paternal roof had visited half the ports of the world. Furthermore, to hear Mike talk, there had been many thrilling and dangerous adventures in the strange places he had known. The Little Virgin would sit for hours, with the greatest credulity, listening to the Newark boy's stories. Then he would dream of the things that would happen to himself someday and how he would go back home and tell the fellows in his little village about them while they stood open-mouthed and amazed around this wanderer returned.

So the days passed and the *West Illana* put in at a port in Senegal. That night after dinner almost everybody went ashore. There was good business in the French wineshops where seamen and native women gathered before the night grew late. Porto Rico, Jerry, and I were sitting at a little table in the crowded Bar Boudon when we saw Mike, the Virgin, Chips, and Paddy enter. They were accompanied by four little dark girls and they all sat down at one table at the far end of the room. Drinks were brought. There was much talking and noise—a tangle of languages and sounds. A smell of beer, wine, and smoke floated under the murky yellow lights. The blue blouses of seamen, the white coats of the native waiters, and the black faces of the little girls spotted the room.

An hour of drinking and laughter must have passed when suddenly there was great turmoil at the other end of the place and somebody yelled, "Fight!" I climbed on a chair just in time to see Mike from Newark strike the Little Virgin full in the face and send him sprawling backwards among the tables and the feet of sailors. Then I saw a black woman spring at Mike, her fingers like claws, and in her turn fall backwards, struck in the face, among the tables and the feet of sailors. Then somebody threw a bottle and the free-for-all began. The lights went out. And I went out, too—into the cobblestone street and safety from the flying missiles. By and by I saw Chips emerge from the mêlée and I asked him how the fight started.

"Over nothin'," said Chips. "All them darn fools drunk and one of the girls knocks a glass o' beer over on Mike and gets his pants wet, so he up and slaps her face and she cries. Then the Little Virgin hops up and says no gentleman would hit a woman so Mike up and hits him, too. The kid tries to come back at him but he knocks him sprawlin'. Then the girl tries to come back at Mike and he knocks her sprawlin'. Then somebody throws a bottle and hell breaks loose. And I comes on out . . . Paddy is carrying the Little Virgin back to the ship now and the kid's cryin' like a baby and sayin' over and over, 'No gentleman would hit a woman. No gentleman would hit a woman.' He's drunk. But Jesus! All that fuss over a African gal! And Mike and the Virgin being such good friends, too . . . Licker'll cause anything—the rotten slop . . . Let's go down the road and get another drink." And the carpenter took me jovially by the arm.

"No," I said. "I'm going back to the ship. I'm tired o' this stuff." And I went off alone through the quiet street toward the dock where the ship was lying under the stars against the vast blackness of the harbor, infinitely calm and restful.

I met Paddy staggering down the gangplank, returning ashore to join the drunken sailors. I said hello to the man on watch as I went aboard and crossed the deck toward the bunkhouse. It was very quiet on ship and the seamen's quarters were warmly lighted but empty save for one figure—the Little Virgin, who lay sobbing as though his heart would break, face downward on his dirty pillow. It was strange to see someone crying in that room.

"What's the matter, kid?" I said.

"He oughtn't to hit a woman," sobbed the Virgin. "Mike oughtn't to hit a woman." And the young boy kept repeating the phrase over and over and cursing between sobs, awkwardly like a child. "He oughtn't to hit a woman." His breath smelled of wine and beer and his face was flushed, damp, and warm.

"You're drunk," I said. "Go to sleep . . . Mike was drunk, too." And I pulled off his clothes, put a blanket over him, and went to my own quarters to bed. But for a long while the sobs of the youngster disturbed the quiet of the empty fo'c'sle and I could not close my eyes for strangeness of the sound.

The next day, when we sailed, the Virgin was unable to rise from his bunk. His head ached. His hands were hot and he felt dizzy. That afternoon at sea, he began to sob again deliriously. Someone told the steward that the boy was ill and when the chief mate came back to take his temperature, he pronounced it a severe case of tropic fever and ordered him removed at once to the hospital in the forward part of the boat. As soon as the bunk was ready, Mike picked the boy up and carried him there himself. And for three days, during hours off duty, Mike sat near the Virgin as he tossed and moaned, and turned from side to side, or sobbed, or talked aloud when the delirium returned.

Meanwhile the *West Illana* steamed slowly through a tropic sea. On the third morning the ship anchored at Calabar, the French doctor came aboard, and the sick boy was sent ashore to the European hospital. As they carried him down the gangplank in a blanket at high noon while the sun blazed, he kept sobbing over and over in the raucous voice of delirium, "Oughtn't to hit a woman . . . No, no, no . . . Mike oughtn't hit a woman . . . God knows he oughtn't . . . hit . . . a . . . woman." And the blanketed figure trembled with chill in the heat of the African day. And his voice rose shrill against the rattle of the cranes lifting cargo. "He oughtn't hit a woman . . . Oughtn't . . . never to hit a . . . woman."

Luani of the Jungles

"Not another shilling," I said. "You must think I'm a millionaire or something. Here I am offering you my best hat, two shirts, and a cigar case, with two shillings besides, and yet you want five shillings more! I wouldn't give five shillings for six monkeys, let alone a mean-looking beast like yours. Come on, let's make a bargain. What do you say?"

But the African, who had come to the wharf on the Niger to sell his monkey, remained adamant. "Five shillin' more," he said. "Five shillin'. Him one fine monkey!" However, when he held up the little animal for me to touch, the frightened beast opened his white-toothed mouth viciously and gave a wild scream. "Him no bite," assured the native. "Him good."

"Yes, he's good all right," said Porto Rico sarcastically. "We'll get a monkey at Burutu cheaper, anyhow. It'd take a year to tame this one."

"I won't buy him," I protested to the native. "You want too much."

"But he is a fine monkey," an unknown voice behind us said, and we turned to see a strange, weak-looking little white man standing there. "He is a good monkey," the man went on in a foreign sort of English. "You ought to buy him here. Not often you get a red monkey of this breed. He is rare."

Then the stranger, who seemed to know whereof he spoke, told us that the animal was worth much more than the native asked, and he advised me softly to pay the other five shillings. "He is like a monkey in a poem," the man said. Meanwhile, the slender simian clung tightly to the native's shoulder and snarled shrilly whenever I tried to touch him. But the very wildness of the poor captured beast with the wire cord about his hairy neck fascinated me. Given confidence by the stranger, for one old hat, two blue shirts, a broken cigar case, and seven shillings, I bought the animal. Then for fear of being bitten, I wrapped the wild little thing in my coat, carried him up the gangplank of the *West Illana,* and put him into an empty prune box standing near the galley door. Porto Rico and the stranger followed and I saw that Porto Rico carried a large valise, so I surmised that the stranger was a new passenger.

The *West Illana,* a freight boat from New York to West Africa, seldom carried passengers other than an occasional trader or a few poor missionaries. But when, as now, we were up one of the tributaries of the Niger, where English passenger steamers seldom came, the captain sometimes consented to take on travelers to the coast. The little white man with the queer accent registered for Lagos, a night's journey away. After he had been shown his stateroom he came out on deck and, in a friendly sort of manner, began to tell me about the various methods of taming wild monkeys. Yet there was a vague, far-off air about him as though he were not really interested in what he was saying. He took my little beast in his hands and I noticed that the animal did not bite him nor appear particularly alarmed.

It was late afternoon then and all our cargo for that port—six Fords from Detroit and some electric motors—had been unloaded. The seamen closed the hatch, the steamer swung slowly away from the wharf with a blast of the whistle and began to glide lazily down the river. Soon we seemed to be floating through the heart of a dense, sullen jungle. A tangled mass of trees and vines walled in the sluggish stream and grew out of the very water itself. None of the soil of the riverbank could be seen—only an impenetrable thickness of trees and vines. Nor were there the brilliant jungle trees one likes to imagine in the tropics. They were rather a monotonous gray-green confusion of trunks and leaves with only an occasional cluster of smoldering scarlet flowers or, very seldom, the flash of some bright-winged bird to vary their hopelessness. Once or twice this well of ashy vegetation was broken by a muddy brook or a little river joining the larger stream and giving, along murky lengths, a glimpse into the further depths of this colorless and forbidding country. Then the river gradually widened and we could smell the sea, but it was almost dinnertime before the ship began to roll slowly on the ocean's green and open waters. When I went into the salon to set the officers' table, we were still very near the Nigerian coast, and the gray vines and dull trees of the delta region.

After dinner I started aft to join Porto Rico and the seamen, but I saw the little white man seated on one of the hawser posts near the handrail so I stopped. It was dusk and the last glow of sunset was fading on the edge of the sea. I was surprised to find this friend of the afternoon seated there, because passengers seldom ventured far from the comfortable deck chairs near the salon.

"Good evening," I said.

"*Bon soir,*" answered the little man.

"*Vous êtes français?*" I asked, hearing his greeting.

"*Non,*" he replied slowly. "I am not French, but I lived in Paris for a long while." Then he added for seemingly no reason at all, "I am a poet, but I destroy my poems."

The gold streak on the horizon turned to orange.

There was nothing I could logically say except, "Why?"

"I don't know," he said. "I don't know why I destroy my poems. But then there are many things I don't know . . . I live back in that jungle." He pointed toward the coast. "I don't know why."

The orange in the sunset darkened to blue.

"But why?" I asked again stupidly.

"My wife is there," he said. "She is an African."

"Is she?" I could think of nothing other to say.

The blue on the horizon grayed to purple now.

"I'm trying to get away," he went on, paying no attention to my remark. "I'm going down to Lagos now. Maybe I'll forget to come back—back there." And he pointed to the jungles hidden in the distant darkness of the coast. "Maybe I'll forget to come back this time. But I never did before—not even when I was drunk. I never forgot. I always came back. Yet I hate that woman!"

"What woman?" I asked.

"My wife," he said. "I love her and yet I hate her."

The sea and the sky were uniting in darkness.

"Why?" was again all I could think of saying.

"At Paris," he went on. "I married her at Paris." Then suddenly to me, "Are you a poet, too?"

"Why, yes," I replied.

"Then I can talk to you," he said. "I married her at Paris four years ago when I was a student there in the Sorbonne." As he told his story the night became very black and the stars were warm. "I met her one night at the Bal Bulier—this woman I love. She was with an African student whom I knew and he told me that she was the daughter of a wealthy native in Nigeria. At once I was fascinated. She seemed to me the most beautiful thing I had ever seen—dark and wild, exotic and strange—accustomed as I had been to only pale white women. We sat down at a table and began to talk together in English. She told me she was educated in England, but that she lived in Africa. 'With my tribe,' she said. 'When I am home I do not wear clothes like these, nor these things on my fingers.' She touched her evening gown and held out her dark hands, sparkling with diamonds. 'Life is simple when I am home,' she said. 'I don't like it here. It is too cold and people wear too many clothes.' She lifted a cigarette holder of platinum and jade to her lips and blew a thin line of smoke into the air. '*Mon Dieu!*' I thought to myself. 'A child of sophistication and simplicity such as I have never seen!' And suddenly before I knew it, crazy young student that I was, I had leaned across the table and was saying, 'I love you.'

" 'That is what he says, too,' she replied, pointing toward the African student dancing gaily with a blond girl at the other end of the room. 'You haven't danced with me yet.' We rose. The orchestra played a Spanish waltz full of Gypsy-like nostalgia and the ache of desire. She waltzed as no woman I had ever danced with before could waltz—her dark body close against my white one, her head on my shoulder, its mass of bushy hair tangled and wild, perfumed with a jungle scent. I wanted her! I ached for her! She seemed all I had ever dreamed of; all the romance I'd ever found in books; all the lure of the jungle countries; all the passions of the tropic soul.

" 'I need you,' I said. 'I love you.' Her hand pressed mine and our lips met, wedged as we were in the crowd of the Bal Bulier.

" 'I'm sailing from Bordeaux at the end of the month,' she told me as we sat in the Gardens of the Luxembourg at sunset a few days later. 'I'm going back home to the jungle countries and you are coming with me.' "

" 'I know it,' I agreed, as though I had been planning for months to go with her.

" 'You are coming with me back to my people,' she continued. 'You with your whiteness coming to me and my dark land. Maybe I won't love you then. Maybe you won't love me—but the jungle'll take you and you'll stay there forever.'

" 'It won't be the jungle making me stay,' I protested. 'It'll be you. You'll be the ebony goddess of my heart, the dark princess who saved me from the corrupt tangle of white civilization, who took me away from my books into life, who discovered for me the soul of your dark countries. You'll be the tropic flower of my heart.'

"During the following days before our sailing, I made many poems to this black woman I loved and adored. I dropped my courses at the Sorbonne that week and wrote my father in Prague that I would be going on a journey south for my health's sake. I changed my account to a bank in Lagos in West Africa, and paid farewell calls on all my friends in Paris. So much did I love Luani that I had no regrets on taking leave of my classmates nor upon saying adieux to the city of light and joy.

"One night in July we sailed from Bordeaux. We had been married the day before in Paris.

"In August we landed at Lagos and came by riverboat to the very wharf where you saw me today. But in the meantime something was lost between us—something of the first freshness of love that I've never found again. Perhaps it was because of the many days together hour after hour on the boat—perhaps she saw too much of me. Anyway, when she took off her European clothes at the Liberty Hotel in Lagos to put on the costume of her tribe, and when she sent to the steel safe at the English bank there all of her diamonds and pearls, she seemed to put me away, too, out of her heart, along with the foreign things she had removed from her body. More fascinating than ever in the dress of her people, with the soft cloth of scarlet about her limbs and the little red sandals of buffalo hide on her feet—more fascinating than ever and yet farther away she seemed, elusive, strange. And she began that day to talk to some of the servants in the language of her land.

"Up to the river town by boat, and then we traveled for days deep into the jungles. After a week we arrived at a high, clear space surrounded by breadfruit, mango, and coconut trees. There a hundred or more members of the tribe were waiting to receive her—beautiful brown-black people whose perfect bodies glistened in the sunlight, bodies that shamed me and the weakness under my European clothing. That night there was a great festival given in honor of Luani's coming—much beating of drums and wild, fantastic dancing beneath the moon—a festival in which I could take no part, for I knew none of their ceremonies, none of their dances. Nor did I understand a word of their language. I could only stand aside and look, or sit in the door of our hut and sip the palm wine they served me. Luani, wilder than any of the others, danced to the drums, laughed, and was happy. She seemed to have forgotten me sitting in the doorway of our hut drinking palm wine.

"Weeks passed and months. Luani went hunting and fishing, wandering about for days in the jungles. Sometimes she asked me to go with her, but more often she went with members of the tribe and left me to walk about the village, understanding nobody, able to say almost nothing. No one molested me. I was seemingly respected or at least ignored. Often when Luani was with me she would speak no French or English all day, unless I asked her something. She seemed almost to have forgotten the European languages, to have put them away as she had put away the clothes and customs of the foreigners. Yet she would come when I called and let me kiss her. In a far-off, strange sort of way she still seemed to love me. Even then I was happy because I loved her and could hold her body.

"Then one night, trembling from an ugly dream, I suddenly awoke, sat up in bed, and discovered in a daze that she was not beside me. A cold sweat broke out on my body. The room was empty. I leaped to the floor and opened the door of the hut. A great streak of moonlight fell across the threshold. A little breeze was blowing and the leaves of the mango trees rustled dryly. The sky was full of stars. I stepped into the grassy village street—quiet all around. Filled with worry and fear, I called, 'Luani!' As far as I could see, the tiny huts were quiet under the moon and no one answered. I was suddenly weak and afraid. The indifference of the silence unnerved me. I called again, 'Luani!' A voice seemed to reply: 'To the palm forest, to the palm forest. Quick, to the palm forest!' And I began to run toward the edge of the village where a great coconut grove lay.

"There beneath the trees it was almost as light as day and I sat down to rest against the base of a tall palm, while the leaves in the wind rustled dryly overhead. No other noise disturbed the night and I rested there wide awake, remembering Paris and my student days at college. An hour must have passed when, through an aisle of the palm trees, I saw two naked figures walking. Very near me they came and then passed on in the moonlight—two ebony bodies close together in the moonlight. They were Luani and the chief's young son, Awa Unabo.

"I did not move. Hurt and resentment, anger and weakness filled my veins. Unabo, the strongest and greatest hunter of the tribe, possessed the woman I loved. They were walking together in the moonlight, and weakling that I was, I dared not fight him. He'd break my body as though it were a twig. I could only rage in my futile English and no one except Luani would understand . . . I went back to the hut. Just before dawn she came, taking leave of her lover at my door.

"Like a delicate statue carved in ebony, a dark halo about her head, she stood before me, beautiful and black like the very soul of the tropics, a woman to write poems about, a woman to go mad over. All the jealous anger died in my heart and only a great hurt remained and a feeling of weakness.

" 'I am going away, back to Paris,' I said.

" 'I'm sorry,' she replied with emotion. 'A woman can have two lovers and love them both.' She put her arms around my neck but I pushed her away. She began to cry then and I cursed her in foreign, futile words. That same day, with two guides and four carriers, I set out through the jungles toward the Niger and the boat for Lagos. She made no effort to keep me back. One word from her and I could not have left the village, I knew. I would have been a prisoner—but she did not utter that word. Only when I left the clearing she waved to me and said, 'You'll come back.'

"Once in Lagos, I engaged passage for Bordeaux, but when the time came to sail I could not leave. I thought of her standing before me naked that last morning like a little ebony statue, and I tore up my ticket! I returned to the hotel and began to drink heavily in an effort to forget, but I could not. I remained drunk for weeks, then after some months had passed I boarded a riverboat, went back up the Niger, back through the jungles—back to her.

"Four times that has happened now. Four times I've left her and four times returned. She has borne a child for Awa Unabo. And she tells me that she loves him. But she says she loves me, too. Only one thing I do know—she drives me mad. Why I stay with her, I do not know any longer. Why her lover tolerates me, I do not know. Luani humiliates me now—and fascinates me, tortures me and holds me. I love her. I hate her, too. I write poems about her and destroy them. I leave her and come back. I do not know why. I'm like a madman and she's like the soul of her jungles, quiet and terrible, beautiful and dangerous, fascinating and death-like. I'm leaving her again, but I know I'll come back . . . I know I'll come back."

Slowly the moon rose out of the sea, and the distant coast of Nigeria was like a shadow on the horizon. The *West Illana* rolled languidly through the night. I looked at the little white man, tense and pale, and wondered if he were crazy, or if he were lying.

"We reach Lagos early in the morning, do we not?" he asked. "I must go to sleep. Good night." And the strange passenger went slowly toward the door of the corridor that led to his cabin.

I sat still in the darkness for a few moments, dazed. Then I suddenly came to, heard the chug, chug of the engines below and the half-audible conversation drifting from the fo'c'sle, heard the sea lapping at the sides of the ship. Then I got up and went to bed.

Notes

The Ways of White Folks

1. At the request of Carl Van Vechten, the Mexican caricaturist Miguel Covarrubias designed the jacket of Hughes's first book, *The Weary Blues* (1926).

2. On July 28, 1932, Herbert Hoover directed officials to disperse thousands of World War I veterans who had come to Washington in the Bonus Army March to urge Congress to approve immediate payment of the bonus certificates they had received for their war service.

3. The tenor Roland Hayes (1877–1977) was the first African American male to gain international recognition as a concert artist.

4. In reprinting this story in *Something in Common*, Hughes substituted "right out of the Copa or the pages of *Playboy*" for "right out of the Scandals or the back pages of Vanity Fair."

5. In reprinting this story in *Something in Common*, Hughes substituted "a *New Yorker*, so he could sober up on cartoons" for "an American Mercury, so he could sober up on Mencken."

6. "Hinkty" is slang for snobbish, aloof, stuckup.

7. Ada "Bricktop" Smith (1894–1984), an African American singer and entrepreneur, was the owner of Bricktop's, a nightclub in Paris frequented by American and European celebrities, writers, and artists.

8. Gilbert Seldes (1893–1970), critic, novelist, editor, playwright, and screenwriter, is credited with being the first American intellectual to give legitimacy to popular culture. His book *The Seven Lively Arts* was published in 1924.

9. Raphael Merry del Val (1865–1930), Spanish prelate and cardinal of the Roman Catholic Church.

10. Vivi may be modeled on Hughes's one-time lover, the Chinese dancer Sylvia Chen. For detailed information, without my implication, see Arnold Rampersad, *The Life of Langston Hughes*, 2 vols. (New York: Oxford University Press, 1986, 1988), 1:264–65.

11. In reprinting this story in *Something in Common*, Hughes deleted the word "nigger-like."

12. In reprinting this story in *Something in Common*, Hughes deleted the phrase "old knotty headed."

13. In reprinting this story in *Something in Common,* Hughes changed "Marconi" to "Gandhi."

14. Perhaps no contemporary event infuriated Langston Hughes more than the famous Scottsboro trials. On March 25, 1931, nine young blacks were arrested in Scottsboro, Alabama, for allegedly raping two white girls. Despite the lack of solid evidence, eight of the youths were sentenced to death. For more on the trials and Hughes's responses, see *The Collected Works of Langston Hughes, Volume 10, "Fight for Freedom" and Other Writings on Civil Rights.*

15. In reprinting this story in *Something in Common,* Hughes added "yet shared in common."

Laughing to Keep from Crying

1. In reprinting this story in *Something in Common,* Hughes added "in those days."

2. The American photographer Man Ray (1890–1976) experimented with transferring the artistic techniques of Cubism, Dadaism, and Surrealism to new technologies, thus creating a photographic art with chance effects and startling juxtapositions. Introduced in 1921, the theremin, a musical apparatus assembled in part with cathode tubes, was one of the first electronic instruments. The American composer George Antheil (1900–1959) became prominent in 1921 as a leader of the musical avant-garde in France. After returning to the United States in 1933, he worked as a composer and producer for motion picture companies. In addition to symphonies, quartets, and sonatas, his work includes *Ballet méchanique* (1926), which makes use of electronic props such as electric bells and propellers.

3. In reprinting this story in *Something in Common,* Hughes added "—or anybody else who might at the moment come between them."

4. In reprinting this story in *Something in Common,* Hughes added "where the mutterings of independence had not yet penetrated, nor the voice of Azikiwe from far-off Lagos."

5. In reprinting this story in *Something in Common,* Hughes changed "dime" to "quarter."

6. In reprinting this story in *Something in Common,* Hughes added "and money got to circulating again and that Second World War had busted out."

7. In reprinting this story in *Something in Common,* Hughes added, "We's got something in common."

8. In reprinting this story in *Something in Common,* Hughes added, "as long as it remains *Negro* and does not get tangled up in integration."

9. In reprinting this story in *Something in Common,* Hughes changed "six thousand dollars" to "ten thousand dollars."

10. In reprinting this story in *Something in Common,* Hughes added "during the war."

11. Nora Bayes (1880–1928), comedienne and vaudeville singer of the early twentieth century; Egbert Austin "Bert" Williams (1876–1922), legendary comedian many observers consider to be the greatest vaudeville performer in the history of the American stage and one of the foremost pantomimes of all time.

12. The Alhambra is a threater in Havana, named for the Moorish fortress and palace in Granada, Spain.

13. Vladimir Vladimirovich Mayakovsky (1893–1930), the foremost poet of the Russian Revolution, began writing in earnest when his political activity led to his imprisonment during the czarist period. Federico García Lorca, one of the most admired poets of the Spanish language and a leading dramatist of the modern period, was assassinated by Franco's Nationalists on August 19, 1936, during the Spanish Civil War.

14. *Baño de vapor,* steam bath.

15. *Mestiza,* a half-breed woman.

16. Zócalo, the public square.

17. *Portales,* entrances or doorways.

18. *Cines,* pictures or movies.

19. "In 1946, [George Washington University] opened Lisner Auditorium for public performances with an inaugural performance by the well-known Swedish American movie star, Ingrid Bergman. Bergman, a European unaccustomed to Southern racial protocol, found that Lisner seated black customers only in segregated upper balconies and refused to perform. Facing a large penalty for breaking her contract, Bergman acquiesced and performed. But she called in Washington and European journalists to run the story and welcomed pickets who paraded with signs protesting the insult of public segregation. WWII veterans, GIs who had filled college campuses after the war, and many of whom believed the wartime professions of equality, joined the picket line to demand that Lisner Auditorium's managers treat all customers fairly. Lisner did integrate in 1947" (Phyllis M. Palmer, "Reflections on Black History

Month," *By George, The Newspaper of the George Washington University*
12 [February 2000]: 2). This topical reference was added after the original publication of "Trouble with the Angels" in *New Theatre* in July
1935.

Something in Common and Other Stories

1. William Franklin "Billy" Graham (1918–), an American evangelist,
has been one of the foremost leaders of the televised ministries. The title
character of Sinclair Lewis's 1927 novel *Elmer Gantry* is an ex-football
player who through various opportunistic but fraudulent means becomes
successful as an evangelist; Burt Lancaster won an Academy Award for
his portrayal of Elmer Gantry in the 1960 film. Charles M. Bishop "Sweet
Daddy" Grace (1881?–1960), a captivating African American populist
minister, founded the United House of Prayer for All People in the
1920s; although he became wealthy while leading a national congregation, his church has developed a reputation for feeding and clothing the
poor.

2. William Ashley "Billy" Sunday (1862–1935), an American evangelist, made an attack on liquor the mainstay of his campaigns. In *The Big
Sea* (1940), Hughes says of the Reverend, "Dr. Becton was a charlatan
if there ever was one, but he filled the huge church—because he gave
a good show." "The Angel of Angelus Temple" is a reference to Aimee
Semple McPherson, who completed the $1.5 million Angelus Temple in
1923.

3. The reference is to George "Father Divine" Baker (1882–1965),
an African American religious leader and founder of the Peace Mission
movement.

4. *Tessitura* refers to the general range of a voice in singing. Hughes
means a very high male register of the sort that Sam Cooke could reach
for.

Index of Titles